Praise for Designer You

"A tenderly written story of a mother and daughter's struggle to move on after loss, with characters so authentic you find yourself cheering and laughing."
Kelly Simmons, international best-selling author of *One More Day* **and** *The Fifth of July*

"Sarahlyn Bruck's touching debut is a beautifully written novel about love, grief, redemption—and the art of personal and professional recreation. This is a tender mother-daughter story that will stay in your heart long after you turn the final page."
Dawn Ius, author of *Anne & Henry, Overdrive,* **and** *Lizzie*

"Sarahlyn Bruck's debut novel *Designer You* is a story about the unexpected, and the hope that can be found after a tragedy. Once I started it, I didn't want to stop reading. This well-written and intriguing novel will draw you in and take you on an emotional and satisfying journey."
Elizabeth LaBan, best-selling author of *The Restaurant Critic's Wife* **and** *Not Perfect*

"Can a professional fixer-upper repair her broken family and business after the tragic death of her husband? *Designer You*

is a story of grief, motherhood, reinvention and growth…told with humor and an unwavering belief in the power of love."
Sonya Terjanian, author of *The Runaways* and *The Objects of Her Affection*

"This is a gorgeous debut from Sarahlyn Bruck. Heart-wrenching and beautifully-written, *Designer You* starts with a gut-punch and only gets better. My soul ached for Pam from page 1, and I didn't want to stop reading. I can't wait for Bruck's next book."
Laura Heffernan, author of the *Reality Star* series

SARAHLYN BRUCK

Designer You

First published by Hamilton Street Press 2020

This novel is entirely a work of fiction. The names, characters and incidents portrayed in it are the work of the author's imagination. Any resemblance to actual persons, living or dead, events or localities is entirely coincidental.

First edition

ISBN: 978-1-7344343-0-9

Editing by Maureen Vincent-Northam
Cover art by GoOnWrite.com

*Dedicated to my mom,
who is the strongest woman I know.*

Chapter One

P am found him.

Thank God she'd made the gruesome discovery herself. If she'd been held up in traffic or stopped someplace else on the way, Grace would've arrived home first after school.

And Pam would never have forgiven herself.

Now, a mere twenty-four hours later, she could no longer avoid it.

It felt too soon, too unreal to share the unavoidable news with their legions of followers. She closed the door to her home office, sat at her laptop, and forced herself to type.

It's with a sad, heavy heart I must inform you, our faithful readers: Nate died yesterday.

She paused after she typed that sentence. Her husband would've hated having his death announced on their lifestyle blog. *Better than on Good Morning America or in the pages of This Old House.* An inappropriate giggle escaped Pam's lips, followed by more tears. In one day, she'd cried more than maybe her whole life. She grabbed a Kleenex and blew her nose. This was the hardest thing Pam had ever written, but it was necessary. Their fans deserved to know, and the full story needed to come from her.

You may have already read about it in the 'People' section of the newspaper, or heard about it on a brief report on the local news last evening, or this may come as a complete shock to you. It did to me. And I'm still in shock. I haven't fully absorbed the fact that Nate is gone. That he's never coming back.

Pam wheeled her desk chair away from her computer and rose, pacing the length of the tiny room. The converted home office-slash-guest-room closed in on her – the dresser and queen bed and file cabinet and bookcase and TV encroaching on her personal space like domestic topiaries sprung to life. With the door shut, she had no space to roam, no way to avoid this awful task that idled on her screen, patiently waiting for her to return.

He's never coming back.

It seemed impossible. Pam almost expected him to burst through her office door asking, "Hey, hon…help me pick between these two ties. Got an on-camera interview in New York and I can't look like a slob."

Pam sat back at her desk.

He's not going to return home from doing an interview in New York or consulting with a client in Lambertville. That's over. You've all been so kind to follow us, some for a matter of days or weeks, many for years. We've met some of you at design shows across the country and at book signings. We could not have built Designer You without your support. And I feel a responsibility to be open and honest with you, our loyal fans.

Pam closed her eyes, which in her mind, only seemed to sharpen the horrific discovery of her husband's lifeless body and made her dizzy with despair. She opened her eyes and pushed away from her desk, knowing there was no facing this vision without help. Pam cracked open her office door and peered out. Down the hall, muffled music drifted out from Grace's room. She let her alone this time – the perpetual checking in on her shocked and grieving daughter had become a writing avoidance technique. Maybe a reality avoidance technique, too.

Pam crept down the stairs to the dining room, opened the door to the buffet, and inspected the meager selection of alcohol – a warm bottle of chardonnay and a near-empty liter of tequila. She grabbed the Patrón and squinted at the contents – maybe a couple shots worth? *That'll do*, she thought, and wandered into the kitchen.

She pulled off the top, poured the remains of the bottle into a juice glass, and sipped. The alcohol clung to her throat and made her cough. Pam didn't drink much hard alcohol. Wine? Yes. And an occasional margarita or gin and tonic? Sure. But straight shots? Hardly ever.

Last time she'd felt compelled to drink a shot was last year at her sister-in-law's bachelorette party, where she'd suffered through the usual bride-to-be silliness – paper hats and feather boas and male strippers – with a group of women fifteen years her junior. Taking the shot had been more of a way to get through the evening.

Booze, the world's #1 coping mechanism. She took another timid sip of the tequila. Smoother. Glass in hand, Pam walked upstairs to her office and settled into her desk chair.

Nate died yesterday while installing a deck I'd been pestering him to build for the last four years. Ever since we moved into this old house, I thought it'd be fun to write about a home project again – our home this time, not a client's – and I imagined we'd be sipping a glass of wine out there by the end of May. We thought that by chronicling our progress in early spring, we might inspire some of you to tackle your own outdoor projects and enjoy the finished products all summer long. Anyway, this winter Nate mapped out the design, I had a few ideas for lighting and furniture – it was meant to be fun and a way to return to where we started.

A way to 'reinvigorate' the brand, their nervous publisher had advised in February, when Pam had bounced blog ideas to them that could provide a lead up to their third book, a book she'd hadn't even finished outlining and had already missed a deadline on. An outdoor project would also pair well with their new line of gardening tools set to launch that spring. And when the deck was finished, Pam had envisioned that she, Nate, and Grace would eat dinner out there on a warm summer evening while watching fireworks blast over clear skies above the Art Museum on the 4th of July.

That would never happen now.

Pam took another helping of tequila. It burned as it slid down her throat. She fixed her gaze on the computer screen and raised her fingers to the keyboard.

Designer You began with home projects just like the roof deck, and we were so excited about it. Nate thought he could get a jump on building it as soon as the weather turned, which those of you East Coasters know it did...sort of. Our spring has been all over the place, with snow showers one weekend to temps in the 70s the following week to thunderstorms again the weekend after that. Those of you who follow our blog know that this past week we had a patch of dry weather at last, which we'd been waiting for, and Nate wanted to take advantage of it. The support beams were up from the week before, and he was in the process of installing the wooden framework when he died.

Pam withdrew her fingers from the keyboard and stared at the screen. *When he died.* The words stabbed at her. It would be easy to just stop. Let the mainstream media do its job of offering this bit of salacious news to hungry consumers and give Pam permission to step away from the computer and begin the grieving process in peace.

She imagined the likes of twenty-four-hour news channels and celebrity websites offering digestible tidbits such as, 'Nate Wheeler, DIY guru and one half of the popular brand, Designer You, died yesterday while installing a deck on the roof of his Philadelphia home.' Or, 'Design genius, Nate Wheeler, succumbed to gravity yesterday and died. He was forty-five and is survived by his Designer You partner and wife, Pam, and their teenage daughter, Grace.' Or maybe, 'Nate Wheeler was found dead after a fall yesterday. In a dazzling career spanning almost twenty years, Wheeler was a pioneer in the lifestyle blog trend of the early 2000s. Often described by their predominantly female fan base as 'brilliant,' 'funny,' and 'gorgeous,' Wheeler founded Designer You with his sidekick wife, turning their popularity into multiple book deals, appearances, and high-ticket clients.'

Gorgeous, funny, brilliant – Pam had always been the 'lucky' one according to the press. A sidekick. An afterthought.

Still, their fans didn't deserve to find out about his death through the press.

Pam and Nate had built Designer You by reaching out to the very people who felt that they knew them. Their beautiful, restored home, Grace's private school, all of the spoils of their success resulted from that personal touch.

It's been a difficult and surreal twenty-four hours – I lost a husband and partner of twenty years. Over the last day, I had the worst news to give our daughter, Nate's parents, my parents, and our dearest friends. In truth, I haven't had the time to process anything. I almost expect him to walk through our front door and ask when dinner will be ready and I have to remind myself it's not going to happen.

As horrific and shocking as this news is, I wanted to be the one to tell you, our DIY community. I owe it to you. As the writer, I feel a special connection to you. Many of you have followed our work for years, and I feel a particular responsibility to reach out to all of you, just as I have our friends and family. I know how much you adored Nate because I was as much of a fan of Nate's as anyone. I was floored by his talent and ambition right from the start.

A sad smile crawled across her face as she remembered how they'd met during their last year of college. By the time she was twenty-two and in her final semester at Penn State, Pam still didn't know what she wanted to do – she had no plan. It seemed everyone she knew had secured jobs or internships or accepted offers from grad schools. Panic about her post college no-plan had started to invade every corner of her life – her friendships, her school work, her sleep. And then she'd met Nate in her last class. Charming, brilliant, gorgeous Nate. She was smitten, and lucky for her, he was just as attracted to her.

Turns out, she *did* have a plan. It was Nate. She would have followed him anywhere...and had.

Please keep us in your thoughts during this difficult time. And thank you so much for your support.

Pam exhaled, her muscles depleted as if writing the post had sapped all of her strength. She was done for the day and hoped that after the tequila, which was already making her eyelids heavy, she would sleep better tonight.

* * *

That night, Grace, who'd just turned fifteen in March, crawled into bed with Pam like she used to when she'd been spooked in the middle of the night as a little girl. Grace drifted off as soon as her head hit the pillow and slept like she was in a coma, but not Pam. Invasive thoughts danced in her head. The looming urgency of planning Nate's funeral, making arrangements for the cemetery, flowers, catering, finding places for family from out of town to stay, and dealing with everyone else's grief on top of her own had become separate fists squeezing her throat. At last, she nodded off sometime after three in the morning, slept fitfully, and awakened just a few hours later at dawn confused, relieved that the day before had just been a bad dream before realizing it wasn't.

Instead, she experienced his death for the first time all over again.

* * *

Chapter Two

I n the moment that Nate had died, Pam had been out shopping at one of her favorite local haunts, Artifact Salvage, which sold anything that could be reclaimed from demolished row homes and brownstones. Unaware of the tragedy at home, she'd been sifting through old light fixtures and door hardware such as hinges, doorknobs, mail slots.

In the twenty-four hours since, Pam's mind had that doomed afternoon on repeat, and she wished she could rewind her life by one day and make the choice to stay home.

She tucked a loose strand of dark brown hair behind her ear and pawed through the doorknobs, picking out a large brass piece with an intricate pattern on the handle. *This would be perfect on the Meinhardts' front door*, she thought, which she and Nate had just stripped. The door itself was more than one hundred and fifty years old, and for decades, the wood finish had been hidden beneath layers of dark forest green paint. Once they stripped that off, a beautiful walnut revealed itself like buried treasure. A door like that needed a touch of bling to show it off, and this intricate brass doorknob would do the trick. She grinned, thinking about how much Nate would love it. So would the Meinhardts. *See? I have ideas, too.*

Pam handed over her credit card to the cashier, while stealing one last longing look around the large, open space. She didn't get the opportunity to visit Artifact Salvage and its artful arrangements of treasures often enough, and she soaked it in now.

In one section of the expansive warehouse, doors and windows hung with care from their displays, so that customers could flip through them like pages in a book. Kitchen and bathroom sinks engulfed another section, where century-old porcelain was polished to a pristine sheen. A neat row of elevated toilet tanks stood in their own designated area. Overhead, chandeliers twinkled and captured the light of the afternoon sun. Pam and Nate frequented this place all the time while renovating their first house, but over the last few years, Pam came alone. Nate's schedule often meant that the details were left to her. She didn't mind – her obsession with details served a vision that was all her own.

Pam scowled at her watch. It was getting late. Grace would be home from school soon, and Pam couldn't put off the day's blog post any longer. *Until next time, my love, my Artifact Salvage*, she thought as she signed the credit card receipt.

She opened the front door when she arrived home and shouted, "Home!" to Nate, wherever he was. She hung up her parka and purse on the coat rack in the entryway and slid off her shoes. It was early April and the snow was gone for good, but not the cold. Rubbing her bare arms that prickled in the drafty entryway, she pulled on a discarded cardigan draped over the banister of the stairway.

"Nate?" Pam padded into the kitchen and placed her doorknob on the butcher block, running her fingers over the texture of the handle one last time. She half expected her husband to be standing at the kitchen counter, a cup of coffee in his hand, waiting for her and Grace to come home, impatient to impart deck details so she could start on the blog. He wasn't. "Nate, let's talk deck!" she called up the stairs. "I gotta write the post."

Feeling a familiar pang of irritation return, Pam started up the stairs. *It's just like him. I wait while he is immersed in his project. And I have to write about it – now.* As she arrived on the third floor and walked to the rear room's door that led outside to the top of the third-story roof, her annoyance increased. She opened the door, surprised that Nate was nowhere to be found. His tools were out. The steel beams were in place. Pam reached for a discarded Coke can to bring downstairs to recycle, but it was still full…and cold, with drops of condensation clinging to the outside of the can. *He just opened this and left it? What a waste. Where the hell is he?*

"Nate?" she said again, quiet this time, thinking maybe he hadn't gone far. Pam peered over the railing down into their backyard and spotted something. Her stomach clenched. *No, that can't be…* She raised her hand to her mouth and stifled an anguished scream.

Nate had fallen off the roof and now lay still with his back on the collapsed, wrought-iron patio table, facing skyward with his arms open wide. An alarming amount of blood pooled onto the bricks below.

* * *

One glance was all it took for Pam to be certain that the sight of a lifeless Nate was not an image her daughter would ever witness and have imprinted into her brain for the rest of her life. *Is it too late?* she thought, slipping her cell from her pocket and running back inside the house. With her heart in her throat, she scrambled down two flights of stairs while punching 9-1-1 on her phone.

"9-1-1, where is your emergency?"

"Please come now," she said, her voice shrill. "My husband—" Pam couldn't form the words. The grotesque image of him in the backyard looped through her mind. Maybe it was some sick hallucination?

When she reached Nate, Pam stared at his body, praying for some kind of rise and fall of his chest. Nothing. She placed her hand over his wrist and then his neck, but couldn't detect a pulse. His eyes were sightless through half closed eyelids. This was no hallucination.

Pam started to hyperventilate. If she didn't get help right that second, she might pass out. Once the 9-1-1 operator collected her address, she hung up, and then called the one person she knew who might be able to help her, help Nate right now: her closest friend, Becky, who lived just a few doors down. Becky was about the strongest person Pam knew. She was a nurse-midwife, and Pam was sure she'd seen it all – though the sight of her husband sprawled out on the patio table could traumatize her friend forever. She also knew that Becky would be home today.

"Please, something's awful happened to Nate. I think he fell off the roof. It's bad, Becky." Her voice shook into her phone. "I didn't know who else to call."

"Did you phone 9-1-1?"

Pam nodded.

"Pam, are you there? Is 9-1-1 on the way?"

"Yes, yes. But can you come? Are you home?" Pam said, her

voice high pitched and raw.

"You stay put," said Becky, with authority. It didn't hurt she was British and sounded authoritarian to begin with. "I'll be right there."

Pam pocketed her phone and with tears streaming down her cheeks, she crouched beside her husband and cradled Nate's still face in her arms, not caring who saw or what nosy neighbors thought. Maybe she wanted them to know. If it was all too real for her it would be real enough for them too. She looked up at the backs of the row homes behind her house, defying anyone to gawk at her from the windows above. No one. She was all alone. She was exposed and helpless and one hundred percent unequipped to handle any part of this horrific scene – in her backyard, of all places. Pam knew just by looking into his blank, staring eyes that Nate was gone. There was nothing she could do. He couldn't be saved.

Seconds, minutes later – time seemed to have stopped – Becky swooped in and took over just as the ambulance arrived. As Becky explained what happened as best she could to the paramedics, Pam took Nate's right hand in hers – it was still warm in her palm, and though lifeless and beginning to stiffen, felt so familiar. It was the same hand that had just made steak tacos for dinner the night before. It was the same hand that had grasped (and learned to let go of) the seat of Grace's bicycle as he ran along beside her when she first learned to ride. It was the same hand that kneaded away the knots in Pam's shoulders after a long day sitting at her writing desk. It was a hand she'd known for more than twenty years.

"It's time to say goodbye, just for now, OK?" Becky gently separated Pam from Nate's hand and led her down the side path to the front porch, where they sank on the steps facing the street. Pam's chin started to tremble again and the hot tears returned to her eyes. As if she was floating outside of herself and watching down on some, poor, grieving, middle-aged woman, whose insides felt raw and on display. She didn't even know this person crumpled on her front steps, her sweater and jeans spotted with Nate's blood. Couldn't identify with her, let alone *be* her. Her brain hadn't caught up with her reality yet, and all she could envision was the gruesome image of her husband dead on the patio. She started to sob again with forceful breathlessness, as a small circle of bystanders gathered across the street – neighbors and passersby probably wondering what was going on at the Wheelers' and why there was an ambulance parked outside. She hated the gawkers and their idle curiosity, while she melted down on her front steps.

Becky hugged Pam to her as the EMTs wheeled Nate's body to the awaiting ambulance. The one thing on earth she was grateful for at that moment was her friend for being there, protecting her. Pam leaned into Becky's strength.

And now it was unpretentious, unafraid, understanding Becky, who was there to hold Pam up as the paramedics closed the back doors of the ambulance and drove away with Nate inside. Pam realized there was, all of a sudden, a mountain of things to do – clean up the back yard, funeral arrangements, and dozens of excruciating phone calls – but nothing could be done until she could break the news to Grace. She'd called the school, but Grace had already left on the school bus.

For this brief moment, her first without Nate, Pam existed in a weird holding pattern. She couldn't call or text anyone, not even her or Nate's parents, until she'd told Grace. She would be violating the first in a long line of unwritten codes and rules about death and dying and the grieving process, all things she knew next to nothing about. Over the span of about ten years, after college and into her early thirties, all four of her grandparents had died. Pam remembered there were rules in place that everyone seemed to come to the table understanding but her: on her father's side, there was a proclivity toward open casket, on her mother's, closed, the order in which family and friends filed in and out of the sanctuary, who took care of the funeral arrangements, who was in charge of food, and which unfortunate family member was assigned the task of sorting the estate.

Pam's head swam with all of these urgent responsibilities and it had not even settled into her chest that Nate was…gone. Poof. Just that fast. It didn't feel real. *Can't be real.* She shut her eyes with the brief hope that when she blinked them open again, she would return to the roof and discover Nate setting wooden slats over the steel support structures. She'd try to persuade him indoors to go over that day's blog post.

She opened her eyes to her unfortunate reality. Everything about her body – her dark hair and inky eyes, her pale face, her legs and arms – felt heavy as she waited for her daughter to appear from the school bus. Moments later, it pulled up to the curb. She shook her head back and forth, not even knowing how to begin.

Becky gave her arm a gentle squeeze. "You just need to tell her," Becky said, quiet but firm. "I'm here. I'm not going anywhere. But you need to do this."

Her eyes red and brimming, Pam met Grace at the sidewalk. Grace emerged from the bus with her backpack dangling from her shoulder, laughing and waving her goodbyes to her friends. But as soon as she caught sight of her mother's stricken face and bloodied cardigan, she sobered, as if she knew something was wrong.

"Mom?" It took just a second for Grace to absorb the scene. "Is it Dad?"

Pam nodded and folded her arms around Grace, hugging her close.

Grace buried her face into the crook of Pam's neck and sobbed. What Pam would do next, she had no idea.

Chapter Three

Pam stacked the last of the dessert saucers on the remaining space on the counter and surveyed the kitchen. Stacks of plates, piles of forks, serving trays, serving ware, cloth napkins, coffee cups, and glassware covered most of every available surface. She sighed and opened the empty dishwasher. Now that friends, family, work associates, a few top clients, their editor, agent, publicist, and Nate's high school and college friends had all left, Pam was alone to face the dishes.

Finally alone. She couldn't believe how much she longed to be alone, but after days of people – the constant presence of well-meaning friends and family – descending on her like she was an unhinged person on suicide watch, Pam craved space. She didn't want to kill herself, she just wanted a few moments to hear her thoughts.

"It takes time to *process,*" said Pam's widowed Aunt Martha, who'd cornered her during coffee in the sanctuary after the funeral service that afternoon. Pam tried to remember that Martha was trying to be helpful, but it was like she'd appointed herself as Pam's personal expert on dead husbands. "It gets easier," she assured her when she'd arrived with Pam's parents that morning. And "Nate would have wanted you to be happy," she'd mentioned an hour ago, as she gripped a tiny plate of cheese and crackers in their living room, pointing at Pam with a slice of cheddar for emphasis. Martha, Pam decided, had no clue. She was in her mid-seventies and Uncle Larry in his eighties when he died three years ago. They'd enjoyed a long and happy life together, raising their family and seeing their grandchildren come into the world. They traveled. They sized down. And when Uncle Larry got sick, Martha was by his side. Together. Pam didn't want to diminish Aunt Martha's grief, but this was not the same.

What is 'happy' without Nate? Pam wanted to ask. *What is life without Nate?*

But she didn't even have a chance to entertain the questions that had started to bloom in her head. Between the day of Nate's death and the funeral today, Pam's only time to herself was when she closed herself off in the bathroom for a few minutes of peace. And still, beyond the closed door, she could hear the steady murmur of voices downstairs peppered with 'Nate' this and 'Pam' that. She resented everyone trying to understand how she felt – guessing wrong some of the time and more infuriatingly, guessing right. How dare they try when she hadn't had the opportunity to begin to 'process,' as Martha had so aptly put it?

Pam reminded herself that all of these people, too, were heartbroken and in shock. Nate attracted almost everyone he came in contact with, and Pam discovered early on she was far from alone in her grief. In countless ways, she was grateful so many loved Nate; he could make anyone feel like they were the most important person in the room. But she was also very protective and territorial about her grief. Nate was *hers*. She was the one who would wake up every day without him lying by her side from now on. She was the one who had to cope with their teenage daughter's anguish in all its unpredictable glory day in and day out. She was the one whose tiny family went from three members to two in a split second.

But he was also *not* hers. She thought about how Grace clutched to her and Pam's parents today. How Nate's parents shook with sobs in the front pew at the funeral. The service overflowed with mourners this morning and Pam guessed she had at least two hundred people through her house today to pay their respects.

But she was grateful to take off her brave face like it was a mask and relieved not to have to make small talk with the people she'd invited to share something uniquely painful and private. Now that it was all over, without the immediacy of a funeral to plan and all of the other arrangements surrounding Nate's death, Pam saw little beyond the stacks of plates and cups that surrounded her in her kitchen. What was her purpose beyond these dishes? She had no clue.

Pam peered out the window at her bare patio. She'd had the grisly furniture hauled away to the landfill and the bricks scrubbed clean after the accident. Two weeks into spring, no signs of life appeared in the backyard yet, no buds had popped through soil. The beginning of April looked just as cold and lifeless as the end of winter. She never wanted to go out onto that empty patio ever again.

"Pammy." Her father, Thomas, ambled into the kitchen. "Can I help you with these dishes? I'll scrape, you load."

She snapped out of her daze. "Sure, Dad."

In his mid-seventies, her dad remained trim and robust, though he'd slowed bit by bit through the years, and his salt-and-pepper hair was just starting to recede. Pam had inherited her compact physique from him, and the two stood side by side as he rinsed the dishes and she loaded them one by one into the dishwasher.

"I'm so proud of you today, honey. So's your mother. We're heartbroken, but we've never been prouder of you either," Dad said. Pam watched her father's chin quiver for a second before he forced a tight smile. "To be honest, I don't know if I would have handled it as well or with as much class."

Pam looked at her feet. She was grateful for the sentiment, for sure, but she was so…lost. What, exactly, was handling the death of one's husband 'well' or with 'class'? 'Stunned,' 'numb,' and 'wrung-out' better described her feeling. And God, trying to be there for Grace – how many times had she paused outside Grace's closed bedroom door and lacked the courage to knock? She didn't know how to comfort her own child. And her father couldn't have known that beyond the loss of Nate – her love, her partner, and Grace's dad – she had no plan. There was no Plan B. In fact, she and Nate had been working on Plan A since they were in their twenties, chipping away at it together. That was it. If she didn't do something soon, Plan A would be gone just as sure as Nate was.

With the plates and bowls loaded, Pam placed the forks, knives, and spoons into the dishwasher's silverware section. "Thanks, Dad. I don't know what's going to happen tomorrow, though. Grace goes back to school and I have to go back to…I don't know what. My life isn't my life anymore." She squeezed liquid detergent into the dispenser, closed the door, and started the dishwasher. Her gaze skimmed across the remaining dishes on the countertop. "You and Mom don't need to stay up. There are at least two more loads after this."

"I don't mind," her dad said, reaching out to hug his

daughter's shoulder. "There's a lot of work to be done, and it'll feel nice to wake up to a clean house tomorrow."

"An empty house is more like it," Pam said. She cocked her head. "It's quiet. It's unnerving. Where's Grace? And Mom?"

Her dad sank into one of the chairs at the butcher block. "Last I saw, they were going through Nate's Facebook page on Grace's iPad."

"I can't bear to look at those photos or read the comments."

Pam scanned the kitchen, which was in many ways also an album of the life she and Nate had put together, just as those Facebook photos. The whole house was. The floors were the original wood, which Nate refinished himself before they moved even one box in four years earlier. Pam's blog posts those weeks when they were moving into their current house were so popular – over six thousand clicks on each bi-weekly post – she and Nate decided to compile all of the posts plus bonus material in their second book, and *This Old House* had given them a photo spread.

Pam had found the butcher block. She loved trolling the big-garbage pick-up days in the well-to-do Philadelphia and New Jersey suburbs. One September morning, three and half years ago, just as the sun was starting to rise, she stumbled across it. She'd pulled over and was pleased to see that she'd discovered an old, beaten up John Boos butcher block out on the curb in front of a very large Morristown, New Jersey McMansion. Pam couldn't contain her excitement as she heaved the thing into the back of her Subaru and drove off, a big smile spread across her face. The table needed a lot of work – the top required sanding and one of the legs had broken clean off. This allowed Nate to re-imagine the piece, and he ended up lopping off the legs and using the top to create a large butcher block table the family could sit at on barstools and eat breakfast. It was Nate's genius to re-imagine that butcher block, but Pam loved to remember it was *her* find. Details – she loved the details. Still, the butcher block was little comfort to Pam today. She couldn't look at it, or anything in the house, without it all reminding her that Nate was gone forever.

She rubbed the worn edge of the table with her thumb. "This whole house is like a museum to Nate."

"I know it's hard now, Pammy. But it'll get easier," her dad said, his tone uncertain.

She hoped that was true, but for the first time since she was a teenager, she doubted her father. Every night since the accident, Pam lay in her bed, the bed that less than a week ago she'd shared with Nate as man and wife for more than two decades, wondering if it really would get easier. It didn't seem so. *I can't even bring myself to wash his scent from the sheets yet, let alone even think about life after Nate.* But now she couldn't put it off much longer. She would need to start wrapping her foggy head around running Designer You without him.

Pam had avoided her computer since the blog post the day after Nate's death, which was unusual. On any given day, she could be found hunched over her laptop, not only writing, but answering email, scheduling design projects, and managing the website. But she couldn't face the feedback, knowing it would be a combination of sympathetic well-wishing comments and messages from fans mixed in with a dash of vitriol from internet trolls. All of it, she could do without.

She was going to have to figure out a next step whether she felt up to it or not. Usually, she could plan her time away from her laptop. Even when they went on vacation, Pam made certain she had a few blog posts stored to upload like magic into the universe at their scheduled days and times. Was there a virtual version of the sign in the window that could read something like, 'Grieving: Be back soon!' with a little clock she could position to a particular time? *How long was considered long enough? How long was too long?*

Pam cozied up to her dad and wrapped her arm around his, resting her head on his shoulder like she had when she was a little girl. "It's official. I think I'm overwhelmed. I wish I could just crawl into a hole. Maybe I'll bring a case of merlot with me."

Her father kissed the top of her head. "Mom and I are here for you. We're going to get through the rest of this day together. And we'll get up and do it again tomorrow and the next day and the day after that."

Pam raised her head and looked in her father's warm brown eyes. "You'd stay for me?"

"We'd stay for both of you. As long as you need. I can always ask Jimmy to step in and run the diner on his own for a few days. Your brother pretty much does it all himself anyway. And he's desperate to help you in any way he can." He offered her a sad smile. "We'd do anything for you, you know that, right?"

"Thanks, Dad. I do know that."

"So your mom and I moved all the furniture back to their original spots in the living room," said Becky, as she wandered into the kitchen. "The dishes are cleared out – wow, looks like they all made it in here. Can I help you wash these by hand while the dishwasher runs?"

Pam shook her head. "You should go home." She walked

over to her friend, whose bloodshot eyes and slumped shoulders gave away that she was as drained as Pam. She hugged Becky. "Thank you. I couldn't have gotten through the day – this whole long weekend, actually – without you."

"You are very welcome, honey," said Becky, giving Pam a quick peck on the cheek. "I'll stop in tomorrow after Grace is in school – see how the morning went, OK?"

Pam offered a weary look. "Thanks," she said, waving off her friend.

The front door opened and closed with a click in the distance.

"I don't even know where to start with Grace," Pam said to her father. "It's like real life starts again tomorrow, but it's going to be so hard on all of us. And Grace going back to school – do you think it's too early?"

Her father shook his head. "She's going to have to go back sometime. You can't just shield her from life."

Pam agreed. "You're right. I keep telling her that I'm here if she wants to talk, but she doesn't. Not that she was all that into confiding in me before…" She cleared her throat. "She's been so up and down lately, which I guess is part of being a teenager. But I think I thought she would come to me over the last few days, and instead she spends all this time crying and listening to music alone in her room. Aside from the first night, she doesn't seem to want to have anything to do with me. I don't know if she blames me a little, or if she's angry, confused."

"You both lost the most important person in your lives. Your family is hurting. You need to give her – and yourself – a break," her father said. "And know when to maybe give her a little space."

"Maybe we should go to counseling or something, I don't know." Pam sighed and looked up at her father. "Just you and Mom being here helps. At least she's got Mom to talk to now."

He smiled. "I'm glad. They've always had a special bond."

At that moment, Pam thought she knew what could make things better, at least for the time being. "You and Mom – can you, just, stay?"

"Yeah, I told you. We can stay the next couple of days. It's no problem."

"No, I mean, can you move in for a little while? A few weeks? A few months, even?" Pam put her hand up, curling her fingers into her palm. "Just think about it. I know you need to discuss it with Mom and it's a big commitment. And I know you have your own lives that you enjoy very much." She shook her head. "I'm scared, though. We've got the insurance money in a trust that I don't want to touch – that's for Grace. Or emergency, I suppose." She swallowed. "But I have to think how to keep Designer You afloat right now. Nate and I were partners, but it was *his* baby. If I don't start paying attention to it right away, I could kill it. And I would never forgive myself if I were responsible for ruining his legacy. He worked so hard – *we* worked so hard – and I could so easily just screw it all up by doing nothing because I'm too overwhelmed doing it myself."

"A few months is a long time, honey."

Pam looked at her father, eyes shimmering. "Please, Daddy. I could really use the help around here."

Chapter Four

"The Utah home expo's at the end of the month," announced Liz, Pam's assistant, over the phone one afternoon, a mere week and a half after the funeral. After almost a decade, Pam considered Liz, who was in her mid-sixties and seemed to favor wearing tailored jackets and pencil skirts 365 days a year, like a second mother. A much more formal, scolding, disciplined mother, who delivered gentle prodding and kind reminders whenever she needed them, which was often.

Pam cradled the phone between her chin and shoulder and smeared jarred frosting onto her fifth graham cracker with a knife. Lunch. She closed her eyes.

Utah home expo. Shit. Part of the job as a popular 'lifestyle brand' – Pam cringed at the label attributed to Designer You, even more so since they helped define the term – included presenting at several home expos throughout the year.

Liz continued, "You both killed it last year and I know they were eager to have you back. It's been on the schedule for months. Think you could manage it?"

"Do I have to?" Pam touched her slick dark hair, now piled on top of her head and precariously secured with a plastic clip. She recoiled, as her fingers slipped through the greasy strands.

Did I shower yesterday?

The days melted into each other, each as indistinguishable as the previous. Liz would be disgusted if she saw her now. "Where's the adorable wife?" Pam heard her say in her head, in a tone that admonished her slovenly appearance in the nicest possible way.

Liz sighed into the phone. "Look, it's an easy gig. Utah loves you. You need to start hawking the gardening line. And quite frankly, it's a good way to get you out of the house."

Pam looked down at her pajama bottoms and a ratty tank top, which she was still wearing at two in the afternoon. "It feels too soon. We can't cancel? I'll do the next one."

"Pam," said Liz. "I know you don't feel ready, but it's time. We have to publicize the garden line now before summer. If we don't, you can say buh-bye to any further Lowes contracts. And they may decide to sue you if you don't play your part in the marketing."

"What if we hire out? Hire an actor or something."

"Designer You was always you and Nate, which is now just you. If you hire an actor or anyone that's not *you*, people are going to feel cheated," said Liz. "*You* need to get out there and represent."

Pam fought back the rising, angry tears. Her tears were always at the surface now, ready to spring into action the moment she became upset.

"It wasn't me! It was *never* me. They want Nate," she said, all of a sudden overwhelmed by resentment toward her charming, dead husband.

"I think they'll love you even more for coming out, showing the product, signing a few books. You'll see." Liz's voice had turned soft and soothing. "They love you and want to see that you're OK."

"But I'm not OK. That's the point. I'm not OK and I don't feel like putting on heels and getting on a plane to go to this damn home expo." Pam swallowed the emotion in her voice. She was too raw. It was too soon. The sight of the frosted graham cracker idling on the kitchen counter now turned Pam's stomach. "It's only been a couple of weeks. I'm not ready." An extended silence made Pam think the phone had cut out. "Liz?"

"Lowes needs you to be ready. Your publisher needs you to be ready. Your clients are starting to wonder if their projects will ever be finished," said Liz, like someone who was about to lose her patience with a petulant child. Pam detected a quiet desperation in Liz's voice. "You need to do this whether you think you're ready or not. You have a mortgage to pay, food to put on the table, Grace to take care of. You lose Lowes, the future of Designer You will be in jeopardy. I know you don't want that. Nate wouldn't want that, either. You need to take action now."

Pam was glad Liz couldn't see her bent over her kitchen counter, hand cradling her forehead.

"I'm emailing you your flight details."

"Shit, OK," Pam said, sobering. It wasn't fair. It was too hard to be an adult right now. It dawned on her that her days of extended self-absorbed grief were over – her non-decisions were starting to affect the people she loved and needed, like Liz and her agent, Jackie. And paying clients. And Grace. "I'll be there."

When Grace arrived home from school later that afternoon, Pam had showered, changed, and was hunched over her laptop sipping a cup of coffee and nibbling a plate of cheese and apples.

"You're up early today," Grace said, as she stood in the doorway.

"Ha ha, funny," said Pam, swiveling around in her desk chair to see her tall, ponytailed daughter. Even with no make-up and sweaty in her workout clothes, she looked more grown up every time Pam saw her, which, now that she thought about it, wasn't much these days. She'd foisted the bulk of the household responsibilities – meals, laundry, cleaning – on her parents, probably too much. And Grace got herself to and from school and practice. Any spare time, Grace spent with friends. It was as if they all existed in separate bubbles.

And in this rare, brief moment, Pam took in her daughter, the girl-woman standing in front of her. Worry, grief, and love pinged inside her chest. Pam ached to share the uncomfortable combination of joy and sadness with Nate that she felt as her little girl grew up before her eyes.

"How was school?" she said.

"Fine."

"How was lacrosse practice?"

"Fine." Grace narrowed her eyes. "What are *you* up to?"

"I'm making arrangements to present at a home show at the end of the month."

"You're going back to work?"

"I'm going back to work."

"Why?"

"I have to."

Grace raised an eyebrow. "Do you want to?"

Pam thought about it for a moment. Want didn't have anything to do with going back to work at this point. She needed to. "I do. I think." She forced a smile, as if to twist her words into truth. "Yeah, I think I want to."

* * *

From the moment she stepped off the plane at the Salt Lake City International Airport, Pam's body buzzed with anxiety. Liz had arranged for all of the materials for the garden line to be shipped direct to the Dream Home Expo, a detail that Pam was grateful not to worry about, yet she still fretted about how *she* was going to get there. Should she catch a cab to the Dream Home Expo just outside Salt Lake? Or maybe she should call for an Uber? No, cab – cab drivers didn't have to rely on Google to tell them the fastest route, and today she needed as many people surrounding her who knew what they were doing, because she sure didn't. She cursed herself for being so nervous and second-guess-y. After all, this was the part she was supposed to be good at – packing an overnight bag, having Liz arrange the flight, calling for the black town car to pick her up. She'd almost remembered everything but forgotten about the town car. Of course, none of this was why she was such a wreck, why her armpits felt damp with sweat despite the cool, dry, Utah air.

Every cell in her body screamed that she didn't belong here – not without Nate. She'd gone from a supporting player in a two-person show to its unlikely and unwilling star. And it was laughable that she had anything to offer anyone, let alone design advice or gardening tips. Who the hell was she? Nate was the brains and heart of Designer You. So what did that make her? Something superfluous. She was an ornament, a painted fingernail or a pierced earlobe. For one fleeting moment, Pam entertained the impulse to turn around and get back on the plane, which after fueling up and boarding another wave of passengers, was on its way to Honolulu, its final destination according to the pilot. She would have traded a trip to present at a home show in Salt Lake for a few days on a Hawaiian beach in a hot minute. But no, she was certain Lowes would swim out to the island, pluck her off the beach, and throw her in a plane bound for Salt Lake City.

Last year's line proved to be a moderate success, and this year they had even higher hopes for the garden line. But that was before Nate died. Still, she had no choice but to deliver today, or else she could expect no more ware sponsored by Lowes and designed by Designer You. Pam also couldn't abandon either her responsibility to their brand nor her agent, who would be meeting her at the expo with another suitcase full of her and Nate's latest books to sell and sign at one of the vendor tables.

In just a few queasy hours, Pam would be up on the Expo's main stage. Last year, when they debuted their gourmet knife set – a product launch that still perplexed Pam since they were DIY designers, not cooks – Nate did most of the demonstrating. *Thank goodness I'm not performing a knife demonstration*, Pam thought. *I'd likely slice my thumb off.*

In the past, Pam and Nate would come in with a loose agenda of what aspects of the products they wanted to showcase. Nate loved to improvise and banter with the audience, which for each day they were there, swelled in numbers as word went around that the semi-famous pair were in town and answering questions, signing autographs, and taking selfies with fans. Happiest in the background, Pam let Nate steal center stage, but she could keep up wherever he led her. She could draw names out of a hat for giveaways or slice through a tin can using a serrated bread knife as Nate babbled away about the quality, the price, and the lifetime warranty, but she always felt like the magician's assistant. Nate never needed her at these expos like she needed him, and boy did Pam feel that need acutely today. She was sick with rage and fear that Nate had the audacity to be dead on today of all days. *Insensitive jerk.* Just the idea of getting up on stage by herself made her stomach cramp and she'd been in and out of the bathroom during the entire flight.

Pam arrived at the convention center in just enough time to change into a cream-colored blouse, black pencil skirt, and black heels. She fussed with her hair and refreshed her make-up in the greenroom's full-length mirror. Her pale face looked even more sallow under the florescent lights. Pam's agent pulled out a packaged salad and a plastic fork she'd picked up from Trader Joe's.

"Eat up, girl," said Jackie. "You've got your presentation and a book signing this afternoon. You don't want to be doing this on an empty stomach."

But Pam couldn't bear to even look at the spinach salad. The shriveled cranberries and candied pecans floated atop the bed of spinach leaves.

Nope.

"Maybe when I'm signing." The pungent bleu cheese almost knocked her out. It seemed impossible to her that she could keep down even one bite. "I can't eat right now." She waved it away with a shaky hand.

Jackie shrugged. "It's up to you. You just need to get this presentation over with. After this, it'll be smooth sailing." She squeezed Pam's shoulder. "You look gorgeous. I'll be rooting for you front row, center."

The stage was arranged with several set pieces including a swatch of plastic grass covered with fake yellow and orange leaves, rectangular boxes filled with potting soil and herbs, a coiled hose and sprayer, and an overgrown, potted rose bush. The entire line of garden tools were featured in a prominent position stage right. Pam took a deep breath and entered from the left.

She squinted and took a few seconds to let her eyes adjust to the lights and gauged the crowd. If Pam were being generous, she'd say the audience was about half full, with no one sitting in the first two rows besides Jackie. A year ago, the seats filled early, with audience spilling out to stand in the aisles. First row was always the most coveted seating. *Are they scared of me now? Worried they're going to catch 'widow' or something?*

She shook off her nerves and centered herself under the hot overhead lights, launching into her presentation, first demonstrating the garden lighting, which she'd had a hand in designing. Although if she were asked how it was going, Pam would say 'fine' – she had to acknowledge that it felt much more like a school lesson or a business presentation. She might as well have been up there with a PowerPoint diagramming sentences. Today lacked the fun and humor that Nate always lent to a presentation. While Nate engaged the audience with his warmth, today Pam was formal. When Nate dared to flirt with the chiefly older crowd, Pam was stiff. She was, as Jackie advised, just going to stick to the script and get this over with. She could reassess and then sparkle tomorrow.

Next, Pam grasped the pruning shears off the velvet display table and rolled the overgrown, potted rose bush to center stage. She hadn't yet held a finished production model, and she was quite pleased at how sturdy they felt in her grip. The hand-held shears sported green handles and six-inch, razor sharp blades.

"Pruning your rose bushes on a regular basis is an important component of your gardening regimen in the spring and summer," Pam started, gesturing toward the plant. "On a repeat bloomer, like this one, you'll want to keep an eye on it all season. Once the bush has bloomed out, cut them back to allow for regrowth." Pam's heart raced. She snipped a few of the blooms off the bush in an attempt to slow herself down.

Breathe, you fool!

"Beautiful, see?" She showed the audience a fistful of roses in her shaking hand before placing them in a clear glass. She smiled a fake smile, as a flash of intense yearning to be back home in her kitchen in a dirty tank top and yoga pants smearing frosting onto one graham cracker after another taunted her mind. She'd told Liz, *too soon*. Too fucking soon.

Pam returned to the rose bush and grasped one of the stalks. The lights beat down on her like the sun on a cloudless July afternoon. As if in protest, her stomach roiled with hunger. "Using these shears, most stalks will be easy to cut. But they also cut through just about everything, including thick stalks such as this one, just be careful you cut it cleanly." Pam pivoted toward the audience as she cut through the thickest stalk of the rose bush. Right away, she heard gasps from the audience and saw dozens of faces register shock. She frowned and looked for Jackie in the front row, whose face had paled.

What are they staring at? she wondered with growing alarm. Beads of sweat surrounded her hairline, and she felt a heavy drop of perspiration fall from her temple down the side of her chin and onto her white shirt.

She needed to get back on track. "A clean cut," she began again and turned back to the rose bush and saw blood gushing from her fingers and down her forearm. "Oh, Jesus, sorry." Pam dropped the shears.

When she realized she'd lopped off the fleshy tip of her middle finger, she fainted.

Chapter Five

When Pam came to in the greenroom, her cream blouse now stained with her own blood and her left hand wrapped in a bulky bandage of paper towels and masking tape, Jackie was stooped over her, fanning her face with an expo program. She handed Pam a cup of water, who struggled to sit up. Pam took a sip and winced at the pain in her hand. She glanced down at her shirt. "I look like a horror show," she said.

"We need to get you to an emergency room for at least a proper bandage, maybe stitches," said Jackie, whose usual calm-under-stress demeanor was visibly shaken. "When you fell over on stage, I knew it was serious."

Pam groaned. "What about the signing?" she asked.

"Fuck the signing." Jackie shook her head, her dark ponytail bobbing back and forth. "I knew I should have made you choke down that salad."

"How were you to know I'd chop off my own finger?"

* * *

The second day of the expo, her left middle finger wrapped stiff in a large, white bandage, Pam presented the garden line again as best she could, this time with Jackie as her assistant. Although she and Jackie managed to pull off the demonstration without cutting off any more digits, she was discouraged to find that the size of the audience had shrunk, made up of a handful of onlookers.

"I think they were just bored," Pam said to Jackie over lunch after the presentation. "I can't figure out how to make these Lowes lines fun and sexy like Nate did."

"Don't beat yourself up about it. You're here, and that's progress. It's more important that you get your first one on your own out of the way and do better next time," said Jackie, dipping a French fry in a puddle of ketchup and popping it into her mouth.

"The weird thing is we – Nate, mostly – didn't have a learning curve at these home shows. We could work a crowd and make it grow each day." Pam picked at the sandwich on her plate. "I'm doing the opposite – I'm *driving* people away. I'm wasting their time. What's Lowes going to think of that?"

"You're being *way* too hard on yourself. Everyone has an expo or two that's a total bust. Maybe it's you, but maybe it's not? Maybe it's a shitty audience. Maybe it's Utah. Who knows? And we're fortunate that your brand's success isn't dependent on this *one* appearance. Just take a breath, eat your lunch, and get ready to sign some books," said Jackie, raising an eyebrow at Pam's barely-touched sandwich. "Seriously, eat."

After lunch, Pam sat on a plastic folding chair at a rectangular banquet table covered in a white tablecloth in a convention booth flanked with stacks of her and Nate's latest bestseller, *Designer You: Garden Edition.* Multiple blown up poster boards of glowing reviews of their books, magazine articles, and their blog perched on tripods on the table, surrounding her. Along the periphery of the booth, Jackie had set up large, imposing photographs of the two of them on the *Today Show* couch being interviewed by Hoda Kotb, waving to the camera during an HGTV appearance, and sitting in a studio to record a podcast, grinning like idiots with bulky headphones covering their ears and microphones at their mouths. Pam tamped down the overwhelming urge to sob at the unexpected images of her handsome husband smiling back at her from another time, blissfully unaware of his impending and gruesome demise. But all of their latest publicity material featured the both of them, and it would be a while before she would be the sole face of Designer You, at least in print.

During the months following the launch of a new book, healthy lines for signings were frequent at these home shows. Nate and Pam could count on staying over their allotted two hours to keep up with demand. Pam relished this time – after all, they were flocking to get a book that she wrote signed. Yes, the book jackets featured both of their names. And most of the ideas were Nate's. But the *words* were hers. Every time a reader gushed about learning how to knock down a wall to expand a kitchen or find attractive paint combinations for the exterior of a Victorian home, internally Pam took her share of the credit. She wasn't just the cute sidekick. This was a team effort. *You're welcome.*

Today, Pam hoped she could live up to both the ideas and the words. That sounded optimistic. Maybe instead, she hoped that their readers would forgive her for not living up to both the ideas and the words. That they would forgive her that she didn't have Nate's smile, which was like a gravitational pull.

Did they miss his tall, strong frame, a body that could heave a sledgehammer, carry drywall up three flights of stairs, and lift and position a bathtub? She longed to lean into that frame today, feel his hand resting on the curve of her back, smell his aftershave, confident in the knowledge that he was hers and hers alone later on that night.

Could they forgive her for not possessing an accessible genius and creativity? The magic he worked on people's homes, including his own, inspired devotion in their fans in ways that Pam could only label as bordering on religious. That was all him, not her. Pam often wondered what he even saw in her. She had nothing to offer that was anywhere close to his genius. If he had the ability to phrase a sentence with finesse – take his jumble of ideas, smooth them out, and breathe logic into his brilliance – she may have never gone any further with him than that spring semester, their senior year at Penn State.

Pam looked down at her left hand where the bandaged middle finger protruded crudely. If Nate were alive, this would become an amusing story, for sure an anecdote worthy of a blog post of the 'Don't Do What I Did' variety. Instead, alone, it was a visible reminder of her incompetence. That she had no business going it alone. Their readers had no obligation to her at all. In fact, their readers would know better. Nate was the brains and heart of Designer You, and without him, well, she could count herself lucky that the tip of her finger was the only casualty. It served as a warning shot. As if to say: get out of here before someone really gets hurt.

The book signing ended up feeling more like a wake or Shiva call for Pam with somber readers trickling in, expressing how sorry they were about Nate, and Pam nodding her thanks, the cute sidekick wife reduced to middle-aged widow with an injured finger. One gray-haired woman set down a box of home-baked cookies for Pam and in tears, recounted what their early blog days had meant to her, back when Grace was a toddler and Pam and Nate were remodeling their first home. The woman went on to explain that their bi-weekly blog got her through when her mother had died and left her with an old house that was practically falling down.

"Restoring it was like therapy for me," she confided. "Our relationship was always so fraught. We butted heads. And when I read your blog one day – when you repainted the cabinets in your kitchen in your first house that lovely slate blue – a light bulb went off in my head. *I could do this!* This house didn't have to be a disaster. I could fix it, and in a way, I felt like I was able to make peace with my relationship with my mother." Her eyes filled with tears again. "I'm so sorry for you," she said, her voice hoarse.

Warmth stirred inside Pam's chest. Here was a woman sharing her own personal pain. She was thankful for this simple act of kindness that reminded her she wasn't alone in her suffering. And equally disturbed that her grief would never disappear altogether just like this woman's grief hadn't. Pam had endured enough sympathy but was grateful for the sentiment. And for the reminder of why she and Nate did these personal appearances in the first place. She offered her a tired smile. "Thank you," she said with genuine affection. "Did you have anything you wanted me to sign?"

When she returned home from the airport, her parents already long asleep upstairs on the third floor, Pam crept up the stairs to the second floor and paused by Grace's room.

The light flooded out from under the crack of the darkened door. She gave the door a soft knock.

"Gracie?" she asked, turning the knob. A single reading light clamped to the double bed's wrought-iron headboard illuminated the room with a dim light and shone a spotlight onto the dark wavy ponytail that splayed out on the pillow. Still wearing her grass-stained lacrosse uniform, Grace lay on her side on top of the down comforter and snored softly. Her expansive bedroom occupied the last room on the second floor, and although it lacked the drama of their formal living room, Pam always thought Grace's room was the best in the house. Quiet and furthest from the street noise. The high ceilings sported the original crown molding. The beveled bay window that overlooked their blooming backyard was the perfect space to read on the cozy window seat.

Pam tiptoed into the room and slid the cell phone out from Grace's loose grip. Grasping the edge of a blanket folded at the base of the bed, she crawled in and pulled the blanket up, covering them both. She knew her daughter got home so tired and often put off showering after games until the following morning, and she inhaled the odd but comforting scent of teenage B.O. mixed with fresh cut grass of Grace's hair. Pam was already drifting off when she clicked off the reading light. Despite her throbbing finger, everything about being home right here, right now, felt one hundred percent right.

This. This is what you're fighting for, she reminded herself as she drifted into unconsciousness.

Chapter Six

Pam knew enough to bring Dennis, Nate's trusted foreman, along with her to the work site. She couldn't go alone. She needed someone she trusted to check out the rebar on a basement that was in the midst of being dug out on a huge townhouse in Old City before giving them the go-ahead to start pouring concrete. She always steered clear of both dirty work and basements, but lately she found herself once again, way out of her comfort zone.

Since her return home from the home expo, Pam pieced together the status of all of the unfinished client projects Nate had going before he died. It was like cramming for a midterm exam. She could grasp the arc of progress in a design project enough to write about it, but had just a vague idea of the day-to-day process. One week after the home expo, she received a call from an ongoing basement project in Society Hill. There was a problem that demanded her immediate attention. One of the new support beams they'd installed had buckled and snapped, and when she and Dennis arrived on the scene, they could both see the first floor already starting to bow.

What if the family had been home? Pam swallowed hard, horrified at the possibility that someone could have been hurt or even killed, robbed of a spouse or parent just like she and

Grace, because of an egregious error on the part of one of the workers. *Her* workers. These were people Designer You had hired and trusted with their select clients. This almost-disaster was on her.

Standing there with nothing to do but gape, Pam turned to Dennis and shrugged. She wasn't Nate. She could (and would later decide to never, ever) recount the details of this problem on the blog, but as far as how to solve it, she hadn't a clue. Pam's ego took another small hit as her complete uselessness registered on Dennis's face. He was a short, stocky man of Polish descent with weathered blue eyes and hair the color of iron. He pulled his gaze from Pam and shook his head in disgust at his men.

"You didn't plumb the beam properly. This is Contractor 101, guys," he said to the trio of workers. "This whole structure could have collapsed."

Pam watched as Dennis took immediate control. There was so much for her to learn. He read the situation and directed the men to install a temporary support post into an adjustable floor jack to prop up the sagging floor. He showed the two men how to install a load-bearing beam. When she returned that afternoon, the beams were in place and the men working with a newfound energy and efficiency. As far as she was concerned, Dennis had saved the house and the day.

"Looks so much better," said Pam as she descended the wooden stairs. "I think we averted a disaster."

Dennis approached, mopping his face with a dirty towel. "Yeah, well, we got lucky."

She nodded. "It's a good thing the Montanaros are spending the next few months in a rental. This morning was not an image that would instill confidence."

"No," said Dennis, his voice sober. "It would not." He looked back at the men as they poured concrete into two-feet deep holes dug into the dirt floor to secure the beams. Dennis turned back to Pam and pointed up at the ceiling. "Can I talk to you?"

"Sure," she said, and headed back up the stairs into the expansive kitchen. The Montanaros seemed to have an endless supply of money and were longtime clients of Nate's. He loved the Old City townhomes and their rich history, many of them dating back to the eighteenth century. This particular house stood just a few blocks from where the Declaration of Independence was signed and represented the tiny neighborhood well. Nate was in the business of preserving the integrity of these stately homes while also updating the interior features to make them suitable for modern living. He was an expert at merging traditional sensibilities with modern practicalities, and Pam noticed his fingerprints all over the sleek kitchen he'd redesigned for them a few years back: the heavy wood cabinets, copper lighting, and the slab countertops balanced out the look of the latest appliances and modern seating. She now had to become the expert or expect to lose contracts, get sued, even lose her own house. The realization made her turn cold. Pam took a seat at the kitchen island and wiped her clammy hands on her chinos.

"Well?" she asked. *Just tell me I'm an idiot who doesn't know what she's doing, and then fix the problem and move on.* She needed to get back home in time to write the day's blog post. These days, the blog was the one piece of her life where she felt in command. Behind the closed door of her office, it didn't matter that she was failing to connect with Grace or that the basement ceiling from one of Philadelphia's most valuable properties had almost collapsed. All Pam longed for was to get away from the dust and grime of her work and life and return to the safety of her office and laptop, where she would pick just the right combination of words and photos to showcase the transformation of space from drab or ugly or outdated or even dangerous to clean and useful and beautiful.

Dennis grimaced. "I'm not so sure about those guys Nate hired. Digging out the basement is a tricky job, and they just don't seem to know what they're doing without a lot of supervision."

"I remember. Nate mentioned that in March – that they seemed to lack experience. He was out here all the time. But–" Pam shrugged. "He hired them for a reason. What do we do? Fire them? After all this time, we hire a new crew? It sounds crazy this far into the project."

"I get it, I do. But this *cannot* happen again. We could have been looking down the barrel of a lawsuit." Dennis rubbed the back of his leathery neck, averting Pam's eyes. "These guys need more guidance and it's got to come from you."

His words took her aback. How was *she* supposed to act like she was in charge when she didn't know how to do the job herself? What would Nate do? Delegate. He delegated and still remained in complete control. The difference was, he knew what he was doing and she didn't. She cleared her throat.

"Dennis, I'm probably not the right person to—" Pam's cell interrupted. She took it out of her pocket and looked at the screen. Belfield Friends – Grace's school.

Shit. One more thing.

She offered him an apologetic look. "Sorry, I gotta take

this."

Dennis backed off, as Pam lifted the phone to her ear.

"Hello?" she said, as multiple reasons for the phone call whizzed through her brain – *is Grace sick?* She hadn't noticed that Grace was feeling under the weather this morning. Or maybe she'd hurt herself at lacrosse practice? Or maybe Grace had forgotten something at home – a book, her lunch. But then she would have just texted Pam what she left (and would she please, *please* drop it off at school?)

"Hello, is this Grace Wheeler's mom?"

"Yes." Panic rose in Pam's throat. No one ever began a happy, good-news conversation with "Is this Grace Wheeler's mom?"

"This is Teri Brown from BFS. I'm calling because Grace did not show up to fifth period after lunch. Did you pick her up from school?"

Pam wracked her brain. Did Grace have an appointment today that she'd forgotten about? Maybe her parents picked Grace up from school early? Her lips pressed together in instinctive annoyance at them for failing to communicate with her. Now *she* was in trouble. She cleared her throat. "Hi, Teri. I'm so sorry. I'm sure it's a misunderstanding. I didn't pick her up, but my parents are staying with us and helping out, and I bet they picked her up."

Papers rustled on the other end of the line. "I don't see that they signed her out," the school receptionist said. "I know it's been…hard, but as I'm sure you're aware, attendance is a serious issue, here, especially in high school. We have a strict attendance policy and a limited tolerance for unexcused absences. All children must be signed out."

Pam took a deep, cleansing breath. She didn't like being

lectured to by her daughter's hoity-toity private school. She loved that Grace adored the school and had grown up there, having attended from the age of four, but there were times when a few curt words from the school community could toss Pam right back into her lower middle-class station and remind her she was nothing more than a child of uneducated, small-town bumpkins. Bumpkins who had forgotten to sign Grace out of school today.

"I understand," Pam said, trying to keep a grip on to her patience. "I'll talk to her grandparents. It won't happen again."

"Yes, please see that it doesn't," Teri said. "Thank you."

Grimacing, Pam hung up and slipped the phone into her bag. "Sorry about that, Dennis."

Dennis, who'd been admiring the woodwork in the kitchen, spun around. "No big deal. Grace's school?"

Pam forced a feeble smile. "I think I'm in trouble," she said. Her parents thought they were being kind by taking over so many of the duties at home and with Grace and allowing her to focus on Designer You. Anything she needed to take even remotely serious, they would have told her right away. And she was grateful for their help. Still, something about the phone call niggled at Pam. Probably just the icy tone of the receptionist.

Dennis raised his eyebrows. "Sounded like you got a bit of a scolding. I hate it when they do that."

"It's not fun." She offered a thin, nervous laugh. "I'll sort it out." She met his eyes. "So, the guys – you think they need some supervision."

"Yeah, they need *a lot* of supervision. If it were me, I'd be here once a day to check on their work and make sure they're staying on track and doing it right." He scratched the scruff on his chin. "Where'd Nate find these guys?"

Pam blinked. It sounded like he was questioning Nate's judgment.

"Look, I don't know. But Nate always went with recommendations from guys he's worked with. Guys he trusts." She folded her arms across her chest. "They've always gotten the job done."

"Well," said Dennis. "These guys are pretty green. I'm surprised someone recommended them for this job in particular."

"Dennis." Pam's chest tightened. "I don't need to be in the position to defend all of the decisions Nate made. He was spreading himself pretty thin. I do think he took on too much there toward the end, but he'd always stood by his crew." *Toward the end.* Pam shook her head, turning away from Dennis so she could get her chin to stop trembling. She took a breath and faced him. "And now it's just me."

Dennis softened. "I know, kiddo." He sounded almost paternal, even though they were almost the same age.

"Can you help me on this one?" Pam loathed herself for having to ask. It made her feel small and helpless. But Dennis was Nate's most trusted supervisor. They'd worked together for more than a decade, and he'd helped Nate oversee the jobs he couldn't handle alone. "I'm afraid I just don't have the expertise to keep everyone on task and doing good work. The entire house will literally cave under my watch."

Dennis massaged the bridge of his nose with the tips of his fingers. "I'd like to, Pam, I would. But I don't see how that's possible. I'm overseeing the Ungers' project up in Lower Merion, the Campbells' all the way out in Westchester, and I've been flying out back and forth between here and a craftsman in Arizona. I'm swamped."

Pam knew it was true. Nate often gave Dennis the jobs that demanded a lot of travel so he wouldn't have to do it as much himself, though she did inherit a dining room conversion in Brooklyn that was now at the halfway point. She made a mental note to see about contracting that one out. But now that it was early May, one month after his funeral, it still seemed too soon, too overwhelming to be knee deep in Nate's design projects when she had just a cursory understanding of what needed to be done and how it was done right. She didn't have time to drop by this project every day. And for what? Stare at something she didn't understand? Clients who hired Designer You spent a lot of money for an expertise that Pam didn't possess. All she wanted was to hire someone else to make all the decisions.

"I know you're swamped, Dennis," said Pam, hating herself for having to push him. He was so *nice*. He and his wife, two high school age step-daughters, and their three-year-old twin sons lived out in a spacious colonial in Mt. Airy. They didn't get to see him enough. But if he didn't help her, Pam was certain she was going to lose her mind. "Could you just help me, then? For the next couple of weeks? I'll do my best to catch up on what goes into these basement projects, but from the technical side, I really know nothing."

Dennis sighed and gave her a sideways glance. "Julie's going to have me tarred and feathered for this, but OK, I can help you out. Temporarily."

On impulse, Pam reached out and enveloped him in a grateful hug. Dennis wasn't much of a hugger, but she couldn't help herself. "Tell Julie she can have you back in two weeks. I'll hand deliver you myself if it will keep me in her good graces."

* * *

Two weeks later, Dennis crouched by Pam's side as he pointed out the steel reinforcements along the wall of the basement. She chewed the inside of her cheek. The last fourteen days had felt like a contractor's master class on steroids.

"This is looking better," he said. "I think we're ready."

Pam sighed with relief. They were ready to put in concrete. After that, wallboard. And flooring. Finally. Each problem – the sagging ceiling, leaking pipes, outdated electrical wiring – needed addressing right away. It seemed endless, like they would never get traction to move forward. Each problem took them farther and farther away from completion. Pam couldn't allow the Montanaros' home to collapse or flood or burn down. But now, the space would start to take shape. She just wanted to fast forward to the end at this point, but at the same time, this project had forced her to learn a lot more about the structure of homes. She wasn't even close to an expert, but over the last two weeks as Dennis pointed out how he solved the myriad problems in this basement project, Pam felt she now had a rudimentary understanding and didn't need to interrupt every sentence to ask basic questions. This was progress. Her cell buzzed in her pocket. Grace's school again. It was the third call in two weeks.

"Excuse me," she said, climbing up the stairs to the kitchen. She'd had more conversations with BFS lately in the Montanaros' kitchen than she had in her own. Even though Pam had reminded her parents to sign Grace in and out of school via text message, she made a mental note to follow up maybe in person this time. "Hello?"

"Mrs. Wheeler, it's Susan Hicks from BFS. Do you have a

minute? I won't take up much of your time."

Pam's stomach sank. Principal Susan Hicks. Pam suspected she wasn't on the receiving end of a call from Susan Hicks for something Grace had done right. Susan Hicks was a strict but fair woman with a dominant no-nonsense streak. Her style worked well for the high-achieving children of Philadelphia's well-to-do, but Pam never took to Principal Hicks. She wasn't one of the parents who made small talk with the principal in the yard after school or during the fall book sale or spring fundraiser. Principal Hicks intimidated Pam, which made her feel dumb and small and not good enough, and for over a decade, she'd managed to avoid her, letting Nate take on the bulk of communication with her.

Pam learned that Grace had missed more than a week of school – *was everything OK?* Principal Hicks had asked, not unkindly. Pam swallowed her shock and managed to croak in embarrassment that she was not aware that Grace had skipped out on all her classes. Though, with all the time that Designer You stole lately, Pam almost never saw her, and the two had exchanged maybe a few sentences in the last two weeks. Someone, Principal Hicks continued, had called the school each day and informed the receptionist that Grace was sick and not coming in. They'd learned today that those phone calls weren't coming from either Grace's mother or her grandparents.

This is all Grace.

Pam's head buzzed and she sat on one of the barstools to steady herself, keeping her cell to her ear.

The principal then calmly (*too calmly*) invited her and Grace to meet with her this week in her office to "troubleshoot" the problem of Grace's truancy.

Troubleshoot. It was as if Pam had a problem connecting to the internet, not an issue of what to do with her sad and angry teenage daughter, who seemed to have been dodging her classes since Nate's funeral. Or so she gathered. She hadn't been around much to even notice. On the days she'd rush home to eat dinner with Grace and her parents, Grace would be having dinner at her best friend, Hannah's house. Or after putting in another marathon day, she'd hurry home to say goodnight to Grace, but when she'd arrive, the lights would already be off in her bedroom.

When Pam thought about it, she had very little idea what exactly Grace had been up to for weeks. Her parents made sure she was fed and clothed. They helped out with laundry and cleaning. And she knew they were there for Grace if she needed a shoulder to cry on. But for the first time, Pam wasn't on top of All Things Grace. She wondered what movies she had seen, how she'd performed on her last math test. *What was she eating for lunch? Did she go to spring formal?* It appalled her to think that she had no idea. Just trying to keep up with all of the unfinished client projects had monopolized her focus. When she was home, she retreated to her office and caught up on the blog and completed paperwork. She'd foisted the parenting onto her own parents. This situation, they'd reminded her in gentle voices reserved for children and widows, could not be sustained. They were happy to help out, but there would come a time when they would need to return to their own lives and Pam would be forced to figure out how to run Designer You on her own, as well as pay attention to Grace.

"Your father and I need to return home. Not right this minute, but soon," said her mom, leaning in the doorway of

Pam's office. It was after 11 p.m. the previous night and Grace was in her room and her dad asleep upstairs, while Pam wrote the day's post for the blog. She looked up at her mom and blinked, allowing her eyes to readjust from the glare of the computer screen. Deep lines surrounded her mother's eyes and lips, and Pam thought her mom appeared like she'd aged ten years in the weeks since Nate died. "Grace needs you. She loves your father and me, but she's running circles around us. All of us. She's fifteen, Pam. She may not show it, but she still needs her mom."

The heat rose to Pam's cheeks. Couldn't her mother understand the immense amount of effort it took on a daily basis just to keep up with the near constant demands of Designer You? Being a good mom right now meant keeping Designer You alive and well so they wouldn't starve or have to live under the Spring Garden Street Bridge.

Until now. Her parents lived to fawn over their grand-daughter and do whatever they could to take away her pain. Pam knew that in their eyes, punishing Grace for trouble they weren't even aware of was pointless and cruel. And not their concern. Pam didn't have a problem with her parents playing 'good cop' but it left the entire role of 'bad cop' up to her. A lonely role at that, now that she wouldn't get to share it or commiserate with a partner who understood and shared her frustration. Pam wished she could face Susan Hicks with Nate at her side. That evening when Pam got home, Grace's door was closed, but she could hear talking and music playing in the bedroom. She knocked.

"Yeah?" Grace called.

Pam let herself in.

Grace's bedroom, while not always the vision of pristine

orderliness, was usually at least neat enough for Pam to run a vacuum through. Today, grass-stained lacrosse gear, scattered papers, school textbooks, and what looked like at least a week's worth of dirty clothes covered the floor. In one corner, the formal dress that Grace had picked out on a shopping trip just before Nate died was piled in a crumpled heap. Pam paused in the doorway. She couldn't recall the last time she'd witnessed her daughter's room with so much debris on the floor.

Grace snapped her laptop shut and looked up. "What?" she asked, her tone curt and annoyed. She was sitting at her desk, which featured an overflowing collage of photos of her friends from school, summer camps, and her sports teams pasted on a corkboard and hanging on the wall above. Pam guessed her daughter had put in more mental energy in her collage of photos than she had her midterm geography project.

"I don't think I've ever seen your room this messy. Not even when you were, like, four."

Grace swiveled in her desk chair to face Pam. "Well 'hi' to you, too, Mom. I didn't think you'd be home until late."

"Something came up," said Pam. She made her way through the maze of clutter to the dress and lifted it up, pinching it between her thumb and forefinger. "What's this doing on the floor?"

Grace's face reddened. "I don't know."

"Did you leave it there?"

"I guess," said Grace, who'd now swiveled away from Pam and picked up her phone, swiping her finger along the screen.

"Why?" Pam glared at the back of Grace's head. "Look at me. Put the phone down."

Grace let out a heavy sigh. "I don't know, Mom. I guess I

just forgot. I don't need the stupid dress anymore anyway."

Pam's heart sank. This was a surprise.

"Did the formal…already happen?" Pam began, trying in vain to remember when that dance was supposed to take place.

"*Oh my God, you don't even know,*" Grace said under her breath.

"I don't know what?"

She shook her head. "I can't even talk to you."

"Yes you can," said Pam, feeling the desperation start to rise in her throat. "Please, tell me what's going on."

"I don't even know where to begin," Grace said with a sneer. "You haven't been home in like a month."

Pam blinked. Grace nailed the point that had been gutting her for weeks. She hadn't been around very much. Work had taken everything out of her and so far she was just barely hanging on, but performing both her and Nate's jobs was an unfortunate necessity if they were going to keep their house, pay the exorbitant BFS tuition every year, and well, eat. But Grace could not just bail on school when she felt like it. They both had responsibilities to keep up despite losing the most important person in the world to each of them. Simmering rage at Nate for having the horrific timing to die on them now, to abandon them when they needed him the most, threatened to boil over.

Pam took a beat, inhaled and then smoothed out the dress and draped it over the window seat. "I have to work, honey. We have to have income. If I lose the business, then we have nothing." Her breath hitched in her throat. *If I lose Designer You, then I lose all I have left of your father.*

"I hate that dress," said Grace. Pam recognized that stubborn streak well. She'd inherited it from both her and Nate – double whammy. What was Grace hiding? Pam gazed at the two framed posters hanging over the headboard of Grace's bed, one of a popular boy band and another that read, Keep Calm, Kill Zombies.

Has she grown up without me? Has she moved beyond her teenybopper obsessions?

Pam softened. "Did something happen? I still don't know if the formal has come and gone."

"The formal hasn't happened," Grace allowed. "It's this Friday."

"OK, then why isn't your dress in your closet on a hanger?" The exasperation rose in her chest again. "I don't get what it's doing on the floor."

Pam startled as she watched how fast the rage returned to her daughter's face.

"I'm not going!"

"To the dance?" As frustrating as it could be trying to pry two words from her daughter, Pam wondered how in the dark she was. Up until that moment, Pam allowed herself to take comfort in knowing that although Grace was deep in grief, she was still participating in school, still playing her sports, still going to the dance with her girlfriends. Pam had envisioned whole gaggles of girls dancing together in groups, stealing glances at the boys all the way across the gym, like she did when she was the same age. Boys, as far as she knew, were not yet much of an issue that loomed large. But they lurked on the horizon, probably closer than that, and Pam began to fear that hormones and broken hearts had sneaked in while her back was turned.

Grace rose from her desk and flopped onto her bed. "Ugh,

you do *not* understand, Mom!"

Once again, her words rang true. Pam *didn't* understand. "You're right. I don't get it. Why aren't you going? Did you and Hannah get into a fight over something?" They'd been excited about their first formal dance since winter break.

"Not really," Grace said and huffed. "I'm just not going."

Pam sighed. Round and round they could go. She sensed there was more at stake here than what Grace was letting on – this couldn't just be about missing a dance – but as always, the more she pushed, the more Grace backed away. She suspected it didn't seem to have anything to do with her grief, though. For now, Pam needed to address the thorny, missing-school issue. "Well, I just got off the phone with Principal Hicks. That's my news."

The color drained from Grace's face. "You did?"

"Yeah, and she is not too happy with you at the moment." Pam walked over to the bed and sank down. "And neither am I. What's with skipping whole days of school? You've missed more than a week?"

She didn't respond. Pam could see her seethe, the anger and maybe – *hopefully* – embarrassment and shame simmering inside of her.

"We need to talk about this. It's serious," said Pam. "I don't want the first conversation we have about you bailing out of school to happen in front of Susan Hicks. Right?"

Grace remained stubbornly silent.

"Listen," said Pam. "I know it's been a hard time. It's been tough on the two of us, carrying on after Dad died. The world doesn't stop, though. If you don't do your part by going to school and trying your best, well – we need to hang on to what we have. We can still lose. Everything. Our house, our car, our whole way of life, meaning no sports, no extracurricular activities, no dances, no going to the movies, no hanging out with friends. You know that, right?"

Frowning, Grace looked away.

"And calling in to school, pretending to be me or Grandma excusing your absence—" Pam shook her head. It was tough getting past the lies. Grace had never been dishonest like this, and for the first time, she found it unsettling and frightening how easily it seemed Grace could just lie without breaking a sweat, like it didn't affect her at all except to get her what she wanted. "That is so baffling to me. I've never known you to be someone who's dishonest." She fought back the raw anger that if Grace saw surface, would diminish everything she had to say to her. "I'm so disappointed. I don't know what to say."

"Seems like you're saying plenty," said Grace.

Pam's anger flared. "You're seriously talking back right now? You don't have an argument here." She inhaled, trying to calm her temper. "But why? Why don't you go to school? Where do you go? What do you do all day?"

Grace kept her eyes down and traced the butterfly design on her comforter with her index finger.

"What do you do, Grace?" Pam's patience waned as she sought anything, any sort of sign from Grace's face. She'd had enough. "I don't get this. You go to an excellent school. It's an absolute privilege to attend that school and it opens a gazillion doors for you, and I'm watching you piss it all away. And for what? To go downtown? Go to the movies? What are you trading your education for? I can tell you right now, your dad would be just as disappointed as I am."

That did it. Grace's eyes reddened and one by one, tears fell down her cheeks. "Nothing," Grace croaked. "I don't do anything."

"What do you mean, you 'don't do anything'?" Pam said.

Grace looked up and met her mother's eyes. "I walk around. I think," she said. "I ride the bus sometimes, see where the different routes end up and then turn around and come back."

"But why do you have to do this during school? Why can't it wait until after school or on the weekend?"

"It's quieter during the day. Everyone's at work or, obviously, *school*. I can miss Dad and no one stares at me. No one cares, no one judges. No one even knows. I can just disappear and get away from all the pressure for a little while."

"You want to disappear?" Concern and worry edged into Pam's voice.

"Sometimes. I don't like the stares."

"You feel like other people are staring at you?"

"Or asking if I'm OK." Grace sniffed and ran the back of her hand under her nose. "I know everyone means well. But don't you get sick of the pity looks? And the 'are you OKs?' Or worse, the people who don't have anything to say, but just *stare* at you like you're a freak and then look away when you catch them. Like they'd sooner die than be in your shoes right now, which is what I know they're all thinking. So yeah, I don't really want to go to school much these days."

Pam paused and absorbed Grace's confession, her mind returning to the home expo when everyone had seemed to stare and pity her. Pam had no desire to present at any more expos in the near future. No wonder Grace didn't want to go to the dance. She wasn't ready to jump into this new life without a father yet. Pam nodded. She wasn't ready for it either.

"OK. I hear that," she said, rubbing Grace's back. "When

we go in to see Principal Hicks on Thursday, you need to be ready with an apology and promise that this isn't going to happen again – and you need to mean it. My bet is Ms. Hicks will probably lecture you and give you a stern warning, maybe some time to catch up on any tests or assignments. Maybe detention after school. You might have some extra work over the summer." Pam watched Grace's eyes widen in horror at the thought of summer school. "But don't count on any more second chances. Her patience with you is pretty thin at this point."

"But I hate it. I can't go back," said Grace, sniffling.

"You can and you will," said Pam, resolving to be firm. "We have to be strong. We're a team of two now, and we need to do our best to keep up. You have less than a month left of school. I think if you can ingratiate yourself to Principal Hicks, you can fix the damage and move on this summer. Next year, you'll start over. It'll feel fresh. It might even feel great to be back at school to see everyone. But for now, you need to dig deep, just like you do at the end of a tough lacrosse match."

Grace sat up and wiped her eyes with the sleeve of her t-shirt. "It's not lacrosse, Mom, it's life. Lacrosse is so much easier."

Chapter Seven

At four o'clock the following afternoon, Pam drove across town to Belfield Friends and glided into the visitor parking spot. She placed a shaky hand on the key and killed the ignition. *Just breathe*, she told herself for the thousandth time since the phone call forty minutes earlier. She took in two, deep, jagged breaths.

"There's been an incident," said Principal Hicks over the phone. "She's safe, but I need you to come down to the school right away and pick up Grace."

So much for them meeting over her cutting school. *There's been an incident.* Pam's head swam with limitless possibilities of 'incidents' – all of them much worse than truancy. And without Nate, how was she supposed to smooth things over? She was never the 'smoother.' She was the 'hand-wringer.'

Pam looked out the driver's side window and took a visual assessment of the school that had been Grace's second home since she was four. When she and Nate first interviewed at BFS, following a lengthy application, an afternoon 'play date' with one of the preschool classes, and a not-insubstantial processing fee, she felt a nagging suspicion that she didn't belong. She would *never* belong. Nate belonged and Grace would for certain. But not Pam. She remembered sitting in this very parking spot with Nate at the wheel. He'd put the car in park, switched off the engine, and slipped off his seatbelt.

'Wait,' she'd said, placing her hand over his. They were alone in the car, as four-year-old Grace was staying at a neighbor's that afternoon. This interview was for parents only. The car ticked as it cooled.

'What's wrong?' Nate had asked. In his typical fashion, he wasn't worried at all about the interview. This was how he'd grown up: private schools and tennis clubs as a regular part of his world. Pam could tell he just wanted to get on with the interview, get Grace admitted, and move on to the next thing. She longed for the same effortless confidence and couldn't help but resent him a little for it, too.

'Nothing,' she said. She gnawed the inside of her cheek. 'I'm just...' She'd let her words hang.

Nate settled back in his seat and squeezed her hand. The keys dangled in the ignition. 'Don't worry. Grace is going to get in. Application's complete. The check cleared. Grace charmed everyone at her preschool play date. This interview is just a formality. And you know what, if she doesn't get in? So what? We're out $500, and we'll accept Penn Charter's offer.'

It was true. Grace would go to a top notch preschool that fall, that was a fact. But Pam wasn't nervous about that. She would come face-to-face with Principal Susan Hicks for the first time, a woman Pam had met in passing when dropping Grace off for her afternoon class play date. Tall and slender, Susan Hicks had cropped, near-black hair, surrounding an angular face with a strong jaw. She exuded a cold confidence and a ready toughness. Pam knew as soon as she shook Susan Hicks's hand, she did not want to get on this woman's bad side.

During the interview, Pam fidgeted and talked too much, which she always did when nervous. She wanted so desperately to appear as if she belonged there, even if she didn't feel it on the inside. She would have loved to go to a school like this, but growing up in rural Chester County, she didn't have an option like BFS. Quiet but determined, Pam had worked her way through grade school and high school. She was the steady worker, always keeping her head in a textbook while economic uncertainty hovered over their household. Her mom stayed home to raise Pam and her older brother, Jimmy, while her dad followed his dreams of owning (and then losing) a series of restaurants.

When Pam was still just a baby, her father opened his first restaurant – an old-style Italian place, the kind that featured red and white checkered tablecloths and simple pastas with rich sauces. At first, it served as a perfect date night destination for the town's residents. But her dad never secured a liquor license – Pennsylvania was known as a state that was particularly stingy with them – and therefore never had the ability to serve the expected Chianti with the popular spaghetti and meatballs. Any initial interest in the small town restaurant waned after a new place opened a few blocks away that could serve wine and beer and was owned by Italian immigrants.

After the Italian joint was forced to close, her father opened and operated an off-brand, fast food franchise. Although the restaurant had steady customer traffic, it was an exhaustive venture and in the end, just wasn't enough to keep their family afloat. He kept taking out loans and resorting to his stack of credit cards solely to keep the lights on and (fast) food on the table. There were two Christmases in a row that they celebrated a few days late, so her parents could take advantage of the after-Christmas sales just to put a few presents under the tree for Pam and Jimmy. Her dad learned that the best way to make ends meet in the franchise business was to own multiple businesses, which wasn't going to happen with the amount of debt he'd taken on. His only choice was to sell the franchise, which relieved Pam, though she knew to keep her mouth shut. She was twelve at the time and imagined she was the one kid in middle school who would have been happy if she didn't have to look at another French fry for the rest of her life. To this day, the slightest whiff of fry oil kicked in her gag reflex.

The summer after Pam turned thirteen, the restaurant business had started to turn around for her dad at last, but only when he cajoled his wife and kids into taking on roles as cashiers, servers, hosts, and even cooks. He bought an established diner after the owners had retired and decided to sell. It was situated in the middle of their small town and served as a central meeting place for everyone from teenagers grabbing a burger and Coke after school, to the Chester County Agricultural Development Council, to the local rotary club, to motorcycle enthusiasts, to public meet-and-greets with the mayor.

Pam spent her weekends, most days after school, and her summers fulfilling Cobb salad, club sandwich, and French onion soup orders for friends from school, local farmers, retailers, Harley Davidson riders, and small-time politicians. She knew how proud her father was of his success, but for Pam, every day was a constant reminder of her small town, blue-collar upbringing. It felt like her whole life she'd dreamed of getting out, getting away from rural 'folks' with thick Pennsylvanian dialects to someplace larger, where she had the freedom to figure out who she was in a large, urban, and diverse environment, where she didn't have to worry about the burden of being under a microscope all the time. Those roots were hard to shake sometimes, even as an adult, educated and successful by anyone's standard, and removed from her lower middle-class past, and especially later as she competed for spots in the best of private education for little Grace. Her parents didn't even go to college and here was Grace on the academic fast-track. Pam felt so small time, always proving that she belonged in this world of BMWs and private schools. She found this an unfortunate truth as she sat in a hard, plastic chair outside of Susan Hicks' office waiting for her interview about Grace's preschool.

Nate had leaned over and whispered in her ear, "Just remember, they need us as much as we need them." She smiled and gave his hand a quick squeeze. He always knew just the right thing to say at the right time, and she loved him for it. And even though she was nervous and talked too much and too fast, she and Nate interviewed well enough to get Grace into the school, which had been the perfect fit for her from day one.

Until today.

When she saw the school from the window of her Subaru, Pam tried to conjure up that unassuming structure, that friendly, nurturing environment that had been so good to Grace for more than half her life. Would they be good to Grace today? She sat glued to the driver's side seat, gripping the wheel with both hands. At least the large bandage had come off of her left hand middle finger and was replaced by two smaller Band-Aids wrapped in a neat and dainty white strip of first aid tape. She was grateful she didn't look as broken as she had following the Dream Home Expo. Maybe a *little* broken. She'd just keep her left hand in her lap for the duration of the meeting.

"Well." Susan Hicks offered Pam a bony but vigorous handshake and ushered her into her office. Pam looked around. Although she'd caught brief glimpses of the principal around campus and at events over the years, she hadn't entered her office since Grace's preschool interview. Not much had changed. The large, L-shaped desk took over much of the window side, which looked out over the expanse of lawn and the flagpole at the front of the school. In the middle of the room were two midcentury wooden chairs with orange cushions that faced a coffee table and love seat. "Thank you for meeting with me on such short notice," said Principal Hicks, her tone cordial.

Pam scanned the room. Judging from the photographs in tasteful frames that littered the desk and windowsill, it seemed Susan Hicks had married and produced a couple of babies – twins, it looked like – since Pam had last sat in this office, more than ten years ago. It was funny, though. She couldn't ever remember Principal Hicks as pregnant. She hoped motherhood had softened her, but she doubted it. Her hair was still short and very black, which accentuated the sharpness of her facial features.

Grace emerged from the front office, her face angry red and tear stained, her hair a tangled, frizzy mess, and sat in the other orange chair beside Pam.

"Hi?" Pam offered, blinking in shock at the image of her daughter. She couldn't begin to imagine what had resulted in such a fearsome look. Grace peered back at her with a pained face.

"So," Principal Hicks began, as she perched on the over-stuffed loveseat. It appeared almost as severe as Susan Hicks herself. "I received a report this afternoon from Coach Briggs, who told me she had to break up a fight between Grace and Darla Zipperstein today in the girls' locker room before lacrosse practice. Witnesses – all lacrosse team players – reported that Grace started the fight. I wanted to get both of you in here to discuss the incident and figure out what, exactly, happened." The principal sat back into the sofa and crossed her legs. She gazed at Grace with an expectant look on her face.

A fight? Grace? Pam thought she might pass out – just slide into unconsciousness as surely she would slide to the floor. Instead, she stared at the floor, shaking her head back and forth in disbelief. She turned and looked at Grace. "Is this true?"

Grace, still dressed for lacrosse practice, leaned her elbows on her knees and cradled her face in her hands. "Sort of," she said, her words muffled through her fingers.

Pam turned away from Grace and gave Principal Hicks a loaded look.

"What do you mean, 'sort of'?" Pam asked, stealing a sideways glance at Grace, who seemed to want to disappear. She slumped in her chair, arms folded across her chest, and stared at the Turkish rug that bridged the short distance between the armchairs and the love seat.

Principal Hicks sat forward. "Tell us what happened, Grace. I want to understand why Darla went to the emergency room today with possibly a fractured nose."

"A fractured nose? Are you serious, Grace?" Pam could feel the color draining from her face.

Grace straightened, her mouth set in a slash. She faced her mom. "Yes, Mom. I punched her in the nose." She looked down at her feet, her voice lowered. "The bitch deserved it."

Pam closed her eyes, blocking reality for a moment. Since when did her sweet, sensitive girl morph into a vicious, violent menace? "Really? Now is not a great time to be using language like that."

Susan Hicks stiffened.

"I should watch *my* language? After Darla called me a 'whore' and a 'slut' to the whole school and the 'c' word to the team? That's bullshit." She crossed her arms over her chest. "I hope her nose *is* broken. I hope it heals like a hockey player's nose."

"Grace!" said Pam, as if she were the shocked mom in a television sitcom. Like saying Grace's name in a stern enough voice would solve anything. She'd never felt more incapable of handling a disciplinary action against her daughter. And if she was being honest, if Pam had found herself in the locker room with the two girls, Pam wasn't certain *she* would've been able to resist punching Darla in the nose for calling Grace the 'c' word, either.

Grace slumped in her chair. Pam determined from the defiant glint in her eye that Grace was nowhere near backing down. She reached out and touched her daughter's arm. "What's going on, Grace? Why would you hit someone? A *teammate*?"

Grace ripped her arm away and looked away from both her mother and the principal.

"Please tell us," urged Principal Hicks in a tone that bordered on soothing. "I want to understand what happened."

"You'll never understand," Grace said, under her breath. "Why should I tell you anyway? You'll just try to use it against me. I'm amazed no one bothered to film it with their phone."

"Well," said Susan Hicks settling back into the sofa. "Then I may have no choice but to base all disciplinary action on what I've heard from the coach and the girls."

Pam looked up at the principal. "Which was…?"

The principal folded her hands in her lap and offered a humorless half smile. "That Grace instigated an assault on another team member before practice in the girls' locker room," she said. "Darla and her cohort of friends insist Grace attacked Darla unprovoked, though three more members of the team came forward, revealing there had been some 'drama' going on between the two for weeks, now. And that, and I quote, 'Darla deserved it.'"

"She *did* deserve it. She deserves worse." Grace's face was pinched, her arms folded across her chest.

"Between the assault and cutting weeks of school, you're looking at level three – maybe level four – offenses."

Pam recalled the days and weeks she'd spent poring over the *Welcome to BFS!* manual they'd received in the mail after Grace was accepted to the school. She nodded as she remembered with horror, what 'level three' and 'level four' offenses equated to as possible consequences for Grace's actions: expulsion. Her eyes darted back to Grace. There had to be an explanation. Grace wouldn't just hit someone for no reason.

"Why did Darla 'deserve' to be hit? What did she do?" Pam asked keeping her voice as gentle as possible.

Grace covered her face with her hands and crumpled. "She's just so mean," she said through tears.

'Mean' isn't going to cut it.

"OK, but what did she *do*?"

Grace wiped her eyes with the sleeve of her t-shirt. "She humiliated me in front of the whole school."

Pam looked over at Principal Hicks, whose patience, judging by the look on her face, seemed to be waning.

"How, hon?" prodded Pam. "How did she 'humiliate' you?"

Grace took in a deep breath and let out a sigh. "Darla knew I was cutting school. She knew it and got so jealous. She's always been jealous – jealous that my parents are on TV or popular or whatever, and now that my dad is dead, it's like I'm getting even more attention." She narrowed her eyes at the colorful strip of rug at her feet. "Whatever. Like she'd ever want to trade places for my life."

Pam resisted reaching out to her daughter and instead held her breath, worrying that any movement, no matter how loving, how supportive, how mom-like, would break Grace's momentum.

"So when she found out I was cutting school, she sneaked a photo of me when I was standing next to some guy, waiting for the light to turn – a guy I don't even know or remember but from the angle, it looked like we were holding hands or cuddling or something – and sent mass text messages to everyone telling them I was hooking up with older guys and that I'm a slut and that I need the attention of older men now that my dad is dead. It was vicious and spread so fast." She dropped her head onto her hand. "The more lies she spread, the more I wanted to disappear. Never come back to school. And the comments after were worse than the rumors in the first place. Some of my friends stood up for me online, but a lot didn't. A bunch of the douchebag football players now ask me every time I pass them in the hall in front of everyone how much I charge for a blowie."

Pam's stomach dropped. She wanted to murder those assholes. This was her fifteen-year-old daughter they were harassing. Horrific rumors, of course, had always been an unfortunate part of high school probably since its advent, but now all students seemed to carry around with them cell phones with cameras and Instagram accounts and Snapchat that tracked and logged each ugly moment. Even reclassifying something innocent into something tawdry. Every vulnerable, pimpled, hormonal teenager had to be on guard at all times and pray that nothing caught on camera was going to bite them in the ass either thirty seconds later, or when they started looking for employment after college graduation.

Grace straightened in her chair. "To get her back, I took an old piece of salmon out from the freezer and let it defrost on top of the deck for a few days." She allowed a slow smile to spread across her face. "I knew no one was going up there, so I gave nature plenty of time to do its job on that fish."

Pam swallowed hard, thinking Grace had been up on the same roof that Nate had fallen off of just last April. Grace was right, Pam was certain no one had been up there, except for Nate's guys who'd cleared off the decking supplies a few days after his death and left only the steel beams, which were bolted to the roof.

"Then today," Grace continued. "I took it to school, unsealed the package, and dumped the fish in Darla's locker during first period. By lunch, people were gagging as they walked by. I heard everything in her locker got fish juice on it – her binder, textbooks, letter jacket, backpack. It was epic."

Frowning at the note of satisfaction she heard in her

daughter's voice, Pam tore her eyes from Grace and turned to Principal Hicks, who appeared as flummoxed as Pam felt enraged.

"Did you know this was going on? Did you know that the whole school was calling my daughter a slut? That she was seeking attention from older men? All this after she had just lost her father?" Pam could feel the heat rising from her gut, traveling up her chest and neck, and spreading to the top of her hairline, like she was a human thermometer. Pam lowered her voice and enunciated for the principal. "Did you know?"

Principal Hicks shook her head. "No, this is all news to me." She leaned forward and set her gaze on Grace. "This was *this morning*? The fish incident?"

Grace sank lower into her chair. "Darla was pissed. She and her group cornered me when I was getting changed for practice and accused me of putting the fish in her locker. They knew it was me because I wasn't hiding anything. I didn't sneak like she did." She shrugged. "So she called me a stupid 'c' word and a drama queen with daddy issues and that's when I punched her."

Pam took a breath and pinched the inside of her thumb, a little trick she used to remind herself to breathe and not lose focus. Instincts to both comfort her hurting, bullied daughter and crush her vengeful, violent behavior vied to expose themselves, but instead she swallowed her impulse and sat mute in Principal Hicks's mid-century orange chair.

The principal regained her composure. "None of this new information takes away from the fact that Grace assaulted another student. We will reach out to Darla and her family for more details surrounding the, uh—"

"Bullying," said Pam, straightening in her chair. "I don't

condone punching anyone in the nose, but Grace wasn't unprovoked. This didn't come out of nowhere."

"OK." Principal Hicks flashed her palms as if in surrender. "Look, I will make it my personal mission to investigate the situation, but Grace's behavior has all gone far past what is acceptable at BFS." She turned toward Grace. "Before all of this nonsense with Darla, you made the choice to skip school and lie about it, even after several warnings and revoked privileges."

Pam's eyebrows shot up. "Wait, what? There were warnings?" She stared at Grace. "What privileges?"

Grace brushed a wisp of hair from her eyes, squeezed her arms tight to her chest, and sank lower into her chair.

"Has there been some sort of disciplinary process going on that I haven't been aware of?" Pam asked.

"We always try to communicate with the parent first about absences. When these first started, of course, we understood we were speaking with you and that you had excused these absences. The moment we found out that Grace was lying, we put her on academic probation," said Principal Hicks in a level tone that Pam noticed was not judgmental, but clear and factual, and left no room for argument.

"Huh," said Pam, letting the weight of Principal Hicks's words settle in. Grace was in far more trouble at school than she'd thought.

Grace continued to look down, refusing to make eye contact with either Pam or Principal Hicks.

"I see," said Pam, eying her daughter. "Do you have anything to say for yourself?"

Grace shook her head.

"She is also banned from attending the formal dance this

Friday," Principal Hicks said.

Pam almost burst into laughter. Of course! The books and paper everywhere, the overturned art and craft supplies, the dress in a heap – Pam surmised that Grace had probably been furious and took out her anger on her poor bedroom like a toddler having a temper tantrum.

Pam glared at her daughter. "Really?" Grace did not respond.

Principal Hicks stood and walked over to her desk to pick up a folder. "I hope you understand – our patience is wearing thin at this point." She opened the file and scanned the top page. "Legally, the student may be removed from the school after ten unexcused absences, and even with the allowed five absences for the loss of the father…" Pam winced at the clinical way Principal Hicks tossed out 'loss of the father' "…there are still thirteen unaccounted for days. We are within our rights to expel even before we take the assault into consideration."

Pam's heart dropped. "We are within our rights to expel?" She'd expected a slap on the wrist for the absences and imagined the three of them negotiating ways Grace could perhaps make up some tests and school work. *The fucking Welcome Manual.* Its very existence was an extension of the school covering its own ass. She looked over at her daughter, whose face had gone white. Grace straightened in her chair. Pam's hope that this conversation would head in the 'stern warning' direction began to evaporate.

"I was thinking more suspension than expulsion, which is what we would have been talking about Thursday. And then today happened. It's quite alarming, this assault on another student on top of the truancy," Principal Hicks continued. "And even as I take into consideration your situation, with the death of your husband and the emotional turmoil that creates when families are making that transition, I can't dismiss the combination of the amount of missed school – the sheer number is at best egregious and irresponsible – and the fighting, which is totally inappropriate and goes against everything we stand for. We take the safety of our students very seriously." She sat back on the love seat and crossed her legs. "On top of that, BFS is a very competitive school with one of the best reputations in the state. We are forced to turn away students every year, even in high school. These are students who would sacrifice almost anything to attend BFS and reap the benefits that this school has to offer."

"I understand," Pam said.

"The bottom line? We want students who want to be here," said Principal Hicks, folding her hands in her lap.

Not only had her expectations for this meeting fallen far short, but any amount of control Pam might have started with was now slipping through her fingers. She pinched the inside of her thumb again. *Focus.* "Grace wants to be here, believe me."

Principal Hicks offered them both a closed-lipped smile. "I understand that this may come as quite a shock. We can make arrangements for assignments and tests to be completed over the summer at a local public high school, one that is convenient to your home, if you like. But I think it's time that BFS and Grace part ways."

Part ways. This can't be happening. Pam shot Grace a desperate look. "Please, honey. Tell Principal Hicks how much you want to stay and that you'll do anything to return in the fall."

"Yes, it's true," mumbled Grace, whose eyes were rimmed

with red. "I don't want to be kicked out." Her chin quivered.

Principal Hicks appeared unmoved. "Well, you should have thought of that before you racked up more than ten unexcused absences and punched Darla Zipperstein in the face."

Grace's mouth contorted into a sad grimace and the tears flooded down her cheeks. "Expelled? I'm expelled?"

Principal Hicks offered her a somber look. "I'm afraid so, Grace."

Pam looked from Principal Hicks to Grace, Grace to Principal Hicks. "There must be something we can do. Pass a test? Community service? Probation? Or something? Anything?" she pleaded. "This just seems so rash. So sudden. I assure you. Grace wants to be here. She wants to graduate from BFS. She wants to be a very generous alumna in the future."

Principal Hicks remained solemn. "We did not arrive at this decision lightly, Mrs. Wheeler."

"Please, then. Give her – us – a second chance. Grace just lost her father and I lost my husband. We're both not ourselves right now," said Pam. "We will not mess this up again, and if we do, well, I guess we'd deserve to be kicked out." She swallowed, hoping her tone didn't give away how desperate and frightened and angry she was at that moment. "I'll do anything. Volunteer me for the gala fund raising committee or the fall's pancake breakfast. I'm begging you."

Principal Hicks closed the file and shook her head. "I'm sorry. The decision's been made."

Pam wanted to smack the self-satisfaction off of Principal Hicks's smug face. *We are not a problem you can solve.*

"You don't know what's going on in your school," said Pam.

"You don't know what's going on with your daughter," said

Principal Hicks.

Their words hung suspended in the air like smog above the principal's Turkish rug.

Pam sighed. She could cry so easily at that moment – burst into furious tears like she was five. Stomp her feet and hurdle her body onto the carpeted floor and just wail. It hurt her chest just to breathe in and out.

"When I drove out here today and sat in that parking lot, I thought about Grace's first few days here as a visiting preschool student, the spring before she was admitted. And I thought about how perfect this school was for our little girl. What a perfect fit. Great teachers, nice kids, a beautiful program that promotes the 'whole child' – which I found a little mystifying at first, because I'm not an educator. But I've seen with my own eyes what that means and how BFS has shaped my daughter and helped her grow into a loving, kind, funny, smart, confident little girl and now teenager, though, I admit, a troubled one. But it's temporary." Pam reigned herself in. She was talking too much again. "With Nate gone, I just feel like the rug has been ripped out beneath us once again." Saying his name brought tears to her eyes. She could hear him whisper in her ear all over again: *They need us as much as we need them.* That's it! She felt for her checkbook in her purse and turned toward Grace.

"Grace, please wait for me outside."

Grace furrowed her brow before standing and slinging her backpack over her shoulder. She closed Principal Hicks's office door behind her.

Principal Hicks tilted her head. "What's this about?"

Pam sat straighter in her chair. "I'd like to write you a check for next year's tuition as well as a large donation."

Principal Hicks hesitated. Pam shifted in her seat. She hoped Principal Hicks was considering her offer. She hoped she didn't just commit an obscene error in judgment.

Pam decided to push ahead anyway. She'd nothing to lose at this point. "I remember chatting with Grace's sixth grade teacher at the winter concert last December, and she mentioned the school wanted to send both her and Mr. Henley to South Africa this summer to conduct research for the Africa unit next year, but the school didn't raise enough money. I'd like to fill that gap."

Principal Hicks blinked. Pam wrote a large check that not only covered tuition but also an additional $15,000, a total amount equivalent to her latest book advance payment. She gulped. She ripped the check out of the checkbook and slid it over to Principal Hicks. "Think about it."

Principal Hicks looked at the check for what seemed like an eternity and then met Pam's eyes. "OK, you don't give me much choice. Grace can stay on a probationary basis." She narrowed her eyes. "Grace lays one finger on anyone in this school, she is out. There are no more chances after this."

Pam's heart lifted. For the first time, she felt like she belonged.

Chapter Eight

The day that Nate had secured the popular ex mayor's new-old brownstone project in Rittenhouse Square had been one for celebration. Bernie Scott had approached both Nate and Pam at a fundraiser for a parent of a member of Grace's club lacrosse team, who was running for city controller. He'd just closed on a Civil War era brownstone corner property that needed to be converted from four separate flats and returned to a four-story, single family home. The projected budget was upwards of a half million, but Nate considered the visibility of the project worth more – it was priceless. Bernie Scott was looking for publicity leading up to a possible run for governor and Pam was cleared to write and photograph every step of the process for not only her blog, but *Philadelphia Magazine* and *This Old House*. TLC was slotted to film some segments about the project as well.

"You can't *buy* that publicity," he said to Pam later that night in bed, after a little too much wine and just enough celebratory sex.

That was last October, when Pam and Nate soared with confidence. In the ensuing months, Nate had his guys scoop out the insides of the house, bring it down to the studs, and then start from scratch. Nate relished a raw space. His brain flooded with ideas. Pam loved watching him sketch out each floor, determining where the kitchen would go, the living room, library, media room. The house would include five good sized bedrooms and six gorgeous bathrooms, including a gigantic master suite on the fourth floor. Nate came up with an ambitious plan of having Bernie Scott in the house a year later, by the end of October. But now that it was mid-June and Nate gone, Pam felt a little too visible taking a shaky lead on a project for a rich, charismatic ex-mayor with an oversized presence in the city that loved him so much, they'd elected him in two landslide victories. *Nate*, thought Pam, *you really left me in the lurch with this one*. This was a huge house for an even bigger personality. *Why would a single man in his mid-fifties need that much space?* Pam often wondered, now that she was forced to take on the project alone, though the thought did make her feel a little judgy. *He doesn't even have kids.*

The sketches and the empty brownstone were all she had of the project before Nate had fallen off the roof. And because of mutual 'scheduling conflicts' that put off this meeting until mid-June, Pam was just now getting around to meeting with Bernie Scott about the designs. She wondered how he'd take it when she'd have to 'fess up how little qualified she felt for a job this 'visible.' It was one thing to take on the Montanaros' relatively humble basement project, and quite another to convert an entire mansion of a beloved public figure. Pam cursed Nate's ambition that got her into this mess and half hoped Bernie would just fire her and find someone else who knew what they were doing. That didn't sound bad to her at all – more like relief.

She'd been waiting a half an hour, and her nerves were on

high alert. Bernie's assistant brought her a bottle of water and then left her there to freeze in the over air-conditioned conference room of Bernie's downtown law office, a high-rise on the 51st floor of one of the city's newer buildings that appeared from the outside as if it was made entirely out of glass. Pam shivered and rubbed her bare arms. She got up once again to stretch her legs and look out the window, which looked out over City Hall and Dilworth Park. Now that summer was in full swing, the city felt alive and vibrant, teeming with tourists and pop up parks and joggers, all of whom seemed to be having far more fun than she was. She looked down the more than fifty stories and the vertigo kicked in, leaving her a little dizzy.

"Pam," said Bernie, as he entered the conference room. Pam turned from the window, heart thumping, and met his outstretched hand with her own. He clasped hers in both of his. He had the hands of a politician – dry and warm. Bernie had gone back to practice law after his tenure as mayor had ended, though she wasn't certain how much law he actually practiced, considering that maybe he was in a holding pattern until election season. "I'm so sorry about Nate. What a devastating loss – for you and your family, for the architecture and design community. I can't believe it." He shook his head in sympathy.

Pam nodded her acknowledgment. She'd become adept at hearing people tell her the same thing over and over again over the last two months. "Thanks."

Bernie offered her a leather swivel chair and sat at the end of the long wooden conference table. Pam surmised there were twenty chairs around this huge table and wondered what the conference room looked like when it was full. *Was it warmer with more people?* she wondered. *Is that why they keep the conference room so cold?* Now, with just the two of them, to an outside observer it must have looked a little ridiculous and extravagant to use such a large space for something that wasn't even business related.

She sat and unrolled Nate's plans for the house. "When we talked over the phone in March, Nate had just put the finishing touches on these plans. As you know, the house is just a raw space waiting to be put back together into the beautiful brownstone it was designed to be – a large, single family residence for a family of prominence." Pam cleared her throat. *He* wasn't a *family*. He was a prominent single person, not a prominent family. Ugh, she hoped she didn't sound as sanctimonious as she felt. "Anyway, I need your approval on these plans before we proceed."

Nate had mapped out each floor on his computer over the winter, and yesterday, Pam had Liz print them out on large drafting paper at Kinko's. She hadn't viewed them since Nate giddily called her into his office one morning after Grace had left on the bus for school to take a look at them. He'd been up the whole night working on the plans on his iMac and reeked of sweat and stale coffee.

Today, Pam smoothed the printouts on the conference table. Nate's vision of the home was a marriage of meticulous research and his own brilliant design. He waved his magic wand and turned a building of modest flats into a single-family home, replete with a shimmering kitchen, grand dining room, magnificent living room, and even a gorgeous parlor on the first floor, luxurious bedrooms, bathrooms, a library, a den on the second and third floors, and then a sweeping bedroom suite on the fourth.

When Bernie slid his reading glasses from his dress shirt pocket and bent over the plans, pride for Nate surged through Pam like an electrical current. It didn't matter what Bernie thought. The plans were a brilliant use of a large space for a single, prominent, middle-aged man. Pam smiled just thinking about the historical details she could add to make the house a home – two bold, brass chandeliers in the formal dining room, the crown moldings, the wooden window seats in the bay window on the second floor, the gargantuan mirror in the entryway. She'd bring back the hardwood floors to their original gleam. She would attempt to talk him into a historically accurate but tasteful wall paper and sconces in the upstairs hallways. One striking detail for Pam was that Nate had thought to bring back the secret hallway on the first floor that joined the kitchen to the entryway and was designed for nineteenth century house staff who needed to scurry between the kitchen and living rooms without being seen. It almost felt like she and Nate were working together again after a short hiatus. *Go Team Wheeler.*

Pam held her breath as Bernie scrutinized the plans. As much as she wanted to tackle those details, she was a long way off. The house didn't even have walls yet, let alone wallpaper.

Bernie straightened and took off his glasses, squeezing the bridge of his nose with his thumb and forefinger. "And this is according to historical records? We'd be restoring it to its original footprint?"

Genuine enthusiasm coursed through her. "Yes, with updates." She stood and placed her finger on the plans and pointed to one of the bathrooms. "The bathrooms, for example, aren't quite as large as most modern luxury bathrooms today because we're putting the house back to the way it was before the conversion, but they will have all the modern comforts and conveniences you can expect – roomy tub, glass shower, heated flooring."

He grinned. "Good, I like a heated floor." He pointed to the fourth floor plan. "And what about the master suite?"

"Nate made sure you had a sitting room by the window. This is where the fireplace will go, and on either side will be full-length bookcases. I imagine it's going to be a very comfortable place for you to read." She smiled up at him. During Bernie's tenure in office, his hair had turned from dark brown to salt and pepper. Now, Pam noticed that the hair at his temples was turning white. It suited him. "Along this wall is the bed and nightstands. Other side of this doorway is the master bath. On the west facing wall is your wardrobe. And this little room here," Pam pointed to a small rectangle on the plan, "is going to be your walk-in closet."

Pam wondered if she needed to reel herself in a little. She was talking too much and too fast. Her nerves were getting to her. Was she selling this too hard? Wasn't she *just* fantasizing about being fired from this job? She pinched the inside of her thumb. *Breathe*, she told herself.

"This looks great," said Bernie. "I knew it was going to take a lot of research to turn this beast back into a beauty, and you both came through."

"Really?" said Pam, who wasn't sure she'd heard him right.

"I love it. Nate spoke with me about it over the phone in early March, but this is the first I've seen of it with my own eyes." He smiled down at her again. Pam watched as the corners of his eyes crinkled into a dozen tiny wrinkles that to her surprise didn't age him, but instead made him look younger, more vibrant, and a little mischievous. "When can we start?"

That was not the answer Pam expected. She'd spent the greater part of the last week since they rescheduled the meeting thinking about the ways Bernie would break it to her that they were going another way, they would find a team that wasn't in the middle of a big transition, he hoped she would understand. And secretly pleased and so, so relieved, Pam had in her mind rehearsed her graceful step aside.

"Oh, well, I guess we need to talk about next steps," she said, flustered. She was glad for an excuse to sit down in the protection of her leather swivel chair, away from Bernie's warmth. She slid her binder-sized planner out of her messenger bag and opened it to July. "I can have a contractor in there pretty much any time. But Bernie, I have to be honest. This is all Nate's work, not mine. I'm much more useful when there are walls and plumbing and electricity. And that's just scratching the surface. We're going through, I'm sure you know, a big transition." She cleared her throat and looked him in the eye. "If you want to go with another design team, believe me, I'd understand."

"Are you looking for an out?" Bernie's tone was not unkind, but direct. Pam got the sense he wanted to know if he needed to move on.

Am I?

Pam looked down at her calendar. Something urgent was written into every box in July. Giving up Bernie's brownstone would possibly allow her to tackle and finish all of the outstanding projects she'd been struggling to complete all spring. She was already way too busy. Maybe she could spend some time with Grace. Speak more than two words to her and her parents at the end of the day. Or go on vacation? Was that even possible? She could get started on that third book she was supposed to be halfway through drafting but hadn't even touched for six months. But she would be breaking Nate's promise to Bernie and more important, to Nate himself. This house, the scope and visibility of this project was what Nate's dreams were made of. Pam had no doubt of the significance of this project for him. He had the opportunity to take a prominent piece of historically significant property in his adopted city and restore it to its newfound glory. And the fact that the ex-mayor hired them – one of Philadelphia's treasures – meant that the likelihood of more of these projects would be rolling in. If she blew off restoring Bernie's brownstone, she'd be betraying Nate.

"No, of course not," she said quickly. "I just wanted to make sure you were comfortable working with me as I figure out how to do this solo."

Bernie reached over and covered her hand with his and gave her a warm smile. "I think you can handle my little old house."

Chapter Nine

Pam and Bernie agreed to an early July start and set the completion date as late fall for photos, December for move-in. Although she was grateful for an extension, Pam knew she was in over her head. She barely had enough time to get a team of contractors together to wire the house and configure the plumbing. Every day, Pam needed to take some action, whether it involved going on-site and checking in on the Weinbergs' kitchen or signing off on the Siefkens' master bath or going to City Hall and filing for permits. And all while finishing the basement project with a frustrated Dennis, blogging about key projects' progress and holding off the impatience of Jackie, her agent, who wondered why she hadn't submitted any chapters of the new book for her to look over yet. Becky – not quite joking – told her she was revoking their friendship if she didn't meet up for a drink with her that week. Pam agreed, as long as it was a glass of wine in her kitchen at the end of another very long day.

"Hello, lovely," said Becky, clutching a bottle of rosé in one hand and attempting to shake the rain off of her umbrella with the other before coming inside. Her hands were flecked with green, white, brown, and blue paint spatters.

Pam took the bottle and motioned to Becky's hands. "New

project?"

"I stayed in today and painted my view from my third floor window," she said, following Pam into the kitchen. "It's impossible to get oil paint off my hands. Where's Gracie?"

"Good question," said Pam. "We're like two ships in the night. I come home after dinner and leave early in the morning. She sleeps late and stays out late and doesn't come home until after I've gone to bed, which these days is pretty much when I walk through the front door."

Pam rooted around in the silverware drawer before finding the wine opener.

Becky frowned. "Doesn't that bother you?"

"Of course." She poured them each a generous glass. "I don't like it at all. It's scary. God it's awful, when the weather's crappy like this. People continue to drive like maniacs even when there's a monsoon going on outside. And, to be honest..." Pam touched her fingertips to the stem of her wine glass.

Becky raised her eyebrows.

"When we do see each other, we just fight," Pam said. "About stupid stuff. I'm always riding her about her make-up work for school. And then she's angry at me for never having the stuff she likes to eat in the refrigerator. Oh, and I've 'abandoned her,' leaving her stuck with my parents." She sipped her wine. "I feel like there's this unspoken understanding between the two of us that it's almost better that we just *not* see each other." Pam turned to Becky. "God, that sounds so depressing."

"So why don't you do anything about it?"

"Who says I'm not doing anything about it?" Pam sighed in weak defense. "You're right. I'm not doing anything except fretting about it. I've been relying too much on Mom and Dad to do my parenting for me, when in reality, they don't want to. They're done. They raised my brother and me, and now they're done being the bad guys. They just want to enjoy their grandkids. Spoil them for as long as they can." She took in a mouthful of wine and shrugged. "I can't blame them. Though I will, anyway."

Becky plopped down onto the barstool. "I used to pull the same shit with my poor mother," she said. "I'm surprised she put up with me all those years."

Pam nodded in agreement. "Teenagers are difficult even when they haven't just lost one of their parents."

"And it's funny," said Becky. "Most of the time, we come back. I'm closer to my mum now than ever, even living across an ocean. Lately, she's been calling me once, sometimes twice a day."

"Really? What do you have to talk about?"

"Nothing, really. We talk a lot about the weather over here – she worries, you know, and in England it's cold and damp year round. Not Philly. She wants to hear about the snowstorms in the winter, humidity in the summer. If she hears about a hurricane in Florida, she tracks it, assuming I'll be affected by it sooner or later." Becky took another sip from her glass. "She just wants to hear my voice. I think it comforts her."

"That's sweet. She misses you."

"I suppose so." Becky gave Pam a sad smile. "I miss her too. If anyone told me when I was Grace's age how much I'd miss my mum now, as a middle-aged adult, I would have died."

Pam laughed. "Right."

"So what do you think Grace's up to?"

"I think she's doing what she says she's doing," said Pam. "I know, naïve, right? But look at this."

Pam pulled her cell out from her front pocket and tapped on the screen. "What does this look like to you?"

Glass in one hand, Becky squinted at the phone. "It's a bunch of goofy pictures. Pretty girls making funny faces."

"I think those were taken over at Hannah's house tonight." She reached for the phone and tapped again.

hey mom. staying over at hannah's 2nite, k? will text when home 2mrrw

"It's a bit presumptuous, don't you think?" said Becky. "Even if they are just having some innocent fun posting silly photos online."

Pam groaned. "This summer officially sucks." Fingering the edge of her wine glass, Pam wondered if she was letting everything that meant the most to her – including Grace – just run out of control. "It's not all her fault. I haven't been around all that much."

"You're telling me," said Becky, with a sly smile. "I was ready to just write you off. Of course now I know it takes a bottle of booze to get your attention."

"I am not defending myself to you. You know that right?" said Pam, taking another sip.

"I miss the days when you'd be able to come for a run with me or sit on my porch for afternoon tea. I used to be able to count on you for free decorating advice for God's sakes and now I have to make my own design decisions. I hate making design decisions!"

"Believe me, I miss those days, too." Pam could hear the undignified hitch in her voice. She wanted to avoid getting sad, but there were too many plates spinning and dropping.

"Sorry, hon. I know it's hard." Becky squeezed her hand.

She offered Becky a grateful smile. "I'm so glad you're my friend. It sounds cheesy, and we're not supposed to say stuff like that out loud, but I am."

"You've been there for me. I'm here now. We got each other's backs." Becky drained the wine from her glass. "What about a job?"

"Huh?" said Pam, confused. "I have one. I have, like six, actually."

"Not for you. For Grace." Becky uncorked the wine bottle and refilled her glass. "Hmm?" she asked, gesturing toward Pam's almost empty glass. Pam pushed it toward Becky. "Our pool club is still asking for more lifeguards. Begging is more accurate. At fifteen, Grace is the right age for that, and it's just the beginning of summer. She could be occupied with something healthy and fun all season. It would give her day some structure. And she'd get paid a little. She can start chipping away at that month she skipped at BFS. What's that, like four thousand dollars of your money she's wasted?"

"Oh my God, you are not kidding. You should have seen that check I wrote to them at that meeting with the principal a few weeks ago. I paid for all next year plus a five-figure donation, which took up the bulk of my latest book payment. Sickening. I better make some of that up this summer."

"I would have fainted," said Becky. "I almost fainted just putting the deposit on the house. Dan and I were newly divorced with two littles, and we split the proceeds from the other house, the one we shared. There's nothing like parting with large sums of money to crystallize your focus, eh?"

"It's a kick in the pants, all right." She looked Becky in the eye. "You've been on your own for how long now? A decade? Longer?"

Becky smirked. "I stopped counting after fifteen."

Pam pressed her fingers to her eyes, like she was warding off a headache. "I don't know how you did it. It takes superhuman strength to do this alone."

"I *wasn't* alone. I leaned on anyone I could, particularly that first year. It took a while, but I got my shit together and figured it out. It wasn't instant." Becky placed her hand on Pam's shoulder and squeezed. "You have got to give yourself a break."

Pam frowned. "I don't have time. I wish I could. I wish I could scoop up Grace and take her someplace far away for the summer, where we could heal and cry and get angry and miss Nate and maybe start getting along again."

Becky nodded. "Those teen years are the worst. Have you thought about therapy? Grace just lost her dad. At the very least, she's sad. The kids and I went to therapy after Dan and I split up. I think it helped."

"I've thought about that, especially after the 'incident' last spring. I was just hoping I'd have more time to set it up over the summer. But I don't. I'm busier than ever." Pam sighed and closed her eyes. "Sorry. I'm sounding like a broken record."

"You are sounding like a broken record, sweetie. But you're not listening to yourself. You keep plugging away without taking any time for yourself or Grace."

Pam sat onto one of the barstools. Could she take any time off? To her, it sounded like the most exquisite luxury just to take off on a trip somewhere away from a bi-weekly blog, unfinished basements, cranky contractors, home expos, and Bernie Scott's townhouse. She would have loved to not have had to think about any of that for a week or two or three, or even a whole summer. The only way she could even think about entertaining the idea of a break would be to quit altogether. Close up Designer You forever and she could say goodbye to her source of income. She'd also be walking out on Nate's wishes. She'd be giving up on his dream. Just the thought of disappointing Nate, even in death, felt like the ultimate betrayal.

Not an option.

She offered a patient smile to her friend. "I know you mean well, Becky. And I do want to take time for myself. But fantasizing about it is not helpful. You know how it goes. You've been in my shoes. I'm in the situation I'm in whether I like it or not, and I'm not getting out any time soon."

The hurt flickered across Becky's face. "Sorry, hon. I was just trying to be helpful."

Pam's hands fluttered to her chest. "You *are*. Really, you are! I think what I need right now is a good friend just to listen to me bitch and moan about the craziness. And to remind me I'm not alone." Pam picked up her glass. "And to stop by for a glass of wine or two just to talk. I need that, OK?" On instinct, she grabbed Becky's hand. "You're the best, you know that? You have made the last two months tolerable."

Becky softened and squeezed back. "It's too bad your parents can't help more with Designer You."

"I know. Keeping anything other than their diner afloat is not their thing. They do love Gracie and have been such good sports, but I think I need to send them back to Chester County."

Becky grinned. "Chester County needs your parents back. They are maybe the nicest people I know."

"They can't keep Grace out of trouble, but at least I know

she hasn't been alone at home."

"That's definitely something." Becky tipped her glass, swallowed the last of her wine, and stood. "Tell Gracie to get a job. I'll be back to check in."

"Good," said Pam. "Please do."

* * *

Two days later at breakfast, Grace considered Pam's suggestion to get a job.

"My friends all have jobs," she said. She squinted at Pam. "I thought you didn't want anything to get in the way of me catching up in school over the summer."

Pam raised her coffee mug to her lips. "A part time job won't get in the way. It had better not."

Grace looked away. "It's not," she said. "It *won't*."

"Good," said Pam. "Becky tells me the pool club is dying for lifeguards. They throw in Red Cross training and have flexible hours. I bet you could teach lessons, too."

"Little kids?" asked Grace. Pam could see her daughter mulling it over as she picked the sesame seeds off the top of her bagel. "I guess I'm OK with little kids."

It was easy for Pam to envision her daughter in a Red Cross one-piece swimsuit, sitting atop a wooden, white-painted lifeguard stand, twirling a whistle while watching the swimmers enjoy the pool below, and barking at kids running along the deck to slow down.

When she was in high school, Pam always worked at her father's diner. By college, she'd hung up her apron for good to try her hand at retail. She snagged a sales position at a small, but exclusive boutique called Urbane on College Avenue, a short walk from the residence halls on Penn State's campus. It was working at the boutique that allowed Pam access into a world much different than any she'd been exposed to before. She learned just how to give compliments to people who received them on a constant basis, without appearing like a parasite. She learned how to listen to customers and gently make suggestions. But for the most part, she learned that the way to help these women spend their money was to steal some of their behaviors. She learned how to move and speak like she'd grown up with money, and wasn't the daughter of the owner of a small-town, greasy spoon. Although going to work sometimes felt like an acting job, Pam enjoyed appropriating the easy confidence of the rich and pretending like she had no worries other than selling expensive clothing to them. And she discovered the skill came in handy much later in life as a partner in Designer You, when she and Nate advised their clients how to spend their money.

After four semesters of waning profits, Urbane filed for bankruptcy and was forced to close. Pam then took a part time job working as a secretary's assistant in the Engineering department and later on, when Nate entered graduate school in Philadelphia at Penn, they scraped by on his minimal stipend and her hourly wages working at Blockbuster Video, which took up part of the first floor of their apartment building in West Philly. The convenient location wasn't the only draw for Pam. In fact, there were aspects of the job she loved – the order and rhythm of moving and displaying merchandise, featuring new releases, moving last week's new releases, and shelving the old stuff. The job was social – she often ran into neighbors and friends of Nate's from Penn. And of course, she had access to all the free movies she wanted to watch whenever she wanted to watch them. *Not bad for a girl from Chester County*, she used to think. On the other hand, Blockbuster was like a magnet for drunk college kids on Friday and Saturday nights, and the place was robbed on a semi-regular basis. But in the end, Pam stayed on for two years, ending her tenure as assistant manager. She liked to think Blockbuster made her more adaptable in her and Nate's own business and ready to handle crises on the fly. After Blockbuster, she and Nate began building their empire in the DIY world. Her adult life had officially begun.

Pam brightened at the memory of those jobs. She had way more fun working in so-called menial jobs than what she was enduring now, though all of that experience working with people came in handy when she needed to impress politicians, tell a coherent design anecdote to a podcast host, and prod picky clients into choosing a light fixture. Working at the pool could be a wonderful opportunity for Grace, and who knew what those skills could lead to? Maybe she would discover she was a brilliant teacher or natural leader?

"Why don't you swing by the pool this morning and fill out an application? I can drop you on my way."

"And how will I get home?" Grace demanded, tension building in her voice. "Who knows *when* you'll be home tonight?"

Pam gave her question some thought. "You're right. Grandma or Grandpa can pick you up. Just text them when you're done."

"I heard you gave them the boot yesterday."

Pam detected the slightest bit of resentment in Grace's voice. "I didn't 'give them the boot.' I'm just releasing them to go back home. They have a life other than us, you know."

"Grandpa says he needs to get back to the diner," said Grace. She sipped her orange juice. "I'll be all alone."

Was Grace feeling relief or regret at the thought of her grandparents returning home? Either way, her heart swelled at the thought that Grace was opening up to her, even if it was just a little.

"He's right. It's time that life goes on for all of us." Pam walked toward a seated Grace and kissed the top of her head. "And for you, that means a job."

"Yeah?" Grace looked up at her and raised an eyebrow. "What about you?"

"One foot in front of the other." Pam drained the coffee in her cup and looked down at her phone. "Grab your bathing suit and a towel – they may ask for a swim test. And finish your bagel in the car. It's time to get moving."

Chapter Ten

Pam fanned her face with a pizzeria menu she'd picked out of the junk mail. Every day she visited the work site, a pile of restaurant menus, credit card offers, Bed Bath & Beyond coupons, and realtor mailers greeted her on the floor of the marbled entryway in Bernie Scott's unfinished brownstone. It was six o'clock in the evening the third week of July and the city was in the midst of the summer's longest heat wave so far. Even in shorts and a tank top, Pam felt like she was cooking in the spacious but stifling mansion. The walls weren't up yet, but the plumbing, electrical, and heating and cooling duct work were all in place. Pam wanted to eyeball all the systems before giving the go ahead to put up the wallboard the following morning. She was up in the sweltering fourth floor master suite, sweating.

Let's start with the air conditioning, she thought, as she stood in front of the large compressor stashed in the back of Bernie's gigantic walk-in closet.

"Helllloooo?" boomed a man's voice from far below. "Pam? Are you here?"

What's Bernie doing here? Pam backed away from the compressor. She walked to the stairwell and peeked down four flights, spying the top of his tanned, somewhat balding head below.

"Hey!" she called down the stairs. "I'm on the fourth floor. Come up!"

Bernie looked up and grinned. He gave her a thumbs up.

"You're just in time. I'm testing out the systems today. First is the air conditioning," she said, as Bernie reached the top floor.

"Gad, it's hot." He mopped his forehead with a handkerchief he'd pulled from his lapel. Pam led him back to the walk-in closet.

"It gets pretty bad in the afternoon, but I wanted to take a look at what they've finished so far. Now the duct work will all be walled in, obviously, and the compressor will have its own compartment. You'll barely hear it and won't know it's even there, when we're done. But, I'm glad you dropped by so I can show you where it is." She cocked her head at him. "Just curious – what *are* you doing here? This house is not a great place to be in a suit in the middle of a heat wave."

"Believe me, that thought crossed my mind as I just climbed four flights of stairs. Jesus, I should have bought a ranch out in the 'burbs.'" Bernie had taken off his blazer and draped it over his arm. He continued to dab at his neck and forehead as his eyes wandered through the space. He whistled. "Wow, it's coming along."

Pam beamed at the praise and smiled for real in what felt like the first time in months. *He likes it!* "It is. It'll be more dramatic when the walls go up and the rooms take some shape and character. But yeah, it's coming along. We've got a great crew." Internally, Pam thanked Dennis a thousand times over for steering her toward a group of experts that ensured Bernie's home didn't flood or burn down. At least, so far. She motioned toward the compressor. "I was just about to test out the air conditioner. You want to do the honors?"

Bernie laughed. "I don't even know what I'm looking at. Why don't you do it?" Most of the time, Pam would know that feeling all too well, but right now, she knew precisely what she was looking at. She shrugged and pressed the switch to 'on.' The compressor belched to a start and then began its quiet hum, pushing cool air into the stuffy closet.

Bernie gave her a sheepish look. "Heh, I guess I could have figured that out."

"Oh my gosh, this is amazing," said Pam, almost to herself as she closed her eyes and the cool air blew over her skin. "It's working. I can't believe it."

"It's fantastic. Almost makes me want to move in right now," said Bernie.

Pam basked in this small victory. In the three months since Nate had died, she felt she could do *something* right on her own. Sure, she had an entire crew doing all the work, but she was forging ahead and implementing Nate's plans. She was taking the lead. And so far, the ex-mayor's house hadn't fallen down on her watch. In fact, now the mansion had the ability to cool itself in a sweltering July heat wave. She smiled again.

"What?" asked Bernie, grinning.

"Oh." Heat rose to Pam's cheeks. "It's a relief to get the AC going and I'm glad it worked out. Sometimes it's tricky in these old homes with three or four floors."

"I think you've done a fantastic job. You're *doing* a fantastic job," Bernie corrected. "I'm so glad you took on what many see as maybe too much of a challenge."

"These are the projects Nate lived for," said Pam. "And I'm happy to see his vision through."

"But not you?"

Pam furrowed her brow. "I don't know what you mean."

"But not you – *you* don't 'live for' projects like these." Bernie's face was serious.

"I don't know." Pam rested her gaze on the view outside one of the large bedroom windows, which looked out onto the thinning rush hour traffic below. "I need to be heading home."

"Let me take you to dinner," said Bernie as he loosened his tie. "I'm starving. And it's late."

Pam shook her head. "I can't. I need to be home when my daughter gets home from the pool."

"Saturday, then."

Pam knew Bernie Scott was a man who liked to have his way. What if she did just drop everything and go to dinner with him? She had to eat. Whether she ate at home or in a restaurant, what difference did it make?

She peered into his tanned face. He looked rested and relaxed after his two week vacation in Italy. Handsome, really. She could see why people took a liking to him. No wonder he was elected mayor twice; he had an intangible magnetic pull about him, not unlike Nate's own charm. He was so different from Nate, though. Nate was no politician. Brilliant, driven, the most creative person Pam had ever met, but you'd never catch Nate in a button-up shirt kissing babies on the campaign trail.

"I can't," she said.

"Too soon?"

Pam felt like a nervous teenager all of a sudden. "What?"

"You're not ready to date yet?" Bernie persisted.

Date?

"No, I don't think so," she blurted, feeling the heat rise to her cheeks once again. Just the word 'date' had sent her stomach off a cliff. She hadn't been on a date in over twenty years. "It's not a good time. I need to focus on work."

"I understand." He grinned. "I know my timing's probably off, but I had to give it a try before someone else swooped in."

Swooped in?

Pam wasn't sure if she should feel flattered or more like a forgotten sandwich on the beach scooped up by a passing seagull. Her head swam. "Heh, I doubt that," she mumbled, as she fished the car keys from her purse. "Um, I have to go. But thanks for stopping by today."

"Right." He nodded. "Let me walk you out."

* * *

When Pam arrived home, the house was silent. With her parents gone and Grace spending most days lifeguarding at the pool, Pam found herself coming home to a silence that often crushed her. She hoped Grace would come home soon, before Pam fell into bed. She rubbed her shoulders. The heat of the day was wearing off and the central air in her house was maybe a bit too cold. Grace had draped an inside out BFS hoodie on the coat rack, which Pam slipped on over her tank top as she made her way to the kitchen. She opened the refrigerator.

She didn't have to be alone tonight. Didn't have to eat leftovers while sitting in front of her computer editing a blog post she needed to have up the following day. She could have accepted a casual invitation to dinner. It didn't have to mean anything, not even 'date.' Not to her, anyway.

I'm not ready.

She wasn't even ready to pack up and donate Nate's shoes and clothing to the Goodwill. With some regularity, Pam still needed to visit the inside of Nate's closet and inhale the scent from his faded jeans and polo shirts and flannels and work boots. She kept his old deodorant in there, too, swiping it across the inside of her wrist so she could inhale his scent until it wore off. This provided Pam comfort and pain and shame all at once. It made her think Nate would walk in at any time and catch her in the act of sniffing an undershirt. She could just see his lips curling into an amused smile and ask, "What the hell are you doing in my closet?" But of course, he couldn't – and that realization alone had the potential to send Pam over the edge into despair. How could someone who still needs to swipe their dead husband's deodorant on their wrist be ready to go to dinner with another man?

But Pam didn't know how to *not* be married. The last time she was single was in college. She'd never lived alone. She'd never had to be the sole breadwinner. The responsibility of parenting and general adulthood she'd always shared with Nate. Pam didn't know how to be alone and over the last few months, she wasn't any closer to finding even a sort-of groove in her home and work life, and she had few examples to help guide her through this awkward transition. Her older brother had been single for most of his adult life, until he impregnated and then married his much younger girlfriend almost a year ago. But for someone who was so single for so long, Jimmy took to marriage and fatherhood at once, like shrugging on a well-worn sweater when the weather turned.

Becky was single. Becky was a single *mom*. But Becky had asked for the divorce. She didn't love her husband anymore. She'd wanted to split from her ex – wanted to be single – so there was some forethought to her and her kids' survival. As hard as life was for her when she and her husband separated, Becky had carved out a career for herself, made mortgage payments every month, and raised two, upstanding, productive adults, one of which was now in law school.

I can barely keep Grace from getting kicked out of high school.

The one widow who lost her spouse young was someone she knew from childhood. She'd grown up living on the same block as Pam. *Louise.* They walked to school together every day and because Louise hadn't moved far from her old neighborhood, the two had remained in touch through the years. Louise came to her and Nate's wedding. She'd known Grace since she was born. When they were both thirty-one, Louise lost her husband, Paul, after a year-long battle with an aggressive bone cancer. Two weeks after his death, Pam and Grace made the first of several special trips out to Chester County to bring her frozen meals or dessert and keep her company on weekend afternoons. When Grace had fallen asleep for her afternoon nap, Pam had excused herself to use the bathroom. She was struck by the unopened boxes of fancy creams and make-up that cluttered the ordinarily neat counter.

"What's with all the make-up and stuff?" Pam asked upon returning to the living room. Two-year-old Grace snored in a Pack 'n' Play in the middle of the room.

"I had a moment of weakness at Sephora the other day," said Louise. "I've had lots of those moments, actually."

"Oh yeah. Their make-up counter is intense," said Pam, who sipped a mug of coffee. "Sometimes a little makeover, a little shopping spree, can be just the right thing to pick you up."

"I think I panicked, you know?" said Louise as she glanced at the napping Grace in her crib. "I'm not getting any younger, and one day, I'd love to have a little one like Grace."

Pam nodded. "That'll come. I can see you as a mom someday." Though it was hard for Pam to see past the pale pinched face of her friend who had just gone through the most excruciating year of Paul's chemo and radiation and homeopathic treatments, and then scarily no treatment and toward the end, hospice.

Louise's lips twisted into a hard slash across her face. "I don't want to be a mom 'someday,' I want to be a mom *now*."

"Oh my God, Louise, you need to give yourself time." Pam leapt from her seat and sat next to Louise, patting her back. "There's no rush. Paul hasn't even been gone two weeks. Give yourself time to grieve."

Louise stared down at her hands. "It's weird, Paul and I met, fell in love – it was so fast – in less than a year. We were married and then bam, cancer. A little more than three years from the day we met to when he died. It was no time, really. But at the same time, I can't imagine my life without him. I can't imagine going back to that single girl in a studio apartment above the Chinese takeout place downtown. Remember that?" Louise turned to face Pam and gave her a sad smile.

Pam nodded. She agreed. It was depressing. Like going backwards.

"I bought contact lenses, too." Louise sniffed and laughed to herself. Her eyes were red through her glasses; Pam had always thought they looked cute on her and accentuated her quirky, artistic personality. "I thought, I'd better make myself look as presentable as possible, especially now. Because I feel like shit on the inside." She grabbed a tissue from the box on the coffee table and wiped her eyes. "I'm lost, Pam. I just don't know what to do."

Pam wasn't sure how to respond. She didn't know what Louise should do either. It was a position she couldn't even dare to imagine herself in. Paul's death was an anomaly, horrific luck. He'd drawn the short straw. Pam and Nate wouldn't have to worry about cancer and heart disease and high blood pressure until…when? When Grace was in her twenties? And Louise's answer was to find Paul's replacement as soon as possible. Pam swallowed. To consider searching for a second husband when she'd just buried her first seemed at best premature, and at worst, insensitive, impulsive, and potentially damaging. Pam had tried to reel in her judgment. She wasn't successful.

"I think for now, you're doing what you need to do – grieving Paul's loss. Leaning on your friends and family. We miss him too and want to help you as much as you'll let us."

"Thanks." Louise's eyes glistened. "I feel my life moving backwards. This little house already feels too big. Will I go back to a studio apartment? Or move back home with my parents?" She shuddered.

"I don't know," said Pam. Louise's words unsettled her. She rested her eyes on her sleeping daughter and thought fleetingly about what she would do if she were single all of a sudden. Just her and Grace. She shook off the thought. "Just do me a favor and don't rush into anything."

"Last night, after a little too much Pinot Grigio, I posted a profile onto OK Cupid." Louise gave Pam a terrified look. "Is that the stupidest thing you've ever heard? Am I a horrible person for wanting to move on as soon as possible?" She dabbed at the corners of her eyes. "Since when did I become someone who can't live without a husband? I woke up this morning with a headache, thinking, who *am* I? What is this person I've become?"

Pam grimaced. "Maybe lay off the wine?"

Louise smirked and leaned in. "You always made me laugh, Pam." Her eyes swam with tears again. "Paul made me laugh *so hard* sometimes. We could always crack each other up. I want to find someone who's funny. And kind. And a democrat."

Pam nodded. "You'll find someone."

She wasn't so sure.

But Louise had. And she wasted no time. Online dating had worked. By the end of that year, Louise was engaged to a man named Allen Henkel, a community college professor who was sweet and funny and leaned left in their conservative home town. Pam had heard snippets of Louise's life after she remarried – they moved to upstate New York when Allen got a job offer for a full time position at Jefferson Community College. From what Pam's parents had told her, Louise and Allen were raising a daughter and a younger son, and as far as she knew, they were happy. Louise had moved on and Pam was happy for her. Louise knew what she wanted and got it. *Good for her*, she remembered thinking.

Now, Pam found herself in a much different position. Unlike Louise, she had *not* set up a profile at an online dating website. Just the thought jangled her nerves. What would she say? Who could she possibly meet? It was much different for a woman in her early thirties and without a child to find a man than it was for someone more than ten years older and saddled with a teenager. Over the years, Becky complained about the dismal prospects for single, middle-aged women to find anyone interesting and age appropriate. Becky said divorced men in their forties and fifties considered women their own age too old and nine out of ten times chose younger women. And as she got older, the more rigid and set in her ways Becky became. As wonderful and open and funny and artistic and smart as Becky was, Pam didn't think she'd been on a date in a year. Would Pam find herself in the same position spring of next year? She shivered. A year alone sounded devastating, depressing, and lonely. It might even drive her crazy. If she didn't move on, her odds of finding another husband were lowered with each passing year. Did she want to remain alone? Pam took her phone from her pocket.

If you're free, she typed into a new text message. *Dinner Saturday sounds good.* She hit 'send' feeling dizzy and impulsive, like she'd just made a too-big purchase at the Apple Store.

Her phone pinged. She looked down, her heart in her throat and read Bernie's message.

Great. Pick you up at 8.

Holy. Shit. Pam stared at her phone. *I think I have a date.*

Chapter Eleven

As she waited for Bernie on Saturday evening, Pam smoothed out the skirt of her dress and checked for stray hairs clinging to the back. She fiddled with the necklace she borrowed from Becky earlier in the day, now half wishing Grace was home to give her a final inspection. But on the other hand, Pam knew enough to call Grace's absence tonight and unawareness of the dinner itself a blessing. Dinner with Bernie was best left a mystery until Pam could figure out a better way to define it. 'Date' seemed too loaded a word for this dinner – meeting? Event? – yet, there was something about Bernie that drew her to him.

Pam checked herself out for the eighth time in the mirror above the fireplace. She looked…good? Becky had mercifully come over that morning to help her choose an appropriate outfit. Pam's panic had been on hyper drive, and when Becky arrived, Pam had nine outfits laid out on her bed and the guest bed to choose from.

"It's a date, my love, not a meeting with the Queen," Becky said. Hands on her hips, she scrutinized the selections.

"What?" Pam asked, gnawing the inside of her cheek.

"You're over-thinking this." Becky picked up two leggy dresses by their hangers and handed them to Pam. "Back in the closet."

"Nate always said I looked 'hot' in both those dresses."

"I'm sure you do, but not tonight," Becky said. "Trying too hard."

Pam lifted a colorful maxi dress and held it to herself. "Hmmm? What about this one?"

Becky wrinkled her nose. "Not trying hard enough."

Pam pointed to a short-sleeved sweater dress. "This one's cute when I wear it with tights."

"Too hot," Becky said, shaking her head. "It's July, babe – you'll be a puddle by the end of the evening."

"What about this skirt and blouse combo?"

"Looks like you're going to work in an office."

Pam sat on the edge of the guest bed, defeated. "Becky, I'm starting to regret asking you to help me."

"Look, the key to a good first date outfit is that it one, must match the occasion – a nice dinner in this case. And two, it needs to look like you give enough of a shit to look nice, attractive, that sort of thing, but *not* desperate."

"I'm not desperate," said Pam, her tone defensive. "I don't even want to go to dinner at this point. I'm not even hungry. I wish I'd never sent that text."

"Relax. It's just dinner."

"With my client who also happens to be a super visible ex-mayor. Just last month he was quoted in *The Atlantic* about Philadelphia's public education. I'll consider it a miracle if I get through the night without passing out."

"That's the spirit, Pam." Becky gave her a wry smile. "Here, what about this? Lose the pumps and pair it with some cute wedges. What do you think?"

Pam glared at the dress. It was a simple black sleeveless

dress that skimmed the knee. She'd picked it up on sale at Ann Taylor one day while shopping downtown last summer. She and Nate were appearing on the Lowes decorating web series, and she needed something that wouldn't steal focus. "I thought you'd tell me this one was 'too boring.'"

"No, it's perfect. And I have a chunky necklace that will go with it."

As she sat waiting in her living room, flipping through magazines and trying to calm the pounding in her chest, the chunky necklace hung around her neck like a weighted chain. Pam wasn't used to wearing such large jewelry and considered ditching it when the doorbell rang. She glanced at the time on her phone. 8:11.

"Hi," she said, after opening the front door. The air was thick with summer heat. Bernie wore a long-sleeve, gingham dress shirt from Burberry tucked into pressed trousers. The casual but sophisticated ensemble was punctuated with polished black oxfords.

Bernie grinned. "Aren't you a sight?" Taking her hand, he leaned in to peck her cheek. She detected a hint of eucalyptus after shave.

Pam tensed. *Relax.* Becky's words reverberated in her head: *It's just dinner.* "Thanks," she said, reddening. "You, too. Let me grab my purse."

After she locked the door, he led her out to his black Audi and opened the car door for her. She was a little surprised – and pleased – that the car wasn't his chauffeured town car she'd seen him shuttled around in before.

"Thought I'd drive tonight," he said, reading her mind. "Give Fred the night off."

Pam settled into the plush seat and marveled at the restrained luxury of the sports car – the leather seats, hand stitching on the steering wheel, Bang & Olufsen sound system – it wasn't overly showy, but it was obvious he was driving an exquisite car that most people who voted for him could never afford. Even though she and Nate had enjoyed a more than adequate lifestyle through the success of Designer You, neither had taken much interest in fancy cars. Nate had driven a beat up pick-up and she drove an eight-year-old Subaru station wagon. *Bernie doesn't have kids to schlep around. And he's not hauling heavy building material, either.*

"So where are we going?" she asked.

"To my favorite steak place in the city. You like steak? I should have asked that before I made reservations. If you don't, they've got chicken, seafood, whatever you want, OK?"

"Yeah, sure. Steak's fine." Pam liked steak well enough, but couldn't remember the last time she'd eaten it. And she wasn't sure how much her nerves would allow her to eat tonight anyway. *Calm down.* She pinched her thumb.

A short time later, Bernie rolled into the valet parking spot in front of Barclay Prime. Pam had never eaten at the celebrated steakhouse, but had heard about it. The valet opened her passenger door and another opened the front door to the restaurant. *Will they wipe my mouth for me? Help me retouch my lipstick?*

"Welcome back, Mr. Scott," said the hostess as soon as they approached the podium. She was sleek and stunning in a black buttoned-down dress shirt tucked into a pencil skirt and her blonde hair slicked back into a low ponytail. She grabbed two menus. "Right this way," she said, as she turned and walked toward their table, revealing a peek at the red leather soles of her four-inch heels with each seductive step.

Along the way, Pam and Bernie were interrupted every few feet.

"How are you doing, Mr. Scott?" asked a short, bearded man bussing a nearby table.

"Thanks again for coming, Mr. Scott," said a slim waiter carrying a tray as he passed by.

"Nice to see you again, Mr. Scott," nodded a man in a suit and tie, as he whisked Pam and Bernie to their table. She guessed he must be the restaurant manager.

Pam basked in all the fawning attention and offered a wide smile. "Nice!" she said, and meant it.

Maybe too nice, she thought as Bernie pulled her chair out for her when she sat down.

They sank into cozy club seating across from each other, Pam in a banana yellow chair and Bernie in lime green. She took in the atmosphere of the restaurant – both contemporary and old school. The space was open and bright for a steakhouse, yet each table felt private, intimate. Bookcases filled with old, hardbound books lined the paneled walls of the restaurant, giving it a retro library feel. Crystal chandeliers hung from the high ceilings. Pam noticed the room also felt clean and new, defined by subtle contrasts and straight edges. She smoothed the cloth napkin onto the lap of her year-old, on-sale shift. Pam thought her entire outfit didn't cost half as much as the shoes the hostess was wearing. At once, she felt too young and unsophisticated, like the kid at the adult table at Thanksgiving who longs to be back at the kids table with her younger cousins eating turkey in front of a Disney cartoon. "Sounds like you come here a lot."

"Now and again." His eyes twinkled. "They'll treat you like a queen here. Make you forget about, oh, I don't know, your pain in the ass politician client for a little while."

Pam mustered a pained laugh. *As if I needed to be reminded I'm having dinner with my client.* She opened her menu and tried to focus. "So, what's good?"

"Everything." He opened his own menu and squinted at the pages. "Seriously, it's all great. Even the $120 cheesesteak is worth it."

"Really?" Pam scanned the page. Sure enough, the restaurant offered a cheesesteak served with wagyu beef, truffled cheese, and foie gras. "At least it comes with champagne. That way you get your money's worth."

"It's to die for. And I don't say that lightly. My own cardiologist has warned me to stay away from cheesesteaks, but this one is last-meal worthy."

"Are you going for it?"

"Not this time. I'm in the mood for rib-eye – also something my doctor has told me to avoid – but I can't resist."

"Your doctor sounds really bossy," said Pam, grinning.

Bernie laughed. "That's what happens when you get old. You, my dear, don't have that problem yet."

Pam blushed. *Is this flirting?*

"So nice to see you again, Mr. Scott," the waiter said as he approached. "May I get you both something from the bar?" He turned toward Pam, his expression expectant. Pam passed a panicked look to Bernie.

"Shall we go sparkling on this warm summer evening?" he asked.

Pam nodded, relieved she didn't have to make a decision.

Bernie snapped the wine list shut. "Two glasses of the Prosecco, thank you."

The waiter walked away and Bernie leaned forward. "Isn't

this fun?" Pam watched his mischievous eyes crinkle.

She took a breath. "Yes, actually. It's a nice change from standing at my butcher block eating cold leftovers straight out of the refrigerator."

Two flutes of sparkling wine appeared at their table. Bernie lifted his glass. "To eating sitting down."

Pam raised her glass in return. "I'll drink to that." She took a sip. The bubbles tickled her nose. She cocked her head. "May I ask you something?"

"Course!" Bernie sank back into his chair. He appeared so at ease to Pam who sat with her back stock straight, like she was still in college waiting for her professor to call on her.

"This big townhome…why do you or why would you…?" Pam tried to think of a delicate way to ask but faltered. It was none of her business.

"What would I, an unattached guy in his mid-fifties – no kids, no wife – want with a big old mansion? Is that what you want to know?"

Pam reddened. "Yes. I mean, I'm only asking out of curiosity. I just want to understand." She took another sip from her glass. "You have this gorgeous condo – I know, because I've seen the photos in *Philadelphia Magazine* – a job that's demanding, a lifestyle that takes you to restaurants like this one on a regular basis. I would think the simplicity of living in a building where everything is taken care of for you would be both desirable and necessary for a man like you."

Bernie looked away.

Pam's eyes widened. "I'm sorry. I'm being nosy and offensive." She took another long mouthful of the Prosecco. "Ignore me."

"No, it's a good question. Believe me, my financial planner

is wondering the same thing. I *am* a single guy. I don't have a family. And this year I turned fifty-five." He chuckled. "Can you believe it? Fifty-five and never been married or had kids. But I'm amazingly fortunate. As mayor, I got paid for trying to make people's lives better. How lucky is that?"

The waiter returned and took their order. The sommelier followed with a bottle of Bordeaux and two glasses.

Pam had finished her sparkling wine and took a sip of the red the sommelier had poured for her. "Yum. I could get used to this."

"I know. Good food, great wine – these are nice perks of what I do, too. And I get more opportunities to meet people in all situations, whether it's at a fancy place like this, a beef and beer fundraiser in Kensington, a neighborhood block party in North Philly, or a meet and greet and Famous 4th Street Deli – precisely because I have nothing tying me down."

"So, then why the house? That's like six thousand square feet of Civil War era townhome that not only needs to be designed, but will need upkeep and constant care. It's an expensive and time-consuming project. It's not a home for someone who will hardly be there."

"Is that what you're worried about? That the house won't be loved the way it should be?"

Pam took a second to think about it. Was she worried that the historically significant mansion wouldn't get the level of care it needed and deserved? That it would sit empty half the time, gathering cobwebs while Bernie was out traveling or campaigning? She didn't think so. That concern sounded more like Nate, not her. As far as she was concerned, the townhome was just a building. If she were honest with herself, Bernie's house was part of Nate's dream, one step closer to Designer You's world DIY domination. She was proud to transform the house, shape it into a custom home for a prominent local figure. And she hoped she got it right. But still, in the end, it was just a building.

She shook her head. "I guess I'm just curious why you'd want it in the first place."

At that moment, the waiter appeared with a tray carrying two steaks and sides of roasted cauliflower, whipped potatoes, and creamed spinach. The executive chef trailed close behind. To Pam, he appeared almost too young for a chef, with a waifish build and clean-cut baby face.

"Welcome back to Barclay Prime, Mr. Scott," he said. "We are honored to serve you this evening."

Bernie rose from his seat and shook his hand. "Good to see you, Ross." He gestured toward Pam. "This is Pam, Pam Wheeler. She's a friend."

The chef clasped her hand in his with enthusiasm. "Ms. Wheeler, it's a pleasure. Actually, I'm very pleased to meet you." He glanced at Bernie and back to Pam. "I'm a big fan of yours."

"Of mine?" asked Pam, confused.

"Yes, of course. I've read your books and love your blog." He offered a sheepish smile. "I'm a bit of a do-it-yourselfer, at least, on the weekends. My wife and I learned how to strip and refinish furniture thanks to you. Our new house in Fishtown is full of old garage sale finds." His face became somber. "I'm so very sorry about your husband. My sincerest condolences."

Pam looked down. "Thank you," she said, jarred by the reminder of Nate on her first date since his death. *It's not a date!*

Ross gave a slight nod to the both of them. "I'll leave you to it. Please enjoy your meal."

As she watched Ross retreat, Pam noticed for the first time the furtive glances she and Bernie were getting from the patrons at the surrounding tables. And they weren't just staring at Bernie, but at *her* and Bernie. When Nate was alive, every now and then when they were out and about – at dinner or CVS or the farmers market – someone would approach them, like Ross had approached her or the woman at the home expo had in May, and tell them something about their home projects. It didn't happen all that often – they weren't that famous – and when it did, it was always about them, not Nate and Pam. But now, sitting in this restaurant, Pam was aware that the stares were about her and Bernie. She lowered her gaze to her plate, wishing she could crawl under the table.

"Nice guy," said Bernie, unaware of, or more likely accustomed to, the stares.

They probably don't even faze him, thought Pam, both baffled and impressed.

"He donated his time to cook at one of my biggest fund raisers when I was running for mayor the second time around," Bernie said. "I attended his wedding. He's a hard worker too. Smart. I watched him rise through the ranks here. He and his wife are about to be parents." He cut into his steak. "I look at him and think, I could have a son that age. Ross is what, early thirties you think?"

Pam nodded. "At the most. He's great. And this," she pointed her fork at a piece of cauliflower. "This is how I want cauliflower for the rest of my life. My God, it's fantastic." Pam had grown up with vegetables that had been boiled within an inch of their lives. Cauliflower, broccoli, green beans –

they'd all tasted the same. But this cauliflower was a little smoky with flavors of olive oil and garlic and pepper. It almost tasted…meaty. She stabbed it with her fork.

"You have kids, right?" Bernie asked.

"Daughter. She's fifteen."

"What's her name?"

"Grace." Pam sipped her wine.

"Beautiful," he said. "I love that name."

Pam put down her wine glass and shook her head. "She is not exactly living up to her name these days. Teenagers are…a challenge."

"So I've heard." Bernie patted the edges of his lips with his napkin. "And I'm sure it can't be easy these last few months."

"No," said Pam. She didn't want to talk about this right now. She couldn't open the conversation up to her worries about Grace for fear of letting her raw anguish escape from her chest. The very thought of speaking about Grace and her troubles with school and staying out too late – those behaviors that were inevitably linked to her grief surrounding Nate's death – filled Pam with a kind of guilt and dread that turned her stomach into knots. She watched Bernie recoil.

"I'm sorry," said Bernie. "You don't want to talk about it – I understand."

Pam offered him a tight smile. "Thanks." She looked past him to the tables of couples, smiling and leaning into each other. Or sharing bites of each other's entrees. Or holding hands across the table. No longer stealing glances at her and Bernie, they were all in their own worlds, making her feel like an outsider. She didn't belong here, not with Bernie Scott. "I'm sorry," she said. "It's still hard to talk about my family. We're—" *What?* She tried to think of what she and Grace were right now. "Healing, I guess."

Pam's thoughts flashed back to Louise. Louise had thrown herself into the dating pool so soon and with so much force, it had stunned and confused Pam at the time. And what did she have to show for it? She was no longer single a year after Paul's death. She had her babies. She got what she wanted. Just thinking about Louise's courage and audacity made Pam feel weak, gutless, and judgmental, like she wasn't getting what she needed – a husband. Isn't that what she wanted? If Pam was smart, she'd take her cue from Louise's example. *Pam* was the one who needed to be first in line at the Sephora counter for a makeover. Couldn't she benefit from an updated wardrobe? A trip to the salon to freshen her hair color? A little Botox to soften her crow's feet like countless other forty-something women she knew?

Ugh, she thought. *Why does there have to be so much work to be single?*

Pam looked across the table to Bernie and met his eyes. He was attractive, and Pam could see why he charmed so many women. He lacked the effortless attractiveness of Nate, but his face radiated warmth and vibrancy. She liked the gray in Bernie's hair. She liked the wrinkles around his eyes. She liked the casual polish of his blazer and button down oxford. Bernie Scott was not a bad first not-date.

"Your daughter is lucky to have you," he said. He sipped his wine. "Taking the time to heal is important. I lost my father when I was nine. It was just me, my mom, and my baby brother. It was the early seventies, you know? All of a sudden, I was the man of the house, and my mom had to go to work and I had to take care of myself and my brother. We didn't have time to heal or grieve or any of that. We were in survival mode."

"Yeah, wow." Pam nodded. "It was a different time. Did it ever get easier?"

"Oh sure. I grew up. My brother grew up. Whatever your new reality is becomes your routine. Your new normal. And my mother later found someone very nice and married him in seventy-nine. They're both still around – in their eighties and closing in on forty years together, living in a condo in Florida."

"'Florida: God's waiting room,' my father-in-law likes to say," said Pam.

"That's good." He chuckled. "Your father-in-law sounds like a funny guy."

Pam laughed, nodding. "Nate got his sense of humor from him, that's for sure." Her mind flashed to a vision of Nate's father's anguished face during the funeral. Pam closed her eyes, willing it away.

Bernie leaned back in his chair. "I'm at kind of a midpoint in my life and career and starting to take a good, hard look at what I want going forward. I love my work and find incredible meaning in what I do. But I have no one to share that with."

Pam raised her eyebrows. "Oh?"

He gave her a warm smile. "It's OK. I'm not in any hurry, believe me." Bernie folded his hands behind his head and crossed his legs. "But as I start looking into running for governor, I know I don't want to do it alone. I want a wife by my side."

"Uh huh." Pam felt the color drain from her face. All of the restaurant noise, the conversations that hummed around them and the clinks of silverware on porcelain and soft music, shrank. Their table and chairs suddenly felt like a remote island in the middle of an ocean.

"Please don't misunderstand, I have no expectations of you or of 'us.' But I do feel a responsibility to let you know that I'm not playing around here." Bernie took a slow sip of his wine. "I know what's been written up about my personal life. Some of it's true, a lot of it isn't. I do enjoy the company of beautiful, interesting women. I have been, as the press likes to say, a 'serial monogamist.' I do not, as *The Inquirer* and *The Post* have reported, have a personal collection of hidden sex tapes or fathered any illegitimate children."

Pam forced a laugh. "Well, I'm glad you put those rumors to rest."

Bernie placed his chin in his palm. "You're easy to be around. I can see why Nate was so crazy about you."

Pam's breath caught in her throat.

Nate. Why does he have to bring up Nate now?

She looked down at her dinner plate. The meat practically throbbed beside the whipped potatoes and the half-eaten cauliflower. Her appetite vanished. She wondered what it would be like to just be swallowed up, engulfed in this yellow chair and never to be seen again.

"I hope I'm not scaring you," he said, sitting back in his chair.

"No," Pam lied.

"But to answer your question about the house – it's perfect for a family. I think you even said it yourself, calling it a home for a 'family of prominence' or something like that."

Pam stared at him, confused. "Wait, what? You want to have children?"

Bernie shook his head. "My own kids? No. I'm afraid that ship has sailed. I'm not interested in bringing any babies into this world." He smiled. "But I'd make a pretty darn good step-parent."

"So let me get this straight. You bought that house because you want to get married and move the new wife and her children, if she has any, into it?"

"Eventually."

"OK, eventually." Pam drained the wine from her glass. "Because you're running for governor? And if you win, wouldn't you live in Harrisburg, not Philly?"

"When you put it that way, it sounds awfully calculated."

Pam shrugged. "Well, yeah."

"Truth is, the campaign heats up in two years. I have to think about how my personal and political lives will intersect. I always have to think about that anyway, because I'm a public figure. You probably know what I mean."

Pam thought about the stares she and he had garnered moments ago. Or was that just her imagination? She understood perhaps a tiny bit about living as a public figure, but not to the extent that Bernie Scott knew. She raised her palms. "I don't think it's quite the same."

"Bottom line is, I don't want to be alone. I want to be ready when I meet someone who is mature and my intellectual equal. I found from experience, I'm just not attracted to women in their twenties or early thirties anymore. One reason is they want babies. I don't. But I also don't have a lot in common with these younger women. Less and less as I get older. I want to fall in love with a woman who enjoys a good glass of wine. A woman who reads novels. A woman who could name at least one Bruce Springsteen song. And if this special woman also has one or more children, I would welcome them into my home as if they were my own."

"Huh," said Pam. "You've really given this all a lot of thought."

She averted her eyes.

"But?" he asked, leaning in.

"But what?"

"But I'm missing something, aren't I?"

"Well," she started, unsure of how to respond. "Yeah, totally."

He grinned. "Like what?"

"Like kids are difficult. A lot of the time they can be tough. Parenting a teenager – or any kid – is not for the weak. Every age has its challenges, believe me."

"I bet, but I don't expect it to be smooth the whole time." He uncorked the wine bottle. "My sister has kids. I get it."

"Your vision, as sincere as it may be, sounds a little naïve." Pam nodded as he topped off her wine glass. "I imagine being a step-parent would be even more complicated than straight parenting. At least as a parent, when your kid tells you he hates you or something for taking away his cell phone, neither the parent nor the kid can just quit. The parent is still the parent and the kid is still the kid. Nothing can change that. But a step-parent sort of has more wiggle room; it's a fuzzier relationship, which may make certain potential mates a little nervous. If you're not in it for the long haul, you're doing both your future wife and step-kids an immense disservice by getting involved in the first place." She met his eyes. "I hope I don't sound condescending."

"You don't. You sound honest. I appreciate it, I really do. It's refreshing. And I hope you're not scared away by my honesty."

Later, Bernie dropped Pam off after dinner. He walked her onto her porch and gave her a dry kiss on the cheek.

"I'd like to see you again," he said.

She wasn't sure how to respond. Unlike him, she'd given almost no thought to her love life and she felt like she'd stepped onto a ride that was now spinning too fast for her. Agreeing to dinner, agreeing to this non-date, now seemed impulsive and foolish. She was still mourning Nate. What was the hurry? She wasn't Louise. She didn't feel a need to jump start her life. Sure, she didn't want to die alone and held some vague hope of finding someone at some point, but it was a little jarring to put an actual face to that blurry vision that earlier in the week seemed so far away. And that face was that of Bernie Scott, no less.

"I'm going to have to think about it," she said, unlocking her door. "Good night."

She closed the heavy door, and for the first time in months, took comfort in her solitude.

Chapter Twelve

The only fallout from her 'date' with Bernie was with Grace.

Pam should have predicted she'd find out about it sooner or later, but because she'd hardly seen her since she'd gotten her lifeguarding job, Pam didn't give it much thought. But Grace was home. And she was sitting up waiting for her in the living room.

"What the hell, Mom?" said Grace from the living room, as soon as Pam shut the front door.

Still standing in the entryway, Pam called back, "Hi to you, too, honey." She hung her purse onto one arm of the coat rack.

"So, you're dating Bernie Scott now? After three months? It's like you can't wait to replace Dad with someone else."

"I'm not—" Pam stopped herself. She'd texted Grace that afternoon not to wait for her and to help herself to leftovers in the fridge for dinner, but kept the details to herself. How would she know she was out with Bernie? Pam swiveled around to find Grace sitting on the sofa with her laptop open on the coffee table, the screen tilted toward Pam, revealing a photo of her and Bernie out at Barclay Prime. Someone had taken a surreptitious photo of the two of them, smiling and looking into each other's eyes, holding their glasses of Prosecco in mid clink. She'd been caught doing…what?

"You're not 'what', Mom?" asked Grace, her tone filled with fury.

Pam couldn't figure out what she was or wasn't doing. Dating? Waiting? Remaining celibate forever? She walked into the living room and sat in one of the reading chairs. "I went out to dinner. That's all."

"Right. With Bernie Scott. He's a politician. He's your *client*." Grace leaned forward. "Did you kiss him? The caption under the photo says you're 'canoodling.'"

Pam squinted at the computer screen, trying to get a better look at the photo and caption. They looked cozy. She shook her head. "I didn't kiss or 'canoodle' anyone tonight." She bent over and slid off her heels and rubbed her feet. "Honestly, sweetie, I don't know what I'm supposed to do. It's not like they hand you a rule book to follow when your husband dies. Bernie asked and I said yes." She leaned back in the chair and took in her tall, suntanned daughter. "How did you find the photo?"

"Hannah. It's making the rounds as we speak." She slammed the top of the laptop shut. "It's so embarrassing. My mom and Bernie Scott. Gross."

Gross. "There's no 'Mom and anyone', sweetie. That I can assure you." She checked the time on her phone – it was almost 11 o'clock. "When did you get home?"

"A little after nine."

Pam wondered how long Grace had been sitting there seething with the intrusive photo on the laptop. It'd probably interrupted her lounging and watching YouTube videos. And now she was sitting straight up, her body tense and pulsing with questions.

"Are you seeing him again?" she asked.

Pam sighed and met Grace's intense, fervent eyes. "I don't know, Grace. Not any time soon. I don't think I'm ready."

"Why not?"

"Well," Pam got up and sank into the couch beside Grace. She pushed a loose piece of wild, sun-kissed hair behind her ear. "I think that dinner clarified some things for me. Finding a partner isn't my main concern. I've got work. And I've got you. We have this life I'm trying to keep together, you know? Seeing someone isn't high on my list of priorities right now. Caring for you and continuing Designer You far outweigh any fears of being single at this time in my life."

Grace's brow softened. "I don't understand, then." She bit her lip. "How come you have time to go to dinner with Bernie, but no time to come to any of my games?"

Pam didn't have an answer that could make Grace feel any better.

Because I'd miss work if I came to your games? Because dinner with Bernie was less about having fun and more about keeping a client happy? Because I'm a shitty mom? Because going to your games was more your dad's job?

"I don't know, sweetie. Is that what's bothering you? That I don't come to your lacrosse games?"

Grace shrugged. "Dad always tried to make time."

"I know he did." She looked down at her hands, touching the empty space where her wedding band had been for two decades. She felt for the little groove that her ring left behind when she took it off a few weeks ago. The ring was now tucked away in her jewelry box upstairs in her bedroom, but the indentation had persisted for a long time, until finally she couldn't feel it any more. It was as if the flesh in her finger was ready to be single before Pam was. She got up. "Are you staying up? 'Cause I'm beat."

"Nah," said Grace, looking down at her feet almost sheepish. "Can I sleep in your bed tonight?" Her voice was small, like a child's.

Pam cocked her head at her. "Everything OK?"

Grace nodded. "Yeah, I just got worried, that's all."

"Worried I'd move on with Bernie? Or someone else?"

She nodded again, her chin trembling.

"Leave the worrying to me OK, Gracie?" Pam threw her arms around Grace and hugged her close. "Let's go to bed."

Chapter Thirteen

For the rest of the summer, Bernie didn't ask Pam out again. In the couple of times she'd seen him, he was friendly and warm and kind as always. When she met with him about the progress of the townhouse, he was generous in his praise of her work. But he didn't follow up on his professed desire to see her again for dinner and kept a professional distance. Pam wondered if he had lost interest in her and moved on with someone else. Or maybe he'd taken her at her word – she needed the time to think and he was giving it to her. Or maybe he'd forgotten all about it. But it was strange and a little terrifying to think she held his attention in any sort of romantic way. For her, it was something that always lingered at the edges of her mind whenever she came into contact with him. So she tried to push the thoughts aside and dig into her work.

From Pam's view, it seemed Grace had dug into her new job as well. By mid-summer, Grace had passed her exams at school and was poised to begin her sophomore year with a clean slate in September. And judging by her browned skin and endless appetite, Grace was spending all week lifeguarding and teaching swimming at the neighborhood pool club. Most days they didn't see much of each other. And when they did, they squabbled over dirty dishes left in the sink and the 'pig sty' Pam called Grace's room. They were more like bitchy roommates than mother and daughter, which made Pam's chest ache when she thought about it for too long.

We've got to try the therapy thing, she thought with dismay, for what seemed like the hundredth time that summer. But when could they schedule that? Between their two crazy schedules, it seemed an impossible task.

Before she could take a breath, Labor Day had come and gone and Grace was back in school, starting her sophomore year. Pam was already so behind. She never had a chance to catch up over the summer, like she'd hoped. The final details of the basement project and Bernie's townhouse loomed. She had to prepare for another demonstration of the gardening line at an expo in New Jersey. The Goddamn book she still hadn't started. Jackie was starting to worry they'd lose the contract. On a Thursday evening in mid-September, Pam plopped down in front of her laptop after a long, exhausting day to write responses to interview questions to go along with a profile on Bernie's townhouse that were going to appear in the November issue of *Home and Design*. She'd been dreading this and putting it off for weeks and still wasn't sure how to tackle the author, Hilde Mesick's, questions about her design process and the progress of the project.

"What inspired you to study and pursue design?"

"What aspects of your upbringing and background have shaped your design principles and philosophies?"

"Who or what has been your biggest design influence to date?"

"In terms of your skill as a designer, what is your strongest asset and how have you developed that skill over time?"

Pam was tempted to answer every question with 'Nate'. Who had made her want to pursue design? Oh, Nate. Her biggest influence? Nate. Pam swallowed. The idea of clinging to Nate, the golden child, was so overwhelming, Pam didn't feel she had much of a choice. If his passion was picking up trash, she was sure she'd be discussing the ins and outs of garbage disposal. What shaped her design principles and philosophies? Not that she really had any of her own, so the obvious answer to that question was Nate. Biggest influence? Strongest asset? Duh…Nate. This interview was going to be easy. Pam pressed her palms to her eyes. Magazines like *Home and Design* wanted to hear about a designer's passion for the work. *Her* passion for design was buried with a man who had been gone for more than five months now. She glanced at the clock. 6:45 p.m. *Maybe I'm done for the day. I've got nothing in the tank for this.*

What struck Pam as even more dreadful was that the magazine was slotted to take photos of the townhouse's progress early next week. They'd already snapped a few photos of the 'before' – ancient apartments with peeling wallpaper and stained wall-to-wall carpeting. They returned when the house had been hollowed out. She'd made more progress, but hardly dramatic to the naked eye. How could she make it look more 'done' as soon as possible? Refinish floors? Put walls up? Paint? Pam made a mental note to ask the contractor how much they could squeeze in before the photographers showed up.

Pam clicked to her email tab. One hundred and thirty-four unread emails. *Ugh.*

She sifted through the junk and important emails and clicked on one from her agent, Jackie, who asked Pam so very nicely, "How's the draft coming? Publisher is getting antsy! Please ballpark when I can have a look. Thanks." *Shit.* Pam hadn't even outlined the first draft nor looked at the document in months. Next.

God, the nightmare basement project. The owners complained that the basement *still* wasn't complete, and the family wanted to be able to take over the space before the start of school. Demanding to know timeline. Forward to Dennis.

And speaking of Dennis, he had sent her an email about a plumbing emergency on a bed-and-breakfast project in San Francisco. *Who should I call? I don't know anyone here.* Neither do I. *Contract this job out.*

This evening was starting to look like an all-nighter. With her parents back home and Grace – at Hannah's? Grabbing a bite with friends after study hall? – Pam felt like there was no one she could complain to. Becky was working at the hospital tonight. And Becky had been so distracted because of her mother lately; Pam would have felt terrible about complaining to her. Just a few days prior, Becky had learned that her mother had fallen in her bathtub during her evening shower and broken her hip. The pain knocked her out at first, and when she came to many hours later close to dawn, she managed to drag herself, still naked, from the bathroom to the bedroom where her phone was, plugged in on the nightstand. She called herself an ambulance. Becky didn't find out that her mom was hurt until late next morning, east coast time, when the hospital called.

"I'm so upset," she told Pam that afternoon. "My mum's eighty. Broken hip? Wet and cold after a shower?" Becky ran her fingers through her cropped hair. "She could have easily died in her own bathtub."

"Thank God she's OK," said Pam. Becky was right. Her mother, who was otherwise a healthy and active eighty-year-old, lived by herself in the country. A broken hip could be all it took to do the poor woman in.

"And there's nothing I could've done about it. That's the worst part about it. Here I am, an ocean away, helpless in my mother's time of need." Becky sighed. "I'm gonna have to figure out how to get out there as soon as possible."

"You need some miles? I've got hundreds of thousands."

Becky's eyes widened. "Seriously?"

"I'm not kidding. Mine and Nate's. And I can't even begin to use them right now." Pam made a note in her phone. "I'll call tonight. When you know, just tell me the dates and I'll have Liz set it up."

"Oh my God, thank you!" Becky hugged Pam.

"It's nothing," said Pam, warmth spreading across her chest. It was sort of nothing, but it felt good to Pam to help Becky in this small way. She could afford the miles and Pam knew a last-minute trip to London would wreck Becky's budget.

"It's not nothing," said Becky. "I'll talk to my work and then just go. Thank you. And my mum thanks you."

Pam sat in front of her computer, the needy emails glaring back at her and demanding her immediate attention. It was in these stretches when, feeling overwhelmed, she'd lose all patience if it weren't for Nate. Tonight, he'd probably tell her to shoot off a quick email to Dennis to solve the plumber problem.

Tell Dennis to call Gary's. One of their guys will be out within an hour. Tell him to tell them I recommended them. They'll come.

Or about the never-ending basement project: *Give them a call in the morning. They just need reassurance. It'll be done, but in order for it to be done right and safely, we needed more time than we anticipated. Something like that. You want me to make the call?*

Yes, thought Pam. He was an expert at smoothing those rough edges and reminding people why they hired him in the first place. *Could I do that? Why the hell would the Montanaro family trust* me? *I'm surprised they haven't gotten over feeling sorry for me and just sued me already.*

She positioned her cursor over the 'x' to close the email tab. She pressed down and felt relief wash over her, as if she'd just 'x'ed out her building anxiety. She could deal with all of those emails tomorrow. When Nate was alive, after a frustrating day, she could close down her computer and join him for a drink sometimes in the kitchen or outside. *On the patio, ugh.* Or in the living room on the couch. She'd drape her legs over his and complain about all the people demanding their attention. He'd rub her feet and listen as she complained. And then she'd get it out of her system and they'd move on to make dinner. He was like her personal pressure valve. No more. She no longer had a partner to tell her she was right, that getting back to them in the morning wasn't going to hurt anything.

And anyway, the beauty of their marriage – any marriage – had been that she and Nate were in it day after day. He knew the context. She could get right to the heart of the problem without providing any back story because he'd have been there when the back story happened. Would she ever get to a place in a relationship where she'd feel as comfortable with someone? She thought about Louise again, who'd found someone so soon after Paul died. It seemed miraculous and shocking at the time, but Louise was happy. She got what she wanted. Pam wondered how long it took before Louise was cuddling up to her new love and complaining about her day. How long before Louise could complain unencumbered by back story? Was Louise's new husband her personal pressure valve? Probably.

What was that dating website she used?

Pam couldn't remember. She'd told Grace she wasn't ready to date, and she wasn't. But she never predicted just how excruciating and lonely it would be without Nate. He filled in so many blanks – as a partner, lover, friend, companion. Her life right now, as busy as it was, was far less full without him in it.

She opened a new tab on her computer and clicked into the search box and typed: 'match.com.' Pam felt her throat begin to close and swallowed down her anxiety. *I'm going to need to wade into this online dating thing at some point,* she told herself. *And I'm just looking, not posting.* That made her feel better. All she needed were a few self-imposed parameters. Online dating was something that took hold of the singles community during the time she was already married and starting a family. Of course, other than Louise, she knew plenty of couples who had met through Match or eHarmony or J Date and marveled at how acceptable, efficient, and even preferred it was to meeting someone in a bar. Even Tinder was getting some traction in the over-40 set. But it was all still a mystery to her. She wasn't so sure about going out to dinner with Bernie again, but she did know she wasn't about to be alone for the rest of her life, either. She needed someone to complain to about her overflowing email box.

The website wasted no time. It asked her immediately – before she could have a click around – if she was a man or woman seeking a man or woman, age range, and zip code. All this before she would be allowed to 'View Photos.'

Ack!

Pam wasn't sure she needed to view photos just yet, but she filled in the information anyway and clicked. The page opened to dozens of pictures of men staring back at her. Many looked like casual profile shots that one might see on Facebook or Instagram. Many men posted what looked like vacation photos – with beaches or mountains a prominent feature in the background. Some posed with their hobbies, perched on motorcycles or holding up a fishing pole. One man posted a photo of himself crossing a marathon finish line, his fists raised in a triumphant 'V'. A handful stood beside what Pam hoped were their grinning children, which Pam thought was weirdly honest. Like, *I have children. Deal with it.*

She clicked on the marathon guy, which revealed his responses to several questions such as, what he likes to do (run, swim, compete in triathlons, travel) and his favorite hot spots (Kelly Drive running trail, new restaurants). Pam considered how her future husband might respond to 'what he likes to do' and 'his favorite hot spots.' She wasn't sure she cared. Would she learn anything about someone who listed Five Guys as his favorite hot spot? After all, Nate's favorite spot was probably any empty old building.

How could she determine the person who she could complain to about needy clients or frustrations over replacing the printer toner or Grace's utter silence by how they responded to 'A Few of His Favorite Things?' But still, she couldn't look away, profile after profile. They spanned all ages, income brackets, education levels, race, religion. Some were divorced, separated, never married, still married (!). Some had kids, many did not. And a lot of these people, Pam had to admit, were attractive. No one appeared desperate. No one looked strange. Just normal people.

Pam thought about how she would fit in the online dating community. How would she define herself? Middle-aged mom? Young widow? How would anyone browsing her profile see her? She felt at once too old and too young. She clicked on the questionnaire. The first questions asked: About Your Date.

Wow, we're getting right to it, aren't we?

She squinted at her computer screen. 'What does he look like?' 'What's his hair color?'

Hair color? That's easy. She eyed the checklist.

No Preference

Auburn / Red

Black

Light brown

Dark brown

Blonde

Salt and pepper

Silver

Dark blonde

Gray

Platinum

Bald

MORE

Oh my gosh, there's 'more?'

Pam gawked at the choices in hair color alone. She wasn't sure she had a preference. Nate's hair was brown, and he didn't have even a strand of gray. Red? She'd never dated anyone with red hair before Nate and hadn't found herself drawn to red-headed men. But on the other hand, she hadn't been a part of the dating pool in more than twenty years. She had a working relationship with a red-headed decorator, who had an awful comb-over. The thought of those long strands of orange hair piled over a freckled scalp made her shiver. *Bad example.* How would she know if she was attracted to red-haired men? Salt and pepper. Well, Bernie certainly could check that box, and she found him kind of attractive. Silver? Gray? Pam hoped there was a section on age coming up soon. She didn't want to date anyone too much older than she was. Or too much younger.

This is too hard. She clicked back to check her email. There was a new message waiting for her from Bernie: update on the brownstone. She blushed. *Ugh, not now.* It was like she was being watched.

She clicked back to Match.

Bald? *If he looks like Ed Harris, then sure, why not bald?* Pam clicked No Preference.

I may need to keep my options open. Aren't most men my age married? She scrolled to the next option – eye color. No Preference.

OK, I think I'm getting the hang of this.

'What's his body type?' Pam thought the only body type she could love was Nate's. But Bernie wasn't so bad either. Bernie didn't have the understated musculature that Nate did. He never had a gym membership, but putting up wallboard, climbing ladders, sawing two-by-fours, and lifting cans of paint kept his core, chest, arms, and legs in gym shape. Bernie had the body of a former athlete. He was solid – she could see that through the tailored pants and expensive dress shirts – but he also sported a well-established paunch, probably from too many dinners at places like Barclay Prime.

Pam gazed at the body type choices: About average, Athletic and Toned, Slim, Heavyset, Stocky, A few extra pounds, Large, and No preference. There was also an additional box for DEAL BREAKER.

Oh God, so guys are going to set their preferences for women, too, she thought. *Am I, 'average?'*

Pam thought so, but her exercise regimen had vanished since Nate died. She was heavier now than when Grace was little, but not by much. She didn't feel particularly slim or athletic. Her body these days felt flat, which there wasn't a check box for. Average?

What if my 'average' isn't what my date thinks is average? What's the deal breaker?

All the focus so far on looks seemed so surface and judgmental. It *was* judgmental. But of course it was. Pam wondered if she could see herself dating someone who considered himself Large or Stocky. She sighed. She clicked 'average,' 'athletic and toned,' 'a few extra pounds' and 'deal breaker' – and hated herself a little bit for being so picky.

After going through height, education level, race, religion, whether and how much he drank or smoked, Pam now had to size up herself. She found it far easier to check off the boxes for hair (black), eyes (brown), height (5' 6"), body type (average), have kids (yes), want kids (no, but it's OK if my partner does), marital status (widow), language (English). She had no choices to make. But when she came to the box where she needed to write something about herself or about her ideal match in about two hundred words, the answers dried up.

Don't overthink it, the website reassured her. *You can always change it later.*

But it didn't make her feel any better. Pam saved her profile and opened up a blank Word document. The security of a word count and spell check made her feel a little better, but not much. She padded downstairs to the kitchen and poured herself a large glass of red wine. She came back upstairs, took a mouthful, and started to type.

I'm a newly widowed mother of a teenager. Just want to get that out there right off the bat. These are no doubt two major road blocks for most men. I understand. Feel free to move on to the next profile. I'm also trying to hang onto our livelihood. I fear I'm not doing such a great job and it's a lonely feeling – all this work, this time away from my daughter, this need to keep from drowning in projects my husband started and that now I need to finish – makes me wish for someone to lean on. When I used to have free time, I liked cooking dinner at home for family and friends. I liked spending long afternoons rummaging through architecture salvage warehouses, poking around flea markets, wandering second-hand furniture stores. I love walking through the old neighborhoods of Philadelphia, or any city, really. Nate and I used to take long walks as dates before Grace was born. And after Grace was born, we'd do the same thing, but this time pushing her stroller. She's fifteen now and doesn't want to have anything to do with me.

Pam sat back in her desk chair, disgusted with herself. *Well don't I sound 'fun'? This is pathetic.* Pam took another sip of wine. *Who in their right mind would want to email me after reading this profile? And would I even want to date someone who is attracted to this pathetic, needy, lonely woman? Delete.* She took a breath and raised her fingers to the keyboard.

I am a kind-hearted, hard-working, and fun-loving person. There's nothing I like more than trying new restaurants or taking a quick trip to the beach or New York. I like an excuse to let loose and dance to current hits or songs from the 1980s and 90s at weddings and bar mitzvahs. Going for a hike in the Wissahickon or riding my bicycle along Kelly Drive are two of my favorite ways to spend a Sunday afternoon. I'm looking for someone who also likes to have fun. I'd like someone I could go to a Phillies game with or to Reading Terminal Market. I'm interested in someone who is non-judgmental and likes to travel. I'm not interested in serial daters, hook-ups, or games. I'm looking for someone who can make me laugh. I'm looking for intelligent conversation. Are you that person to share in the fun?

No. A hundred times no. This is all wrong. Delete. Pam scowled at her blank screen. *Why is this so hard?*

She leaned back in her chair, sipping her wine. How would others see her? How would they define her? Explain her to someone else? *What would Becky say about me? What would my parents say? What would Nate say?*

I think if you asked the people closest to me what they would say about me, their answer would be that I'm kind and sometimes funny. I'm loyal, compassionate. That I get chatty when I get nervous. That I'm cautious one moment and carefree the next. That I'm a homebody. That I love to travel. That I love sharing food and wine with friends and family at my dining room table. That I love my kid with everything I am and want the absolute best for her. That I had a fantastic marriage and amazing partnership with an honorable, sexy, hilarious, brilliant man, whom I miss and still love. That I'm still sad and continue grieving his loss. But also that I don't want to be alone. That I'm ready to see if there's anyone else out there I might get along with. I think my friends would say that I could even fall in love again.

Pam heard the front door lock click and the door shudder

open. Grace was home. She looked at the clock on her laptop. 8:35 p.m. She'd been sitting at her desk browsing Match.com for almost two hours.

"Mom?" Grace called from downstairs. Pam clicked out of the Word document.

"I'm in my office!" Pam shouted back. She heard Grace ascend the stairs. She appeared in the open doorway.

"You didn't make dinner for me, did you?" asked Grace, leaning into the door frame.

Pam looked up from her computer. She shook her head. "I didn't make dinner for myself, either. Did you eat?"

Grace nodded. "At Hannah's."

"Did you finish your homework?"

"Yeah." Grace looked down at her feet.

Pam watched her daughter for clues, to see if her body language gave anything additional away. If she thought too long about Grace's disastrous spring semester – skipping school and brawling with another girl – she could feel that deep familiar terror, anger, and despair awaken inside of her. Meeting with Principal Hicks, writing that humongous check – it all made her innards churn.

"Are you sure?" she asked, wishing she could sound a little more detached, less desperate and untrusting.

Grace looked up and narrowed her eyes at Pam. "Yes, Mom. I'm sure. Hannah and I went to the library and worked on it."

Pam pressed for details. "What'd you work on?"

"I had a geometry worksheet and studied for a history quiz and vocab quiz in Spanish." Grace looked up at the ceiling, thinking. "Um, bio reading and questions. Oh, and for health, we had to fill out this questionnaire about college and career. We're supposed to find out what majors or whatever we're most suited for."

Pam sat up in her chair. "Really? That's interesting. Must be useful, too, to find out what you would naturally lean toward, right? I'm sure you and your friends have already started talking about college."

"I wish they'd all shut up about it."

Pam frowned. "Who, your friends?"

"Everyone. Friends, teachers, coaches, parents. Any grown up." Grace clenched her jaw. "You know who didn't care if I went to college? The pool club kids I taught how to swim. Not one of those little assholes asked me one time where I wanted to go to college."

"Language, Grace."

Grace ignored her. "Or what I wanted to major in. What I wanted to be when I grew up. All they cared about was that I taught them how to float or dive off the diving board." She folded her arms across her chest. "I wish it were summer."

Pam raised her eyebrows. Grace had always resisted any conversation that related to goal setting, and Pam didn't think Grace could plan beyond the following weekend. Having conversations about college and career seemed like a smart, logical topic for high school. It was one of the major reasons she and Nate chose BFS for Grace.

"College is all anyone wants to talk about with me," Grace continued. "Adults think that the only thing teenagers care about is college. Well I'm tired of it. I don't want to think about it but you all keep forcing the subject on me."

"It's something you're going to need to face, hon. The sooner the better. Your father knew what he wanted to be when he was your age, and that gave him a big advantage," said Pam.

"I *know*, Mom."

Pam shrugged. "You've got to think about it at some point. Don't you have the first round of PSATs coming up?"

"Ugh, Mom. It's almost the weekend. The last thing I want to think about are those stupid tests."

Pam didn't push it. They'd had versions of the same conversation for years. But it was obvious to Pam that Grace did not inherit Nate's focus.

Grace cocked her head. "What are you looking at?"

"Huh?"

"On your computer." Grace walked behind Pam's desk chair so she could take a better peek at Pam's computer screen. "Is that a dating website?"

Pam felt the flush surge from her chest and burn her cheeks and temples. "Oh, yeah," said Pam, flustered. "I was just poking around."

"Right," said Grace, in a mildly accusing tone.

Pam clicked her email tab. "Just taking a break from answering emails. I should get back to that, actually."

"You should eat something, Mom. Take a break and eat *dinner*."

Dinner. For months, meals were the furthest thing from her mind, with the exception of her dinner with Bernie. That seemed so long ago. "What are you up to tonight?"

"YouTube. I'm beat."

Pam nodded. She felt a tinge of envy for the window of free time Grace had to just watch videos on her computer. Here she was, guilty of wasting her time just browsing around on Match.com when she had what seemed like an infinite number of other, more pressing projects demanding her attention. "I'm going to fix myself something to eat."

"Good," said Grace turning away. "You're looking a little ragged these days."

A little ragged?

Pam wished Grace would sometimes keep her opinions to herself. But Grace was right. Pam felt ragged, so there was no reason she wouldn't look it, too. She clicked back to her unfinished profile. Just answering the questions and writing up a statement explaining who she was in two hundred words was too much. She clicked out of the website without saving her profile.

I'm too ragged to be date-able.

Chapter Fourteen

During the fall months, Bernie's brownstone ate up every working minute Pam could spare. Once the walls went up, she needed to make decisions about colors, fabrics, light fixtures, and window treatments. She ordered a claw-foot bathtub for one of the guest bathrooms and hired a craftsman to create the glass shower and tile work for the master bath. She refinished floors, ordered rugs, and installed tile. She culled through Bernie's art collection and decided what to keep and what to send to storage, as well as what additional pieces she would need to buy. When she wasn't at the work site or out shopping for Bernie's house, she was writing all the details down in bi-weekly blog posts, which seemed more popular now than ever. For Pam, September, October, and November blurred into one, long, exhausting span of nonstop, pressing tasks. Pam looked forward to not being needed for a time so she could catch her breath.

These months all led to final preparations for the photo shoot scheduled for the Tuesday before Thanksgiving. After an all-nighter Monday, moving and arranging Bernie's furniture, Pam was still putting the last touches on the place when the *This Old House* staff writer and camera crew showed up at nine Tuesday morning.

Among all the last-minute craziness of the day, her email pinged. Jackie. *We need to talk.* That was all.

Shit.

Pam felt her throat close up. Jackie, who she'd worked with since the first book, was Pam's fiercest and most tireless advocate. But she knew that despite her loyalty, Jackie was losing patience with her lack of progress on the latest project, and there were only so many times Jackie could go back to the publisher and ask for another extension. Was this her last chance?

Pam pushed the thought aside, vowing she'd find a way to smooth things over tomorrow. The packed day went off without too much drama. Bernie arrived late, but he charmed, and the brownstone shined. All proved photogenic. And when everyone had left, Pam felt a tidal wave of relief wash over her. Not pride, not satisfaction, not joy. Not even happiness for accomplishing Nate's vision. The job was over.

Now I can stop thinking about it. Cross that one off my enormous fucking list.

Pam couldn't help but think how different this day would feel if Nate were around. He would be buoyant, energized, celebratory. Nate would have already been scheming how to turn Bernie's brownstone into an even bigger opportunity for Designer You. And she knew a lot of that would have rubbed off on her, too. But not now. Now she just wanted to move onto the next item on her list. Even if she felt differently, Pam had no time for a self-congratulatory glass of champagne.

By Wednesday afternoon, she was sitting at her desk ready to trade one headache – Bernie's brownstone – for another potential problem: Jackie's mysterious email. She wrote, *Hi Jackie, OK, let's talk. Bernie's brownstone is done and we can make a plan for the book. ~ Pam.* But a full day later, Pam hadn't heard a word of reply from Jackie, and she thought the silence might drive her crazy.

She checked her email again as she sat on her parents' reading chair by the window in their living room. The Thanksgiving smells of roasted turkey, glazed carrots, green bean casserole, and pumpkin pie permeated the entire house. Sounds of cheerful banter between Becky, Jimmy's wife, Vanessa, and her parents emanated from the kitchen. *They're probably helping, while drinking chardonnay or sparkling wine,* she thought, both jealous and grateful at once. No new emails. *Is that a good thing or a bad thing?* She glanced up from her phone. Grace was on the floor with Gus, Jimmy and Vanessa's six-month-old. She laid on her back and had the boy perched on her shins, his arms outstretched and her hands clasped his. His gummy mouth opened in a gleeful shriek.

"Airplane, Gus! Up, up, up! Wheee!" she sang, laughing. Drool pooled along the brim of Gus's lip. A long strand emerged and dripped onto Grace's chest. She bolted up and wiped the spit from her shirt. "Wow, super gross, little man." She kissed his fat cheek. "No worries. You'll get the drooling thing under control in a few years. It just takes practice. C'mon, let's go find Mama."

Jimmy, clutching a bottle of beer, smiled at the cousins on the living room floor as he appeared from the TV room. "Gus treating you OK? He's not being rude or inconsiderate, is he?"

Grace offered a polite laugh. "No, Uncle Jimmy. Gus's only crime is he's too adorable. And a little drool-y."

He laughed. "Yeah, well, you can probably count yourself lucky he didn't spit up on you. Drooling is definitely a minor infraction." He watched as his son beamed at Grace. "When did you get so good with kids?"

Grace looked back at Pam, who shrugged. "I don't know, maybe working at the pool club last summer? I taught kids how to swim and was a lifeguard during recreation hours. It was really fun."

"Wow, that's impressive. What were we doing when we were your age, huh, Pammy? Not teaching kids how to swim, *that* I know."

Pam raised one eyebrow. She knew what Jimmy was doing when he was in high school – a lot of sneaking out and partying with his soccer teammates. And avoiding working in their dad's diner as much as possible. Doing the least amount of work to slide by in school.

Which is why he ended up going to work straight out of high school, and I had a scholarship to Penn State.

"*I* was helping out at the diner. *And* working my butt off in school." She smirked at him. "You can speak for yourself."

"Fair enough, sis. I still think teaching the little ones how to swim is far nobler than serving up pancakes and eggs over easy." He turned to Grace. "Want me to take him?"

Grace nodded. Pam sensed that she'd had her fill of baby time and was ready for a break. She handed Gus off to Jimmy. Pam watched her rise from the floor.

"I'm gonna grab a Coke. Anyone want anything from the kitchen?" asked Grace as she edged out of the living room.

"I'm good." Pam refreshed her email again on her phone. Nothing.

"Me too, kid," said Jimmy, sitting down onto the couch and cradling Gus in his arms. He put his beer onto a coaster on the coffee table. He looked into Gus's eyes and nodded toward Pam.

"Aunt Pammy's been on her phone all day, can you believe that, Gus? What is so important on Thanksgiving?"

"I can hear you, you know," said Pam, not looking up. She opened up her to-do list. Since completing Bernie's brownstone for the magazine layout two days before, she had an impossible list of tasks related to stalled projects she'd had to push to the side. Dennis had had enough and had taken the time off that was coming to him. Her progress on the book, for which she'd already received a generous advance, came to a screeching halt since Nate's death. Her publisher had been nice enough to give her extensions, but Pam knew they were losing patience with her. If they wanted to cancel her contract, they had every right.

"I don't know anyone who's checking their email today, unless it's for Black Friday coupons to Best Buy or Banana Republic," said Jimmy. Gus's cheek settled drowsily on his shoulder.

"Yeah, well. I have a ton of stuff I need to remember for when I get home," said Pam, now scrolling through her to-do list again.

"It's Thanksgiving. Why don't you pay attention to your family for the afternoon? We've hardly seen you since, well, late last spring. You and Grace are just getting to know Gus and let's face it, Vanessa too. Mom and Dad want to know you're doing fine." He looked at her, his eyes pleading. "*Are you doing fine?*"

Pam looked up from her phone and scowled. "Yeah. Of course I am," she said, aware she might be coming across like a sullen teenager.

Jimmy pressed on. "You know you can tell me anything. I won't mention it to Mom or Dad. Not even Vanessa if you want. Is there anything wrong? It's the first Thanksgiving without Nate for God's sake."

She crossed her arms. "Just because I'm not crowding into the kitchen making nice with your new wife and going ape shit over your new baby doesn't mean I'm not fine. 'Busy' is different from 'something's wrong,' OK?"

Jimmy reeled back. "OK, geez. Don't have to bite my head off."

Pam set her phone down. "Sorry. You're right. That was uncalled for." She offered her brother a tight smile. "Gus is a doll. Grace and I are both crazy about him, and I'm thrilled for you and Vanessa. I've just got a lot going on that's taking my attention right now. It doesn't look like it's going to let up anytime soon, so I've got to try to keep on top of it. And if you want to know the truth, I'm not doing such a great job of keeping on top of it, so I'm sitting here obsessing over my email and all the crap that's waiting for me when Thanksgiving's over. I have to get a handle on it as soon as possible, otherwise, well—" She shrugged. "No income, you know?"

And I'd have to force myself to think about Thanksgiving without Nate, she didn't say.

"That sounds like a lot," said Jimmy, nodding. Gus gave a slight sigh in slumber.

Pam's face softened watching the two. "Good God, he's adorable." She inhaled and rested her back against the cushions of her chair. "You've got a lot too. I think it's just been a crazy time. Grace and I are still adjusting to life without Nate. We definitely don't have that down. You were helping run the diner while Mom and Dad were staying with us last spring. Vanessa had the baby." Pam left out Grace's close call at school. "It's amazing we didn't all lose our minds."

"It's true," said Jimmy. "But, you might think of letting up a bit. Don't take so much on. Take a break. Get to know Grace again – she's a great girl and growing up so fast."

On one level, Pam conceded he did have a point, but it infuriated her how easy it was for others outside of her immediate day-to-day life to say 'take a break' and 'spend more time with Grace' but not have any clue just how impossible that really was for them right now. If she *could* take a break, didn't he think she *would* take a break? Pam often fantasized about the trips she, Nate, and Grace used to take together, vacations that weren't tied to projects or appearances – just time off to goof off and refresh. They'd traveled to Disney World and driven cross country to San Francisco. They'd rented a motorhome and camped in the Black Hills of South Dakota for two weeks when Grace was five. For many summers, they'd spent a week with friends at the beach in North Carolina or at the Jersey Shore. It didn't seem to matter too much where they went as long as they were together, focusing on anything other than what 'had' to be done at work, at school. Life was put on hold. Pam was dying to put her life on hold. She and Grace needed to find a way to escape and get to know each other again. Be in a different space, smell different air, eat different food, meet different locals. She'd played this game in her head, though, for months. It wasn't going to happen any time soon.

Her mom called Pam and Jimmy into the dining room for dinner. Jimmy laid Gus down in the porta-crib set up in the living room and wandered in after Pam.

"Can I help?" asked Pam. The kitchen buzzed with chatter and moving platters and steaming food and the opening and closing of the refrigerator door.

"Here," said Becky, handing Pam a glass of champagne. "Glad you've emerged from your isolation cave and decided to join us." Becky had spent several Thanksgivings with Pam in recent years. Since her ex-husband was Jewish, they'd decided together long ago that he'd take Thanksgiving with the kids and Becky could have Christmas. Since the moment Pam's parents met Becky more than four years ago, they'd extended standing invitations to all of their holiday gatherings. Becky was always welcome.

Pam gave her a look of mock consternation and took the glass. "Thanks." She would show her family she could stay off her phone for the rest of the day.

How 'bout that? she thought, daring herself. *I will drink this champagne. I will eat turkey dinner. I will make pleasant conversation.* Ugh. She sounded like a scolding mother from the Eisenhower era.

Her parents' home had a pretty big kitchen, but even the expansive space had limits. Vanessa, her mom, and dad jockeyed for elbow room and counter space for all the final Thanksgiving dinner prep – to pour the gravy in the gravy boat, toss the salad, carve the turkey, tong green beans into a ceramic bowl. They looked like amateur dancing sous chefs.

"Hot mac 'n' cheese behind you," said Vanessa. Pam scooched forward so that Vanessa could maneuver behind her out of the kitchen and into the dining room and set the hot pan down onto an awaiting pot holder. Pam sat with her champagne next to Grace, who was already seated and on her phone.

She leaned in. "Who are you texting?"

"No one," said Grace, shielding the screen, her thumbs

tapping.

Right. "'No one' seems to have a lot to say," said Pam.

"Ha ha," said Grace. She didn't look up.

Pam placed a hand on Grace's arm. "Let's put the phone down at the table, OK?"

Grace glared at her mom. "Fine," she hissed, sliding her cell into her back pocket. "So now you're the only one who's allowed to check her phone on Thanksgiving?"

"Yes," said Pam keeping her face straight. Actually, she was itching to check her email, even after only, like, ten, fifteen minutes? "Who are you texting today?"

"Just a friend from school." Grace traced the gold rim of her dinner plate with her finger.

"Do I know this person?" Grace had been spending so much time away from home, Pam assumed she was spending it all with Hannah. Maybe Pam had assumed wrong. *Boyfriend?*

"No. She's new. She just moved here from Arizona."

She? "How does she like BFS?" asked Pam, still not convinced whoever Grace was texting was necessarily just a 'she' or a 'friend.' Her family crowded into the dining room. Jimmy sat across from her and Grace. Her parents, Becky, and Vanessa all set out the food in the center of the table and prepared to sit.

"She hates it," said Grace, matter-of-fact.

"Oh." Pam didn't think Grace knew anyone who 'hated' school, but she remembered having a few friends who proclaimed to despise school when she was the same age as Grace. She hoped Grace didn't feel the same way as her friend.

"Who hates what?" asked her dad, settling into the chair at the head of the table.

"Just a friend from school, Grandpa," said Grace.

"Then she should go to another one." Tom passed the sliced turkey to Jimmy, who forked two slices onto his plate and passed it onto Vanessa. "Her parents are spending way too much money on tuition to keep their kid someplace she hates. Can't she 'hate' attending a *public* school?"

"Dad," said Pam. "We're not criticizing Grace's friend's parents right now. I'm sure they have their reasons for choosing the school. It's normal for kids to go through a bit of a transition, especially when they're at a new school."

Tom shrugged. "Fine," he said as he spooned a dollop of mashed potatoes onto his plate and passed them on. "Do you like your school, Grace?"

Grace's cheeks reddened, and she bit her lip, as if she were clamping down on what her instincts wanted to say but her judgment knew better than to reveal. "It's OK."

Pam felt for Grace. She'd worked hard all summer to make up for the work she'd missed last spring when she was skipping weeks of school. Pam's parents were pretty clueless about it at the time, but Pam filled them in, furious at them and herself for being fooled so easily. It was like how clueless they'd been with Jimmy in high school. Her parents were now aware of how close Grace had come to being expelled and knew that Pam had paid out of pocket so Grace would be given one last chance to stay. Becky knew, of course, but not Jimmy and Vanessa. It didn't take much imagination to know how deeply embarrassed or even ashamed Grace felt about what had happened. Although his comments seemed innocuous, no one needed to be reminded of last spring. Not during Thanksgiving dinner.

"Dad, come on – give it a rest, all right? It's Thanksgiving. I'm going to try not to obsess about work today and I think

Grace should take a day off from thinking about school. Especially since PSATs are gosh, next week?"

Grace nodded. She slumped in her chair. "Monday."

"That seems so fast," said Pam's mom. She sat opposite of her dad at the far end of the table. Pam loved that although her parents were very much partners and equals in life, they hung onto some traditions from the past. Growing up, her mother and father always sat at the heads of the table, while Pam and Jimmy filled in the middle, and that's how it was today with a kid and a spouse extra. Before this year, the spouse had always been Nate. Now it was Vanessa. Cooking the turkey had always been a task for the men in the family. After the pumpkins and costumes and candy were put away or discarded after Halloween, Nate, her dad, and even Jimmy began the yearly preparation-of-the-turkey discussion. Would it be roasted, baked, or fried? Spatchcocked and grilled? Was anyone a vegetarian this year?

Every Thanksgiving, Pam and Nate would arrive after breakfast so that Nate and her father could get started on the turkey, brining or basting it and preparing it before cooking. It was one of the rare moments that Pam got to see the two most important men in her life, two men who couldn't have been more different, unify and collaborate with varying degrees of success. Today, Pam noticed her dad had prepared and roasted the turkey by himself. Jimmy was too busy with Vanessa and the baby. And no Nate. Pam ached for her father, wondering if he felt Nate's absence today as acutely as she did.

"So fast, Mom?" asked Pam. She spooned green beans onto her plate.

"You and Jimmy – you didn't take the PSATs that early, did

you?" she asked. "I don't remember you even thinking about SATs and college or any of that stuff until before your senior year."

"It's changed, Mom," said Jimmy. Vanessa nodded along with her husband. "They start talking about college like in pre-school, right Gracie?"

"Yeah," said Grace, her voice flat. She picked at her food with her fork.

Pam could see from Grace's glum face that she was done with this conversation and wondered exactly how worried or stressed she might be over the upcoming test. Her report card was always all As and Bs, but she never performed well on standardized tests. Since she didn't have to get into a magnet school where test scores were taken into consideration, Pam never worried too much about it. Pam wondered if the PSATs were bothering Grace far more than she was letting on.

"Whoops," Pam said. "I think we're talking about school, and we agreed – no school or work talk for Thanksgiving."

"Sorry, kiddo." Jimmy gave her a little wink, which Grace returned with a small smile. Gus saved them all by beginning to cry in the adjacent room, providing an easy change of topic.

Saved by the wail.

* * *

Pam didn't check her email until later that night, after she and Grace had returned home from their forty-five minute drive. She avoided staying overnight at her parents' house, sensing that both she and Grace wanted to sleep in their own beds. Sure enough, a new email from Jackie waited for her in her inbox.

Ripping the Band-Aid off here – Doubleday is canceling contract over all the delays. I'm so sorry, Pam. I'll call tomorrow. ~ Jackie

Fuck.

Pam had never been fired from anything before in her life. She wasn't keeping up – completing the home projects, pushing the garden line, blogging, and working on the next book were all forced to the bottom of her list. But now she could do it! Just give her three months – one month – two weeks – and she'd have something to hand in to her editor. Crazy desperation flooded her chest like new moths.

Fuck, fuck, fuck, she thought, staring at her computer screen.

The advance. According to the contract, she'd have to give the very generous advance back to the publisher. *Right?* Pam wondered, horrified. And she didn't have it to give back. The advance went toward the mortgage and swim club and putting food on the table and lacrosse fees and two seasons worth of new clothes for a growing teenager. It went toward a full year's tuition plus an extra $15,000 to Belfield Friends School. Not to mention her reputation. *Nate's reputation.* She'd never work with Doubleday again.

FUCK.

She wanted to die. To just disappear right there on the spot. To be sucked through a deep sinkhole into the earth along with her house and her and Nate's precious things like the House of Usher.

It seemed everyone was mad at or disappointed with her. She was late on everything. She didn't feel she could do anything right after Nate was gone. Doubleday cancelling her contract was further proof that she was nothing without Nate.

But Grace. She needed to be there for Grace. She couldn't

just disappear. She wasn't allowed to just run away. She couldn't take off for Disney World or go on a cruise. She couldn't rent an RV and take a year driving all over the United States seeking out who made the best version of baby-back ribs.

But she *could* put an end to the dying Designer You brand. She didn't want to do it anymore.

She didn't have the mental or physical energy for it. It was Nate's baby, not hers. It was so clear in that moment that the right thing to do at that point was shutter the blog, let the Lowes contract expire, forget the books, and cancel the remaining projects.

But what would I do?

The question itself seemed too big, too wide, too open-ended to even begin to consider an answer. She needed to provide for her and Grace. She thought about Nate's insurance money – all of it put into a trust, something she didn't want to touch or even think about until Grace went to college at the earliest, or they ran into an emergency and needed funds to live on.

Isn't this an emergency? I don't have a job, or I won't as of the end of tomorrow. The insurance money could tide us over until I find something else. Like, what? Pam thought about the last place she worked before Designer You took off. *Blockbuster Video doesn't even exist anymore. A Metropolitan Bakery had taken over its spot on Walnut Street more than a decade earlier. I can write, she thought. But who would want me now?*

All at once, Pam's head felt too large for her body. She lowered her forehead onto her arms on her desk and began to weep.

* * *

By Monday morning, Pam had three mostly sleepless nights under her belt and was no closer to a plan; in fact, she felt further away. She'd barely touched the Thanksgiving leftovers her mother had forced on her when she left Thursday night. She *had* gathered the courage to speak with Jackie about Doubleday's contract cancellation that Friday morning as promised. She learned that Doubleday had already been more than fair, allowing her extra time to 'transition after Nate's loss.'

Transition into what? Pam thought. *A complete failure?*

They no longer had enough time to finish the draft, edit, create the book cover, and release the book the following year. The project was abandoned. The one sliver of good news was that the publisher wasn't going to sue her for the first advance, which was lucky, because it was already spent. But they would never offer her another contract. And after word got around what had happened, Pam bet she would never be offered the chance work with another publisher again. Pam had demolished Designer You.

Reputation destroyed.

Pam laughed without mirth.

"What's so funny?" asked Jackie on the phone, sounding a tad unnerved.

"I don't think I have a brand anymore."

"What do you mean, Pam?"

"I'm quitting."

"Quitting? Are you crazy?"

Pam thought Jackie sounded a little unhinged herself.

"Maybe. But I think I'm driving myself insane with Designer

You. I just don't have it in me." She sighed into the receiver. "Jackie, you and I both know that it was always Nate's. Nate was Designer You." Pam swallowed the lump of shame that had risen in her throat. "I'm sorry," she said, her voice barely above a whisper.

Silence on the other end. At last, Pam could hear Jackie breathe noisily into the phone.

"Jackie? Are you OK?"

Pam heard Jackie put the phone down and blow her nose in the distance. "Yeah," Jackie said finally. Her voice croaked. "I'm just disappointed."

Disappointed? "I'm sorry?" Pam was confused. "I don't know, Jackie, but it sounds like I need to apologize for something."

"No, no, Pam. I'll be fine. There's a ripple effect when big brands like Designer You either go under or, in the rare case that the owner doesn't want to do it anymore. It was just a jolt for me." She heard Jackie sniffle. "I'll be fine. I'll bounce back."

Pam hadn't thought too far ahead of the quitting part. Yes, she'd be parting ways with people like Jackie, Dennis, and Liz to start. They'd all mutually benefited from Designer You's success. But Pam knew it could be weeks or months before she'd run Designer You into the ground.

Better to get out now.

"You'll bounce back," Pam assured her. *At least one of us will.*

And now, on Monday morning, Pam stood yawning in front of an open refrigerator trying to decide whether turkey and cornbread or pumpkin pie made for a better breakfast. She slid the cold pie tin from the shelf. For Pam, lack of sleep ensured poor eating choices. She dragged a fork across an uncut portion of the pie and took a bite. Cool and creamy, it tasted like exactly like what she needed today. *Sometimes pie is like a warm hug*, she thought, taking another bite.

Her cell buzzed. Grace's school. *What now?* she thought, annoyed, setting down her fork.

"Mrs. Wheeler?" It was Mr. Callahan, one of the school counselors.

"Yes?" asked Pam, checking the oven clock: 7:10. School didn't start until 8:20.

"We've had a bomb threat phoned in to the school early this morning. We are calling all parents and asking that you not bring your child to school or put them on the bus today. I realize a few students may already be on their way, but we're hoping to catch as many as possible before they leave for school." Mr. Callahan sounded breathless, like he had rushed through the same speech dozens of times already. He probably had. "Has Grace left yet?"

"Oh God, that's terrible. I'm sure Grace hasn't left yet – the bus doesn't pick up until 7:40. But I'll check Grace's room, while I have you on the line."

"Thank you."

Pam ascended the stairs by two and knocked on Grace's bedroom door. No answer. She listened for sounds of Grace getting ready for the day. She often had music on as she got dressed. Nothing. Pam pushed the door open. Grace's room looked the same – a few pairs of discarded shoes and flip-flops littered the floor and the remnants from dessert the night before remained on her desk. Grace's bed, though, was neatly made. Grace was nowhere to be found. Pam walked the few steps to the main bathroom – empty.

"Um," Pam stalled. "She's not here. That's weird." She

covered the speaker with her hand and called out, "Grace? Are you home?" Silence.

Pam's face reddened. "Grace isn't here right now," she said. "I'll try her cell."

"That's fine. Please have her come home right away when you find her," said Mr. Callahan. "If she ends up at school, we'll call so you can pick her up."

"Sure thing. Thanks." Pam hung up and dialed Grace's number. It rang and rang and rang and then switched to voicemail.

"Grace," said Pam. "Please call me when you get this message. It's important. Do not go to school today. Someone called in a bomb threat, so school is closed for the time being. Again, please call me as soon as you get this so I know you're OK."

Pam's hands shook as she clicked to hang up. She opened her text messages and typed: *Call me right away, please.*

Did she have an early practice? Field hockey ended before Thanksgiving. Lacrosse season didn't start until spring. Grace was sort of on a sports hiatus until well after the New Year. Grace was also not the student who got to school early to get a jump on assignments or do any last-minute studying for a test. Pam felt the panic begin to settle into her gut.

Where the hell is she? And why isn't she calling me back?

Pam went into her office and rooted around her desk for the BFS directory. She found it and looked up Hannah's number.

"Hello?" Hannah's mom answered the phone, sounding awake, like she'd been up wrangling kids and making breakfast since the break of dawn.

"Hi—" Pam looked down at the directory to make sure she remembered Hannah's mom's name right. "Deborah. It's Pam

Wheeler, Grace's mom."

"Debbie… call me Debbie. Everyone does."

"Debbie, right," said Pam, mentally kicking herself. Hannah and Grace had been friends since middle school, and she couldn't get her name right? "Listen, this is a bit embarrassing, but did Grace spend the night at your house?"

"I don't think so, but let me find Hannah." Pam heard Debbie put the phone down. "Hannah!" she called in the distance. "Pick up the land line! It's Grace's mom – she wants to talk to you!"

"Hello?" Hannah sounded groggy as if Pam had awakened her out of a deep slumber.

"Hannah, hi. It's Grace's mom. Did I wake you?" Pam bit her lip. She knew Grace probably wasn't even with Hannah if Hannah was just waking up.

"Oh hi, Mrs. Wheeler," said Hannah. She cleared her throat. "No, it's OK. My mom came in like fifteen minutes ago and told me about the bomb thing at school. I think I fell asleep again."

Pam knew the answer before she asked. "Grace isn't at your house, is she?" She let out a frustrated sigh.

"No, she's not." Hannah sounded sorry to disappoint Pam.

"Did you see her yesterday?"

"In class, yeah. But not after school or anything."

"Do you know of any other friends she might have spent the night with?"

"I don't know. We haven't really hung out much lately."

Pam rubbed her forehead. "OK, thanks, Hannah. I'm sorry to bother you." She hoped she sounded reassuring.

"No bother. I hope you find her. I'll call or text if I hear from her." They exchanged cell numbers.

"Yes, please do." Pam was relieved at Hannah's suggestion. *Such a nice girl.* "Thank you. I'm sure this will all be resolved soon."

Pam hung up. She called Grace's phone again. Voicemail. She tried to recall Grace's friends from school – Annalisa, Sofia, Courtney, Elise – the names and faces of girls she'd met maybe once, but often, never.

Who was the girl she was texting during Thanksgiving? The new girl. What was her name? Pam typed a message into her phone. *Hannah, do you know the name of the new girl at school? She's a new friend?*

Pam's phone pinged. *Yeah, that's Lauren Holloway. Not my friend. She and Grace have been hanging out tho.*

'Not my friend.' Weird. Grace and Hannah had hung out with the same group of girls since middle school. They were all jocks and studious. A pretty wholesome group, Pam liked to think. Pam looked up the girl's name in the BFS directory. She was so new, her contact information hadn't even been added. But why would Grace leave so early in the first place? To spend time with a friend?

Maybe she didn't leave early, but sneaked out overnight?

A mix of rage and fear began to bubble within her gut. She feared she was looking at a repeat of last spring's lying and sneaking, only this time, she wasn't skipping school, she was sneaking off at night. For what? Boys? Drugs? Alcohol? Did she know anyone who drove? It seemed all the juniors and seniors at BFS had cars – could she have gotten into a car with a boy who was drunk? She scowled at her silent phone. *Please call me, Grace!* she wanted to scream.

Her phone buzzed. Pam didn't recognize the number.

"Hello?" she asked, breathless.

"Pam Wheeler?"

"Yes, that's me."

"This is Officer Marano from the Philadelphia Police Department. Is your daughter named Grace Wheeler?"

Pam felt the room spin around her. No. Is this what happens when your worst nightmare as a mother becomes your reality? There were so many 'worst nightmares' crowding Pam's brain now: car accident, overdose, sexual assault, murder. It was different from all the other 'worst nightmares' she'd protected Grace from since the day she was born. Like when she switched out the crib pads and placed Grace on her back when she slept to avoid SIDS. Or when she screamed at toddler Grace who had decided to run away from Pam to play hide-and-seek in a parking structure at a shopping mall. Or when she put her on the school bus for the first time alone, leaving the driving to another (hopefully capable and alert and licensed and background-checked) adult. This time it was no fantasy she could shake off by wrapping her arms around Grace and giving her a kiss on the cheek, reminding herself Grace was right here under her own roof.

"Is she OK?" she managed to croak. She almost didn't want to hear his response.

"Your daughter has been arrested for allegedly phoning in a bomb threat. You need to come pick her up from the police station."

Chapter Fifteen

A bomb threat. Not burglary. Not murder. And still, Pam didn't feel relief. The officer's claim seemed unreal and untrue. Offensive. Vindictive. "Is this… a joke?" she finally asked.

"I'm afraid not, Ms. Wheeler. I need you to come in and fill out some paperwork so you can bring your daughter home."

Cradling the phone on her shoulder, Pam was already gathering her keys and wallet from the kitchen counter, the pumpkin pie forgotten on the butcher block.

"I'm on my way," she said before sliding the phone into the pocket of her cardigan.

When Pam arrived, she discovered that Grace and her new friend, Lauren Holloway, had phoned in the bomb threat from Lauren's father's landline very early that morning. Grace later insisted it was Lauren's idea, not hers, to get out of the PSATs by putting the school on lockdown, but that didn't matter in the eyes of the law.

As Pam waited for Grace to be fingerprinted and her mugshot taken, she learned Lauren had just lost her mother over the summer to ovarian cancer and was now living with her father, whom she hadn't seen since she was a toddler.

"I haven't been there for her like I should have," the father monologued as he paced the waiting room. Judging from the dark circles under his eyes and the gray pallor to his face, it looked like this arrest was just the last in a series of incidents he'd had to bail his daughter out of. The guy was short – shorter than Pam – and had huge ears. He looked like he'd been bullied a lot as a kid. He seemed to shrink every time any of the officers asked to speak to him. "And her mother's death was very hard on her. Obviously. She did *not* want to live with me," he said and let out a humorless laugh, raking his fingers through his thinning hair. "It's been a rough six months for all of us."

Pam wished he would shut up. Her reserves at this point held little sympathy for this absent father and his delinquent offspring, which she also knew was completely hypocritical, considering how she'd handled her own challenging child.

"Keep your daughter away from my kid," she said through gritted teeth.

She shivered despite the overheated waiting area. Pam could see why the girls would be drawn to each other. The connection in grief between Grace and Lauren made perfect sense, but it still unnerved her that the girl had been at BFS for a mere couple of months and had already talked Grace into committing what would be a felony if she were an adult. Pam couldn't imagine who this 'young mastermind' might be – someone powerful and hypnotic with the charisma of a politician or cult leader or a rock star like Pink. When Lauren emerged, to Pam's surprise, she was tiny, a good six inches shorter than Grace, and pale with mousy brown hair and glasses with black plastic frames. She was so small and meek-looking, like her father, Pam couldn't reconcile this child with the magnitude of her crime. Still, Pam wanted to throttle her. Wanted to throttle both her and her father. She hoped she never saw the girl again. The father put a tentative arm around the girl's shoulders, which she shook off with force. Lauren stomped out of the station as her father scurried after her.

And then Grace appeared from behind the glass doors accompanied by a female officer. Pam watched as the officer said something to a nodding, red-faced Grace. Grace was still wearing the pajama bottoms she'd worn to bed the night before – a light blue flannel printed with dozens of dozing fluffy sheep. Over the pants, she wore a gray BFS lacrosse hoodie. Her face looked puffy and raw from crying. The officer pushed the door open to let Grace out and be reunited with a stunned Pam.

"Yeah, this is my mom," she mumbled to the officer who nodded in Pam's direction as she closed the door.

Pam and Grace enjoyed a tense drive home from the police station.

"Just because it wasn't your idea doesn't make it any less wrong. It was still stupid. Maybe even more stupid because you just went along with it – you're certainly in the same amount of trouble." Pam tightened her grip on the steering wheel and shook her head in disbelief. "Went along with it!" she said more to herself than to Grace. She narrowed her eyes at her in the rear-view mirror. "Do you realize how deep in the shit you are right now? At least you got out of the Goddamn PSATs. Wasn't that worth it?" Pam abandoned any restraint it took to keep the sarcasm out of her voice.

Grace ignored her and slumped down in the backseat, refusing to return Pam's glare. She stared at the back of the passenger seat. Pam huffed and retreated. She was too tired, too worried, too sad right now to have any sort of logical thoughts come out of her mouth in a way that would make Grace listen to her. That would knock some sense into her. For Pam, it felt like her smart, beautiful daughter had thrown her whole future away this morning with one, very stupid phone call. BFS had yet to decide if they would press charges against Grace and Lauren. If so, she would be forced to sink money she no longer had into hiring a criminal defense attorney. But Grace was not welcome back to BFS. She could consider herself lucky if one of the public high schools would accept her with her record.

When they arrived home, Grace snatched her backpack from the backseat, followed Pam inside the house and made a beeline upstairs. Pam winced as she heard Grace's bedroom door slam shut and decided to give her some space. She wandered into the kitchen.

Pam knew she needed to behave in some way that resembled an adult. She'd just brought home her daughter from jail. She just quit her job. Right now, reality was telling her that she needed to get on the ball. Was now the right time to give up Designer You? Her attorney and Jackie were taking care of the broken book contract with the publisher, and she still had a few more phone calls to make to clients, breaking the news she was out of the design business. The weight of what she had just ended, all of her and Nate's dreams she'd snuffed out, settled into the center of her chest.

She eyed the pie that had been idling on the butcher block since early that morning. Four even lines from the fork tines slashed across the otherwise smooth surface. She picked it up, feeling the weight of the cool tin on the palm of her hand. Drawing back her arm she catapulted the pie at the expanse of wall near the sink, where it slapped against the tile and slid onto the kitchen counter with a satisfying splat.

Pam looked around her kitchen, at the wood countertops, handmade cabinets, and stainless steel appliances. If she wasn't careful, this life she and Nate had constructed together could all go away. She didn't feel the timing was right to downsize, but wasn't that what she was supposed to do? Wasn't it worth even considering? They'd only been in the house for four years, yet it didn't seem fair to yank Grace from her home to go…where? A suburb with a stellar public school district? Downingtown with her parents? No. She wasn't running away from her problems. And she wasn't going to allow Grace to flee in the face of what she did. If BFS was going to press charges, she would face them alongside Pam. And the thought of *not* living half a block away from Becky sounded unbearable. But she and Grace had a lot of empty time to fill over the next few weeks. School – if there was school – wouldn't start for Grace until January at the earliest. And any hope of finding a job would have to wait until after the holidays, not that she knew what she'd be doing, anyway.

And on top of it all, the event that lurked in the background: her and Grace's first Christmas without Nate. The last thing she wanted to do was lug the bin of Christmas decorations and tree ornaments out of the basement. Last year at this time, the three of them walked to Izzy's Deli for an early dinner and filled up on corned beef sandwiches and pickles and matzo-ball soup before picking out a tall Douglas fir from their corner lot, dragging it home in the snow, and setting it up in their front window. Becky joined them when she got off her shift, and together, they'd all decorated the tree. Pam, Nate, and Becky drank spiked eggnog, and Grace sipped hot chocolate. It was joyous and simple. They were all together. This year, Pam didn't have a job, Becky was worried sick about her mother in England, and Grace may or may not be a felon. And Nate was dead.

Filling an entire month of the empty, sad days ahead of them felt like slow torture. Couldn't they just call off Christmas and pretend like it didn't exist? Or instead, they could go through the motions of getting out the decorations, buying a tree, and wrapping presents. Pam couldn't decide which option was worse. They couldn't just sit at home and mope for the month of December.

We could go anywhere and mope. Why don't we just go away?

It sounded almost too pat a solution. She'd been advised by Becky, Jimmy, her parents, even Liz to take some time and go away. Take a break. Yes. She needed a break. So did Grace.

Pam cleaned the pie off the kitchen wall and floor and proceeded upstairs to her office to Google 'winter destinations.' She found lots of skiing destinations like the Poconos, Tahoe, and Colorado, and plenty of popular warm vacation spots such as Hawaii and Florida. Several dude ranches in Nevada, Arizona, and New Mexico all vied for her attention. Pam thought about the first time she'd gone on a real vacation with her parents when she was young. When she was thirteen, her father folded his unsuccessful fast-food restaurant just as school was letting out for summer. He wouldn't buy the diner until that August, and that summer, her parents took the family to visit relatives in Tampa. They piled into the Sweeney mini-van and drove for two days. Pam had never seen her father so relaxed. With every mile he put between himself and that awful second-tier franchise, the more relaxed and happier he became, and the happier the whole family became.

He laughed and joked. He sang along (at full volume) with the radio. They spent two weeks visiting with their aunt, uncle, and cousins (Chad, who was in Jimmy's grade, Nina who was a year older than Pam, and their five-year-old sister, Zoe) in their modest ranch home. They were all packed in the three-bedroom house, but no one seemed to mind. Pam, Jimmy, and her parents slept in the living room, Jimmy and Pam on the sectional, and their parents on an air mattress on the floor. Every day they'd all take a trip to the beach and by afternoon, the sky would darken and a torrential rainstorm would roll in, forcing everyone inside for board games and Cokes in tall, glass bottles. One day, they took a day trip out to Busch Gardens and rode roller coasters until the park closed well after dark. Pam remembered never wanting the vacation to end.

Maybe that's what she and Grace should do. Drive down to Tampa, or some place a little quieter nearby, and rent a little house by the beach. She logged into Airbnb and searched for quaint beach communities along the Gulf, and before she could talk herself out of it, she'd rented an adorable, two-bedroom cottage overlooking the beach in St. Petersburg, FL for her and Grace for the month of December. She already felt better, lighter. She was putting her and Grace's life on hold for the month and maybe they would at last be ready to heal together and return home stronger and more resilient after the New Year. Maybe they could have a relationship again.

That night, Pam finally slept.

* * *

On Tuesday, the morning after she'd made the reservation on the house on Airbnb, Pam broke the news to Grace that they were taking a trip down to Florida for the month and to start packing after they finished breakfast.

"A month? I don't want to go anywhere with you," Grace said, dumping her half-finished bowl of Rice Krispies down the garbage disposal. "If Dad were here, he wouldn't run away. He'd figure it out."

"Well," she said, absorbing the impact of Grace's words. "Dad isn't around now. I'm the one making the rules."

"I wish it were the other way around."

"Too bad," said Pam, solidifying her resolve. "We're leaving today."

The car ride down was grim and quiet; Pam drove and listened to NPR and local talk radio. After a few timid attempts at reaching out with innocuous, self-conscious comments and questions such as 'Nothing better than Maryland crab cakes' and 'When was your class trip to D.C.? Fifth grade?' Pam gave up. On the rare occasions when Grace would speak up, it was to express her displeasure in one form or another: 'It's not fair.' 'What about my friends? I can't live without my friends for a whole month.' 'I don't want to talk.' 'I'm not hungry. I'm staying in the car.' 'I hate you for making me do this.'

But Grace's animosity toward her mom couldn't thwart Pam's mission as they headed south down Interstate 95. They made stops to use the restroom, to eat, to stretch. They stayed in a Comfort Inn when they reached Fort Bragg in North Carolina after dark and walked to an Italian restaurant for dinner in downtown Fayetteville. Pam hugged her jacket to her as they walked – she was glad to have thought to bring her parka with her, not only because of the temperature drop, but also to guard against the chill of Grace's hostility. She wondered if Grace would ever talk to her again like a normal human being.

The next morning, Grace didn't let up. The two suffered the next eight hours in the car in utter silence. Pam gripped the steering wheel, determined to stay resolute. *I'm the grownup,* she reminded herself. *And the aim of this trip is to let it all out and come back stronger.* Pam glanced up in the rearview mirror and caught Grace's beautiful sullen face in the reflection and decided there was no way Grace could stay mad for a whole month, but she'd sure try.

After two days of driving, Pam and Grace pulled into the driveway of 5213 Sunset Avenue. The one-story beach bungalow looked even smaller than it appeared in the online photos and was painted mint green with white trim and white shutters. A large palm tree stood near the right, front window and palm fronds littered the browning lawn. Pam wondered how long the house had been empty.

She was ready to stay in one place for a while. Even though the sun had just set, and the air beginning to cool, the pleasant, fragrant air of St. Petersburg enveloped Pam as soon as she opened her car door on the driveway adjacent to the cottage. It was a tropical heaven. She felt since Nate's death, she'd been so busy and feeling so lousy, she hadn't had the time to enjoy the late spring and summer months, her favorite time of the year. No weekend trips to the shore, no sunning by the pool, no hikes in the Wissahickon. Fall was glorious in Philadelphia, but for Pam, the season always marked the slow, cold march toward winter. Since the start of November, she had been wearing her parka most days and her parka *and hat* since Thanksgiving. And now, finally, on December 1 of all days, she felt a little too warm in her sweater.

"C'mon, kiddo," she said over her shoulder to Grace, who was stuffing her phone and sketchpad into her backpack. "Let's have a look at the house."

She grabbed her purse and popped the trunk for her suitcase, which she rolled up the tidy walkway that divided the brown lawn. She located the lockbox, which was attached to the wrought-iron railing, and punched in the four-digit code that the owners, Mark and Stephen, had sent to her phone via text message. Out popped the key, and she let her and Grace in.

The space was compact, but the floor plan bright and open. The front door opened into the living room which was defined by a modern sofa with clean lines and a reading chair, both of which crowded around a glass-top coffee table (*no wonder the blurb stressed 'no small children'*) and faced a flat-screen television that hung from the east-side wall. Directly to the right of the living room was a small dining room, with a sturdy wood table surrounded by four sleek chairs in clear plastic with chrome legs. *Yard sale chic?* Behind the dining room at the front of the house was a small, U-shaped kitchen with white appliances that looked like they were new about fifteen years ago. Adjacent to the dining room, was a short counter and bar stools for two.

"Not exactly the lap of luxury," Pam noted. "But it'll do."

"It's tiny," Grace said as she wheeled in her suitcase and took a look around. "I'm stuck here with you *for a month?*"

Pam shrugged.

"I want to die." Grace flopped onto the couch and pouted.

Pam thought it better to let the comment go, leave Grace

alone, and wander into the master bedroom. She pushed the handle into her suitcase and surveyed the small space. A full size bed butted against the north wall. To the left of the bed was a modest closet and dresser. Along the south wall, she was greeted by a large landscape window that faced the screened-in porch which both let in a generous view of the gulf and the gentle waves that lapped the edges of the sandy beach.

Whoa. Now this is what I'm paying for, isn't it?

She pushed open the door from the bedroom to the porch, which took up the width of the house and ran about eight feet deep. There were a card table and four chairs on the right-hand side, by Grace's room. And on her end, a wicker love seat and two wicker sliding chairs making up a cozy sitting and reading area. Pam imagined herself sitting out here and staring at the waves every chance she got.

When she emerged from her bedroom to tell Grace that she needed to check out the porch, Grace had already taken over the second bedroom and had closed the door behind her.

"I'm going grocery shopping," she shouted toward Grace's bedroom door. Pam thought she might as well grab a few things they could both eat in the next twenty-four hours.

No response.

"Can you just say 'OK' or something? I need the acknowledgment." Pam cocked her ear toward Grace's door.

Grace's voice was flat behind the closed door. "Fine. Go. I don't care."

Pam nodded and grabbed her keys. *Good enough for me.*

Google Maps led her to a Fresh Market that wasn't too far away. She wheeled her shopping cart up and down the aisles, in no hurry, not unlike so many of the other customers at this time of the evening. It was funny, if she ever found herself 6 o'clock on a weekday evening in a grocery store near her house, she'd be one of the legions of harried moms picking up something, *anything* to serve their families for dinner that night. She made her way to the deli section. Prepared tomato bisque and a cooked chicken? Done. She put both in her basket. But no one tonight was in any hurry. In fact, Pam was one of the younger patrons. She'd noticed when she selected her cart that most of the customers had emerged from a large commuter van from a senior center that had taken over the fire lane just outside of the grocery store. All senses were engaged – they fondled the produce, sniffed the peppers and cantaloupes, rapped their ragged knuckles against the watermelons. They asked the butchers questions about the freshness of the salmon and whether it was farmed or fished. They scrutinized the best price per ounce of salad greens, peanut butter, sliced turkey breast. Shopping for the retired, Pam decided, was an activity to be taken seriously and that could be either won or lost. Pam longed to achieve that relaxed way of life that focus on the here and now for both her and Grace over the course of this month.

That wasn't going to happen for Pam tonight. She'd already raised the white flag when she decided to go for the prepared chicken, but she did take fifteen minutes to acquaint herself with her new neighborhood grocery store. She ended up buying a dozen eggs, turkey sausage, oatmeal, yogurt, raspberries, bread, coffee, a bag of salad mix, butter, cheese, olive oil, apple cider vinegar, and a pocket map guide to St. Petersburg. She picked out a bottle of cabernet from the wine and beer section of the grocery store. As she surveyed her cart, she figured she and Grace had enough to get by over the next couple of days as they acquainted themselves with the neighborhood. Maybe they'd go out at some point tomorrow for lunch or dinner? Pam wasn't so sure Grace would be up for that.

When she arrived to the cottage again, laden with two paper sacks of groceries, Grace was still in her room, door closed. It was after 7 o'clock and Pam was starving. She set the dining room table and cut up the chicken and heated two bowls of soup in the microwave. She tossed a simple salad in a mixing bowl and set it out on the table. She knocked on Grace's door.

"Dinner's ready," she said through the door.

Silence.

"Grace? Are you in there?" Again, no response. Pam turned the handle and let herself into Grace's room. It wasn't much smaller than the master bedroom and had a full size bed and plenty of room for her clothes in the closet, which also housed a short chest of drawers. The room shared the incredible view of the nighttime beach. Pam could see Grace sitting out on the enclosed porch, which she could also get to from her room.

"Hey," she said, pushing the screen door to let herself out to the porch.

Grace looked up from her phone. "Hey," she said, curled up on the wicker love seat with an afghan covering her bare feet.

Pam sensed a renewed softness to her tone. It lacked the edge from the last two days.

"It's nice out here, isn't it?" Pam offered, hoping Grace's anger had disappeared into the ocean breeze.

Grace shrugged, her eyes still glued to her screen.

"Dinner's ready. Let's eat and then we can just relax for the night, OK?" All Pam wanted to do was eat and fall into bed. It was always like that after long travel days – not like they were doing anything other than sitting all day in the car, but for some reason it sapped all her energy.

"Do I have to? Can't I just eat out here?" Grace peered at Pam now, not with narrowed, angry eyes, but almost pleading. *God, she doesn't want to spend one second with me.* Stung, Pam turned, so that Grace couldn't see the hurt register on her face.

"No, I think you can handle eating dinner with me in the dining room tonight," she said as she opened the screen door and let herself back into the house.

They sat and ate. Grace pulled a third piece from the picked-over chicken. Pam took a breath. She knew what she was about to say wouldn't go down easy, but was relieved she didn't have to say it to a ravenous teenager.

"I don't want you to spend the entire vacation just sitting in your room or on your phone. I want to spend time with you – go to museums, go out to lunch, explore downtown." Pam tried to read Grace's face for any sort of reaction, but all that was returned was stony silence. "We've both had a tough year. And we've made a lot of mistakes. Mine is that I didn't pay enough attention to you. I should have, I don't know, I should have spent more time with you."

Grace put down her spoon and wiped her mouth with a paper towel she was using as a napkin. "I don't want to talk about this now."

"Well, it's the whole reason we're here," said Pam. "I worry that if we don't start getting along again, working as a team, then we'll lose our little family. I need you and you need me."

"It's funny, 'cause you never showed it. Over the summer and when school started, I, like, *never saw you.* And now that you don't have a job and I got kicked out of school, it's all *convenient* for you to want to spend more time with me. Well what if I don't want to spend time with you now?" Pam watched as the dark anger returned to her eyes.

"Whether you like it or not, you still need me and you're still a child." Pam knew she was courting disaster by pulling that card. But it was true. Grace needed her now more than ever. And so did Pam.

"I wish we'd never left," said Grace. "You yank me away from home, my friends, with like, *zero* explanation. I'm not a *child*. I'm not your pet. I'm not your dog on a leash you can just lead around wherever you want to go. I'm my own person."

Pam offered a reluctant nod. "I know you're your own person," she said, wishing she could take back her words. "But I wouldn't have dragged you down here if it wasn't important. We both have some pretty big decisions to make over the next few weeks. And we're better together as a family than apart. I'm a better, happier person when we're connected. I know that now. I need you as much as I think you need me."

"I'm happier when I have a job. When I have something else and don't have to spend my time with you. What loser wants to spend all day with their mother, anyway? I'd rather spend my time with my friends," Grace said with a huff. "And I have no friends here."

Pam sat back in the plastic chair, which squeaked in protest. Grace did have a point. Pam didn't think she'd wanted to spend all her time with either of her parents when she was fifteen – certainly not. But she'd never phoned in a bomb threat to her high school, either. This vacation was about getting to know each other again and she didn't expect it was going to be an easy month of ladies lunches, pedicures, and catching up on award-season movies. They needed to sort out why Grace could do something so egregious, so outside of the person Pam thought she knew.

But a part-time job? Grace might benefit from being around people her own age – she might feel less isolated. She'd be serving the public in some way, whether she was scooping ice-cream or waiting tables. She'd have some pocket money, too. And it was a way for Pam to show that she understood Grace enough to know that she was better when she had something like a job to do. Giving her that freedom might make the month easier on both of them.

"OK," said Pam. "But no more than twenty hours per week. You can't work someplace that serves alcohol. And," Pam made a point of meeting Grace's eyes, "you're not going to like this – dinner with me every night, 6 o'clock."

Grace grunted, sat back in her chair, and folded her arms in front of her chest. "No way. *Every* night? 6 o'clock? Uh-uh."

"Then no job." Pam shrugged. "Your choice." She rose and took her dishes into the kitchen. Job or no job, Pam knew, they *would* spend time together.

"What if I want to go out after dinner, like with friends?" Pam sensed a little give in Grace's tone. *Let the negotiations begin.*

"Depends on what you'd want to do. Unlike home, these would be new friends from unfamiliar families. And you'd obviously have a curfew. I'd have to call it, if and when, it came up."

"What about movies? Can I go to the movies?" Grace stacked her soup bowl and silverware on top of her plate, brought them into the kitchen, and placed them on the counter. She leaned back, her elbows resting on the counter.

"I don't see why not."

"Hmmm…" Grace bit her lip and looked down at her feet. Pam rinsed the dishes off in the sink and put them in the dishwasher. "OK."

Pam turned to face her. "OK, what?"

"OK to dinner. I guess it wouldn't be *so* bad."

Pam offered a small smile. "Good. It's settled, then." She didn't want to look smug, but inside she soared. They didn't have to spend every minute of every day together, but they did need to spend *some* time together. And maybe dinner every night could become a practice they brought back home with them to Philadelphia.

Chapter Sixteen

When Pam awoke the following day and padded out of her bedroom to brew coffee, Grace was already gone. Her bedroom door was open, bed made. Pam glanced at the clock – 11:00. Pam blinked to make sure she was reading it right. *Yep, Day Two on vacation and I've officially turned into a lazy bum.* She made a mental note to set her alarm for 9 o'clock from now on. She didn't want to waste her time sleeping away the day, but it did feel nice to go to bed and sleep in with the sound of water lapping at the shore just beyond her back yard. It was like a cross between a hypnotist and Ambien. Pam checked her phone plugged in on the kitchen counter and felt a surge of relief when she saw a text message waiting for her from Grace. *Looking for a job. Already ate.*

Seeing the house in the brightness of the day made the space feel a little roomier, more open and less claustrophobic. She opened the curtain to the window by the dining room table and saw that there was another bungalow just on the other side of a low, white-picket fence. *We're kind of packed in here like sardines,* she thought, gauging the distance. No matter. She was much closer to her neighbors in Philadelphia. Maybe she'd make some vacation friends?

A copy of *The New York Times* stuffed into a blue plastic bag sat on the dining room table. A nice surprise. *Must've come this morning and Grace brought it in when she left.* Pam hadn't sat down to drink her morning coffee and read *The Times* in months. It felt luxurious to take over the table with the paper and coffee. She read everything she wanted, even the Style section as she ate her poached eggs and finished the pot. *I could get used to this. Nate would approve.* The thought of Nate and his absence left her longing for him to be sitting right there next to her. She wanted to trade sections of the newspaper and bicker playfully over what to tour first – a long walk to get a lay of the land or a trip to the Dali Museum? Sit by the beach and read or take a paddleboard lesson? Or would they take advantage of a morning alone and head back to bed? She folded the paper. *Time to begin the day.*

After a shower, Pam decided to explore. The cottage was a (long) walking distance to the arts district and a downtown area with shopping and restaurants. She hadn't exercised with any regularity since Nate died, and her body looked and felt it. Pam never considered herself an athlete, not like Grace by any stretch, but she'd always been active and enjoyed regular walks and jogged when she'd had the time. Today was as good a day as any to start back up again. She had the whole afternoon to roam as long as she was back to figure out dinner and have it ready by 6 o'clock. Grace was probably working with the same math.

She looked at her pocket map and decided she would walk up to Pinellas Trail, which would take her toward downtown, getting her there around 2 o'clock for a late lunch.

At 1:15, Pam's pleasant, tree-lined walk was interrupted by a phone call from Belfield Friends. She paused, looking down at her phone. *Shit, school.*

"Hello?"

"Mrs. Wheeler?" It was Principal Hicks.

"Hello, Principal." Pam's tone switched on a dime and became subdued, contrite. She imagined her sitting in her modern office behind her big wooden desk. She would be wearing a black suit jacket over a crisp blouse and her short severe hair would accentuate the angles and hardness to her face. Pam knew it was petty, but she thought Principal Hicks could suck the fun out of anything, including a Florida vacation. *I wonder how her husband and children feel about that* she thought, imagining the principal, her husband, and twins surrounding Goofy for a photo at Disney World, pained expressions painted on all their faces, even Goofy's.

"I'm glad I was able to catch you." Principal Hicks cleared her throat. Pam sank down on a nearby wooden bench that faced the wide walking and biking trail with the skyline of high-rise resorts facing the water in the distance. Runners and bikers whisked past her. She didn't think she could remain upright and hear that BFS was pressing charges against her daughter. That upon her return…scratch that…that now, *immediately* her first order of business would be to hire a criminal attorney to keep Grace from serving time in a juvenile detention center. There was a good possibility that instead of finishing up her years of high school at home with Pam, they'd live apart, even further separated, a wedge that could sever their relationship for good.

"Yes," Pam stammered. "Me too. I mean, I'm glad you caught me. Did you meet with the board?" The BFS board met once per month to discuss and vote on pressing matters of the school, such as whether there was room in the budget for a new basketball scoreboard or who would replace the high school Spanish teacher, who had accepted a position at another school, or what to do about Grace Wheeler, who had threatened to blow up the school last Monday to get out of taking the PSATs.

"I *did* meet with the board. Actually, I just left the December meeting, our last before the winter holidays." Pam could hear her suck in a breath on the other end of the receiver. She held hers, bracing herself for bad news. "We're going easy on Grace. We're not pressing charges."

Pam's chest loosened and she let out a long, silent sigh. "Thank you," she said. She could have cried with gratitude.

"You're welcome. It was not unanimous, by the way. There are a couple of board members who thought – still think – we need to send a stricter message. But I think we can all agree that Grace, at least, is not a child who would benefit from serving time. In fact, I feel it could do a lot more harm than good."

"I'm glad. Both Grace and I are so grateful."

"Transcripts will be made available to your school of choice." Principal paused. "Pam?"

The sudden informality caught Pam off guard. Susan Hicks had never called her by her first name before. "Yes?"

"Take care of your girl. I do hope Grace can turn it around in time." The principal's tone sounded almost maternal.

Turn it around in time for what? College? Before she does something even more stupid or dangerous? Pam didn't want Principal Hicks to answer that. They weren't friends – they weren't even friendly – and Pam wasn't in the frame of mind to take advice from Principal Hicks. "Thanks, Susan. I appreciate it."

They hung up.

A sense of lightness enveloped her in an instant as she rose from the park bench and continued her walk. Grace would finish high school. She'd live at home. She'd most likely attend college and have a normal life.

And Pam would never have to speak to Susan Hicks again.

* * *

That evening, a little after 5 o'clock, Pam walked up the path to the cottage carrying a plastic bag of groceries for dinner after a day of walking along the trail, taking in the neighborhoods, and local shopping. A man who looked to be in his mid-forties to early fifties was out watering the lawn of the house next door. He was of average height and medium build. His well-defined arms and legs were golden brown and his dark hair lightened by the sun. He didn't strike her as a fellow tourist. She wondered if he might be the gardener. He looked too much like a native in his loose-fitting chambray shirt rolled up to the elbows, khaki shorts, and flip-flops. He looked like an ad for the Gap, hunky middle-aged edition. He glanced up at her as she fumbled for her keys.

Pam offered him a polite smile. "Hello."

He smiled back, revealing his dimples. "Hi."

She turned the key and breezed through the front door of the bungalow. It'd been a great first day. That afternoon, she'd stopped for a late lunch at a quaint coffee shop that roasted their own coffee beans on site and specialized in easy cafe fare such as sandwiches and soups. Pam had lingered over a BLT while reading her pocket map book, still relieved about the board's decision to drop the charges against Grace.

But still, Principal Hicks' hope that Grace could still 'turn it around in time' haunted the edges of her mind. There were countless ways Grace could still mess it all up for herself between now and forever. And the ugly truth was, time was running out for her and Grace. Grace wasn't going to be a child much longer, and people's patience and compassion for her behavior would wane with each escalating offense. If Grace continued to spiral downward, Pam feared that as a mother, she wouldn't have the ability to contain her out-of-control behavior. Would she have to send Grace away? What a horrible last resort to save your child.

After more than four hours of walking, the exercise had caught up with Pam. Her cheeks bloomed with exertion and a little too much sun. On her way back to the cottage, she stopped by Fresh Market to pick up some fresh salmon, more salad fixings, and a six-pack of beer.

When she'd opened the door, Grace was sitting on the loveseat with her laptop balanced on her knees.

"Hi, hon," said Pam, opening the refrigerator and placing the six-pack inside. "I've got some good news."

Grace looked up. "Yeah? What's that?"

Pam turned to face her. "BFS is *not* pressing charges. So that's something."

Grace looked down at her keyboard. She didn't smile, but she didn't look upset either.

"This means we can go forward with registering you for public school. If there's space at Central or Girls' Academy, which I'm hopeful there is, you may be able to start when we get back," said Pam. "You won't lose any time and you'll graduate with your class."

"I won't be graduating with my friends," said Grace, a little sulky. She looked up, registering Pam's reaction. "But I *know* it's my fault and I know I got lucky," she said quickly.

Pam nodded. "You did indeed get lucky. A couple of the board members thought you should have served time."

"Really? What happened to Lauren?"

"You know? I didn't even think to ask. I don't think Principal Hicks would have told me, anyway." Pam took out a sauté pan and the olive oil. She unwrapped the fish. "Personally, I hope Lauren is opening up to her dad and the two reconcile."

Grace shook her head. "Lauren hates her dad." Pam winced at Grace's casual use of the word 'hate' and 'dad' but judging by the tense exchange between her and her meek-looking father at the police station, Pam didn't think Grace was far off on her assessment. "If her mom didn't get cancer and die," Grace continued, "he wouldn't even be interested in getting to know her."

Pam pictured the guy in her mind – this small, mouse-like man sitting and agonizing for his daughter. He didn't look like a father who would abandon his family. "Sometimes things are more complicated than they might appear." She wondered what the mother was like before she died. Was she strong-willed? Difficult? Tough as nails? Crazy? Crazy smart? Where did Lauren get the balls to phone in a bomb threat to the school? Pam doubted it came from the meek man fretting over his daughter in the waiting room at the police station. But the meek man left, Mom didn't.

"Not always, Mom."

Pam prepared the salmon and tossed the salad. She placed the plates on the dining room table. 6:02 p.m.

"OK, dinner's ready, Grace."

Reluctant, Grace put down the laptop and rose from the couch. "Fine," she said and sighed.

They dug in to dinner. "So tell me what you did today. Where'd you go?"

Grace raised her eyebrows. "Well, I got a job."

"Really? And you didn't tell me the second I walked through the door?"

"I wanted to see how long it'd take for you to ask." She stifled a grin.

Pam smiled back at her. "Good for you, hon. What is it? And where? How many hours?"

"You know that resort kitty corner from Fresh Market?"

She thought of the tall high-rise hotel that faced the water. Pam nodded.

"Well, they needed more lifeguards for the pool during the holiday season. The pool is huge – it has a water slide and a lazy river where people float on these oversized inner tubes. Anyway, the hotel is going to be packed with tourists, so they're hiring more guards and staff for the month of December."

Pam was impressed. When Grace was determined, she made shit happen, for better and for worse. "That's awesome! Couldn't be more perfect. They must be thrilled you have your certification."

Grace nodded. "Yeah, they loved that. I can start right away, though it's not as busy now as it will be in two weeks. I'll work in the afternoons and on weekends. No more than twenty hours." She met Pam's eyes. "That OK?"

"Yes, Grace." She beamed at her again. "That's great – I'm really proud you just went out there and got a job."

If only it were always that easy, she thought, pondering her own unemployed status. Unemployed. The word alone gave her stomach a jolt. Was it regret from abandoning Nate's dream and their only source of income? Or fear of traipsing into unknown territory, where she would have to figure out and settle on what she wanted to be when she grew up?

"Thanks." Grace wiped her mouth with a paper towel. "May I please be excused?"

Pam nodded. After she washed the dishes and put away the leftovers, Pam slid a bottle of pale ale out from the six-pack and found a bottle opener from the silverware drawer. She grabbed her cell and headed for the porch to talk to the one person in her life right now who could provide her with solid advice.

She plopped down on the wicker loveseat, put her feet up on the coffee table, and tapped 'Becky' from her contact list of Favorites.

"Hullo?" Becky's voice sounded gravelly and tired.

"Hey, it's me. How are you? You sound awful." Pam took a swig of her beer.

"Sick. I caught something right after you left. Thanks for the compliment, by the way," Becky responded.

"Aw, I'm sorry. Are you missing the staff Christmas party?"

"I think I'm gonna have to. I've been in bed for the last two days and it's tomorrow night – Saturday." Pam heard Becky sneeze in the distance. "Sorry 'bout that."

"You don't think you'll recover in time, eh?"

"No. But quite frankly, I'm just not up for it this year, anyway." Becky blew her nose. "This cold is kind of a welcome excuse."

Pam took another sip of her beer.

"Are you drinking?" Becky asked. "Confess."

"I'm having a beer," said Pam, taking a look at the label on the bottle. It was green with a picture of a blue river surrounded by trees and snowcapped mountains. "It's wonderful. I don't think I've had a beer in almost a year."

"I'm on my fifth cup of lemon tea with honey. I don't think it's doing anything except making me have to pee every hour."

Pam didn't want to dwell on beverages. "So why don't you want to go to the holiday thing tomorrow? I know you can't, but don't you think you'd be up for it if you weren't sick?"

Becky blew her nose again. "This whole thing with my mum has been such a downer. And with the holidays – Christmas – it just feels wrong to be away from her, especially now that she's still healing and can't be up and getting around on her own. England's never felt further away."

"Hmmm, yeah. That's rough, Beck. How does she feel about it, you know? I mean, is it – not to minimize it – but is it sort of in your head because you feel guilty?"

"Nah, I don't think that's it. I *do* feel guilty, don't get me wrong. But it's more like I'm missing out on just being with her. This will be one more Christmas I miss with her and I may only have a handful of Christmases left, if I'm lucky."

"Oh Becky, I wish there was something I could do. Hey – you want to fly down here and spend Christmas with us?" asked Pam. "It's sunny and warm here. Christmas here resembles no Christmas tradition I've ever seen or experienced, which for this year, is exactly the right medicine. Fuck tradition."

"God, how I love that!" Joy crept into Becky's congested voice for the first time. "Fuck tradition!"

"So how about it? I meant it – we'd love to have you here. Even just for a few days if you can swing it."

Becky sighed into the phone. "I can't. Though it sounds quite lovely. The minute I knew I wasn't going to be able to spend Christmas with Mum, I took on the Christmas Eve through Christmas morning shifts at the hospital. They're always needing extra nurses those nights anyway, even though it's usually pretty quiet. And I get a bump in pay those days, too. It's OK. I'll see the kids, too, maybe in the afternoon. I'll be a lot less mopey when you and Grace return in January. Promise." Pam heard Becky muffle the phone and sneeze violently.

"Bless you," she said.

"Thanks," said Becky, when she returned. "Say, how's it going with the girl?"

"A little better. It was awful at first. She didn't want to say two words to me." Pam took a sip of her beer. "But in her quest to spend as little time with me as possible, she asked if she could look for a part-time job. So I made a bargain with her. I'm making her eat dinner with me every evening. You would have thought I'd asked her to have dinner with Mussolini, but she agreed. It's a little early to tell, but I think she's starting to come around."

"Good, Mummy. Look at you go, putting your foot down like that."

"Thanks." Pam was boosted by the compliment. Discipline had never been her strong suit.

"Sweetheart, I've got to get off the phone. But please ring me with updates."

"Give everyone our love. Talk soon." Pam hung up. She missed Becky's friendship when they were away. Even when Nate was alive, she'd text Becky family vacation photos or snarky comments and complaints about the scratchy hotel sheets and local customs that she found illogical or confusing. In Philadelphia alone, she still didn't understand why double parking on certain roads like Girard and adults wearing hockey Flyers jerseys as day wear were viewed as acceptable. In Florida, flip-flops were appropriate footwear in public. She would have a hard time getting used to that one.

"Hey there," said a friendly voice. It came from the right side of the enclosed porch, in another enclosed porch, in fact. The man who had been watering the lawn earlier offered an understated wave as he sat down in a deck chair with his own bottle of beer.

"Oh," said Pam, noticing him for the first time. "Hi. Sorry, was my phone conversation too loud? I didn't realize we were so close together."

"Nope," the man said, propping his feet onto a stool. "Not a big deal at all. I just sat down, anyway."

"Well, good," said Pam, relaxing a little. These bungalows were pretty close. There seemed to be no one at the house to her left, though, only the house to her right.

"I'm Charlie, by the way."

"Pam," she said.

"Nice to meet you, Pam." Charlie raised his bottle of beer. She raised hers as well. "Nice to meet you, Charlie."

"So where are you from? How do you know Stephen and Mark? Airbnb? Friends? Relatives?"

"Airbnb. We don't know each other – just email – though they both seem very nice. And we like the space," said Pam. She thought she should be nice in case any hint of complaint could get back to Mark and Stephen and result in a less-than-positive review. "It's clean and cozy, but plenty of room for my daughter and me. We're from Philadelphia. You?"

"I'm…from here, I guess," said Charlie, with a slight laugh. "A local. I live here full-time now."

"You know," said Pam, turning toward him. "I thought you might have been a local when I saw you watering your lawn."

He laughed again. "What gave me away?"

Pam thought about it. "Maybe it was because you weren't dressed in sneakers and cargo shorts. You aren't sunburned. And, people on vacation don't typically water the lawns of the houses they're staying in."

"All true." He took a sip from the bottle. "So what brings you to quaint, little St. Petersburg?"

"Just vacation. We wanted to relax. We used to go to Tampa when I was a kid and loved it. Thought my daughter and I would enjoy it."

"Yeah, there's lots to do in Tampa. And plenty to do here as well. The holiday season is pretty festive – you came at a good time of year." He leaned forward in his chair. "You like Christmas lights?"

"Um, sure?"

"How long you in town for?"

"A month."

Charlie whistled his approval. "That's a nice vacation." He put his bottle down on the side table. "OK, there's this crazy Christmas display at this house – corner lot – here in town. It's hard to describe, but you have to go just to see it for yourself. They've got lights everywhere, multiple snowmen, Santas, a teddy bear display, mangers, Jesus, of course, snowflakes. I mean, it's like this weird Christmas cornucopia and takes over the entire corner of the street."

"Sounds like a must-see."

"Yeah, totally. Let's see, tree lighting already happened right after Thanksgiving. How about Santa? Is your daughter still into Santa?"

She shook her head. "She's aged out of Santa. She's fifteen."

He sat back in the chair. "No kidding? I've got two daughters in high school as well."

"Oh?" Pam hadn't seen or heard anyone other than Charlie in the twenty-four hours she and Grace had been there. She knew from experience, once you get two or more teenage girls together, they were loud.

"They're with their mom during the week and I get them every other weekend." Charlie shrugged. "This little bunga-low used to be our get-away beach home and vacation rental before we split. Now I live in it and she's got the house in Winter Springs."

"How far away is Winter Springs?" asked Pam.

"Two hours." He grimaced. "I know, awful, right? But, we moved there because of the close-knit community and schools. Jessica's a senior and Lily's a freshman. And I was the stay-at-home dad. So when my ex and I divorced, it just seemed to make the most sense for me to move into the beach house, which is paid for, while I figure out how to make a living."

"Sounds complicated," said Pam, considering that divorce seemed in some respects thornier than the death of a spouse. Messier, too. "What did you do before the kids were born?"

Charlie groaned. "Sales. I was terrible at it. And I hated it. I think the marriage lasted as long as it did because I needed a meal ticket and out of a horrible job, and my wife needed a babysitter."

"You must miss your girls."

He nodded. "Yeah, it's been a rough transition. I've been

out here for about a year and a half. Sometimes they come out here and sometimes I just go back to Winter Springs and rent a room for the weekend or stay in a hotel so their mom doesn't have to drive them all the way out here every time. But I see them as much as I can. Going from seeing them every day – raising them, helping them with their homework, fixing their lunches, driving them to dance and soccer practice and swim lessons…it's hard not being there for the day-to-day things." He smiled and looked out toward the bay. "You know those conversations you have with your kids when you're in the car on the way somewhere – the grocery store, softball practice, whatever – and you end up having these surprisingly deep conversations? We'd talk about everything – issues they were grappling with in school, what they thought about this boy or that girl, or who's a mean girl. And of course we'd talk about dumb stuff like whether Justin Bieber's still cool or what they were going to wear on Pajama Day at school on Friday." He faced Pam. "It's the little stuff I miss."

"I get it." She did. She missed out on most of the 'little stuff' by being so absorbed in Designer You. And the big stuff, too. "So one will be going off to college soon, and the younger one isn't so far behind."

"I know, right? They're leaving the nest soon." He sighed. "I guess your daughter is thinking about all of that, too. What year is she? Sophomore?"

"Yes." *She's thinking about it so much, she phoned in a bomb threat to get out of taking the PSATs.* "College and SATs and AP courses, sports, community service – it all weighs very heavily on both our minds."

"It's crazy how early these kids have to think about college now. It's been drilled into their little minds since kindergarten that they must go to college. And then before they're even out of middle school, they have to start strategizing about how to game the system while in high school. The AP and honors are so demanding. A lot of kids take classes at community colleges while they're still in high school. It's not good enough to have five college-level courses when you graduate, now you have to have twelve. And all the extracurricular activities: sports, clubs, student government, public service. When do they sleep? Jessica's a senior, and she's about out of her mind with stress."

"I know, I don't like it either," said Pam, shaking her head.

At that moment, Grace, holding her laptop to her chest, opened the door from her bedroom to the porch. She paused, seeing Pam out on the loveseat, and then turned to see Charlie in the next porch over.

"Oh, hi," she said, hesitating. "Sorry, I didn't know I was interrupting."

Charlie rose from his chair. "Nope, not at all. I was just getting up." He nodded toward Pam and Grace. "Nice to meet you both."

Grace turned her face toward Pam and out of Charlie's view, gave her a look as if to say, *Who's that guy?*

"Nice to meet you, too, Charlie," said Pam. She heard the screen door thump as he made his way back into his house.

"So we have a neighbor," said Grace, sliding into the reading chair with her laptop.

Pam drained the remainder of her beer. "Indeed we do."

Chapter Seventeen

Pam awoke early the next morning a bit sore from the five hours of walking the previous day. She massaged the sides of her thighs as she sat on the edge of the bed in her thin tank top and pajama bottoms. It wasn't yet 8 o'clock, and the outdoor sunshine intruded into the bedroom, bathing the room in bright light. Pam made a mental note to close the light-canceling curtains that hung on either side of the window that night when she went to bed, though it felt strange and wonderful at the same time to be awash in all this warm sunshine in early December. If she were in Philadelphia now, the heater would be cranking away inside her dark house, while the trees outside her window stood naked and stark against the bone-chilling cold. The trees and shrubs in Florida were lush and full of life. It was a little weird. *Do they ever lose their leaves? Doesn't seem natural to deny a tree its life cycle.* But for now, Pam thought she'd just go with it and enjoy it.

It was Sunday and judging from her long walk the day before, there would be plenty of activity over the course of the day. Pam didn't want to lose sight of things she actually needed to pay attention to, like registering Grace for public school as soon as possible, and starting to think about what she was going to do for a living, so she wouldn't burn through the insurance money so fast. It seemed strange to Pam that just over a week ago, she had been engrossed in finishing Bernie's house and all of Designer You's outstanding projects, writing the blog, and wringing her hands over not starting the latest book. Now, she just felt relief it was all over. Yes, she recognized the achievement in finishing the monster that was Bernie's house, but it was over and she was glad. She did not miss one bit of it. Nate would have seen Bernie's house as one step in a larger process, a larger goal – a step toward something greater. For Pam, every step represented an obstacle, something in the way of what made her blood pulse – the details. With Bernie moving in, Pam was moving on. She wondered whether all the other jobs she'd just bailed on, unfinished, would be completed without her. Probably. Dennis and his team took on a few of the projects she'd left undone and promised to pass on contractor recommendations. But she'd left behind a lot of disappointed clients. She felt some guilt for leaving these people in the lurch, but if she were being honest, she just didn't care. She harbored no ownership over all of that work. That was Nate's dream, not hers.

She got up and made herself coffee, and when she walked to the front door to get the paper from the outside walkway, she noticed something sticking through the mail slot, halfway in and halfway out. She slid it out of the slot. It was an envelope with 'Pam' written on the outside. She slid her finger under the seal.

It was a computer printout outlining the local holiday events by date with the note, *In case you and Grace are looking for things to do during your stay. ~ Charlie.* When she opened the door, a well-worn Tampa and St. Petersburg guidebook lay on the Welcome mat outside. She picked it up along with the *Times* and walked halfway down the walkway to see if Charlie happened to be out watering his lawn again. His yard was empty and Charlie nowhere in sight.

Pam walked back inside, smiling to herself. *That was thoughtful.* By the time Grace emerged from her room at 10:30, Pam was still pouring over the book, making notes on an open file on her laptop.

Grace yawned and stretched and sat down at the table. "What are you doing?"

Pam sat back in her chair and flipped the book face down to save her place. "I'm figuring out what there is to do around here. It's Sunday. I have a day off today. Thinking about checking out the Dali Museum."

Grace regarded her with a disdained look on her face. "Mom," she said. "You have a whole month off. You should do whatever the hell you want."

"I am doing what the hell I want. Why do you think I'm obsessing over all this right now?"

"What are you doing tomorrow?" asked Grace, leaning in.

Pam paused. She didn't know, really. "I thought maybe I'd get the ball rolling on enrolling you in school."

Grace groaned. "It was your decision to take a last minute, month-long road trip down to Florida for the month. Why are you continuing to beat yourself over the head with obligations? I thought the whole point was to get away from obligations."

"School is a pretty big obligation. I would think you'd be pretty interested in knowing that was taken care of. Maybe even grateful." Pam curled her fingers into her palms. She didn't want to start the day bickering with Grace. She just wanted today to be easy. "Besides, we'll feel better once that's off our plates."

'Off our plates. That's all you care about,' said Grace, folding her arms across her chest. "It's like the most important thing is for us to do our parts, but for what? You quit. You drove the company into the ground all by yourself."

Pam clenched her teeth. Grace had hit her where it hurt. She *had* quit…after a long fight. She'd fought hard to save Designer You. She just wasn't the person for the job. Nate was. She had no delusions about that. Pam rose from the table, collecting her empty coffee cup and breakfast dishes. "Thank you for the reminder, Grace."

"You don't have a life. Your life has become all about other people. Making sure that Dennis or Jackie or BFS aren't mad at you. That's so pathetic," said Grace. She looked disgusted with Pam. "You need to get a life. A real one. You'd be a lot more fun to be around."

Pam set the dishes on the sink and spun around. "You know, I'd be a lot more fun with a little help around here. I don't know if you noticed, but I'm all alone here. It's just *me*." She felt tears begin to choke her words, and she swallowed them down. "It's just me who has to worry about where you'll go to high school in less than a month. It's just me who has to figure out how to make our mortgage. It's just me who has to deal with at least a dozen people who are yes, as you say, 'mad' at me. It's just me who has to try not to be too sad all the time because my husband is gone – like that. And it's just me who has to worry about you, because you're sad, too. And desperately unhappy and self-destructive." By the time she was done, the tears had won. She leaned against the sink, putting her hands to her face, covering her eyes and mouth and letting the tears stream down her cheeks. She hated to let Grace see her like this. She wanted to be strong, but she wasn't. She never was.

She ripped off a paper towel and blew her nose and dabbed at her eyes. *Not even 11 o'clock and I'm already crying.* Grace sat at the dining room table, arms crossed. She didn't move. She narrowed her eyes. "I hope you go to the museum today, Mom. And the beach tomorrow. And out for lunch the next day. And for a bike ride on Wednesday. Maybe by the end of this trip you'll figure out what you want and stop caring so much about what other people think of you."

"Is that right?" *Well then who's going to help you get into high school? Who's going to pay for you to go to college?* "Someone has to be the grownup, and in this family the grownup happens to be me."

Grace sighed and stood. "As the only person in this house with a *job*, I'm going to get ready for work."

Pam winced. She wasn't sure what hurt more, the casualness with which Grace could just fling insults at her or the fact that so often those insults were based in truth. Desperate, Pam clung to the small amount of authority the label 'parent' afforded her to say, "Have breakfast first. Please. You know I hate it when you leave the house with nothing in your stomach."

Grace waved her off and walked toward her room. "I'll eat there. It's a resort and one of the perks is that employees eat for free."

"Well, good." Pam hoped it was true. "Maybe I'll swing by sometime and check out where you work."

Grace whirled around. "Oh, Mom. No. Please don't do

that."

"Why?" Pam's ego took another hit. "You never minded when I would come by the pool last summer."

"That's because we were members. Everyone there knew you anyway. The resort is new. I'm new. I don't need you coming by unannounced."

Doubt started to hover over the edges of her mind. Pam wanted to believe Grace did have a job just as she said, but there could be something she wanted to hide there. Maybe it was nothing more than Grace's space versus Pam's space. "Then consider this a formal announcement. I'm going to swing by today on my way to the Dali Museum. Or, on my way back. Either way, I'm stopping by to learn more about where you work, whether you approve or not."

"Fine," Grace said through clenched teeth. "I guess there's no stopping you."

"No there isn't," said Pam to herself, as Grace slammed the bedroom door behind her. *Get a life? I have a life, and her name is Grace Wheeler.*

* * *

The lobby of the resort where Grace worked greeted Pam with an open and breezy floor plan, right away setting off Pam's interior design Spidey sense. The white marble flooring glimmered under the high ceilings made of an opaque glass that let in the natural light. A lounge area featuring worn leather chairs and sturdy tables, a sparse gift shop, and full bar took over the next section. And beyond that was a gym, spa, and the resort steakhouse which looked out over the bay. The atmosphere of the resort was relaxed and casual but still luxurious. Pam felt she could have stepped in wearing flip-flops and a bikini and appeared appropriate and comfortable, but as long as what she was wearing was suitably expensive. As it was, she felt both dowdy and overdressed in a loose, black and white checked button-down shirt tucked into ankle pants the color of pumpkin pie. The wood registration desk displayed a detailed mosaic of an ocean wave and behind it stood a young man – he appeared barely out of high school – in white trousers and a yellow, short-sleeve button-down shirt. His name tag read 'Pete.' Pam approached.

"Hi, Pete." She smiled. "I'm looking for my daughter. She just started working here as a lifeguard yesterday. Part time."

Pete grinned back. He wore clear braces. "They're all part time. She's either at the main pool, the water slide, or the lazy river."

"OK," said Pam, looking around. "And how do I get there?"

"I'll just need to see some ID," said Pete with practiced authority. He pressed his lips together in an awkward pout over his braces, as Pam rummaged through her purse.

Pam handed over her ID, which Pete skimmed. He held up his index finger and turned around, grabbing what looked like a card key and swiping it on a card reader. He held the card up between his middle and ring fingers. "You'll need this to access the pool and beach areas. Just go through those doors over there." He used the card to point toward a pair of glass doors in the opposite direction of the lounge. "Wander around long enough, and I'm sure you'll run into your daughter." Pete pushed the card toward her across the registration desk.

"Thanks," said Pam, taking it. She made her way past the glass doors and swiped the card to get through another set of doors that led out to the outdoor pools, bar, and beach. The sun shimmered off the water and bounced off the pool deck and hot sand. The sun was inescapable and hit Pam with a blinding force. She fumbled for her sunglasses in her purse and slid them over her eyes. *Much better.*

The whole outdoor area bustled. Tanned people looking relaxed in their bathing suits and towels perched atop barstools. Most were coupled off or in small groups, nursing pale beers and snacking on cheese and fruit trays or eating lunch. Pam scanned the pool area for Grace. Mothers, fathers, sons, and daughters all bobbed along the lazy river, which snaked around an expansive pool complete with waterfall. Maybe four or five years ago, around the time that they moved to their current home in West Philadelphia, Pam could envision her, Nate, and Grace in a resort like this, taking an afternoon off from museums and tours to float in inner tubes around and around the pool area.

None of the lifeguards who sat upon high, whitewashed lifeguard chairs watching over these families was Grace. She walked around the perimeter of the lazy river to get a better view of the pool. Lifeguards dotted the landscape of the pool deck, but Grace was nowhere to be seen. *Maybe the beach?* thought Pam, as worry started to invade her chest. She didn't think Grace was certified to watch over swimmers at the beach, and it dawned on her that that could be what Grace was hoping to keep from her that morning. That this was the reason she was so opposed to her visiting today.

Pam slid off her walking shoes and ankle socks, so she could walk along the beach. The sand felt warm and smooth under her bare feet. At least two dozen cabanas lined the beach area just beyond the outer edges of the pool deck. Resort patrons were tucked inside each tented structure that featured seating, lounge chairs, pillows, and blankets. Soaked kids wrapped in towels took a break from playing in the waves to nibble on sandwiches on a chaise, while couples lay sprawled on chairs sunning themselves. A group of tanned young women in bikinis and towels wrapped around their waists played cards and sipped pink drinks with pineapple wedges clinging to the side of the glass. Further down the beach and closer to the water were rows and rows of lounge chairs, and high above, lifeguards in red bathing suits sat on white chairs, with red tubes strapped to their strong bodies. As Pam made her way down the beach, she passed four chairs. None of them held Grace. Pam frowned in frustration. *Where the hell is she?* she thought. *Did she lie about this job? About working at this resort?*

She decided it was time to go meet the pool manager. Maybe he or she could tell Pam where Grace was or if she was even working there. As she made her way back toward the resort, past the lounge chairs and cabanas and into the pool area, Pam spotted Grace. She was in the shallow end of the main pool with a boy, who looked to be about four or five years old. The boy's face was red and blotchy – tear stained, she could see as she got a little closer, though she was still far enough away that Grace hadn't noticed her yet. His hair and bathing suit were still dry. Waist deep in the pool, Grace raised her arms to the boy, who sat on the edge with his feet dangling in the water. But the boy instead folded his arms to his chest and vigorously shook his head. He craned his neck, looking for someone or something on the patio deck behind him – a woman sitting at an umbrella table reading on a tablet. Pam guessed it must have been his mother. The woman looked about the right age and shared the same dark blonde head of tight curls as the boy. She looked up from her e-reader to raise her eyebrow at the child and twirled her index finger, motioning for him to turn back around to face Grace.

Grace smiled up at the boy when he met her gaze. He bit his lower lip and fell into Grace's open arms. She held him close and blew bubbles into the water, inviting him to do the same. The boy's lips hovered over the water and with great caution, blew atop the surface as if he were blowing the downy tufts from a dandelion. Grace giggled and shook her head, demonstrating how to lower her mouth to the water and blow bubbles that burst upon reaching the surface. Fear gripped the boy's face.

"You can do it, Max." Grace showed him again. Max looked back at his mother, who didn't notice. She was too immersed in whatever it was she was reading. He turned back to Grace, his lower lip quivering. Pam wasn't sure if he was just cold or cold and afraid. He lowered his chin to the water, letting it rest on the surface. Pam watched with intense interest. He pursed his lips, dipped them below the surface and blew. The bubbles popped as they rose.

"Yay, Max!" Grace hugged him close and then gave him a high five. "You are *so* brave! You want to show your mom?" Max smiled and nodded.

"Mommy! Look!"

Pam edged out of view. She didn't want to distract Grace or the boy. Her heart was bursting – she was so proud of Grace. Her first day and already she was giving private swim lessons. And she had just the right touch. Knew just what to say, when to nudge the boy out of his comfort zone. That was not a skill many kids her age had. *Too bad the PSATs don't test for teaching fearful kids how to blow bubbles in the water.* It occurred to her that no wonder Grace wanted to find a job so much. She worked at the pool club all summer and loved every minute of it. Sure, she made friends, but it was the job that she found she was good at. No, *great* at. Right now, that confidence radiated from Grace's every pore. She'd found meaning and purpose and joy in teaching swimming. Pam didn't know if Grace had figured it out yet, but she may have found at least the seeds to her calling.

She left the resort almost skipping. Her girl was soaring. She found a life. And now it was time for Pam to get a life too. She'd take it day by day, and today, it would be the Dali Museum.

Chapter Eighteen

Pam vowed the next few weeks would be characterized by a lack of urgency. She was on vacation, dammit, and she would indulge in as much of St. Petersburg as she could. She started with Charlie's list of holiday events. That first December Sunday, she attended the Santa Parade and tree lighting ceremony. The next day, she browsed the booths at the Christmas Faire stationed for the weekend in a nearby park, where she ran into Charlie himself.

"Thanks for the list and the guidebook," she said, approaching. She'd just bought a bag of kettle corn to nibble on as she walked. She held out the bag for him. "Popcorn?"

He patted his stomach. "Late lunch." He smiled at her. "What are you doing here?"

"This place was included in one of the guidebooks and I thought I'd check it out. What about you – shopping?"

"I was on my way home from lunch. With my daughters and my ex." He looked uneasy. "Sometimes we try to do these family meals together and meet up for brunch or lunch or something, rotating her place, my place every few months or so. I keep thinking it's good for the girls, but I don't know. I always leave feeling uncomfortable. I think we all do."

"Ah." Pam looked down. "But you keep doing it."

"Yep," said Charlie, raising his eyebrows. "We keep doing it." They walked in silence for a bit, Pam snacking on popcorn and taking in the displays of handmade scarves and glass jewelry.

Pam broke the silence. "We've got something like this in Philly, though not in a grassy, sunny park like this. It's called the Christmas Village in Love Park."

"Love Park. That sounds nice," he said. They walked.

"It's not really a park, at least not like this one," she said, taking in the green grass and leafy trees. "It's flat and bland, made up of concrete for the most part. It's where the Love sculpture lives right near City Hall."

"Oh, right. I've seen that sculpture. Never been to Philadelphia though. You like it?"

Pam nodded. "Yeah. I grew up not too far away in kind of a sleepy town but moved to Philly after college. I like living in a city. Have you always lived in Florida?"

"No," said Charlie. "I grew up in Wisconsin."

"Wow, that's a big change. What brought you to Florida?"

"College." Pam liked his matter-of-fact demeanor. He didn't seem to have anything to hide. "I was so sick of winters. They just seemed endless. And to my eighteen-year-old self, Florida looked *fun*. Like a party all the time."

Pam laughed. "I can see that. Was it?"

"A party?" Charlie looked thoughtful. "Yeah, sometimes. It couldn't be a party *all* the time, at least not for me. I had to buckle down and focus to even finish. College was a big transition for me and the work never came easy."

"For me neither," Pam said. "I feel like I have to work twice as hard as everyone else. And sometimes I still don't get it." She gave him a sideways look. "Do you ever miss it? Wisconsin?"

"Oh yeah, especially now during the holidays. I still get homesick for a white Christmas."

"Do you ever take your girls back to visit?" asked Pam. "Have they ever experienced a white Christmas?"

"Uh-huh," he said, nodding. "It doesn't mean the same to them, though."

Pam sighed, admiring the ware for sale on square card tables: glass Christmas ornaments, crocheted hats and scarves, leather wallets, handmade jewelry. "I'm glad to be away from a white Christmas this year. I like my beachy Christmas."

"What brings you down to Florida for the holidays, if you don't mind me asking?"

She glanced up at him. The breeze blew a chunk of sandy hair onto his wide forehead. On instinct, she pushed it back and then retreated. "Oh gosh, sorry. I'm not usually so handsy."

Charlie pushed his hand through his hair and laughed. "It's OK." He looked down at Pam and tilted his head. "I'm glad I ran into you."

"Yeah?" Pam reddened. "Me too."

They stopped at a booth triple the size of all the other booths. It featured strings of dozens and dozens of outdoor lights designed for Florida porches and backyards. The entire booth blazed in colored lights, many shaped as tiny Santas, Christmas trees, angels, reindeer, ornaments. Pam spotted a string of lights made up of the manger scene – the three wise men, the angel Gabriel, shepherds and their sheep, and complete with Joseph, Mary, and the baby Jesus. She spied Hanukkah-themed lights made up of glowing stars of David, dreidels, and miniature menorahs. Many more lights weren't connected in any obvious, direct way to the holiday season at all – she saw bright icicles, snowflakes, pizzas, donuts, chili peppers. The effect was otherworldly and magical.

"Wow," said Charlie, his eyes full of awe as he took in the spectacle. "Incredible."

"I *love* lights. I want all of these in my backyard. We used to—" She stopped. *We used to take a trip as a family every year to South Philly and walk among the bright colors of the lighted streets during the holidays.* She turned toward Charlie, her face sober. "To answer your question – what we're doing here in Florida for an entire month – is to be anywhere *but* home for Christmas this year. That's the simple answer. My husband died last spring, and to be honest, being home during the holiday season was like a constant reminder of what we had last year. We couldn't be home this year." She shrugged. "We just needed something different, you know?" She braced herself for the inevitable awkward response. No one knew what to say. Including Pam.

"I do know. And I'm sorry." He ran his hand through his hair again. "That you lost your husband. I imagine it's been hard."

Through the hazy glow of all the lights, Pam recognized the discomfort register in Charlie's face right away, but she was touched by his sweetness. He didn't recoil from her like she had some sort of disease or pounce on her as if she were some impossible conquest that needed to emerge from her hard shell. "Thanks," she said.

Together, they walked the half mile back to the bungalows. Dusk had settled into the sky. Pam felt warm and relaxed. Happy even.

"Come in for a beer?" Charlie asked when they arrived home.

Pam shook her head. "No, I've got a dinner date with my daughter. She's expecting me."

Charlie shrugged. "Sure, no problem."

"But tomorrow, want to take another walk somewhere?" All of a sudden, Pam felt buzzy and a bit outside herself. *You're not asking him out on a date. It's a walk. No big deal.*

Charlie grinned. "Sure," he said. "Anywhere in particular?"

Pam smiled back. "I've got those guidebooks and an internet connection. I'm sure I can figure out a decent destination. I'll surprise you."

* * *

Over the next three weeks, Pam and Charlie didn't spend *every* day together. He didn't have a day job per se, but he did help out landlord friends manage their rentals. And Pam enjoyed long stretches of solitude. But she also enjoyed being around Charlie, especially since Grace spent so much time working at the resort or hanging out with her new coworkers. Grace made good on their 6 p.m. dinners together and slowly seemed to be coming around. The day belonged to Pam, however, and often, Charlie accompanied her to museums and tours, lunches and long, long walks. They talked on their respective back porches after dinner, sipping a glass of wine or beer. They talked about the ups and downs of raising teenagers and juggling work and single parenthood. They debated about reboot movies and bonded over their love of Cuban food. He talked about his ex, and she about Nate. The conversations flowed and there never seemed to be any awkwardness or hesitation.

And he was cute. She liked the way his dimples creased his

cheeks when he smiled and how the gray was just starting to sprinkle his hair. She could tell that when they walked together that from an outsider's point of view, they looked like a couple. Charlie hadn't made a move on her, though, which relieved Pam. Sort of. She still didn't think she was ready to date, but she could tell that he liked her. They laughed a lot together. He always took the opportunity to hold the door open for her. And she could feel him watch her sometimes when he didn't think she'd notice – just inside her periphery – when they shopped or looked at art or walked to lunch. Last summer, poor Bernie had swooped in too soon. She cringed, just thinking about their awkward 'date' at that ostentatious steakhouse, and later her pathetic attempt at an online dating profile, and wondered when would be the appropriate time to take another crack at it.

And now, a few weeks into the trip and nearing Christmas, Pam was comfortably stretched out on the portable lounge chair. She'd bought the chair right after her inaugural trip to the beach when all she'd brought with her was her purse, sunscreen, an *In-Touch Weekly*, a bottle of water, and a beach towel. Rookie mistake. If she was going to read and people watch and maybe eat a sandwich, she needed to be sitting in something that kept her off the sand. But now, after a few weeks of Florida living, she almost felt like a native, especially compared to the pasty tourists that crowded the beach over the last few days, fresh off airplanes from Minneapolis, St. Louis, Newark, Toronto. Today, she soaked in the bright Florida sunshine like this was what she was born to do. She wore a one-piece swimsuit that in past she reserved for lap swimming, a simple black number and she felt confident in it. She liked the crisscross shape the straps made in the back, liked the modest cut of the leg, and she liked how the front of the suit ensured her boobs stayed in one place.

Pam took a sip from a can of iced tea and then placed it back in its cup holder. She sighed as she watched families on their winter vacations frolic in the waves through her Ray-Bans and then returned to her book on her iPad. With no pressing projects, no Bernie Scott breathing down her neck, no Liz to remind her of what she needed to do and where she needed to be, Pam was burning through books this month. She'd just downloaded the latest Jennifer Weiner novel the night before and she was already at forty-three percent. If Grace was going out with the resort crew again tonight after dinner, she might even finish it before the day was through.

Pam placed her tablet in her lap and settled back in her beach chair, closing her eyes and enjoying the gentle warmth of the sun on her skin. A slight breeze played with the strands of her not-quite-black hair, now tinged with amber, an effect from all the sunshine. It was also getting a little long, as it fell long past her shoulders now. Pam thought back to the last time she'd had it cut. Was it more than six months? Before Nate died? *Valentine's Day – that was it.* How did she go ten months without a trim? She made a mental note to look for a salon in town. She'd touched up her roots on her own, but she hadn't had a proper hair appointment in far too long. If she was going to be a lady of leisure, then a trip to the salon seemed like 'must-do' on her short to-do list.

What about Charlie? whispered a voice in her head. *Add him to your 'to-do' list. He's right here. He's cute. Single. You like him. He likes you. You're on vacation.* Pam opened her eyes and looked out toward the ocean again. She spied a man and a woman with a little girl who looked to be about four walking along the beach. The three held hands and swung the little girl every few steps. She giggled and lifted her feet into the air. Pam remembered walking like that with Nate and Grace when she was about that age. They would have had a great time together here in St. Petersburg. *What would Nate think of Charlie?* She couldn't be sure. They were both so different. Nate would sympathize that Charlie was struggling since the divorce, but deep down, he would find little to relate to in Charlie. Charlie's low-key job was managing rentals. *Where's the fire under him?* Pam could hear Nate asking. *He's got two kids about to leave for college. You think he'd be hustling his way back to a career, burning calories to find something that pays, but no. He's living it up at the beach, while he lets his ex-wife take all the financial burden. Where's his pride?*

Charlie was no Nate. But Nate could be unfair and jump to conclusions.

And now, four days before Christmas on a warm beach, Pam felt the familiar ache of Nate's loss rise in her chest.

Her cell phone buzzed in her canvas beach bag. She rooted around in the bag, feeling for the source of the vibration. She snagged the phone and looked at the number – an 865 area code. *865? Is that real? It's probably one of those scammy credit card calls.* She hesitated, thinking, maybe there was a chance that Grace was calling from a friend's phone, which seemed like a reach but enough of a possibility to justify answering.

She tucked her hair behind her ear and tapped the green button on the screen to answer. "Hello?"

"Hello. Is this Pam Wheeler?" asked a woman's voice on the other end of the line.

Pam swallowed. Recent history had proved that conversations that started by asking her if she was Pam Wheeler were not 'good news' phone calls. "Yes, this is Pam. May I ask who's calling?" The sun felt too hot all of a sudden, too bright.

"My name is Holly Peto, and I am an editor for *HGTV Magazine.*"

Heat rose up Pam's spine and settled into the back of her neck. The blood throbbed in her cheeks. *Shit. Are they at a loose end? Do I owe HGTV work?* She thought she'd backed off every single job – the home projects, the book deal, the magazine gigs, the blog. Frantic, her brain tried to recall any assignment she could have missed, an article that was unaccounted for.

"Oh?" she managed to squeak.

"Yes, well," the woman went on. "I'm sorry to bother you during the holidays. The magazine mostly shuts down for two weeks at the end of December." She laughed lightly into the phone. "In fact, the office is pretty dead today."

Oh God, I must be in real trouble if she's making an exception to talk to me. I hope I don't owe them money. "OK?" *Just tell me. Rip the Band-Aid off.*

"But," she continued. "I ran into your agent at a publishing event in New York over the weekend. Jackie mentioned you were taking some time off to...regroup." *That's an understatement.* "And that you might be thinking of taking your career in a new direction? Do I have that right?"

Pam hadn't given one thought to her career since she'd arrived in Florida. "A new direction? Um, yes, I suppose." *No direction was technically a new direction, right?*

"I wondered if I might persuade you to write for us. For *HGTV Magazine.*" Pam heard Holly take in an excited breath. "Once I heard you were sort of a free agent, I knew I needed to act fast."

Pam paused. Was this a *pitch?* Did she just offer Pam a *job?* Her heart began to pound. "I'm listening," she said, feeling a little lightheaded.

"I'm thinking a monthly feature with splashy photography, great exposure. You'd travel all over the country and cover make-overs of older homes. So you'll be doing a lot of back and forth between the 'before' and 'after' and of course, the 'during,' too. You'll be busy. Each article will end up around a thousand words, so there's a lot to pack in not a ton of space, especially with the photo spread and all." *Feature? Photo spread? Travel?* Pam's brain stalled as Holly forged ahead. "For a name like yours, our pay would be quite competitive. I assume you and Jackie would want to negotiate, but we're starting in the low six figures."

Not a fortune, but Pam could and was living on much less than what she and Nate had brought in together last year. And with no private school tuition, she and Grace would be fine. *Fine. Holy shit, we'll be fine!* "Tell me more about the travel."

"Right, the travel. You'll be traveling every month, probably two to three times for a few days at a time. Some locations won't be too far, but we want to extend our reach and be open to cover locations in all fifty states." Holly paused briefly. "Is it scaring you off a bit?"

Pam thought about Holly's question. She wasn't *thrilled* with more travel for work, though she and Nate did it for a decade for Designer You. At least this travel would be somewhat predictable – show up at someone's old house and chronicle the transformation. No designing. No making tough decisions. The job sounded just about ideal for her right now. Even though Grace was getting older and more independent with each passing day, Pam hated the thought of being away from her for so much, but they'd get used to it. Grace might even like having even more independence. Or maybe she'd want to tag along sometimes. "I think I could handle the travel," she said. "It'd be worth it for an opportunity like this."

"Believe me, we would be the lucky ones to snag someone like you with your experience and your audience. We're huge fans," said Holly. "So, interested?"

Pam nodded, feeling a bit dizzy, wrapping her brain around the fact that this editor called her – *just her* – for a job at *HGTV*. "Yes. Interested. Definitely." *Breathe, you dork!* "But I'll need some time to think about it. What's the next step?"

"Sure, take a few days. Talk to Jackie, think it over."

"I'll be in touch."

She couldn't wait to talk to Grace that night about the offer over dinner. *Finally*, Pam thought, *I may have done something right, something to make Grace proud.*

* * *

Grace slid into her seat at the dining room table. It was ten after six, and Pam could see from her pink cheeks and sluggishness that Grace was exhausted and a bit sunburned. She eyed the chicken bucket, biscuits, and tossed salad in the center of the table.

"Fried chicken, Mom?" she asked, a grin starting to form at the edges of her mouth. "What's the occasion?"

"Who says I need an occasion for fried chicken?" Pam wiped her hands on the kitchen towel, poured herself a glass of chardonnay, and sat across from her daughter.

"Are you kidding? We NEVER eat fried chicken. EVER. It's like against your religion or something."

Pam tilted her head at Grace. "Never? Ever?"

"Last time we got fried chicken was after my piano recital in fourth grade." She reached for a drumstick.

"That was a long time ago, I'll give you that, but not never," said Pam. She took a thigh and a biscuit. Tonight was cause for celebration. Pam envisioned a future of economic certainty, of sending Grace to college, of paying off her house. The insurance money could be saved for Grace's future. Pam wouldn't need to depend on anyone but herself and that was worth celebrating. Fried chicken would not have been her first choice – spending all of high school working in her dad's diner meant she'd eaten enough fried food for multiple lifetimes – but she wanted Grace ready to be as excited about the new job as she was.

"Something's up," said Grace, taking two biscuits and a butter packet. "But I'm not complaining."

After three weeks of dining together every evening, Pam and Grace were back to having some of the same conversations they'd share when she'd shuttle Grace to and from practices, rehearsals, and games. Sure, Grace was still pulling away from her, her fierce independent streak something she inherited from both her and Nate, but now the time they spent together was more concentrated and thus felt more special to Pam.

"Where'd you get it? It's good." Grace licked the grease from her fingers.

"A chicken and waffle place between here and downtown. Charlie recommended it."

"Oh, OK." Grace lowered her drumstick to her plate. She

looked like her appetite had wilted. "Is that what this is?"

Pam looked across the table at Grace, confused. "Is that what 'what' is?"

Grace made a face. "Are you guys a thing now? Because if you are, I think I'm gonna barf."

"What? No!" Grace had caught Pam off guard. "Why? I mean, what's wrong with Charlie?" Now she wanted to know.

"He's a loser," said Grace, like it was a matter of fact. She wiped her hands on her napkin. "He's a bum." *God, she sounds like my dad when I'd bring boys around during high school.*

"He is not a loser or a bum, and I kind of resent you judging him like that."

"It's not a judgment, Mom. It's an observation."

"An observation of what?" Defensiveness rose up in her like a shield.

Grace shrugged. "I observe that he has an awful lot of free time during the day to hang out with his lonely, pretty, widowed, vacationing neighbor, that's all."

"Wow, just wow." Pam wiped the corners of her mouth with her napkin. "That was not the news I was going with, but at least now I know where you stand with Charlie."

Grace narrowed her eyes. "So there *is* something going on. I knew it."

"Jesus, no, Grace. There is nothing going on. We're just friends. But—" said Pam, deciding to ignore Grace's look of utter disbelief. She clasped her hands and placed them in her lap. "I *do* have some good news."

"Really?" Grace smirked. "What?"

"I was offered a job today. A good job," said Pam, brimming with pride. *HGTV Magazine* wanted her and her alone. Nate wasn't part of the package any more, but they didn't seem disappointed about that. She wasn't going into the situation as the less talented half of a DIY empire. Here, she was the star. She was the expert. Just thinking about it made her dizzy with excitement.

"So soon?" asked Grace, her smile fading. "I didn't know you were even looking." Pam thought she detected a note of disappointment in her voice.

"Aren't you happy?" For a second, Pam didn't want Grace to answer her question. She feared she wanted Grace to tell her what she wanted to hear, that she was feeling happier and hopeful, instead of what she probably needed to hear, that she was still angry, despondent, directionless. "This job could save our financial asses."

Grace folded her arms. "I don't care. It's fine."

"'It's fine?' Judging by that sour look on your face, it doesn't seem fine. I haven't even told you about the job yet." She wasn't hungry anymore. "What's wrong with me working? Don't you want a roof over your head? Don't you want nice things? Don't you want to go to college?"

"I guess I should be thankful that you went a whopping three weeks without thinking about work. Like, we're on vacation. Vacation is about forgetting the daily grind and having fun. Is three weeks your 'fun' limit or something?" said Grace, as if she herself forgot that the first thing she did on her vacation was find a job. Grace's face softened. "What's the job, then?" she asked without a note of curiosity or feeling in her voice.

Pam sighed, her enthusiasm and excitement for the new opportunity evaporating. "It's for *HGTV Magazine*. I'll be writing feature articles on make-overs of old houses all over the country. It pays well, it'll be secure, and I'm going in to negotiate the contract next month." She raised her shoulders. "What do you think?"

The creases between Graces eyebrows returned. "So you'll be traveling again," she said in her flat voice.

"Yes, it will require some travel, but I'll do a lot of work from home, too," said Pam, selling the idea. "What do you think?"

Grace shook her head. "No."

"No?" said Pam, crumbling.

"I vote no."

"Huh." Stunned, Pam leaned back in her chair. Was Grace just being defiant? Did she not understand that the sooner Pam had a job, the sooner they could start over again? The insurance money was temporary, not long term. *HGTV* had solved a big problem for both of them. "I don't think you understand just how terrific this opportunity is. If I say no, then it's back to square one. There is no guarantee for me out there, especially with how it all ended with Designer You."

"Then don't ask me for my opinion." Grace wadded up her paper napkin and threw it on her plate. "If you don't want to know what I think, don't ask."

Grace was quiet for a moment and then she started to cry.

Pam leapt out of her chair and went to her. She put her hand on Grace's back which shook as she sobbed. Grace shrugged her away. "Leave me alone!"

Pam sank into the chair next to Grace. "Honey, Gracie, why are you so upset? It's just a job. Is it about the travel?"

Grace sobbed into her hands. "Stop it. Stop talking to me." Her left arm shot out and shoved Pam away from her.

It was all Pam could do to *not* talk to her, to *not* try to comfort her, to *not* throw her arms around her and let her cry into her shirt like she used to as a little girl. She wanted to smother her, smother the tears from her like tamping down a fire with a wet towel. But she wasn't a little girl. Instead, Pam rose and gathered her dishes and the unfinished chicken and retreated into the kitchen, where she threw away her hardly-touched dinner.

Grace's sobs transitioned to jagged breaths. "It's like…you can't…wait…to jump…right back into it." She pressed her napkin to her eyes. "It's like…you can't wait…to get away from me." Grace dissolved into fresh tears all over again.

Pam couldn't help it, but now she felt the heat rise to her cheeks. "I can't win," she said more to herself than to Grace. "It's either, I'm in your face too much or I just want to get away from you. You can't have it both ways. You can't just have me around when you want me and then turn around and decide you want me to get lost when it's convenient for you." Her cheeks flushed in anger. "I'm your mom and I have to be *responsible* for both our lives at the moment. You calling in a bomb threat to BFS? That's scary behavior. You're so *freakin'* lucky they didn't press charges, because that would have ruined things for you for a long time. When your kid does that? It's time to start paying attention."

"Then why didn't you pay attention earlier? You're so selfish. You're not the only one who's upset, who's having a hard time, who's sad, who's lost," said Grace, dabbing her nose with her napkin. "It's not like taking two seconds out of your day to pretend I exist too would have made any difference. You still couldn't handle the pressure. You still quit."

Pam felt the air being sucked out of the room. She squeezed her hands into fists. *"I quit Designer You for you. For both of us."* She turned toward the sink. She couldn't even look at her daughter. "And you know what? You're stuck with me." Her eyes felt like hot pokers. "And I'm stuck with you."

Grace pushed her chair back and leapt to her room, slamming the door behind her. Pam almost panted with exertion, like she'd just finished a sprint, and as she stood there in the kitchen, regret for how she behaved began to cave into her chest. How could she have let herself get so angry, so out of control? *And I'm stuck with you?* Good grief, she might as well be chasing Grace around the cottage gripping wire hangers like Faye Dunaway as Joan Crawford. Who is the parent here and who is the child? It seemed the harder she tried to get close to Grace, the further away she drifted.

It didn't help that Grace always seemed to favor Nate over Pam. They both shared a fierce love for him – he was their world – and now that he had been gone for a good part of this year, they couldn't seem to align. If anything, she and Grace were more removed than ever. This vacation was beginning to feel like an exercise in one more failure in a long string of failures. The cottage that until that moment felt breezy and cozy now felt much too small for the both of them, as if it were closing in on her, crushing her. Maybe they should just pack up and go home, where she could fail as a parent in her own rambling house, where she and Grace could stay out of each other's way and be angry in peace.

Why was she always wrong when it came to Grace? It seemed every other mother on the planet had a close bond with their daughter, something special that only they shared. Facebook was crammed with photos of mothers and daughters getting mani-pedis or attending Taylor Swift concerts or shopping for prom dresses or just in general having a far easier time of it than Pam felt she was. Of course, not all mothers and daughters were close. And Pam didn't feel like she was a monster to Grace. But she certainly didn't feel like the inside of a Mother's Day card either.

Pam rinsed the dishes and put them into the dishwasher. She packed away the leftovers. *I have every right to be proud of this job opportunity. The responsible decision is to take it.* But Pam couldn't shake that Grace had a point. Maybe she didn't want her mother smothering her, but she probably didn't want to be alone either. Because of the travel, these dinners together wouldn't happen every night. Once again, Pam would miss out on a lot of the day-to-day with Grace – homework, classes, college worries, friend drama. She didn't want Grace to feel she was her last priority. She couldn't be an afterthought. Pam dried her hands and looked toward the closed door to Grace's bedroom. *I promise you, Gracie, I will do whatever it takes to make you feel important and keep our family unit together.*

She took out her phone, opened a new email, and typed: *Holly, I'd like to know more. Let's set up a meeting with you and Jackie after the New Year and go over the details.*

Chapter Nineteen

The next morning, Grace emerged from her room while Pam read the paper and drank coffee. They eyed each other warily. Pam couldn't get a read on Grace's mood from her face alone and wasn't sure if she'd snap her head off or begin the day pretending the ugliness from the night before had been a bad dream.

"Hey," she said as Grace trudged to the kitchen to pour herself coffee. Pam watched as she spooned an absurd amount of sugar into the cup and stirred.

"I need a new bathing suit," she said after taking a first sip. "Mine's on its last thread."

"Do you have time to go shopping today?" asked Pam. Grace's lifeguarding shifts and swim lessons always took place in the afternoons, and she hoped that Grace might be up for a little mother-daughter shopping time this morning. She brightened at the thought. "I can take you after breakfast and have you back by lunch so you can get to the beach club in time for your shift."

Grace shook her head. "I can go myself. I have the day off." She walked to the kitchen table and stuck out her palm toward Pam. "Credit card, please."

Pam's eyes moved from Grace's hand to her ungrateful face.

"No," she said, working hard to keep her tone light. "I'll take you myself. We can go to lunch and have a shop."

Grace narrowed her eyes at her mother. "I don't want to 'go to lunch' or 'have a shop.' I just want to replace my bathing suit. You've never had a problem before giving me your credit card and letting me take care of it. I'm not a moron."

Pam took a slow breath through her nose. "I know you're not a moron," she said. "But since you have the day off, we can spend time together. We've had these dinners every night, but we've been doing our own thing pretty much every day. I want to spend some time with you."

"Why?" Grace snapped. "Because you'll have no time for me once again when we get back home? Forget it. I don't want your credit card. I'm making my own money. I'll get the suit on my own."

Pam could see that Grace was digging in, but she'd inherited that stubborn streak in part from Pam herself. "You will not get the suit on your own," she said, her heart beginning to pound. "After breakfast, we're walking into town to buy you a new bathing suit. After, we're going to lunch. You may not like it, Grace, but we need to learn how to get along."

"I hate this." Grace folded her arms across her chest. "I hate you."

Pam nodded and looked down at her hands which held her coffee mug. She gripped it so tightly she thought she might shatter it with her bare hands. She looked up and met Grace's angry eyes. "This is not a negotiation. We'll leave in one hour. End of discussion."

* * *

The late morning sun burned high and bright above them as they came out of the bungalow. Pam squinted before pushing sunglasses over her eyes and spotted Charlie out watering his lawn. He waved at them.

"Ladies' day out?" he asked, pausing the sprayer.

Pam nodded. "Yep."

Grace slouched and jammed her hands in the pockets of her jean shorts.

Charlie's eyes moved from Pam to Grace and back to Pam again. "Well, have fun, you two." He gave her a little wink. Pam returned it with a grateful smile.

"We'll do our best," she said as she and Grace made their way down the path to the sidewalk, where they began their walk to downtown.

Pam had walked miles and miles since the first day of their vacation, and had felt and seen the effects. When she'd arrived, her body had been soft and shapeless, a result of months of neglect after Nate's death. She'd always considered herself an active person – in the past, she'd jogged and biked and when she had a choice, always chose to walk instead of drive. But Nate's death meant she'd had to shuttle between one project and the next. She'd spent way too much time in the car and not enough time moving around on her own accord.

As a little girl learning how to play soccer with her older brother, to leaping over hurdles for her high school track team, to taking an African dance class at Penn State for her P.E. requirements, Pam had always found ways to stay in shape. After she and Nate got together, they were so poor at first that the only exercise she could afford was to run. And she did. She'd trained for and ran her first race – a 5K – the May after she turned twenty-four. Six months later, she ran the Rothman 10K. A year later in the fall, she registered for and ran the ING Distance Run Half Marathon. Although Pam was never fast – she'd always joked that she 'trotted' more than 'ran' anything – she prided herself on always being in good enough shape to run a 10K at a moment's notice. But since Nate's death, her will to run had vanished.

She kept thinking that the desire would return, especially as a way to keep herself sane amidst the craziness and grief of losing a husband, scrambling to keep Designer You afloat, and keeping half an eye on Grace. But she found she had zero time for exercise and didn't want to make time, either.

So when she and Grace arrived in Florida, her body resembled lumpy raw dough in both consistency and texture. The numbers on the scale hadn't changed much, but she'd felt so weak and soft that if someone had poked her arm, they'd have left a dent. But now, after three weeks of walking between five and fifteen miles a day, Pam's legs were lean and strong. The muscles in her thighs and calves had become more defined. Her core felt stronger, more solid like an actual tree trunk. And emotionally, Pam experienced a sense of balance that she hadn't felt in nine months. She felt *good*. And though she was still sad sometimes and unsure of herself, she was far more resilient and confident than she'd been in way too long.

They walked in silence for a few blocks. Pam resisted the impulse to grab onto Grace's hand, like when she and Grace would walk home from preschool or stroll to the local tot lot. She never worried that Grace would run away from her into the street or down the block, but liked the simple act of holding onto her, liked the closeness she'd felt when she clasped her fingers through her daughter's. Grace had seemed to like it too, until they came to their gate or they arrived at the park, where she'd make a beeline for the slide. Today, Grace's hands remained jammed into her pockets and Pam folded her arms across her chest, mostly to ward off the slight chill that remained from that morning. She was surprised when Grace spoke first.

"He likes you, you know," she said. She kept her eyes fixated on the sidewalk in front of her.

"Charlie?" Pam said, flashing back to their uncomfortable, though short, exchange about him last night over dinner.

Grace gave her a sideways glance. "Who else? You're not *that* clueless, are you, Mom?"

Pam shrugged. "I don't know, sweetie. Maybe? He hasn't said anything. To be honest, we're just friends."

"He looks like he'd like to be a lot more than friends with you, if you know what I mean."

Pam smiled at her. Grace still hadn't mastered subtlety.

"I think I know what you mean."

"He's always staring at you with those moony eyes," Grace said. "Like a teenager with a crush."

"I don't know what to tell you, Grace. There's nothing going on and there won't be. Does that make you feel any better?"

"Whatever."

Whatever. It was her answer for everything these days. Pam sensed she wasn't so ambivalent. When they got into town, she and Grace found a Play It Again Sports and located the swimsuit rack. They both leafed through the red, one-piece suits to find a size and style to replace Grace's thinning suit she'd been swimming in all last summer and over the last few weeks at the beach club.

"It has to be red, right?" asked Pam, pausing at a patterned tankini that sported swirls of blue and green and turquoise. "This would look darling on you."

Grace scowled at the suit Pam held up. "Red only, Mom. And a one-piece."

"Well, at least you look good in red," said Pam, returning the tankini to the rack. "Just like your dad. I think it's your eyes. I look terrible in red."

Grace ran her fingers over the tops of the smooth metal hangers. "I think I'm just like Dad," she said, her voice quiet.

Pam nodded. "I think you are, too," she said, though she did not, actually, think Grace's personality was much like Nate's at all. She could see glimmers of Nate in the shape of her mouth, in her gait, in the spray of freckles on her nose and cheeks. But Grace didn't have Nate's natural confident brilliance. She was a much quieter child. The things that came easy to her were athletic rather than cerebral. But when she put her stubborn streak to work for her and determined she was going to ace that geography quiz or memorize something that had eluded or frustrated her, nothing could stop her.

"I think I'm going to be an architect."

To Pam, it sounded like Grace was trying the sentence on to see how it fit her.

"Really?" asked Pam. "That's not a bad job, as you know. You'll have to study super hard, though. It's not an easy profession to break into, but I know you can do it."

Grace shrugged. "I don't know." Sadness crept into her daughter's eyes, which made Pam's heart hurt. She reached out and gave Grace's hand a quick squeeze.

"I miss him too," she said. "Every day."

Grace gave Pam a lukewarm smile and picked out two red swimsuits. She hugged the garments to her chest and frowned.

"Do you ever worry you're going to forget about him? Like, forget little pieces at a time? That after a while, you'll forget maybe about how you felt when he'd come home from a trip. I remember I used to run to him when I was little. I could smell the faraway cities and airports and restaurants in his suit jacket."

Pam remembered those travel smells too – often consisting of some combination of food, cigarette smoke, face powder, power tools, and wood chips. But she more worried that she'd start to forget about the everyday, mundane things, like his favorite brand of peanut butter (Trader Joe's creamy salted) and how he loaded the dishwasher (crammed full). She always wanted to remember that he folded socks to resemble tubes so that he could fit more pairs into his dresser drawer. Or the way he poured a beer into the glass so the foam never spilled over onto the kitchen counter. Or his easy way with Grace. He never hovered. Never raised his voice. As she got older, they seemed more like friends. He was proud of her will and determination. Loved watching her play sports – it didn't matter what sport, his favorite thing in the world was to watch her play. Pam didn't want to forget that, ever.

"I don't think you'll forget, honey." Pam hoped what she said was true, though she doubted it. Nate himself would never fade, but those little details would start to get fuzzy in the same way any memory blurs over time. She clung to the impossible wish that she could hold onto everything about Nate, save it all onto a disk or a thumb drive, and whenever she wasn't sure about the details of an experience she'd had with him, she could pull it up on her laptop and experience that trip, that meal, that birthday, all over again.

Grace took the suits to the ladies' dressing room, while

Pam waited outside the door on a bench beside a three-way mirror. She hadn't shopped like this since Grace was in fifth grade. They'd bought the bulk of her clothes online and when Grace went to the mall, it was always with friends. No parents allowed. "It's boring just the two of us," said Grace through the door. "Home feels so empty. It never felt empty before."

Pam raised her eyebrows. "You're bored by me?"

"Not really bored, maybe just lonely."

Pam grimaced to herself. She could see that. "Yeah."

After Grace chose her new swimsuit, they paid for it and left for lunch. The sidewalks were alive today with a steady stream of holiday shoppers and tourists.

"It's a long transition," said Pam as they walked side-by-side. "We're still getting used to not having Dad around. I'm getting used to…" She paused, searching for the words. "Finding work on my own. Running the house by myself. Your dad and I were such a team, and we saw it that way. Like you're part of your travel lacrosse team. You all have your roles on the field."

"They're called 'positions,' Mom. I play a *position* on my lacrosse team."

"Right," said Pam, nodding at her. "Positions. Well, Dad and I had a version of that at home and in work. Can you imagine if you were out on the field alone all of a sudden, the only one on your team, and you had to go against a whole team in a game? It'd feel really hard, right?"

"That would never happen, Mom. This is a ridiculous example."

"Fine. But my point is, it's tough doing everything that Dad and I did together by myself. It means I'm not home as much. It means my time is stretched." She felt Grace's eyes on her as they strolled. "And on top of it, I'm so sad. I miss your dad every day."

Grace stopped mid stride and folded her arms. "Well so do I."

Pam let the words hang for a moment. She gave her a conciliatory smile. "Of course you do, Gracie."

Grace straightened her posture. "I don't think you get it, Mom. I'm stretched and sad too." Pam could hear the frustration in her voice. "It's scary enough just being a teenager, with college looming and tests and homework piling up and friends who like you one minute and then talk about you behind your back the next. It's not being invited to anything anymore because no one wants the sad girl at their party or to go to the movies with." She squeezed her hands into fists. "And I get that I messed up big time. Phoning in that bomb threat with Lauren was the stupidest, most dumb-ass thing I've ever done. I get that. But I'm still, like, lost, Mom."

Pam looked up, furrowing her brows. They were holding up traffic, and people kept having to step around them. She motioned for Grace to sit at an empty table in front of a Starbucks. "Lost – what do you mean?" Her heart broke for her daughter, and she thought again about how she could have failed her. She should have gotten Grace, maybe even them both, into therapy a long time ago. She should have realized her priority after that first phone call from the school when Grace had skipped out. Not Designer You. Not Bernie's flashy townhouse. Not a blog post. Not even herself.

Her daughter.

Grace sat and put her hand to her cheek. "Like, I still don't know what I'm doing. I don't know what I want. Or what I should be. It seems like everyone I know has this clear picture of what they want and how they're going to get it. They're so *confident*, you know? Like Hannah has known from day one she wants to be a pediatrician. She wants to go to Penn and study pre-med just like her parents. Jacinda does play after play after play. She was one of the leads in *Measure for Measure* this year and does tons of theater at Walnut Street Theatre and The Arden. She's probably going to go someplace like Juilliard or Yale. Abby just got her short story published in the *Weekly*. Mai is already taking pre-cal as a sophomore. I feel like I'm surrounded by these kids who all know something I don't. I wish I could be sure about something."

"Oh, honey," said Pam. *I wish I could be sure of something, too.* "You don't need to have anything figured out yet. You're fifteen."

On the other hand, she was dying to learn what the parents of those freakishly focused kids were doing different than what Pam and Nate had done with Grace. Was it the fact that Grace was an only child? Did Pam indulge her to just be who she was at whatever age and neglect to push her when she should have? Or maybe she should have zeroed in on a specific talent and nurtured it – gone all stage mom on her and shaped it into something marketable that could earn a salary when Grace graduated college? Sure, Grace loved playing sports and crafting. She liked playing computer games and texting with her friends. What major did any of that translate to?

Pam thought back to what she'd been doing at fifteen. Chipping in at her father's diner. Working hard at being the best student she knew how. All she wanted was to make her parents proud. Be better than her older brother. Escape Chester County.

Early on, Pam had known she wanted to be someplace that offered her choices and opportunity. Someplace where she'd be surrounded by smart, talented people. It occurred to her then that although she felt most comfortable basking in others' genius, Grace conversely felt intimidated and second rate. "Just because you don't know that you want to be a math whiz or pediatrician doesn't mean you don't have tons to offer right now. And you'll keep growing and learning about yourself, and I'm sure you're going to grow up into a fabulous adult who's going to help make the world a better place."

Pam knew she sounded like a life coach or a cheerleader, pumping her daughter full of meaningless platitudes. But they weren't meaningless to her.

"Honey," she said, leaning in and lowering her voice. "I saw you at the beach club. I will never forget just how good you were with this one scared little boy in the pool." She could see Grace in her mind's eye, that soft way she'd talked to him and then coaxed him into the water. "That you *love* to work, and when you put your mind to it, you work as hard as your father or I ever have. You're such a natural with kids. Maybe you'll become a teacher? Or a social worker? Or a therapist?"

"Mom." Grace drew out the 'o' sound in the word, making it sound like it had two syllables instead of one. She reddened and looked around at the empty tables and teeming sidewalk. No one was paying them any attention. "Embarrassing," she said in an understated, sing-song voice.

"Why don't you teach swimming?" asked Pam, thinking maybe Grace had stumbled into something career worthy after all. "Run a swim school or something like that?"

Grace looked at her like she'd just offered her a dead rodent on a porcelain plate. "Mom, no. Just no."

Pam shrugged. "I don't know. It just seems like you're good at it. And you love it. Why not go with what you love?"

"Because it's a stupid job. It's a job for teenagers. No one goes to college to teach swimming."

"I don't know, Grace. I'm just trying to help you understand that if you don't know what you want now, it's OK. You are normal. *I* never knew what I wanted until I met your dad and that was at the end of college. I think I turned out all right." As the words came out of her mouth, Pam was already second guessing them. *Had* she turned out all right? Was she OK? Did she really hope that what had happened to her would happen to Grace – to hitch her dreams onto someone else's wagon?

Grace waved her off, dismissive. "Even *you* say that was a long time ago – a different time."

Pam gave her a reluctant nod. Grace was right. It was different for high school kids now. They had different pressures on them that she hadn't in the late 1980s and early 90s. "Yeah, it's different. But I still don't think you need to know everything at this stage. And I'd be surprised if your friends didn't have doubts about the future, too."

"And next month, I get to start at a brand new school. Yay me," Grace said, her voice flat.

"Well, it's either Girls' Academy or homeschooling." Pam cringed at the thought of that huge check she'd written to BFS. She couldn't afford private school again, not this year. "Our choices are pretty slim at this point," she said, considering her scheduled meeting with *HGTV Magazine* after the New Year, feeling both guilt and comfort at the same time.

"What if no one likes me? What if I don't fit in?" asked Grace. "It's the middle of the school year. Everyone will already have their friends, be in their groups. I'll just be some private school drop-out or whatever." She picked at the cotton handles of her shopping bag. "And once you have a job again, I'll be alone at home, too."

Pam didn't know how Grace would fit in to the public school. She'd spent so much time being grateful she'd been given a chance at any school, fitting in and making friends seemed secondary. But of course Grace would worry about that. It wasn't considered the best school in the city, but it was decent with bright students and a dedicated staff. And it wasn't violent, thankfully, but many city dwellers avoided any public school if they could afford it. Pam could think of only one family in their upper-middle-class neighborhood who sent their daughter, a junior, to the local neighborhood high school; everyone else enrolled their kids to the city magnet, charter, and private schools scattered around Philadelphia.

"You'll make friends. Maybe not on the first day or even the first week, but you'll make friends." Pam was aware it was kind of a pat answer to something that bothered Grace, but she didn't want her to get too wound up about it.

But with the possibility that Pam would be working for *HGTV Magazine* soon after they returned from Florida, she realized Grace would spend her high school years alone. It wasn't the first time Pam had wondered if she'd done a great disservice to Grace by denying her a sibling. She'd been alone so much of her life. When she was little and not yet in school, she was portable. She and Nate took her everywhere they went and it worked out beautifully. If they had to make an appearance together, which they were hungry to do back then – a home show, book publicity, interviews – they'd pack Grace up and off they went. When she started pre-school, Grace had visited more states than her parents by the time they had both finished college.

But as she got older and started school, Nate tried to take on more of the travel and on occasion left Pam and Grace behind. More often, though, Pam and Nate needed to present themselves as a team, which they were, and the more popular Designer You became, the more often they'd have to leave Grace behind with their overnight sitter, Olga.

But Pam could sense that the one place Grace spent time with other children was at school. Aside from the occasional play date, Grace grew up knowing how to entertain herself. Pam was proud of that – that her kid wasn't always in her face asking what she could do. "I'm so bored, Mommy," she'd often hear the children of her friends complain. Or she'd know through lived experience the wail of siblings getting on each other's nerves. *Not my kid*, thought Pam, a little too smug. Her family was tidy and neat and happy. And small.

How could she have been so stupid? So selfish? What was it – have one kid so she could call herself a mother? But she'd denied little Grace companionship. A sibling who could share in almost everything from the moment the second child was born. Unfortunately, Grace had too much to deal with right now. If she had a sibling, she would have had someone to lean on when her dad had died. Maybe she wouldn't have felt the need to escape school. Maybe she could have faced relatively benign challenges like the PSATs without threatening to blow up the school. She'd have someone when her mom has to travel for work or when her mom, perhaps, meets and falls in love with someone new.

A rush of guilt took a pot shot at her stomach. But she couldn't help but see their reality for what it was: Grace didn't have a sibling and Pam needed a full-time job. "Grace," she started, knowing she needed to come clean. "I have a meeting with *HGTV Magazine* when we get back home." She winced at the look of utter betrayal on Grace's face. "I wish you could just put the brakes on being furious with me for one second so you could see my side of this."

"Then stop making it so *easy* for me to be furious at you."

Pam twisted her purse strap in her lap. Could mothers of teenage girls do anything right? Ever?

"I don't want to do this alone either," Pam said, lowering her voice. "I never planned on it. And so far, I'm really bad at it." She didn't want to cry, not in front of a Starbucks, but a heavy sadness filled her chest cavity. "When I got the call to write for *HGTV*, I was flattered. They weren't asking for Dad and me, they were just asking for me. Like I had something to offer on my own." As she smiled, the tears spilled over onto her cheeks. She wiped them away with her hand. "They wanted me, just me, you know? After your dad died, I was desperate to fulfill his vision and I failed big time. But now I have this chance to start fresh. To do something that has only my name on it. And I have to admit, that feels really good, really exciting."

"But when you asked me, I said no. You took a meeting knowing it would make me upset. You want me to play along, like we're a team, but you don't treat me like a team member. You treat me like I'm five and anytime you need to get away for work, you can just call Olga."

Pam sat up in her chair. That stung. "Well, I assumed you were too old for Olga. I don't know that I can even afford Olga any more. I assumed you'd be thrilled with a night or two every few weeks where you could be independent. It's good practice. It won't be too long where you'll be on your own at college."

"Fine, just fine. I don't want to talk about it anymore."

Pam didn't either, but she felt uneasy about leaving the conversation open. Why couldn't they arrive to a resolution that would satisfy them both? And if Pam were being honest with herself, she didn't feel 100% comfortable leaving Grace alone to fend for herself overnight a few times a month, either. She had just hoped they'd both adjust.

"What if we got a dog?" asked Pam, feeling a burst of brilliance.

"Are you serious? A dog?" Grace's face was incredulous.

"What? Is that such a terrible idea?" Pam thought about it. *No, it's not so terrible. I've definitely had worse ideas.* "It could protect us. Or at least serve as our alarm system. We'd be adding to the family, filling out the house a little more."

Grace cocked her head. "A dog. I hope you're not trying to replace Dad with a dog."

"What? No, of course not." She shook her head, like she was trying to shake off the thought of replacing Nate with anyone or anything. A dog *was* moving on in a way, though. Nate was allergic to pets, so they'd never even considered it. When they'd brought home Butters the guinea pig for the weekend when Grace was in the third grade, Nate had had to stay far away from Grace's room all that weekend, where Butters' cage was kept, otherwise his eyes puffed and teared and he couldn't stop sneezing. But now? Why not? A dog could do them both good.

Pam grinned stupidly at Grace. "Let's do it. Let's get a dog. Let's at least *think* about it, OK? We can start looking when we get home."

Grace shrugged. "OK. I guess I wouldn't mind having a dog around." A smile tugged at the edges of her mouth. "Can I name it?"

Pam wanted to stand up and break out into song. Instead, she reached across the table and squeezed her daughter's hand. "Yes, my Gracie. You can name it."

Chapter Twenty

Pam looked out at the calm beach from her back porch. It was Christmas, and the temperature hovered in the low 80s. Over the last few days, the beaches crowded with tourists. The hotels all booked up. Vacationing families filled the farmers markets, downtown ice-creams shops, sailing clubs, and restaurants. Christmas would be no picnic even if she was spending it far away from her cold, Nate-less house in Philadelphia.

She took a sip of iced tea and breathed in the sea air. It was thick with the scents of salt and sand and sunscreen. She reminded herself that she loved the beach and felt right about taking this break from her life. But she felt alone today, even more so because she was away from home. Grace had taken an afternoon shift at the club – they were desperate, so Pam let her work even though she was racking up more hours than she'd wanted her to. Charlie took the holiday to spend with his ex-wife and daughters. And now here she was all by herself, not even a blog or a job to keep up with.

She was equally antsy about the potential job that awaited her when she returned to Philadelphia. What if it ate away at every minute of every day like Designer You had in the months since Nate's death? What if she found it too hard, too challenging to come up with a fresh take on old homes month after month? What if Grace couldn't get her footing at her new school? What if she was bullied or didn't make friends? What if she were ignored by all of her overworked and undercompensated public school teachers? Would Pam be able to handle all of that? All of these unknown scenarios played over and over again in her brain. She needed to talk to someone. Becky.

"Hullo?" Becky's voice sounded clear and close, as if she were right next door.

"Becky!" said Pam. "Merry Christmas."

"Happy Christmas to you, my love. How's Florida? Still sunny?"

"It is. It's fine." Pam tried to keep her voice light and breezy.

"What's wrong?" Pam could hear a few people in the background. Becky muffled the phone. "Sorry, the kids are here. I worked the morning shift and am now cooking. Just getting upstairs for a bit of privacy."

"Oh," said Pam. She felt guilty, taking her away from her grown children on Christmas. She didn't get to see them all that much except holidays. "I can call tomorrow and let you get back to Jack and Sophia."

"No, no," assured Becky. "I need a break, actually. Jack brought his new girlfriend over for Christmas. She acts like she's his mother – she does everything. She gets him his drinks, asks if he's too warm, too cold. I saw her reach up once today and wipe off a crumb from his mouth with her napkin while we were having hors d'oeuvres. It's disturbing."

Pam loved this about Becky. Even if she were interrupting, Becky would make her feel like she was doing her a favor and make time to talk for a little bit. "I just wanted to check in and hear your voice. Everyone here is spending time with their families. Frolicking at the beach, that sort of thing. Lots of frolicking."

"How about you? Are you frolicking?"

"Heh, no. Not really." Pam watched a man who looked to be in his thirties, holding the hand of a small boy, who appeared to be around two, and introduce him to the waves that lapped at the edge of the shore. She cleared her throat. "It's just a weird day, that's all. Nothing's open. Grace is at the beach club. Charlie – my neighbor I told you about – he's spending the weekend with his kids and ex. And I'm here, staring out at the beach and feeling sorry for myself. Maybe I'll take myself out to the movies."

"You *should* go to the movies. I do it all the time, especially now when the weather is shit and awards season is upon us," said Becky. "Distractions are what will get you through this Christmas. And then tomorrow, you'll wake up and feel proud that you conquered the stupid holiday and relieved you won't have to deal with it for another three hundred and sixty-four days."

Becky was right as usual. Pam laughed. "You are a wise woman, my friend. What would I do without you?"

There was a slight pause on Becky's end. Usually Becky would come back with something like, "Well you'll never have to find out, because you're stuck with me." Or, "Wouldn't you be so lucky. Unfortunately, I live right up the block." But this time she fell silent.

"Becky?" asked Pam, thinking maybe her phone cut out.

"I'm here," said Becky. "Sorry about that."

"Sorry about what?" Pam sensed there was something off. "Is everything OK?" *Gosh, I've been so self-involved.* She thought about how often she'd taken advantage of Becky's generous nature since Nate died, going on and on about how miserable she was every moment. She'd become a parasite. "Is everything alright with you?"

Becky sighed into the phone. "I was going to break the news to you when you got back."

"What news?" Pam felt panic jolt her spine and she sat straight up in her chair. "What news, Becky?"

"I'm moving. I'm selling the house and moving back to England to be with my mother."

This time Pam needed to take a pause and let Becky's words sink into her brain. She wasn't joking – she could hear the seriousness in Becky's voice. "Is your mother OK? Has something happened?"

"No, she's fine. She's just getting old. I've been feeling bad about being so far away since she fell, and decided I don't have to be far away. I have a choice. I could just go and stay put. It's rather simple, I think," said Becky. "I told the kids today."

"How did they take the news?" Pam gulped, wondering if they were as shocked and upset as she was to lose her.

"They're fine. The kids are moved out and making lives for themselves. They won't even know I'm gone. And not to sound morbid, but to be honest, who knows how long I'll be away? Mum's in her eighties. Theoretically, she could go at any time."

Or not.

Becky didn't sound worried or sad about leaving at all. She sounded great, actually. Like she was just peachy with leaving her best friend in the lurch as she gallivanted across the Atlantic to go home and live with her mother like she was returning after college.

"What about your job?" asked Pam. "You're just going to quit?"

"Look who's talking, you," Becky said. "Yeah I'm gonna quit. And I'll probably find something over there eventually. I'm a nurse for bloody sake. I can get a job anywhere."

She was right. "What about your house?" Pam asked, trying a different tactic. "You're just going to sell it? What if you return?"

"It's not great timing, that's true. Selling a house in January is not ideal. But, we're in a nice area, where people want to live. And," she added. "I bought fifteen years ago. I'm sure to make a little money on it even if I sell it below market."

Pam's world was spinning. She couldn't lose Becky. Not now. Not when she was trying to piece her life back together. She hadn't even gotten a chance to get her opinion on the dog idea. Becky was leaving. Leaving. Fucking leaving. "Well I think it's a crappy idea."

"Oh, do you now?" Becky started to sound a bit annoyed.

Panic gripped hold Pam's good sense and tossed it aside. Heat rose to her cheeks. "You're just up and abandoning your whole life to go and take care of your mother, who's been fiercely independent this whole time. What does she think of that? Of you ditching your job and your kids to go be with her? Any decent mother would insist – no, *demand* – that you stay put."

"This is not a decision I have come to lightly, Pam," said Becky. "I've been thinking about it a long time. Please, I need you to be a friend here."

Pam knew she was behaving horribly, but she didn't care. Why should she if her best friend was deserting her? "When are you leaving?"

"End of January."

Pam wanted to reach through the phone and shake her. "God, Becky. In a month? If you're in such a rush, why wait? Why not just leave after Christmas dinner?"

"Because," said Becky, as if speaking to a child. Pam sensed she was testing Becky's patience like Grace tested her own. "I wanted to have a proper goodbye with you when you returned. I wanted you to help me as I put my house on the market. I need you right now. This is going to be really hard."

"What about me?" Pam was aware of the shrillness that had taken possession of her voice.

"What about *you*? This isn't about you. It's about me. About my mum." The patience had vanished from Becky's voice. "I thought you'd understand, especially now, as you and Grace try to repair your relationship and heal together. You're being really selfish."

"I *am* feeling selfish. I lost my husband. My daughter can't handle high school. I drove Designer You into the ground. And now I lose you too." She wanted to cry. Sobs began to take hold of her chest and throat. She could feel it throttle her vocal cords. She swallowed. "It's like the year Pam loses everything."

"Why don't you talk to me when you're not feeling sorry for yourself? You can't just dump on me right now," said Becky. "If you don't move on, if you don't figure out a way to move on with your life, you'll always be dependent on other people for your happiness."

"It's just not fair," Pam said as her left eye started to twitch.

"I'm hanging up now."

Pam rubbed her eye and stared at the picture on her phone.

A screenshot of a beaming Grace holding a trophy after her lacrosse team had won first place in a tournament the previous year. It was an indoor tournament that Nate had taken her to, and at the end, he took the photo and texted it to Pam. When was it? Last February? March? It might have been the last game he had seen her play before he'd tumbled off the roof. Grace looked so happy on her screen, so proud, so *herself*. Grace hadn't beamed like that since, which made Pam's heart ache. Her daughter hadn't been happy in almost a year. And neither had Pam. *Am I not moving on? Am I feeling sorry for myself? Is all this wallowing preventing me – preventing us – from moving forward?*

Pam heard the lock of the front door click. Grace was home. "Mom?" she called out.

"In here!" Her eyes rested on her phone for a second and then looked away. She was an awful friend. She didn't deserve Becky.

Pam glanced at the wall clock – it was only four. Such an awkward time. Too early for dinner, but late enough for an escape, maybe a holiday walk. Grace came into the porch and flopped down on the love seat. Her skin had browned over the course of the month and her hair sparkled with highlights from the sun. Such a strange sensation to be wearing a t-shirt and shorts, to have the windows open and a lazy sea breeze on her skin. It was Christmas. Last year at this time they were wearing scarves and sweaters and setting the table at her parents' house for roast beef and mashed potatoes.

"Let's take a walk and look at the Christmas lights before dinner," suggested Pam. That sounded Christmas-y.

"What's for dinner?"

Pam thought about the meager options waiting for them in

the refrigerator. She'd put off food shopping until it was too late. Nothing was open today. Her lack of planning had been so liberating up until now.

"Chinese takeout?" she said, her voice small. She didn't even know if anything was open.

Grace sat up in the love seat and faced Pam, looking pensive. "I miss home."

"Me too, sweetie. Me too."

* * *

Pam woke the following day grateful to have Christmas out of the way, but regretting how childish and mean she'd behaved toward Becky. She wasn't a teenager, though she'd had an embarrassing record of giving into her impulses over the last eight months. The world didn't spin on its axis based on how she was feeling during the holidays. Shame clung to her like a hangover, and she decided the remedy was to take a walk to her favorite local cafe, Moods. She thought maybe a coffee and a muffin would help her work up the courage to reach out to Becky and apologize. That was the right thing to do. The only thing she could do. If Becky forgave her, it would be one more in a long list of ways that Becky was a much better friend than Pam deserved.

The bell tinkled as she walked through and made her way to the counter. She couldn't believe she didn't have to wait in line – the place was almost empty.

"Large coffee and a lemon muffin." Eating a Moods muffin was basically having a fat slice of cake for breakfast, but Pam didn't care. She just wanted to read her paper and ingest enough caffeine and simple carbs while waiting until it was a decent time to phone Becky and tell her what a dolt she'd been. And after that, she thought it might be a smart idea to buy a few more groceries to tide her and Grace over for the final days of their stay.

Pam paid and grabbed her coffee and muffin. When she turned, she spied Charlie at the far end of the cafe, reading his own paper and sipping from a cup. He must have been so absorbed in his paper, he hadn't seen her.

"Hey," she said, walking over.

He looked up and smiled, gesturing for her to take a seat at his table. He folded his paper and put it to the side. "Join me."

"I will." Pam set her newspaper, coffee, and plate on the table and sat opposite of him. He looked good, freshly showered and shaved. He wore a clean, heather-gray short-sleeved shirt, slate blue shorts, and sport sandals. "Didn't think you'd be back for a while. Thought I might miss you before we left." She broke a piece of the muffin off the top and popped it in her mouth.

"Yeah, well. Only so much time I want to spend with my ex."

Pam offered her best mock 'not nice' look. "How was Christmas?"

Charlie paused, appearing like he needed to present his answer in the most judicious way possible. "Not fun," he said.

"Oh my, why not?" asked Pam, perking up. *Good! Someone else had a shitty Christmas, too.*

"It was basically a disaster – total mistake for me to join them. Renee and I thought it'd be a good idea. You know, keep the family together for the holidays," he said, taking a sip of coffee. "Thanksgiving was fine. But I think it was fine because there were a lot of relatives around to dilute things. In fact, now that I think of it, Renee and I hardly had a chance to speak over Thanksgiving. Probably a good thing. Christmas Eve and Christmas – it was just the four of us."

Pam thought about what Renee might be like. What was Charlie's type? Who would he marry? She imagined Renee was a go-getter, type-A personality. Maybe she had pretty highlights in light brown hair that reached her shoulders, and intense blue eyes. She would be thin, athletic – as if she did hot yoga or was always training for a new PR for her next marathon. "Too much 'together time?'" she asked, knowing the answer.

"Yeah, pretty much." He gripped his mug in both hands. "We got in a huge fight. And over the dumbest reason – gifts. I thought we'd share in the gift exchange. You know, equally. Every year, we've tried to be generous but not go overboard with presents for the girls. Maybe one big-ish present, like a bicycle or a Kindle – something they've had their eye on for a while. One year it was American Girl dolls, another it was skateboards. And then we fill in with some smaller items. Anyway, this year Renee insisted on doing the big gift and I do the smaller ones. Fine, thinking we'd be spending about the same amount. Well, she went out and bought the girls brand new snowboarding equipment – helmets, boards, and boots. She got top-of-the-line ski pants and jackets. And here's the kicker – a one-week family vacation for the *three* of them in Colorado, which they'll be taking in February."

"Wow, that's a little over the top," said Pam, remembering that divorce could be far more complicated than the death of a spouse.

Charlie nodded. "Just a tad, right?" He laughed. "And here I am, with my lame dad presents like fuzzy slippers, a renewal to

Seventeen magazine, an Amazon gift card, thinking, *she screwed me.* Once the girls unwrapped snowboards, North Face jackets, and a week at a Colorado resort, they were dancing on the ceiling. They couldn't believe it. My gifts? Forgotten. Once they remembered, they had to force themselves to be polite and thank me for the twenty-five dollar gift card, you know? It's like they were thanking their grandma for the crocheted scarf they'd never wear. There's no way I was going to be able to top that, and she knew it. I was furious."

"So you just left?"

"Not right away. I really try not to fight in front of Lily and Jess, but this seemed so aggressive on Renee's part. So mean spirited. After the girls went to bed, I asked what the deal was on the ostentatious gifts. She pretended it was nothing. She got a big bonus this year and wanted to treat the kids to something special, blah, blah, blah. I called bullshit. She should have let me know ahead of time. At least prepare me for it. She blindsided me." He sighed. "It's like it's not enough that she gets to raise them full time, while I only see them every other weekend. She's so Goddamned competitive – she has to win at everything, including Christmas. I just couldn't take her anymore so I made an excuse and left late last night." He laughed again. "Sorry, didn't think you'd be in for a rant this morning, did you?"

Pam smiled across the table. "No, but I'm glad I wasn't the only one who had a miserable day."

His expression changed to concern. "Oh, sorry. Right. I bet the holidays are rough on you two."

Pam looked down at her half-eaten muffin. "It's OK. Or, it's not 'OK,' but we survived." She met his eyes. "We *all* survived, right?"

His expression changed again. "Hey, what are you up to today?"

Pam shrugged. "Nothing much. I need to go grocery shopping."

"Ever try sailing?" he asked. Pam wasn't sure if she imagined it, but it seemed Charlie had almost a twinkle in his eye.

"No," said Pam, elongating the 'o.'

"I've got this buddy from college who owns a small sailboat and keeps it here at the beach club. He's away for the holidays this week and asked if I'd check on it while he's gone and in exchange, he told me I could use it whenever I want. I thought today would be a nice day for a sail. A late Christmas present to myself. What do you say? You can grocery shop any ol' day."

Pam's palm flew to her chest. "Me? You want me to go with you? I don't even know what I'm doing."

"I can teach you. Come on, it'll be fun." Charlie grinned. He *was* pretty cute with those white teeth and dimples that folded into his cheeks. "Why don't you go home, put on your bathing suit, and I'll pack us a lunch?"

She looked away so she could think. It was so easy to say yes to Charlie. Grace was working today. She still needed to apologize to Becky, but she imagined Becky would welcome a little break from her whining. Grocery shopping could wait until the afternoon. And vacation was almost over. *Yeah, why not?* "OK, sounds fun," she said. "An adventure."

* * *

Pam, now clad in her bathing suit, and wet suit top and wet shoes borrowed from Charlie, didn't realize how much work was required in sailing. She'd never thought too hard about sailing or even boats in general, but the one image of sailing that floated into her mind today involved tan people in bathing suits and sunglasses relaxing on a boat deck sipping champagne. That sounded nice. When they arrived at the dock, Charlie's friend's boat was not particularly impressive. At around twenty feet in length and boasting quite a modest cabin, it looked pretty shrimpy compared to the adjacent sailboats and powerboats docked at the club. Before they even launched out into the water, Charlie showed her how to attach and hoist the main sail to the mast, tighten it up, attach the rope that controlled the main sail, ready the jib, and put on the rudder. Pam's muscles felt like they'd already had a workout before they even launched the boat.

But once she and Charlie were out there, and they had a rhythm as they found the wind and skimmed through the bay waters, Pam's exhaustion turned to exhilaration. As they passed the sail back and forth and sped through the water, she experienced both a sense of complete control over nature as well as a submission to it. It was physical almost to the extreme. By the time they docked at Safety Harbor for lunch, her arms were like noodles and her core like it had been wrung out. Pam had a newfound respect for people who did this on a regular basis. *No wonder Charlie is in such great shape. He's got the abs of someone half his age because he sails.* Charlie tied up the boat and grabbed the cooler from the cabin.

"So, what do you think so far?" asked Charlie, taking out sandwiches and lemonade from the cooler, once they'd found a table in the shade overlooking the harbor. "It's my little getaway."

"It's a rush," said Pam, feeling her cheeks for evidence of

sunburn. "It's crazy fun, but my muscles feel like jelly."

"Good thing I've packed us some fuel for the ride back," said Charlie, handing her a sandwich and a plum.

Grateful, Pam took the sandwich. She was starving. "Thanks." She bit into it and had to stop herself from wolfing the whole thing down in seconds. What was it about being around water – pools, lakes, oceans – that made her so hungry? Or maybe she was just relaxed for once. Or maybe it was Charlie? All of her senses were heightened – taste, smell, touch – and she was sure she'd never eaten a more flavorful turkey and Swiss on sourdough bread in her entire life. When she bit into the plum, sweet and sour exploded on her tongue. Juice ran down her chin and she caught it with a paper napkin. She blushed.

"I'm devouring this. It's almost as if I haven't eaten in a week."

Charlie laughed. "Sailing will do that to you. It's a sport for the hearty for sure. And for hearty appetites."

"That's no joke," Pam said. She checked herself. She needed to keep her cool. She was too enthusiastic, too joyful, too out there, too free. She wiped her mouth again and put down the last bit of her sandwich. Pam looked away from Charlie and out into the water, where she saw a school of dolphins swimming across the bay. "Oh my God," she murmured, mesmerized.

Charlie followed her gaze. "Yeah, isn't that great? I see dolphins out here all the time. There are boats that take people dolphin watching, but stay around here long enough, and you'll see 'em."

Pam shook her head from side to side. "It's just…beautiful." She faced Charlie. "I've never seen dolphins swimming like that."

Charlie leaned in and with his fingertips tilted her chin toward him and kissed her lightly on the mouth. His lips tasted a little salty, like the sea, like their whole day so far, and it overwhelmed her senses. She withdrew, sitting back and looking down at her not quite finished sandwich. Just a few minutes ago, it was the most appetizing thing she'd ever eaten. But now, it looked like refuse waiting to be wadded up and thrown away. The plum pit on the napkin appeared naked and shimmering, as if it needed to be covered. She looked up at Charlie. "I'm not…ready," she said, more to herself than to him. "I'm sorry."

He sat back. "I understand. No big deal." He started gathering up their trash. "Anyway, it's time to head back. I don't want to keep you from grocery shopping."

Pam offered him a grateful smile and helped gather up the remaining lunch, but she felt awful all of a sudden. Why reject this perfectly nice, hot guy? *I'm not ready*, she insisted. *It's been less than a year. Who am I? Louise? I'm not desperate to find a husband. I'm not even desperate to get laid. I have a kid and a mortgage to think about. I can't think about hooking up with someone when I have responsibilities! Responsibilities with a capital 'R.'*

"I'm sorry," she said again, only because she couldn't think of anything else to say to nice, hot Charlie.

"Don't be," he said, his tone kind. "I wouldn't have forgiven myself if I hadn't given it a try. You're too special a woman to pass up. But if you're not ready, you're not ready. I don't want to push."

Pam sighed with relief. Jesus, he always seemed to know what to say. "I didn't want to ruin the day. I've had such a good time and so glad you were the one to give me my first sailing lesson." *And my first real kiss since Nate?* Bernie had offered her a dry peck on the cheek after their dinner at Barclay Prime, but Charlie's kiss was less…Pam couldn't put her finger on it. Less polite? Chaste?

They packed up and sailed across the bay back to the dock. They were already deep into the afternoon and Pam felt completely spent, too much sun, sailing, food, and Charlie. After they changed back into street clothes, all she wanted was to curl up and take a nap. They took their time as they walked back to the bungalows.

"So, this is it, right? You leave this week," said Charlie. Pam glanced sideways at him. He carried the empty cooler in one hand and ran his fingers through his drying hair with the other, his muscles in his arm giving a slight flex with each movement.

"Grace starts her new school in a week, so I'll want to get her home by the weekend," she said. "It's been a wonderful month, though. I feel ready to go back and start fresh. We both do."

"St. Pete's will do that to you. I love it, though, I'm not sure how much longer I'll be able to stay out here without a real job. I think this will need to be the year I sell the bungalow and move closer to the girls."

"What about your ex?"

"She doesn't get a say in where I live, and maybe if we could share in more of the parenting responsibilities, she might be less tempted to buy the girls outrageous gifts and take them away on expensive ski vacations." He shrugged. "And maybe not. But I'd like to be more involved. I miss being an everyday dad. This every-other-weekend dad thing doesn't suit me."

They arrived at the bungalows and walked up the driveway that divided the properties.

"Thank you for taking me sailing, Charlie. I loved it."

"I wish I could take you again sometime," he said, smiling down at her. But that would probably never happen. In the next few days, she and Grace would be on their way back to Philadelphia.

Pam looked up into Charlie's warm brown eyes and something inside her shifted. She liked him. He was a good man and so attractive. Why was she trying to deny it? What could she possibly gain by being dishonest with herself? By being dishonest with Charlie? Pam placed her hands on his shoulders – solid shoulders that she knew, she'd just witnessed them at work, were familiar with countless physical hours outside in the Florida sunshine – and kissed him. If he was surprised by her kiss, he didn't show it. His lips were soft and responsive. She could feel that he wanted her, and she wanted him.

She'd always loved kissing Nate, and over the years they had so many different kisses. There were hello and goodbye kisses, just passing through (the kitchen, the office, the porch, the family room) kisses. There were kisses when Grace was born. There were kisses when Grace walked for the first time or scored a goal in a lacrosse game or earned an award in school. There were kisses on the dance floor at bar mitzvahs and weddings. There were the passionate kisses of course, but even those had changed over time. At the beginning of their relationship in college, Pam felt as if she could never have enough kisses from Nate. Embarrassingly, they found they could make out almost anywhere – tucked away in a booth in a near-empty bar or on her parents' sofa when they had the house to themselves. Pam and Nate couldn't keep their hands off each other in those days. And throughout their marriage, even when the passion flagged or quieted, especially the exhausting couple of years after Grace's birth, or when it retreated altogether when she and Nate traveled everywhere the year Designer You blew up and their first book came out, they always returned to each other.

Nate always had a bit of stubble on his face and surrounding his mouth despite his daily shave that she could feel every time her lips met his. She loved the prickly reminder of his masculinity each time they kissed and missed it every day. But Charlie's lips and face were smooth and clean. She inhaled and caught a slight scent of sea and faded woodsy aftershave and pushed her body against his. His hands went to her waist and pulled her in. As much as she worried about her timing – when was it socially acceptable for a widow to date? When was it OK to find love, enjoy sex again? – there was nothing about this that felt wrong. In fact, it felt the opposite. There was nothing wrong with the stirrings she felt deep within her toward Charlie right now. And she felt the stirrings from Charlie as well, which made her want to tear off his shirt, run her hands over his chest, wrap herself around him, and feel him press against her.

Her lips went to his cheek and neck. "I want this," she murmured into his ear.

Charlie stared into her eyes as if confirming for certain that she wanted him as much as he wanted her. "You sure?"

She nodded and took his hand and let him lead her inside his bungalow. As Pam tugged her t-shirt off and stepped out of her shorts, she enjoyed the simple sensation of Charlie's lips on her neck and chest, the feel of her skin against his. His hands caressed her back and moved her closer to him. She felt ready, hungry for him and leaned back onto the bed. All of her nerve endings seemed to tingle with pleasure as he kissed her lips and chin and ears and neck. She'd missed this. She'd missed being wanted like this. She'd missed feeling desired by another human.

* * *

Pam woke in a tangle of sheets, with Charlie's arm draped over her shoulders. She didn't open her eyes at first, but enjoyed the sound of his soft snoring and breathed in the scent of clean sheets and Charlie's warm skin. She felt…great. Relaxed and content, for once. She thought she could lie like this forever. But, no. She opened her eyes. The sky outside the windows had grown dark. *How long have I been asleep?* She lifted her head off the pillow and squinted at the alarm clock on Charlie's nightstand. 7:13 p.m., it read. 7:13? 7:13! *Oh, crap!* She'd missed her 6:00 dinner curfew with Grace. She hoped she was home, hungry and wondering where Pam was, but back at the bungalow waiting for her.

She slid out from under Charlie's arm and sat up, feeling around for her bra and underwear and put them back on. She located her shirt and shorts she'd discarded on the floor. She all of a sudden felt like she had in college on the rare occasion she'd gone home with a guy she barely knew after a big party and had to sneak out in the dark hours of the morning wearing what she'd worn the night before.

She looked over at Charlie whose face looked so peaceful in slumber. At least she could say she and Charlie knew each other well enough before they fell into bed together. He yawned and stretched and patted the side of the bed where Pam had just lain. He opened his eyes, squinting at her.

"What are you doing over there?" he asked, his voice slurry and sleepy.

"I messed up," she said, tugging her shirt on over her head. "I'm supposed to have dinner with Grace – 6 o'clock every night. It's our deal."

"What time is it?" asked Charlie, groggy.

"Like seven-fifteen. I think the sailing knocked me out." *That and the sex.* Pam pulled up her shorts. "I hope she's not too mad."

"I'm sorry," he said. "I didn't realize you had an agreement. That must be nice."

"It is nice, but that's because we've both shown up every time so far. I may be about to face a furious Grace, which I know from experience, is no fun." She gave him a pained expression. "I haven't been the most present parent of late."

"I hope it all blows over and you get in only a little bit of trouble," Charlie said, grinning.

"Me too." She bent and gave him a soft kiss. "Maybe I'll see you tomorrow."

Charlie raised an eyebrow. "If you're not grounded."

Pam grabbed her bathing suit and flew out the door. When she turned the key and opened the front door to her bungalow, it was eerily quiet. She knew right away that Grace was not there. If she were, there would have been evidence – a discarded swim bag and flip-flops on the floor by the front door, her purse on the kitchen table, bread crumbs and an open jar of peanut butter left out on the counter, a closed bedroom door. But now, her bedroom door stood open, the entryway floor clear of clutter, and the kitchen counter as clean as the moment Pam had left it that morning.

Pam frowned. "Grace?" she called, knowing she would get no response. She walked toward the kitchen table and her heart lurched when she saw what was on it: a note that read, *You're such a flake. Abandoned me yet again. I'm going somewhere I'm wanted. Don't bother looking for me.*

Chapter Twenty-One

Pam's heart hammered so hard against her chest, she thought it might split her ribcage. She dropped the letter and pulled out her cell phone. *Call me right now*, she typed, *so I know you're OK*. She hit send and paused, waiting a few seconds before typing, *I just want to know you're OK*, and hitting send again.

She wanted to scream into the phone, '*Call me back now. Now! Now! Now, you ungrateful shit!*' She took a breath. There was an easier way to contact her right, right? She should just call her, old-fashioned style. Pam tapped Grace's name from her contacts list. Her profile picture on her phone was of Grace as a baby, probably right around nine months and she was laughing – not at Pam, who had taken the photo with their new auto focus digital camera, circa early 2000s – but at Nate, who she remembered had been standing to her left and making goofy faces. She loved this photo almost more than life itself, with Grace's shining eyes and bright, gummy grin, long before play dates, chicken nuggets, school, braces, her self-aware, slouching shoulders. In this moment, the tiny photo made her want to weep.

Pam put the phone to her ear, imploring Grace to answer. The phone didn't even ring once. It went straight to voicemail

"Hiyee, it's me! Grace! Please leave a message! Byeee!" Short and chirpy. Pam figured Grace must have recorded that message soon after she'd received the phone for her birthday last year. She sounded so young and happy before Nate died. Not that she wasn't still young. Or acting young. She still acted young, just an angrier, sadder version.

"Grace, please call me as soon as you get this message. I know you're upset, but I need to know where you are and that you are OK. Please call me." Desperation rattled the edges of her voice but she was beyond the ability to tamp it down. Tears of worry gathered in her eyes. She glared at her phone, willing Grace to call, text, anything, and spotted the Find My Phone app. She clicked on it and watched the green dot zero in on her own location. *Well that's not helpful.* Two more names appeared toward the bottom of the screen: Nate Wheeler and Grace Wheeler. Pam remembered now that when Grace received her phone for her birthday, she'd added her and Nate's numbers to the app. She'd had initial plans to stalk her husband and daughter any time she wanted, whether Nate was drinking a beer in front of the TV or Grace was at Hannah's house. But, in typical fashion regarding all things technical, she'd forgotten about the app almost as soon as it finished downloading onto her phone, and it hadn't even occurred to her to use it until now.

Pam clicked on Grace's phone number and watched the green dot try to find her, or at least her phone. It settled on the beach resort, the phone's last known location, which was more than three hours ago. *She's turned off her phone,* Pam guessed. *Or left her phone at work. Well, it's a place to start.* She grabbed her purse and keys.

When she arrived at the resort just before 8:00 p.m., the

dining room and bars were all packed. Guests had changed out of their beach clothes and were wearing jeans and button-down shirts, the women in maxi dresses and skirts, the kids out of their bathing suits and in t-shirts and shorts. The beach outside was dark and empty. She walked through the open glass doors to the pool area and saw a few families in the pool and lazy river, and couples in the hot tub, but no lifeguards were on duty. She walked back inside and approached the registration desk.

Another young – and very sunburned – person in the standard yellow polo and white chinos greeted her as she approached.

"I'm looking for my daughter, Grace Wheeler?" she said searching his face for recognition. Nothing registered in his eyes. "She's tall and tan, hazel eyes. She's got long brown hair that's been lightened by the sun." Nothing. "She's a lifeguard here during the day and teaches swimming."

"Oh, Grace! Yeah, I know her. Or, I know who she is." The guy's face reddened even more through his sunburn. "She's very cool."

"Right," Pam said, inwardly rolling her eyes. *Very cool' my ass.* She stood straighter. "Well, I'm her mother and trying to locate her. She didn't come home for dinner and isn't answering her phone, and I wanted to see if maybe she joined some friends after her shift? Maybe they went to get something to eat somewhere? Or the movies? Or…anything?" she asked. He blinked back at her, his face blank. She'd fibbed a bit about the dinner thing – of course Grace *had* come home for dinner. But where else could she go? The possibilities seemed terrifyingly endless. Surely she'd choose to be with friends tonight. And those friends were who? Pam searched her brain for names she might have mentioned. Someone Pam might be able to say to this poor sunburned guy, who looked hardly older than Grace.

Sun Burn shook his head. "Um, I'm not sure where everyone went tonight. I was part of the lifeguard crew for the first couple of days of my winter vacation, but I got this sunburn and my doctor forbade me from getting any more sun in the near future, which is why I'm behind the desk now." He put a finger to the apple of his cheek and pressed down, leaving a temporary white mark on his skin. "My face is super red, but you should see my shoulders. They're much worse – he said I've got second-degree burns, can you believe it?"

Pam couldn't have cared less about the state of his skin. She wondered if smacking him hard across the face would get him to focus on where her daughter might be right now. It'd probably get her an assault charge. She offered him her patient smile. "Do you know where the lifeguards all went? Was there something going on after their shift?"

"Oh yeah, there's a party tonight. Kevin's, I think. It's going to be a rager."

"Oh is it?" Pam said through gritted teeth. "And all the lifeguards are invited?"

"*Everyone's* invited. Kevin has the best parties. I went to high school with him. His parents are very cool."

"Are they now?" She wondered if everyone was 'cool' to this poor guy – vulnerable teenage girls, loose parents. Pam loathed the 'cool' parents. They ruined it for everyone else with their lax attitudes toward alcohol and cigarettes. They were the ones whose kids provided all the other kids with their booze and weed and maybe whatever was in their medicine cabinets. "And where is this party?"

Sun Burn looked up, as if deep in thought. "Yeah, I'm not sure? Of the address, I mean." He answered like a question. "His house is close to the high school though."

Pam backed away from the registration desk. "OK, thanks."

He grinned at her. "You're welcome, Grace's Mom." Grace's Mom. Like he and Grace were students in the same third grade class.

She got back in her car and turned on the ignition, not sure of where to go. *Where's the high school?* She had no idea. She could pick a direction and just drive. St. Petersburg wasn't that big of a town. She could Google the local high schools. Pam cursed herself for failing to ask the kid *which* high school. *Charlie will know.*

When Charlie opened the door, Pam watched as his face went from pleased to see her standing on his front step to reacting to her anguished expression. "What's wrong?" he asked before she could even get a word out.

"It's Grace. She's missing." Just saying the words out loud made it feel even more real. "She just took off and left this note." Pam handed the note over to Charlie.

"OK," said Charlie, handing it back. "So she went to work today. Did you check there?"

Pam nodded. "Apparently, there's some party at one of the lifeguard's parents' house near the high school. Do you know where that is?"

"Yeah, St. Petersburg has one huge public high school and a handful of private and parochial schools. I bet it's the big public high school. We can start there."

Pam looked up at Charlie's kind face, surprised and grateful. "You're coming with me?"

"Of course. I've got daughters." He offered her a sympathetic smile. "I'll show you where the high school is and we can drive around the neighborhood. We'll find her."

They got in her car and drove north just outside of downtown. The high school was, indeed, huge, and the campus at least twice the size of BFS. The surrounding neighborhood consisted of a mix of small bungalows with spare front yards surrounded by chain-link fencing and larger craftsmen with tidy, well-maintained lawns and gardens and leafy trees lining the street. Pam and Charlie drove up and down the grid of numbered streets and avenues, scanning the dwellings for signs of life. A good number were completely dark or had a sole porch light on.

"A lot of people head out of town this time of year," said Charlie.

"Maybe that will make it easier to spot the wild party?"

They made a few stops at homes that looked as if there was something going on other than the flicker of a TV seen through a living room window or the sight of someone washing dishes in an illuminated kitchen. Now it was after 9:00, getting late enough to where Pam started seeing homes where the only lights on were upstairs.

But as the minutes went by and they exhausted each block, Pam felt her chances of finding Grace in any of these houses diminish. Her stomach sank and her thoughts drifted to thinking the worst possible scenarios. Charlie looked over at her.

"We'll find her, Pam. I'm sure she's fine. It's still early." He reached over and gave her arm a comforting squeeze. "Don't lose hope, OK?"

Pam nodded and turned down a cul-de-sac and at the very end is where she spotted a few, tanned, college-age kids, standing in a group on the home's front porch. *Bingo*. As she approached closer, she could see each holding a red plastic cup. She gave Charlie a hopeful look. In her experience, Solo cups were the international symbol for 'house party.'

They parked and approached the house. Music thumped from inside, but it wasn't blaring. The kids on the porch gave her and Charlie a sideways look, as if trying to determine who they were – if they weren't the parents, then what were they doing there? She skirted past them and let herself in through the front door.

The house itself was a two-story craftsman. The entire first floor had a large, open floor plan and from where she and Charlie stood in the entryway, she could see the living room to the left which led back to an enclosed sunroom, and the dining room stood to the right and led back to the kitchen. Fresh, white stairs led up to the second floor. The living room and dining room were packed with clusters of teenagers and college kids. Pam did a quick scan, to see if she could see Grace right away, but didn't spot her.

"I don't see her yet," said Charlie. "But that doesn't mean she's not here. Let's split up and have a look around."

Pam nodded. "I'll take the living room."

Pam threaded her way through the crowd, searching for her tall, athletic daughter with her broad shoulders and striking eyes. Her fifteen-year-old daughter, who was only visiting St. Petersburg for the month. What would all of these young people see in her? Did they know she was a sophomore in high school? Did they realize that she'd just lost her father earlier this year? Did they know Pam had her baby picture on her iPhone? Did they understand just how vulnerable Grace was? The whole room stank of cheap beer and hard alcohol.

A woman threw back her head and cackled at something the guy she was talking to said and stumbled into Pam, her Solo cup sloshing whatever was in it onto Pam's shoes.

"Sorry," the girl slurred as Pam squeezed behind her. She wondered if that's how she would run into Grace tonight. Would Grace be holding a red cup full of that vaguely orange liquid that Pam guessed was mostly vodka with a dash of an awful, sweet mixer to make it more palatable for teenage girls? Would she be throwing her head back as a leering college-age boy came onto her, hoping that she'd get so wasted, he could get in her pants? Pam refused to let this drunken college party be the time and place where Grace lost her virginity. That was not happening tonight. The living room was sweltering all of a sudden. Pam felt stifled. She needed air. She made her way through to the back porch, where the crowd of kids had thinned a bit.

"Whoa, hey! Grace's Mom!"

Pam swiveled around and found herself face to face with the sunburned boy from two hours ago at the beach resort. "Oh," was all she managed to say.

"You found it!"

Pam stared at him. He was still wearing his hotel polo and khakis, holding a plastic cup.

"The rager? You found the rager?" The boy offered a broad, toothy smile and held up his cup.

She nodded and then grabbed his arm.

"Ow," he yelped. "Watch the burn, lady."

"Oh, sorry," said Pam, removing her hand. She narrowed her eyes at him. "I thought you didn't know where the party was when I asked earlier."

"I didn't," he said. "I swear. I got a ride from someone."

Pam nodded, accepting the explanation.

"But Grace – did you see her here? Did she come to the party?" She had the illogical and impossible hope that Sun Burn would step back and reveal her perfectly perfect Grace engaged in a conversation with another sober girl and upon seeing Pam, would turn to her and say, "Oh hi, Mom. I was just getting ready to leave when I got caught up in conversation with this lovely woman – her name's Esther – who is majoring in child development. Doesn't *that* sound like a great major, Mom? It's just the focus I need to get through high school and into college. Oh, and by the way, I'm not scared of taking the SATs anymore and I think you and Charlie should date."

Instead, the boy's head bobbed up and down. "She was here! I saw her!"

Pam's heart leapt into her throat. "You did? Where is she?"

"Um, I think she left."

Pam grasped the boy's upper arms with both hands. "Tell me *right now*, where she is."

The boy jerked back, but Pam kept her grip firm. "Jesus! I've got second-degree burns. Let go!"

"I said, tell me where she is."

He wrenched out from under her grip. "Shit, lady. I don't know where Grace went. She was here a while ago, but I haven't seen her since I got here."

Pam leaned in again. The boy flinched. "I won't touch your burn, I promise. But what time did you arrive? Do you remember?"

"Yeah," he said in two syllables. He squinted his eyes like it hurt them to think. "I got here with my buddy right after my shift. Like just after nine."

Pam glanced at her phone. It was after ten. "Did she…did

Grace look OK?" she asked, hesitant. She knew Grace had started off the night upset and angry.

"She looked better than OK, I'd say." He practically drooled as he said it.

Pam shook her head. "No, did she look upset?"

"Ah." He grinned like an idiot. "She did not look upset. Not one bit."

"Thanks," said Pam, looking past Sun Burn and spotting Charlie at the far end of the sunroom. "Excuse me."

"Later, Grace's Mom. I hope you find her."

Pam wound her way toward Charlie, meeting in the middle of the sunroom. "So?" she asked as she approached.

He shook his head. "Nothing."

"I heard she was here," said Pam. "But then she left."

The music, which had been on a steady level, loud enough to hear, but not so loud that partygoers couldn't have a conversation, was suddenly turned up to thumping level. Pam clapped her hands to her ears. Charlie motioned for her to follow him outside to the backyard.

"Sheesh, that was sudden," said Pam as they closed the back door. The music blared from the inside of the house, but it was at least contained. Pam wondered how long it would be before the neighbors called in noise complaints to the local police. The two stood just outside the back door on a small deck that stepped down onto an expansive patio and shimmering pool. A handful of young people drinking and talking in pairs and small groups clustered on the patio and sat in circles of chairs.

"How do you know she left?" asked Charlie.

"Some kid she works with at the resort told me. I don't know for sure that she's not here, but he said he hadn't seen her in hours." Pam bit her lip. "Did you check upstairs?"

Charlie nodded. "I didn't check the bathrooms, though. That was my last resort. Why don't you ask these kids out here if they've seen Grace in the last two hours, and I'll go check the bathrooms?"

The bathrooms. That was all there was left. Pam's stomach plummeted thinking that she'd wasted all this time looking for Grace at a party she probably wasn't even at anymore. *Where is she?* Sheer frustration, rage, and fear gripped her all at once, three fists closing around her throat. She thought her heart might beat right out of her chest. She walked toward the pool area, passing young people all talking and laughing in their intimate groups. Grace wasn't among any of them. She reached the far end of the pool area and that's where she spotted her.

Pam found Grace outside curled up on a chaise lounge facing away from the pool. If she hadn't circled the pool area, she would never have seen her. Pam knelt down and felt Grace's hand – it was warm and as she touched her, Grace shifted, her hair falling away revealing her sleeping face. Her eyes were closed and her lips parted as she breathed in and out. Pam was struck by how little her face had changed when she slept. She could still make out the baby face beneath the beautiful teenager with surprisingly well-applied mascara and smeared pink lip gloss.

From the time she was born, Pam and Nate had spent hundreds of hours gazing at Grace in slumber. In those first few days, weeks, months, they'd stared at her in bewilderment and awe. She was the most beautiful, perfect infant they'd ever laid eyes on. "Look what we made," Nate would whisper to Pam as they hovered over her bassinet. As a baby and toddler,

Grace often resisted bedtimes and nap times; sleeping became an 'issue' for all of them, though at the time, it felt like a gross understatement, a cruel minimization of the bedtime battles that played out in their home almost every night. When she would finally collapse in her crib, exhausted from staying up to scream and cry in hysterics for hours on end, bleary-eyed Pam and Nate would watch her slumber in peace, her face angelic, the tear stains and red blotches from her tantrum already fading. She later switched out of her crib to a toddler bed, then to a 'big girl' bed, and at last transitioned to the full-size bed she was in now when she entered middle school. But her face in sleep never changed, even as the circumstances changed.

"Oh, Gracie," said Pam softly, stroking Grace's limp hand with her own. She gave a quick visual assessment looking for missing or torn clothes, bruises or cuts on her skin, anything that would signal damage or violation to her daughter. Nothing, at least not on the surface. As far as Pam could tell, Grace was just passed out. And judging by the overwhelming scent of alcohol that permeated the air around her, very, very drunk. Tears of relief streamed down Pam's cheeks. "I'm sorry, Grace. I'm so, so sorry."

All of a sudden, Grace sat up and opened her eyes, which were wide and blank. It was like she'd woken from the dead. She looked directly at a startled Pam and then threw up onto her mother's lap.

Chapter Twenty-Two

The day after the party, Pam got up early, forced from sleep by the bright sun that beamed into her window, seeking her out like a scolding mother that demanded she get out of bed right this instant. She'd had enough Florida sunshine. Despite her normal aversion to cold, it didn't feel natural to her to have that much sun for so many days out of the year, especially right after Christmas. She felt an intense longing for the gray skies and biting cold of Philadelphia. She wanted to wear tights and boots again under her winter puffer coat. She wanted to wrap herself in a sweater and drink hot tea while curled up with a book on her living room sofa. She wanted to get a move on with her life. And she wanted to get Grace the hell out of here. She couldn't put it off any longer.

Grace, of course, was sleeping off whatever it was she'd drank too much of the night before. Last night, when Pam had picked up Grace's half-empty cup of the stuff – well, she assumed it was hers, it was the only red Solo cup placed on the side table next to the chaise where she was found passed out – she sniffed it and took a hesitant sip. She determined it was some sort of punch made of pineapple and orange juice and plenty of vodka and rum. *Mostly* vodka and rum, she guessed.

Still, it was tasty and went down way too easy, which was the whole point. When she was in college, she'd drunk plenty of potent punch – jungle juice was what she'd called it in the early 1990s – at house and frat parties. But she'd managed to never get herself into the sorry state that Grace was in, sick and passed out.

After Grace had thrown up on her, she'd collapsed back onto the cushions of the lounge and began to snore. Pam surmised she'd had at least a quart of partially-digested jungle juice all over her t-shirt and shorts. When she stood, it dripped down her legs, into her shoes, and onto the pool deck. Charlie ran over with a towel. He dipped it into the pool water and handed it to Pam. She took it, looking at him, surprised.

"I saw what happened as I was coming out. I grabbed the kitchen towel so you could clean yourself off a bit." He offered a wan smile. "It's like the good ol' days, huh?"

You mean college?

Pam started wiping off the vomit from her shirt and shorts and worked her way down. "The 'good ol' days'?"

"You know, when they were babies. Back then, I think my girls threw up on me on a daily basis. I always had a faint spit-up smell." He glanced at Grace. "How is she?"

Pam looked over at her snoring teenager. "She's very, very drunk. Can you help me get her into the car?"

After she and Charlie hoisted her up, each putting one of Grace's arms around each of their shoulders, her eyes closed and head lolling between the two of them, they made their way to Pam's car. Pam prayed Grace wouldn't barf on them on the way to the car. And then she hoped she wouldn't barf in the car. And once again she hoped she wouldn't barf in the house or in the bed that wasn't hers. The drive back to the bungalow was silent. She looked back at her passed-out teenager in the backseat. Pam knew this couldn't happen again. This vacation wasn't ending like she'd hoped. What *did* she hope? That she and Grace would be standing at the beach as the waves lapped the shore singing Kumbaya? Is that what she'd expected? What was she still doing here anyway? There was so much waiting for the both of them back at home in Philadelphia. What was *she* waiting for?

So when she got up the next morning she knew what she needed to do. They needed to leave. Today. She could drive right through the day and into the night. Grace could recover from what would be in all likelihood a massive hangover in the backseat of the car. There was just one, minor factor holding her back from this plan. Charlie. She was going to miss him. Miss his easy, laidback style. His dimples and strong shoulders. She would miss their conversations. And she would miss their not-conversations. She would miss getting to know him better. And she would miss trying out what it would feel like to find someone after Nate, someone she might even fall in love with.

Was she in love with Charlie? She shook her head to no one other than herself. She might have been infatuated with him. Might have been on the path to starting to have feelings toward him. It didn't hurt he was so easy to talk to. Kind. Good looking. And great in bed. And who knows how he regarded her? He knew she was here on vacation. That the vacation would end and she'd drive back up to the northeast to resume her life in Philadelphia. He wasn't stupid. Maybe he thought if he played his cards right this month, he'd get laid by the lonely, middle-aged widow staying in the house next door. What did he see in her anyway? An easy lay?

What had Nate seen? Nate, the golden boy. Nate the brilliant architect and designer. Nate, who could have dated any woman on the Penn State campus he wanted, had chosen her. Chosen Pam, who came from a working-class family who lived in the middle of nowhere. She was the pretty daughter of a man who owned and ran his own diner. A good student. Organized. But what the hell had she *done*? Nothing. Who was she? Nothing. She was nothing until she'd met Nate. *He liked my straight back*, she remembered, despairing. Was that it? Her posture? Was she just a woman who'd been cast under the spell of Nate Wheeler for more than two decades?

Pam bowed her head and pinched the flesh between her eyes. *Stop it. Nate loved you.* He'd given her Grace. He didn't think he wanted to have a child. He thought his life's purpose was his work. And for a while, Pam was patient. But something in her wanted to raise a child, to have a family, in addition to building Designer You with Nate. The desire didn't diminish as they got more successful. It grew. So Nate acquiesced, and they'd had Grace. And he loved being a father. Thank goodness. As soon as Grace was born, and the nurse laid her onto Pam's chest, Nate became a puddle of joyful tears. Maybe that's what he saw in Pam – someone who wanted more than just work, someone who wanted more than just him. Designer You was Nate's baby, and Grace was hers.

Charlie saw her as someone who was more than the lesser half of Designer You and more than Grace's mom. And that felt incredible, too. But she needed to break up with him.

Charlie seemed to know what was up almost the moment he opened the door and found Pam standing there on his front step.

"We're leaving," she said. "Today."

Hurt, disappointment, and confusion registered on his face. "Today?"

She nodded. "I'm sorry."

"Why? I thought you had an extra few days."

"We do have the house until the end of the month, but we need to get back home. It's been wonderful to be down here, but it's time. I can't put off real life any longer." She looked up into his blinking eyes. "Grace and I need to get on track. Last night was really scary."

"Believe me, I know." He sighed and leaned his shoulder into the door frame. "The selfish side of me would like a little more time with you, but I get it. I do."

Pam was surprised by the prickle of arousal that awakened inside her. She moved closer and wrapped her arms around him. "I'm going to miss you."

"Me too." Charlie bent his head toward Pam and kissed her. It felt as if she'd never been kissed before. It felt like the way kisses were supposed to feel. *Like in the movies.* It felt like she was floating above her body, above the trees and into the clouds. When he released her, she opened her eyes and looked into Charlie's face, mentally capturing his brown eyes, golden skin, and dimpled grin.

"I have to go," she said, feeling her feet planted firmly back on earth. She needed to leave before he could change her mind. She was almost certain he could.

"OK," he said, letting go of her hands. "Good luck to you and Grace."

It didn't take long to pack up the car. Grace didn't stir when she went into her room and organized her suitcase and toiletries, just as she'd done when Grace was in primary grades and sporting a Hello Kitty roller suitcase and accompanying her and Nate during book signings and interviews and appearances. Pam crammed her belongings into the bag, zipped it up and rolled it to the car, where it joined all the rest of the luggage in the trunk. All she needed was Grace herself and they were ready to roll.

Grace was in pretty sorry shape. When she sat up – after ten minutes of Pam elevating her whispered, gentle, "Grace, it's time to wake up," while stroking her arm to eventually a far less patient and more exasperated, "Grace, I need you to wake up! Right now!" – Pam wondered if Charlie could hear her in the next house over. Grace stirred and slapped Pam's hand away. She pushed her pillow over her head to drown her out.

"We're leaving," Pam said through the pillow. "If you don't come right now, I'm going to have Charlie help me throw you into the backseat of the car."

Grace sat up. She looked awful. Capillaries blemished the whites of her eyes. Her face looked pale, sallow, and her forehead seemed glazed with oil – or was it sweat? She still wore the rumpled outfit from the night before that reeked of BO and boozy vomit. She looked down at herself. "I'm disgusting," she said, almost to herself.

Pam thrust a small pile of clothes at her. "Here. You can take a shower and put these on. You'll feel better." She handed her a bottle of water. "And drink this. I have plenty more waiting for you in the car."

* * *

The ride home was uneventful and much faster without the

overnight stop. Grace drank water and slept off her hangover in the back seat. When she'd emerged from the shower earlier that morning, scrubbed clean with wet hair and dressed in her clean t-shirt and yoga pants that Pam had picked out for her, her face had already recovered some of its color, though her eyes were still glassy. She got in the car, put on her seatbelt, and stretched out in the backseat, using her sweatshirt as a pillow. They didn't even make it to the end of the block before she fell fast asleep again.

Pam glanced at Grace in the rear-view mirror, her daughter who had trouble making decisions lately, whose belief in herself was at an all-time low. She wondered what was next – would Grace be able to avoid getting expelled from her new school? How would she navigate the expansive field of parties and alcohol and sex and friends? *Not well*, Pam concluded. These next few months she'd need to watch her every move, question where she was going, drive her everywhere, interview parents of new friends. *God, she's going to hate that.*

And what about the new job? Just thinking about their offer made her smile and gave her fluttery feelings in her stomach. She was embarrassed – a bit – by feeling so flattered, but she couldn't help it. No one had ever sought her out for anything. Not without Nate. He was the one they wanted, she was just a tag-along. Like the Girl Scout cookie's name implied, she was a nice addition but not necessary. And she would be working for HG-fucking-TV. To turn down their ridiculously generous offer would not only be crazy, but career suicide. Word would spread that Pam Wheeler, or worse, Nate Wheeler's widow who had run Designer You in to the ground had the nerve to turn down *HGTV* – *what,* she imagined they'd whisper, *did she think she was better? Did she think she was Nate?* – and she could expect crickets when she started circulating her resume. She didn't have the luxury of time to wait for a new opportunity. Certainly not on the level of *HGTV Magazine*. She had a house to pay off, future therapy sessions to pay for, and a credit card bill that had gone into the five-figure zone over the course of the month. At this point, she had no choice. Pam was taking the job.

But something about Grace's words tugged at her – she'd said she felt lost, like she needed someone to guide her through the trials and tribulations of high school, and the one slotted for that job was Pam. Grace wasn't abnormal, Pam knew that. Every teenager felt that they are the only ones who feel isolated, uninformed, on the outs, and everyone else has their shit together. Everyone else is sailing off into the sunset with stellar grades and SAT scores as well as acceptances to the best schools, and then fabulous and influential careers and spacious apartments would fall into their laps after college, along with robust social lives. They were set. If Pam was going to help navigate Grace through the rest of high school, then the most basic thing she could offer was herself. The least she could do would be to help Grace feel less alone.

Pam resolved to make good on getting a dog when they returned. It would help Grace feel more secure when she was away. It would be something she could be responsible for – feeding and walking, at least sometimes. *Right? She's responsible enough to share in the caring of a living creature inside their home.* Pam shook her head. *Maybe not.* A dog walker would probably be a necessity, too. She could see what good ol' Olga was up to these days. Pam imagined informing Grace that her nanny was going to stay over on the nights she had to travel for work. "It'll be like the old days," Pam would say. "Remember how much you loved her rendition of 'Itsy Bitsy Spider'?" And maybe they'd figure it out. Most families had to wing it during these big transitions and most survived. Why not she and Grace? *Because we've been winging it up until now and so far, nothing's worked*, a little voice whispered in her brain. *Fuck off*, she told the voice.

Eighteen hours, six bathroom stops, three gas fill-ups, two breaks for fast-food, and one forty-minute nap later, Pam rolled onto her street and parked the car in front of her house. It was a frigid morning and still dark. A devoted early-a.m. jogger clad in winter weather gear: tights, running jacket, hat, and gloves, ran past her house. Pam smiled. They were home.

* * *

The next day, Pam walked over to Becky's house. She and Grace had slept in (Pam was astounded at how much Grace could sleep over the last two days), and she lingered over breakfast and didn't get a shower in until noon. It was early afternoon, and Pam hoped she'd find Becky in a generous enough mood to even talk to her after their pathetic phone conversation from a few days ago. She cringed thinking of how unkind she'd behaved toward Becky, as if she were the only one in the world who'd suffered. Who was even *capable* of suffering. To make Becky feel guilty about wanting to move back in with her mother was selfish and immature. Pam wished she was better than behavior like that.

In one hand, she carried a box of fruity herbal tea she'd brought back from St. Petersburg and in the other, she held a bottle of the best red she could find in her dining room buffet.

Wine and tea could save a friendship, right? she reasoned as she stood on Becky's porch, finger poised to press the doorbell. Instead, the door opened with its loud creak, making her jump and drop the box of tea on the welcome mat.

"Oh!" said Becky in surprise, her hand flying to her neck. "It's you!"

"It's me," said Pam. "Bad timing?" She raised her wine bottle like a white flag.

Becky shook her head and motioned Pam inside, who picked up the box of tea leaves from the mat. The house smelled like a combination of bacon, cinnamon, and Christmas tree. She led Pam into her living room where the half-bare tree and a half-full box of ornaments lay in wait.

Pam looked at the tree. "You never could wait until New Year's Day to take down your tree."

"Nope. It's just going to lose its needles, which will make a big mess on my floors." She gave Pam a look. "And my floors will need to be clean when I start showing the house."

Pam looked down at her feet like she did as a kid after having been caught coming home after curfew. "About that. I'm sorry. I was wrong. I shouldn't have made you feel bad about moving." She looked up and met Becky's eyes. "Forgive me?"

"As long as your apology includes the wine and tea you've got in your hands."

Pam had forgotten she was holding them. "Oh, right. Here." She thrust the gifts at Becky, who set them down on the coffee table and gave Pam a big hug.

"I missed you this month, but you picked a good one to get out of town. We had a nor'easter pretty much as soon as you left and an ice storm a week ago, all while you were lapping up the sunshine I'm sure." Becky stared at Pam. "My, you've got quite the tan," she said, observing. "Aw, and your booty has returned. I missed it. Have you been working out?"

Pleased, Pam looked behind her in a vain attempt to see what Becky was talking about. She'd gotten some of her strength back with all the walking she'd done in Florida, but hadn't even thought about what the exercise might have done to her backside. "Just walking. *A lot* of walking."

They sat in the living room that still had one foot in Christmas and the other in the rest of the year. Becky sat on the couch and slid her feet beneath her. "How's Grace?"

Pam thought for a moment, not sure how to frame her answer. "She's better." *Sort of.* "I think," she added. "I hope."

"It's an act of hope raising teenagers, isn't it?" said Becky. "And what does she make of the possible new job?"

"She's not a fan," Pam admitted. "We're getting a dog, though," she added.

Becky chortled. "What do you need a dog for?"

"To keep us company," said Pam. "And to keep Grace company when I have to travel. She doesn't want to be alone. I think it will be good."

"Good for what? Grace tells you she doesn't want to be alone and you get a dog?"

Pam frowned, feeling a little defensive. She'd come over to apologize and spend some time with her best friend, not be judged for wanting a pet. "What's wrong with getting a dog?"

"You can't just get a dog and expect everything to be OK. To be hunky dory." Becky said 'hunky dory' in her adorable, imperfect imitation of an American accent.

Pam closed her eyes, trying to remain calm. For someone who hated confrontation as much as she did, she felt like she'd been arguing for a month. "I thought it'd be nice to have a dog around." She opened her eyes and glared at Becky. "Why can't I do anything these days without scrutiny?"

Becky sighed. "Because this is Grace. She's not a quick fix. A dog isn't going to solve anything, don't you see that?"

"It's not a 'quick fix.' It's just for company." As soon as the words came out of her mouth, Pam entertained second doubts. Was she getting a dog, not for company as she insisted, not as a replacement for Nate, but as a replacement for *her*? "I came over here to apologize for being an asshole, and here we are again. Butting heads. Over a dog."

Becky leaned closer to Pam, who sat on the chair opposite the couch. "You know how much I love both of you, right? You're like family to me."

Pam did know. Becky was like family to her, too. She nodded.

"Getting a dog to help your daughter cope with being alone is like using a Band-Aid to cure cancer. It's just not going to do anything. She needs *you*."

Pam didn't want Becky to be right. Pam needed her on her side. The rational side that recognized she needed this job. That this job was actually *saving* them. But still, Pam respected Becky's position so much. She was a single mother who'd raised two happy well-adjusted kids who were making their way in the world on their terms. That's all she wanted for Grace.

She looked up at the intricate trim of the living room ceiling. "I can't believe you're leaving us. I can't believe you're leaving this house." She looked into Becky's eyes. "And your job? Your kids? You're leaving so much behind." She hoped she didn't sound unkind.

"The hospital will do just fine without me. And so will my kids. Jack's supporting himself thank God. And Sophia just landed an internship in the public defender's office in Camden." She smiled. "I will guilt them into visiting as often as possible. And I'll fly here to visit them. But they're grownups now and don't want me interfering in their lives every minute anymore."

Pam looked down. Soon Grace wouldn't need her as much anymore, either. Not now, but sooner than she would think. "I know you think you need to do this. And I know I was a jerk for wanting – begging – you to stay. It's selfish on my part. And it must have been a really hard decision to make."

Becky wore a pained expression. "It wasn't, really. To be honest, making the choice to move back home was really *easy*."

Pam looked at her, confused and trying not to appear wounded. "Seriously?"

"This hip thing she's got now – God it could have been so much worse. A broken hip is nothing to sneeze at when you're eighty." Becky rubbed her arm. "I can feel the time slipping away, Pam. I can't take my mother for granted anymore. She's not going to be around forever. I'm lucky to have her now."

Pam let out a long sigh. She did understand. She wished she'd stopped more often to realize how lucky she was to have Nate when he was alive. How much time had she wasted feeling annoyed with him for failing to clean off the kitchen counters properly or leaving his dirty socks at the foot of the bed? For taking the last tissue and leaving the empty box behind? For insisting on folding her pants in half, as if he'd never noticed in their twenty years of marriage that she liked them folded in thirds? Pam felt so stupid now for wasting precious energy on petty offenses.

"I know how much your life changed when Nate died," said Becky. "I watched how you lost your grip on who you thought you were. I watched poor Grace struggle with the transition. You worked so hard trying to keep Nate's dreams alive. But the best thing you did was quit."

Pam raised her eyebrows. "I doubt it. I think everyone believed I wimped out."

Becky shook her head. "No, you made Grace the choice. Which was really no choice at all, wasn't it?" Becky smiled. "It's the same with Mum. Anything can happen to us at any time. I want to spend whatever years my mother has left with her."

"So you can take care of her?" asked Pam.

"Taking care of her, sure yeah. But just enjoying her too, you know? Paying attention. Listening to her stories. Listening to her talk about Daddy. And about her parents, my grandparents. Hear her talk about what a terror I was when I was Grace's age." Becky giggled. "Oh my, I was horrible. Sneakin' around with boys and drinking and staying out too late. It's a miracle I survived."

Pam felt tears begin to mist her vision. She wiped them away with the palm of her hand. "Oh, Becky."

"I'm going to miss you too, lovey." She reached out and squeezed Pam's arm. "I wanted to ask you something. I'm going to put my house on the market right away, but I want to find a family to buy it. Do you think that's possible? Like, I don't want some developer coming in and ripping out the insides and putting in a bunch of student apartments or something. I want a young family in there. A family where the kids will grow up and remember that house as their childhood home, kind of like Grace and your house. You think that's possible?"

Pam nodded. "Sure, you can sell the house to whoever you want. If a developer bids on it, you don't have to accept it."

"Well that's a relief. I guess I sort of knew that. But how can I make my house more appealing you think to a family?"

"It's in how you set it up. Staging, you know?"

"Staging?" Becky asked. She narrowed her eyes at Pam. "That sounds like a crock of shit to me."

Pam laughed. "It's not in the real estate world. It's a total thing."

"A 'total thing,' eh? I've lived in this house since my divorce. Staging was not a thing when I was in the market for a house. I don't think I even know what it is."

"Staging is when someone comes in and rearranges or even replaces your furniture and takes out all of your personal effects – family photos, clutter, the handmade quilt on your bed or your teacup collection or the pillow with the cross-stitched pattern your aunt gave you for your birthday – all that goes bye-bye. And what's left is this clean, furnished space without all the stuff that reminds a potential buyer that a person actually lives here, so that they can, in fact, envision themselves in the home," said Pam. "Staging can get kinda crazy. Some staging companies bring in their own furniture so the house will be most appealing to a particular market."

Becky appeared lost in thought as she stared at the coffee table. "When I saw my house for the first time, it was empty. Are you telling me, my house will be more difficult to sell if it's empty?"

Pam shrugged. "I don't know. It might not make a difference. But staging can help you sell your house faster, and some say for a bigger price tag. I staged the two houses we sold. And I think it made a difference. You know what?" Pam leaned in to Becky and gave her a playful shoulder bump. "I think it made me feel more in control. Like I was a participant in selling my houses. Which I loved. Both of them." She looked around appreciatively at Becky's house. "I love this house, too. It's got so many of the original details – the molding, the fireplace, the hardwood floor, the mantelpiece. Someone is going to go crazy for this house."

"Are you going to stay where you are?" asked Becky.

"Yeah. Grace still has high school and then college. She needs a place she can point to and call home. The house is an anchor for both of us. If I moved now, I don't know what Grace would do. Join a cult?" She offered a slight smile. "I think I'm a lifer."

"A lifer? Philadelphia is so lucky to call you one of their own."

Pam looked at her hands. "I don't know. But I'm here to stay nonetheless."

Becky cocked her head and put her hand on Pam's arm. "You said you staged your last house you sold?"

"I staged our last *two* houses."

"And you think it made a difference?"

She nodded again. "I like to think so."

Pam watched as Becky's face lit up. "Will you stage mine?"

"Really?" Pam was taken aback. Staging was fun, but she wasn't qualified. Of course, she did have more time these days, at least until the *HGTV* job started. "Sure, but I'm not an expert or anything. You might want to go with a professional."

"Are you crazy? You are a maniac when it comes to details. I couldn't think of a better person to stage my house."

"That's because I'm the only one you know who's had a hand in a design business."

Becky gave Pam a quick hug around her shoulders. "Thank you, my dear."

Pam looked at her. "So we're going to sell your house? You're really going to do it?"

"That's right. Start saving your frequent flier miles."

Chapter Twenty-Three

The following weekend, Pam and Becky hired movers to haul away Becky's roll-top desk, vintage Japanese wall panels, three flat-screen televisions, upright piano, and dozens of family photos to storage.

"The rugs, too," said Pam, surveying the living room. She pointed to a large-scale, gold trimmed mirror that hung menacingly above the fireplace. "And the ancient mirror."

"Really? The rugs are nice. And the mirror came with the house," Becky protested. "Like, it came with the house when it was built in 1870."

"Yeah, parents of kids are going to take one look at that mirror and not know what the hell to do about it. They'll spend the whole house tour distracted and thinking of ways the mirror will kill their children."

They rolled up Becky's antique Turkish rugs from her living room, dining room, bedroom, and hallways.

"Why did I ask you to do this again?" Becky whined. She rubbed her lower back as she stood. "I feel my taste is being questioned at every step."

"Your taste is fine," Pam assured her, rising. "I love this house. *You* love this house – and it shows. But to have someone else fall in love with the house, they need to see themselves living there. We want this place looking light and bright and child-friendly."

Becky crossed her arms in front of her chest. "I just don't want it looking like a Crate & Barrel mailer, OK?"

"No one will confuse the interior of this house with a catalog, trust me."

"It looks like the house of a lonely divorcee." Pam could hear Becky's breath hitch in the back of her throat.

Pam faced her friend. "What has got into you? You knew the deal. I don't have to do this – stage your home so you can move across an ocean. You don't have to move at all, actually. I'd much rather you'd stay." She narrowed her eyes. "What is this? A type of buyer's remorse? Are you regretting your move before you even leave?"

Becky's face fell like a wet washcloth, and she began to sob. "You know how bossy you are? I'm going to miss you bossing me around. Telling me what to do."

Pam smiled in spite of Becky's tears and draped her arm around her shoulders. "Oh, Beck, I'm sorry. You're doing the right thing. What a gift you're giving your mom. You two can get to know each other again and you can help her whenever she needs it. You're a great daughter. And such a good friend. I'm still standing because of you." She couldn't believe she was the one now to hold Becky up after a year of Becky holding *her* up.

Becky wiped the tears away with her hand. She surveyed the bare floors and blew through her lips. "Well, let's make this a little more family-friendly."

A few days later, Becky put up another fight over re-doing her art studio. In the four years that Pam had known her, Becky always had a project going in the studio. Often she'd be working on streetscapes or still-lifes in watercolor or acrylic. She sketched human and animal forms in pencil and charcoal. And the studio was a space only an artist could love; paint spatters littered the wood floor, the lighting was purposeful rather than warm, and art supplies took over every surface.

For Pam, the disorder in the studio gave her a mild panic attack. "You're planning to send your art stuff to England, right?" she asked. The third floor took up two rooms, one large and open, and the other, smaller, felt more like a cozy bedroom. And it also featured a bathroom.

Becky narrowed her eyes at Pam. "Yeeeaaaah, so?"

"Let's send it this week. Sooner rather than later, what do you say?"

"Ha ha, very funny. I'm not getting rid of my art supplies until I know *when* I'm moving."

"We need to do something with this space. It's huge and we have to take advantage of it. And these windows let in so much light." She eyed her friend. "I'm thinking playroom."

"Playroom? I thought you'd say master bedroom and bath."

Pam placed her hands on her hips. "You knew I'd want to make a change to the space."

Becky shrugged. "Well, I know it's not the most attractive space in the house, but it's probably most dear. To be honest, after you and Grace and my own kids, I'm sorriest to leave my studio behind."

"Families aren't looking for the fancy master bed and bath combo, at least not on a different floor from their kids. As a playroom, this third floor could be a huge selling point," said Pam. "Don't think too hard about it."

"What if one of the buyers is an artist?" Becky asked.

"Please," said Pam. "They'll be far more likely to need a

family space than an art studio, even if one or more of them is an artist."

"Can we just say in the ad that the third floor *could* be a family room?"

"Do you want to make this more family-friendly or not? You're going to have to let this go."

Becky gave in. Pam had the wood floors painted black to cover the paint splatters and brought in thick area rugs, a comfortable sofa, plush chairs that faced a flat-screen television. In the smaller room, she set up a ping-pong table.

In two weeks, Becky's house was staged and ready for viewing.

"Fingers crossed," said Becky, as the listing for her house went live online.

"Fingers crossed," agreed Pam. Her stomach churned as she hoped her efforts paid off for her friend.

* * *

The following Saturday, Pam tapped on the door to Grace's bedroom. "Hey," she said into the door.

"Come in," said Grace. Pam swung open the door, not sure what disaster she might find inside.

No disaster at all. Her bed was made. Laundry put away. The floor almost free of clothes and debris, though she did spot a pair of discarded socks at the foot of her desk. Pam's eye scanned up to the desk, which was clear except for a fat, orange binder and Grace's laptop, which she was typing away on.

"Your room's so clean," said Pam, surprised.

"Yeah, I couldn't find one of my shin guards, so I cleaned

up until I found it. It was under a pile of laundry that needed folding."

"That happens. What time's your game?"

"Four thirty." Grace eyed her mother. "Everything OK? It's not even lunch."

Pam ran her fingers through her hair. "Becky's showing the house for the first time this morning."

Grace grinned. "And *you're* nervous."

"Maybe a little," Pam acknowledged.

"Maybe *a lot*. God, Mom. It's not like you're trying to sell *your* house." Grace swiveled to face her mom. "So did Becky call yet?"

"No!" said Pam, with a little more force than she'd intended. "She hasn't. Not even a text. And the showing's been over since eleven thirty."

"Then relax, Mom. It's fine. And there's probably no news. Or maybe she's just cleaning up or something." Grace shrugged. "I don't know. What goes on at a house showing again?"

"If you're lucky, a bunch of strangers and their agents tour your house. If you're unlucky, your agent sits around and twiddles their thumbs for a couple of hours." Pam sighed. "I can't stand this any longer. I'm walking over." Her phone pinged. She pulled her phone out of her jeans pocket and looked at the screen. "Oh my God."

"What?" asked Grace.

Pam showed her the screen: *Sold!*

O-M-G, mouthed Grace.

When she learned all the details, she found out the house had four competing offers, all above Becky's asking price. Pam wasn't about to take credit for the successful sale, but she didn't think her staging hurt anything in the process. Maybe *added* to the process? Oh, she hoped so. Pam's chest swelled with pride. She'd done something. On her own. Nate's fingerprints were nowhere near this project and it felt damn good.

"Sold," she said, letting the word slide across her tongue. She grinned at Grace. "Sold!"

"You did it," said Grace smiling back at her. Pam thought she might have seen a hint of pride in her eyes. Maybe. Since they'd returned from Florida, both Pam and Grace had settled on a modified truce. Pam promised Grace that she was her top priority. She would work her travel schedule as much as possible around Grace's schedule. And they scheduled their first therapy appointment together. Grace promised to do her best in school and pitch in more around the house. After her horrific hangover, Grace vowed to lay off alcohol – she said even the thought of it turned her stomach. But most importantly for Pam, Grace swore that if she felt overwhelmed – in school, tests, college, social life – then she'd come to Pam first. No more running away. No more avoidance tactics like calling in bomb threats. And Pam believed her.

Her face reddened. "It was mostly the house itself. And the real estate agent, let's not forget about her."

"Don't be so modest, Mom. Take a little credit. You're *really* good at this."

I am? thought Pam. She'd always avoided that sort of thinking. It felt like bragging or unearned confidence. But she *was* good at it. A house that might have languished for months on the market was sold the first day. In January. At least part of the reason had to have been her contribution.

Nate never shied away from tooting his own horn. But he was a genius. Pam never considered herself particularly gifted in anything. *But I'm good at this.*

"Thanks," she said to Grace.

She texted Becky. *Can I come over?*

Becky's reply was almost immediate. *YES. Hurry up!*

Pam raised an eyebrow at Grace. "I'll be back with details – stay tuned."

She grabbed her coat and keys, closed the front door behind her, and walked not even a block to Becky's three-story Victorian. She ascended the steps to the porch, where a painted porch swing hung next to a potted bibi plant to the right of the front door, where tufts of little bibi greeted visitors with a purple spray of winter blooms. The door was ajar. She entered the living room, where that heavy antique feel that Becky had favored for fifteen years had been replaced with a lighter, more airy atmosphere. Pam had left the wood floors mostly alone, bringing in smaller, patterned rugs in muted colors for under the coffee table and sitting area. She'd painted the walls cream with white accents, which she thought made the room look even larger than it already was. She'd replaced the large, ornate, mirror framed in gold with a smaller, beveled piece. Pam loved that mirror – it was an antique, but elegant, and not nearly as intimidating as the statement piece mirror that had come with the house. The sofa she chose was a warm sage color piled with colorful silk pillows. It had clean lines and was comfortable to sit on. Instead of the wood shutters, Pam had installed sheer feathery curtains that let in lots of morning sun. She heard voices and walked toward their source – the dining room table, where Becky and her real estate agent, Lisa Giordano, sat looking over paperwork.

Becky rose from the table to give Pam a hug. "Pam, can you believe it?"

"Congratulations!" She shook her head, incredulous. "Well, done, both of you!"

"Brilliant job, Pam," said Lisa, who grasped her hand and leaned in to air kiss her cheek. Becky's real estate agent was short and heavy, with curly black hair pulled back into a low ponytail.

"We had four offers on the table – all above asking and all from young families," said Lisa, beaming. "I haven't seen anything sell that fast since the housing bubble."

"Well, you obviously marketed the property right," said Pam. "Though it almost sells itself. It's a *great* house."

Becky looked up at the light fixture. Pam swapped out Becky's ornate crystal chandelier for a rustic glass fixture that matched the candle sconces that hung by the doorways. "It *is* a great house. I never thought I'd say this, but replacing that dusty chandelier with something more modern was pure genius."

Pam felt her face flush.

"Everything, just beautiful," Lisa added. "But the conversion of the third floor from an art studio to a family room was what did it, I think."

"Oh, I know!" said Becky. "It almost killed me to pack away all my charcoal and canvases and oil paints and easels. I wanted to stab you with my paintbrushes. But I have to admit it – the conversion of that room sold the house."

"The last couple brought their children," said Lisa as they lingered in the dining room. "They each wanted to pick out their bedrooms and when they saw the family room – it was all I could do to pry those ping-pong paddles out of their tiny hands. I can see it in their eyes. They have a mission and it is this house."

"That's so great. If we can't convince Becky to stay on the block, then a family will be very welcome," said Pam, feeling a little overcome all of a sudden at the thought of Becky leaving so soon. And of a new family moving in and reminding her how life was with her, Nate, and a younger Grace. She didn't want to tear up in front of Becky and her real estate agent.

Lisa clapped her hands. "I have to run," she said to them both, and then she turned to Pam. "By the way, I have several jobs that could use someone like you. Do you have a card?"

"Uh," Pam gave Becky a pained expression. "No. I don't really…do…this. Staging, I mean. This was sort of a one-time thing."

"Really?" asked Lisa. "That's too bad. You're truly gifted."

Pam felt her face grow warm again. "Thanks."

Lisa rooted around in her purse. "If you change your mind," she said, digging a business card from a slim, stainless steel case. "Here's my card. I can think of half a dozen houses right now that could use your touch."

"It's too bad you already made up your mind about the *HGTV Magazine* gig, isn't it?" Becky asked, her eyebrows raised. "This staging thing could be good for you."

Pam thought about it. *HGTV* would certainly pay well. She'd be in her comfort zone – writing about others' brilliant designs just as she'd done for more than a decade with Nate. But the travel was something she still hadn't quite gotten a handle on. She didn't want to have to be away from Grace for too long, but that was the job. She could do the job. She would be great at it.

Staging? There was too much uncertainty to even take the idea seriously. What was she expected to do, drop everything and start a new business from scratch? Where would she get the capital? How would she even start? Yes, she loved transforming Becky's home into the home of her ideal buyers' vision. It was a high. And the best part? It was all details. She didn't have to take down walls or change the structure of anything. She worked with what she had. And it would be all hers.

But no. She'd already agreed to meet with *HGTV* and in the end, after running Designer You into the ground and being dropped by her publisher, it would be quite the privilege to accept their job offer. She wasn't about to turn down financial security. And Pam couldn't bear the thought of disappointing anyone ever again. It turned her stomach just thinking about telling *HGTV*, "Sorry, but I've had a change of heart. I'm going to have to decline your incredibly generous offer to start my own business."

"I don't think so," said Pam. "I'm grateful that anyone wants to hire me to do anything. I'd be crazy to turn down *HGTV*."

Becky squeezed her shoulder. "As long as it makes you happy, my dear."

Pam felt the doubt creep in as she ran her thumb over the raised type on Lisa's business card. "Right."

Chapter Twenty-Four

When Pam had returned home that January afternoon, she had a talk with Grace in her bedroom. She sat on the edge of the bed and showed her Lisa's business card.

"She says she has half a dozen other clients' homes that need staging. I could do the same thing for these people as I did for Becky," said Pam. "Best part? It'd be flexible and I wouldn't have to travel." *And it'd be my business, my baby.* "And it's fun. You know how much I love all that detail work."

"What's the worst part?" asked Grace, running her finger over the surface of Lisa's business card.

"Job security. Capital," said Pam. "We'd have to live pretty simply for a while. No more vacations for a year or two. No eating out. And if it doesn't work out, it's back to square one."

"But you'd be home?"

She nodded. "I'd be home."

Grace pulled her hands up over her mouth and almost managed to cover her smile.

Pam thought about what she'd be giving up by turning down the *HGTV* job – money and security, mostly. Depending on the dwindling insurance money made Pam feel like she was still depending on Nate and she couldn't wait to start making a living on her own. Still, the *HGTV Magazine* job was safe. Starting a new business was always risky. But hadn't she and Nate risked everything when he quit his corporate job and started Designer You? They'd bet on Nate's dream and reaped the rewards. Now it was time to bet on her own dream. And betting on a fledgling staging business was betting on herself. And Grace.

Pam met Grace's eyes. "OK," she said. "I guess I better let *HGTV* down easy."

* * *

Pam's phone chirped. She looked down – it was a calendar alert for Grace's final lacrosse game of the spring season, the second Tuesday in May. If she didn't close up shop soon, she'd be late.

She hadn't been late yet, nor missed, one of her games this season, and wasn't about to start now. She made a few notes on her newest project, her latest referral from Becky's real estate agent, Lisa.

He was a client who'd inherited his grandmother's three-story row home on a prime block in the Art Museum neighborhood that hadn't been updated in more than four decades. When she first toured the house, it appeared like a shrine to the 1970s – wall-to-wall carpeting throughout, loud, colorful, and sometimes textured wallpapering on every wall in every room (minus the wood paneling in the den), yellowed pictures in wooden frames of grinning family members dressed in orange sweater vests, with long, starched collars poking out, women with hair spun into tall, dark beehives, and children dressed in their Catholic school uniforms, socks pulled up to the bottom of their knee caps. A 2,500 square foot time capsule. She loved the house and was happy to help the son who had just put his elderly mother into the dementia and Alzheimer's wing of a nursing home. She had no doubt it would sell. Its location alone would make the home very appealing, but any potential buyer would have to look past the decor, the art on the walls, the appliances the color of brown mustard. Ripping up the carpet, painting the walls, installing some fresher furniture in key rooms, and taking out the personal effects could transform the house into a home someone could imagine themselves in and pay a premium for.

Pam hoped the sale of her client's childhood home would pay for his mother's care and relieve some of the stress on the son, who every time they met, looked like he'd been wrung out.

She arrived at the game and found a seat to herself on the bleachers. She'd been to enough games now to recognize a lot of the other parents, and she waved at Jaylyn's mom, Katie's grandmother, and Yu Yan's dad. They made all the games. *Regulars*, she thought, amused. *I'm a regular.* She'd never been a regular. Sports were always Nate's department. He went to as many soccer, field hockey, and of course, lacrosse games as his schedule would allow. He never made *all* of them, though, like she had this season. She imagined she'd be suffering through each game, bored out of her mind and freezing outdoors. She'd brought a blanket to put over her parka and a design magazine to leaf through for the first game in March. The blanket did come in handy, but she never touched the magazine. She was amazed at how Grace and her teammates zipped up and down the field, passing and scooping the ball with their sticks. And today, in May, Pam was a bona fide groupie. In less than the first two minutes of play, Grace received a quick pass from another attacker and flicked it right into the goal. Pam leapt from her seat. Grace pumped her fists and received hugs and high fives from her teammates. One of the defenders on the opposing team threw down her stick in anger.

"Yeah, Grace!" she shouted while everyone around her cheered and whooped. She wished for an instant that she could turn toward Nate with wide eyes and beam, *that's our girl.* Over the last few months, she'd kicked herself for missing out on the experience of watching Grace play with Nate at Pam's side. But she was here now, and that was what was important.

The two teams reset and faced off. One of the midfielders for Girls' Academy cradled the ball and ran with it. Grace crossed up just outside the goal. The midfielder passed her the ball, she caught it, passed it to another attacker, who then passed it back to her. Grace then flung the ball into the back of the net, for her second goal of the game.

"Way to go, Gracie!" cheered Pam, who was now jumping up and down in the bleachers. She couldn't help herself. *She's really on her game today.*

And Grace had been on her game in ways other than lacrosse this semester as well. Girls' Academy had been the change she needed. Initially, Pam had worried that the school wouldn't have been as rigorous as BFS, but the curriculum was challenging and they offered all the AP courses and music and art. The class sizes were larger – much larger – but the student body and faculty were more diverse, which Pam appreciated. But it was an all-girl, college-prep public school, with competitive standards. And in it, Grace found friends, engaging courses, and a lacrosse team.

"God, Mom. Do you realize how horrible it would have been if the only place I was accepted was a community college or something?" Grace had said in February over dinner.

Pam shook her head. "What's wrong with community college?"

Grace glared at her. "If I were still at BFS and I said I was going to community college, I'd have, like, no friends. I'd have to lie and say my fallback school was Rutgers if I didn't get into Brown or Penn or Columbia or wherever."

"Huh," said Pam, thinking. She put down her fork. "Community college doesn't require the SAT, you know. I'd be fine with you going to a CC around here, getting your GEs out of the way before heading off to a four-year university."

"I know," said Grace. "I'll probably go away, but I'm glad that at Girls' Academy the only topic of conversation isn't always about grades and tests and college. Sometimes I want to talk about something else."

Pam nodded. "That makes sense, hon."

The game continued and Pam could see a few more members of the opposing team getting frustrated. One of the players broke away and scored on Girls' Academy. The opposite end of the bleachers erupted in cheers.

"It's OK, girls!" Pam shouted. "We'll get it back!"

The facilities at Girls' Academy certainly lacked in comparison to BFS. That was one of the first things she noticed when she'd dropped Grace off the first day. It was hard to look past the dearth of basics. The building was old, the cinderblock classrooms uninspired, the lockers rusty, and the sparse athletic fields pocked and overgrown. The home and school association held fundraisers all year long for basics like newer books and updated technology.

Pam thought about the check she'd written to send one of the BFS teachers on a research trip to Africa for the unit for the following school year. She now understood what an absurd luxury it was to have the resources to even consider doing that, sending a teacher to another continent. That check would have paid for math curriculum software or current, more inclusive history textbooks at a city public school. So now she attended these fundraisers. She no longer had anywhere near the means to write such large checks, but she could donate her services and pay for event tickets. At the Girls' Academy silent auction in April, she literally bumped into Bernie Scott while perusing the items up for bid.

"Excuse me," she said, looking up, recognizing him right away. "Oh, Bernie. Hi." She reddened. "Sorry, I think I stepped on your foot."

He looked down at the offended foot and screwed his eyes. "No damage from what I can tell." He raised his eyes to meet hers. "I accept your apology," he said in an exaggerated, gallant voice. He gave a slight bow, which made Pam blush again.

She decided to change the subject. "How's the house?"

"The house." He took a sip of what appeared to be red wine from his clear plastic cup. "The house is great. I love it. I officially moved in before Christmas."

She smiled. It was good to hear, though that project seemed like it had happened a million years ago, not five months. "I'm glad. I love that house and was so honored to bring Nate's designs to life."

Bernie smiled back. "And what's this I hear that you're now out of the business? Is that right? Don't tell me Designer You is closed for good."

"Yeah, I needed to scale back," she said. She didn't feel like talking about it, though it seemed a lot of people were interested. "So I closed."

"And now you're in the staging business?"

Pam looked at him surprised. "How did you know that?"

He grinned. "I saw your donation item on the list for the auction. 'Just Details' – that's you, right?"

Pam nodded and looked down. "I didn't expect to see you at something like this. A school auction night." It was then she noticed that some of the other guests had slowed to take a better look at Bernie. When recognition registered in their faces, they would whisper something into their partner's ear who also turned to stare. No one approached and shyly kept their distance, at least not while Pam was talking to him, but she felt a little self-conscious all of a sudden. She wondered if their picture would appear on Instagram later.

"It's not just me, you know," said Bernie, noticing. "They're a bit star struck by you, too."

Pam shook her head. "No, I didn't run a city for eight years. I just wrote about my husband's adventures in design." She cocked her head at him. "Say, what *are* you doing here?"

He laughed. "Good question. It's good to remind people I still exist. And if I can get the funding, I'm making a run for governor next year. I go to these things all the time."

Pam gaped at him. "So this is just *campaigning?*"

"No, Girls' Academy is a very deserving school. It was voted as one of the top public high schools in Philadelphia." He smiled. "And I heard a rumor that you were sending Grace here." He shrugged. "Thought I'd support the school and see if you showed up to their swanky silent auction."

Anyone who attended would agree, it was not exactly a

swanky affair – it was cocktail attire, but the event was held in the school gym, with a buffet dinner and beer and wine bar – though Bernie's presence upped the bar a few notches. Pam caught herself smoothing out the front of her dress and adjusting her earrings. "Right," she said. "And what rumor is swirling around about my kid?"

"My niece attends here. That's another reason I like to support the school," he confessed. "I used to donate a 'coffee and conversation with the mayor' to be auctioned off, but now that I'm just a common citizen again, it's 'coffee and conversation with Bernie Scott.' Maybe someday it'll be 'coffee and conversation with the governor.'"

"Really? And how much does 'coffee and conversation with Bernie Scott' usually go for?"

"Not as much as 'coffee and conversation with the mayor,' I can tell you that." He grinned. "It's great to see you."

"It's good to see you too, Bernie," said Pam. She felt pulled toward him somehow, hypnotized. He had that way of talking to her like she was the only one who mattered. It made her feel so guilty for pushing him away last summer. "I'm sorry I never called. I mean, I'm sorry I never called about going out again. I think it was all too soon for me."

"It was bad timing on my part. No hard feelings." He looked at her and gave her a reassuring smile. He didn't seem heartbroken in the least.

"So are you…seeing anyone?" Pam asked, wondering if it was bad form to even ask.

"Um." Bernie looked up like he was searching for words for a not very hard question. "Not really."

Pam crossed her arms in mock reproach. "What does 'not really' mean?"

Bernie crossed his own arms and leaned in. "It means I'm not seeing anyone serious. Why do you ask?"

Why did she ask? Pam wondered. Was it because she wanted to toy with him? Did she want to go out on another date with him? Did she want to go to bed with him? "I just wondered, that's all," she said, playing it safe.

"Are you seeing anyone?" he asked.

The dreaded question. All of her friends and family had kept their distance when it came to Pam and whether she'd started dating, but after she returned from Florida, it seemed she was all of a sudden fair game for questions. Maybe she gave off some sort of vibe after sex with Charlie. *Good* sex with Charlie. She had to admit, since the trip, she felt more in her body, more sensual. Her senses felt like they had sprung to life after she returned from Florida. Of course she'd blabbed to Becky about the sex ('Way to get back in the saddle, my girl!') and her mother articulated her feelings about Pam's love life during a visit one evening in late January ('I don't know if you're ready yet, but one of Jimmy's soccer teammates from high school has moved back to town after his divorce was final…') But she still hesitated. Her main focus these days was Grace.

"No," she said. "I'm not seeing anyone." She put her hand on Bernie's arm and looked up at him. "But maybe I'll run into you again at one of these swanky affairs." She kissed his cheek. "It was great to see you. I'm going to get a drink."

Chapter Twenty-Five

The score was now tied. Grace moved up the field and passed the ball to an attacker running up the middle. She caught it and scored. Pam's side of the bleachers erupted in cheers. Pam knew Grace was a talented athlete overall and an excellent lacrosse player, but this was the best game she'd ever seen her play. Grace was happy if she came home after a game scoring or assisting on one, maybe two goals in a match. But two goals and an assist in the first twenty minutes? Pam was exploding with pride.

After the players reset, the play began again. More members of the opposing team were visibly frustrated. One committed a foul against one of the Girls' Academy midfielders and was sent to the penalty box. They were now down a player. Grace and her team took advantage and controlled the ball, passing it around amongst themselves, playing keep away from the other team. A midfielder passed the ball to Grace, who then flung it hard to the back of the net. Goal three! Pam jumped up once again and cheered, but as soon as Grace turned, the angry defensive player who had thrown her stick down earlier in the game body checked her. Grace slammed into the side of the goal post and then crumpled to the ground, where she lay motionless in a heap. Pam's heart lurched. The official blew his whistle and both teams took a knee.

Grace's coach sprinted out onto the field. Everyone in the stands was hushed as she huddled over Grace. Pam stood, tense. It was understood that parents were to stick to the stands. Positive comments were fine from the bleachers, but the field was off limits for family and friends. All Pam wanted to do in that moment was rush onto the field and see what was going on with her daughter. And she wanted to punch that kid who had knocked her down in the face. The longer Grace lay motionless on the grass, the more Pam had to restrain herself. Finally, the coach looked up at the official and then toward the stands.

"I need someone to call for an ambulance!" she called out. Right away, half a dozen parents whipped out their cell phones.

Fuck permission. Pam ran out onto the field and crouched down beside the coach. "I'm Grace's mom," she said, by way of introduction. She wasn't certain the coach had put it all together with which players belonged to which parents. She was out of breath with worry.

Grace lay on her side near the goal line. Her eyes were closed and an angry welt was already forming on the right side of her temple. Her cheeks were flushed with exertion and her hair damp with sweat. And to Pam's great relief, she was breathing.

"Can we move her?" asked Pam. She feared the coach would say no, which would mean she thought Grace might have a spine or neck injury.

"Probably," she said. "I think she may have a concussion, but just to play it safe, I think we don't move her and let the paramedics make that decision."

The panic, the same blind panic she felt the day that Nate died returned like a sick dream – spotting him from the roof, scrambling down the stairs, reaching his lifeless body, waiting for the EMT to arrive. And now, there was nothing she could do but wait. Pam took Grace's hand, careful not to move her, but just to feel her warm hand in her own and let her know in the only way she could that she was here. That she wasn't going anywhere.

In the distance, she could hear sirens approaching. She glanced toward the sound and watched an ambulance roar up the street and turn into the parking lot. While her focus was on Grace, most of the girls from the other team had gone to their bench and some to their parents. The girls on Grace's team huddled nearby. Pam noticed a few with tears in their eyes. She turned back to Grace, just as her eyes started to flutter open. She looked blank and then blinked again, trying to focus. Her eyebrows pushed together as she recognized Pam and her coach crouching over her.

"Mom? Coach Marissa?" Grace asked in the softest voice, not yet comprehending. "What happened?"

Pam caught herself before saying something along the lines of, *You got knocked down by that cheating bitch defender, who was probably raised by wolves.* Instead she said, "You got knocked down, kiddo. The EMTs are here to check you out and take you to a hospital."

Tears welled up in her eyes. "Am I OK?" she asked, fear resonating in her voice.

"I think so, sweetie."

"Don't leave me. I don't want to go by myself." Grace sounded like a frightened child.

"I'll stay right by your side the whole time."

"You're a tough player, you know that, right?" offered Marissa encouragingly. "That girl knocked the stuffing out of you, but not before you scored your third goal. Hat trick."

Grace smiled weakly in response, which made Pam want to weep with joy.

One of the EMTs shone a light into Grace's eyes and asked her what year it was, the street she lived on, and who was president. He decided she probably had what's considered a Grade 3 concussion, and they would need to bring her in for evaluation.

Pam rode with her in the back of the ambulance, and walked beside her as they wheeled her into the hospital, and sat beside her cot in the examination room, and stood next to her when the doctor entered. She was a kind, middle-aged woman with a warm smile. She had on translucent glasses and wore her graying hair in a short, smooth bob that she tucked behind each ear.

"Good afternoon. My name is Dr. Prisha Stern." Dr. Stern shook both Pam and Grace's hands. "I hear you had quite a collision today on the soccer field."

"Lacrosse," corrected Grace. "But yeah." Grace was seated on the examination table, her legs dangling over the sides.

Dr. Stern smiled at Grace. "Right, lacrosse." She looked at Grace's forehead. "Quite a goose egg, you've got there. Does it hurt?"

Grace touched the bump lightly with her fingers and winced. "Yeah."

"So." She sat down on a short, rolling stool and swiveled toward Pam and Grace. "I read your file and see you have a Grade 3 concussion. You want the good news or bad news first?"

CHAPTER TWENTY-FIVE

"Bad," said Pam and Grace together.

"I'm keeping you overnight. Just to make sure this concussion isn't more serious than it looks. You lost consciousness for a minute or two, which always calls for caution, OK? I don't play around with concussions, especially in kids."

"And what's the good?" asked Pam, worry fluttering in her stomach.

Dr. Stern offered a warm smile to them both. "Grace, you're going to be fine. You'll be able to play lacrosse again. Probably not for a few weeks, but you'll make a full recovery. In the meantime, if you feel like you're going to pass out, or vomit, tell your mom right away. If your eyes feel like they can't focus, tell your mom. If you can't read or watch TV, tell your mom." She turned to Pam. "You'll be here? Is the father available?"

Pam shook her head. "It's just me. And I'm staying."

"Good. I'll get the paperwork started and you can just rest."

After Dr. Stern left, Pam sat back down in the chair beside Grace. She leaned forward, head in her hands. "What a long day."

Grace was already tapping away on her phone. Pam was sure that Grace's entire team, maybe even the whole school, knew Grace was going to be just fine.

"Mom?" Grace looked up from her phone.

"Hmm?"

"Were you scared today?" Grace set the phone in her lap. "When I hit my head?"

Pam hadn't even had time to replay the scene in her mind over and over again. There would be plenty of time to relive the body slam from that defender, the sickening thump as Grace's skull met the metal goal post, and her collapse at the feet of the goalie.

"Yeah," she said. "It was really scary."

That seemed to satisfy her, and she went back to tapping at her phone. Pam refreshed her email on her own phone.

"Mom?" asked Grace again.

Pam looked up.

"I'm going to be OK."

"You're going to be OK, hon. We're going to be OK."

THE END

Acknowledgements

First off, I'd like to thank Laurence and Stephanie Patterson my original publishers at Crooked Cat Books, who believed in *Designer You* and took a chance on this unknown author, and Maureen Vincent-Northam, my editor, who helped me whip this manuscript into shape.

Special thanks go to my writing crew from Author Accelerator and Pitch Wars, who were generous to take a peek at early drafts of the book and offer their feedback: Jennie Nash, Lisa Cron, Lizette Clarke, Amy Sue Nathan, Margarita Montimore, Heidi Stallman, Mikayla Rivera, Priscilla Mizell, and Chris Swiedler. Huge props to my talented and incomparable book coach, Dawn Ius. In the year that I've worked with you, my writing has improved in pretty much every way imaginable. I no longer look at my work in the same way thanks to you. You are amazing. You're a crazy talented book coach and writer. And please, people, buy her books!

My trusted group of beta readers, namely Anne Pomerantz, Amy Weber, Paulette Greenwell, Heidi Siegel, Joanne Mason, and Kaela Parkhouse, have all provided such unwavering support and constructive commentary that informed this book and undoubtedly made it better.

I wanted to give a shout out to Bucks County Community College, specifically the Language and Literature department and my Tuesday salon. I feel immeasurably fortunate to have these fantastic and dedicated faculty and staff in my corner. I have the best day job!

Finally, I'm grateful to my parents and siblings. You've all inspired me in countless ways and I am proud to be your daughter and sister. And last, to Josh and Virginia, I couldn't be an author without your patience, generosity, and encouragement. And Jazz, my furry writing buddy. Thanks too, Josh, for building that roof deck and having the decency to *not* fall off. I love you guys more than anything. You're the best around…

About the Author

Sarahlyn Bruck writes contemporary women's fiction and lives in Philadelphia with her husband and daughter. She is the author of *Designer You*, first published by Crooked Cat Books in 2018 and re-released by Hamilton Street Press in 2020. *Designer You* won the Indie Star Book Award for 2019 and was included on the 2018 "35 Over 35" list. Her second novel, *Daytime Drama*, will be published by TouchPoint Press in 2020. When she's not writing novels, Sarahlyn moonlights as a full-time writing and literature professor at a local community college.